TRANSF...

VICTIM OF THE ...

TORI K. DOWNS

ISBN 979-8-88540-085-5 (paperback)
ISBN 979-8-88540-086-2 (digital)

Christian Faith Publishing
832 Park Avenue
Meadville, PA 16335
www.christianfaithpublishing.com

Printed in the United States of America

To Brooklyn, a friend of strength who never gave up on me or those around her, even in some of our darkest days. Thank you for always being like a mother, ensuring our safety and teaching me how to show love!

And to my sister, Tacey, whom without, I wouldn't have found the inspiration of a new world or the motivation to continue writing during my toughest phase of life.

CONTENTS

TimeLine and Major Events xi
A Guide to the Creatures of Gossamer xiii
Magia Ore xiv
Stexphin xv
Swiftmaw Wolves xvi
Hollowed xvii
Bandits xviii
Griefolowtros xx
Mislea Raptor xxii
Prologue xxv
Chapter 1:   Survivors 1
Chapter 2:   A Lost Dream 11
Chapter 3:   The Truth 20
Chapter 4:   Declan's Ghost 29
Chapter 5:   Terror at Camino Creek 36
Chapter 6:   Strangers 47
Chapter 7:   The Banister 57
Chapter 8:   A New Instructor 66
Chapter 9:   Second Attack 73
Chapter 10: Beast 82
Chapter 11: Laboratory 90
Chapter 12: Delta's Report 98
Chapter 13: Invention 104
Chapter 14: Run 115
Chapter 15: Deadly Friend 122
Chapter 16: Underground 131
Chapter 17: A Silent City 140
Chapter 18: Smuir 148

Chapter 19: New Journal 156
Chapter 20: Her Second Life 166
Chapter 21: Allred 178
Chapter 22: Left 186
Chapter 23: Storm 198
Chapter 24: Slide 208
Chapter 25: Second in Command 218
Chapter 26: Half of Oracle 228
Chapter 27: Traitor...238
Chapter 28: A New Discovery 247
Chapter 29: No More Secrets...253
Chapter 30: Characters in the Caves 264
Chapter 31: A Shadow Inside...274
Chapter 32: Combative Fight 282
Chapter 33: Foul Play 293
Chapter 34: Darts..306
Chapter 35: Wounded Incomers 317
Chapter 36: Burned 328
Chapter 37: Portal 338
Chapter 38: A War Graveyard..348
Chapter 39: Only Three Left 358
Chapter 40: The Illicit Group 369
Epilogue...377

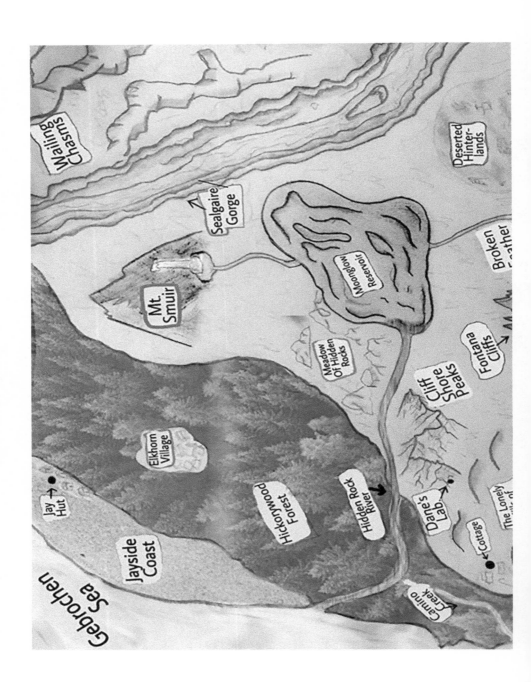

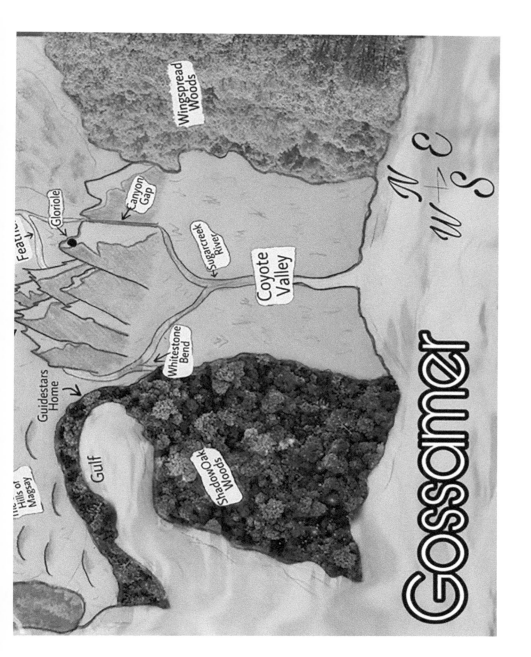

TIMELINE AND MAJOR EVENTS

Energy Cannot Be Created Nor Destroyed, It Can Only Be Transformed

242   The first Magia Ore
247   Colossal Wars began
249   Colossal Wars ended
263   Freddy Blue begins study of Ores
294   Griefolowtros control Swiftmaw territory
296   Captain Dana's sailing around Gossamer
297   Rotto encounters *Arrowbear*
306   Virga encounters the Blind Man
315   Valkyrie arrived in Smuir; fourteen of age
316   The Queen of Smuir leaves the refuge

The Oracle ambushed

317   Crowley returns to the abandoned city
318   Rotto appoints his Second for Command
319   The identity of Declan's grandson revealed

The Lone Ranger

320   The Gloriole Resistance

A GUIDE TO THE CREATURES OF GOSSAMER

Each kindred of species inside the Time Realm has two forms in which they can transform: the form of their Creature and the form of their being titled as their Character Form.

Known races to inhabit Gossamer

>   Stexphin
>   Swiftmaw (Recent)
>   Hollowed (Recent)
>   Bandits
>   Griefolowtros
>   Mislea Raptors *(believed extinct after the Colossal Wars until the recent appearance of Rotto Helman and others)*

Extinct (*) or Undiscovered (^)

>   Silverstreak Wolves. (^)
>   Vitalus Spiris (^)
>   Blue Wolves (*)
>   Lindrum (*)
>   Dearbit (*)

MAGIA ORE

- Jagged outer stone appearance.
- Black crevice throughout the center.
- A strange glow coming from the center.
- If there is a glow, that means the stone is activated. Very few know how to activate these ores.
- Full of strong negative energy.
- If an infant is born near one of these stones, the energy can enter the character.
- Ores are very rare to find.

STEXPHIN

- Ears are focused from the back of the head, not the side nor top.
- Small but long body and legs, giving them incredible speed.
- Hourglass-shaped pupils.

Hair Color: Gray, blond, or brown
Rare: White and red
Eye Color: Green or brown

- Jump max of twelve feet.
- Rarely gifted by Magia Ores.
- Often mistaken for regular alley cat.

Environments:
Elkhorn Village
Kingdom of Smuir
Jayside Coast

Common Weapon(s):
Short Sword
Crossbows

SWIFTMAW WOLVES

- Wolf relation.
- Short ears on top of head.
- Large paws—soundless when stalking.
- Incredible scent.
- White glare above pupils.

Hair: Dirty blond, brown.
Rare: White.
Eye Color: Brown.

- Believed to come from own Island.
- Can swim and hold breath for a long time.
- Imprisoned under Griefolowtros Command.

Environments:
Wingspread Woods
Gloriole

Common Weapon(s):
Long Sword
Compound Bows

HOLLOWED

- Swiftmaw Relation.
- Torn, ragged, short ears.
- Stained, rough fur; covered in brands.
- Dark, stained jaws.

Hair: Black
Eye Color: Black

- Used to be Swiftmaw Wolves
- Under containment of Griefolowtros
- Hard to control

Environments:
Wingspread Woods
Large Armies dispatched throughout the Island of Gossamer.
No known weapon.

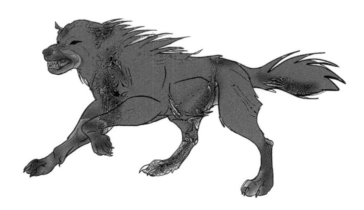

BANDITS

- Only known character to *not* have a Creature Form.
- Pointed ears.

Hair: Shades of black, brown, blond, or red
Eye Color: Brown, blue, hazel, or green

- Bandits are only known to live in one section of Gossamer in a small town called Keoslese located far up north (not shown on map).
- Bandits come from the Mainlands and own the highest tech of machinery.

- Drakewood: The Bandit School of Music
   (As shown in image below)

No known weapon.
Bandits are not a part of the Silent Wars.

GRIEFOLOWTROS

- Lion front/Eagle behind.
- Long ears/Feathered tail.
- Feathered mane.
- Straight pupils.
- Max Wingspan of ten feet.

Hair: Brown, blond
Eye Color: Brown, amber

Character Form:
Feathered Hair
Clawed Nails

- Seen as the most powerful creatures on Gossamer.

Environments:
Wingspread Woods
Gloriole

Common Weapon:
Halberd

MISLEA RAPTOR

- Four-winged creature.
- Star pointed/Open pupils.
- Claw on end of wing.
- A long tail with feathered end
- Small sharp teeth

Hair: Brown, gray, maroon
Rare: White
Eye Color: Yellow, green

- Front wings are larger than back wings.
- Hair is a mix of strands and short feathers.
- Most powerful known Flyers.
- Only five have been sighted on Gossamer since the Colossal War.

Environment:
Wingspread Wood

No known weapon

PROLOGUE

The Silent Wars Inauguration
Rotto—Year 297

Rotto closed his eyes, letting the evening air whisper through his feathers and across his face. Gliding beneath the night sky, he let out a satisfied sigh at the clear weather and cool air. Opening his eyes, he suddenly banked left, dipping dangerously.

He didn't stop to catch himself but instead curled all four wings to his sides and let himself fall like a bullet. He eyed the large tree below where a large platform was built. Light came from the open wall, and inside, he knew—or at least hoped—that's where Slecherick would be.

Nearing the building at a dangerous speed, he unfurled his wings, letting them catch the air.

He may have waited too long to release his resistance and was thrown off balance.

Transforming—wings still intact—he fell, unbalanced. He hit the platform, curling himself into a ball as he rolled across the wood.

As he slowed, he found his footing, shot out his wings, and rose to his feet, taking a few steps forward as he regained control. He was now inside the wooden structure and quickly folded his wings in, letting them disappear as he transformed completely.

"You almost lost that one," a familiar voice chuckled.

In front of him, a man with short white-haired feathers leaned over a table, reading a book. Behind him, shelves bowed under the weight of teetering stacks of even more albums and novels.

Rotto smiled. "I was looking for you, Slech."

Slecherick looked up at him and returned the smile.

"I can't imagine myself being anywhere else. Is this the first location you've checked so far?"

"More or less," Rotto shrugged.

The library had been his last choice.

Looking down at the book his friend was reading, he laughed. "Why are you reading the *Legends of Old*? That's more of a children's book, don't you agree?"

"Perhaps," was his answer.

Slecherick's gaze slid back to his story, and Rotto eyed him curiously. They had been friends since birth, but not even Rotto could deny his companion was different from other Mislea.

For starters, Slech was the only known Mislea with white feathers. Whenever he transformed, he was easy to spot in the sky. His wings had an undertone of black, making them stand out against the rest of his plumage. Some whispered Slech was a higher breed and was destined to be a part of the Blazer Wings.

The Blazer Wings. Oh, how desperately Rotto wanted to join their illustrious ranks! As leaders of the island, Trailblazer, the Blazer Wings held the highest power. Sadly, one couldn't just waltz in, take a test, and earn the privilege of sitting amongst the Head Mislea. If someone were found strong enough to lead, *then* they would be called upon to take the test.

Rotto had been fighting to be the best since he was ten years old, and yet, even now at age twenty-seven, he was still overlooked. This, daily, left him angry and baffled. He didn't have any competition to even choose over him! His family was greatly honored, which automatically gave him a higher rank than others. His grandfather retired from being a Blazer, and his father was the manager of most of the community—not a Blazer but still as respected as one.

Rotto was the oldest son in his family and already treated with honor, but he didn't just want respect from others. He wanted power. He wanted to be looked upon as a king, not a younger prince.

He envied Slech greatly, knowing it wouldn't be long until he would be called to sit among the Head Mislea. Infuriatingly, Slecherick showed no desire to be a part of the Blazer Wings. Instead, too often, Rotto found his friend laughing with the lower citizens and reading fantasies in the library.

Once, Rotto had asked his father if there was a chance for him to become a Blazer. His father had shaken his head and said Rotto wasn't born a leader without even giving him a reason why! Rotto became more angry, leading to an even stronger determination to become the best.

Bored out of his mind and annoyed with being brushed aside, Rotto began to pester his friend for attention. "Come on, tell me what you're reading."

Slecherick looked up at him with laughing eyes. "Please, Rotto," he said, "I know you well. You don't care for books at all." At that, Slech's eyes went sad, and he looked away.

Rotto, not liking the distant look taking over his friend, continued to pester him. "Yeah, I don't like to read. I just want to know why you like to read. Especially all the *fake* stories." He scrunched his nose as if disgusted.

Slech turned back to him, but his melancholy eyes didn't change. "I've always enjoyed the adventures. The stories of war and *actually* trailblazing daring adventures—they fascinate me. Take this book here." Slech pushed the open pages toward him. "It tells of a real war that happened between Mislea Raptors and Blue Wolves decades ago. It happened on a different island called Gossamer and went into books as the Colossal Wars." Slecherick folded his arms and leaned on them over the table, never taking his eyes off the pages.

"I don't understand," Rotto confessed, trying not to sound bored.

"Turns out there might be other islands *and* races out there. Rotto, I didn't want to tell you this, but Briste Blazer told me that I'll be tested tomorrow for—" He didn't get to finish.

"*What?*" Rotto screeched, staring at his friend in bewilderment. He searched for any hint it was a trick, but he knew Slecherick wasn't much of a joker.

"I'm not ready, Rotto," Slech went on, ignoring his friend's accusing expression. "And once I'm a Blazer Wing, you know I can't do anything I enjoy anymore. Reading or searching for more Ores—anything,"

Rotto was quiet when he saw the hollowed look in his friend's eyes.

"What's your plan?" he asked, knowing Slech wasn't finished.

Slecherick looked up at him, his eyes shining soberly and yet with a hint of excitement. "I ask you as my dear friend to fly with me tonight."

The emotion in his words hit Rotto like a punch to the sternum. Although Slecherick didn't want the life that Rotto dreamed for, he pitied his friend. *He doesn't realize he was born to be a great leader.*

"I'll fly with you to the ends of the earth," Rotto said, his voice firm.

"Good because that's where we're going," Slecherick said, standing.

"What?" Rotto straightened, watching his friend return the book to its empty slot but not before tearing a few pages from the binder. He gaped at his friend who never would have vandalized a book before.

"I'm flying out tonight in search of this island, Gossamer," Slech said, not looking at Rotto's gaping mouth. He gently folded the papers and put them into the pocket of his long jacket. "It is the one thing I hope to do before tomorrow. After tomorrow, I'll be grounded here forever. And you, my friend, will never see me as myself again."

Rotto, feeling impish and excited at his friend's daring side, followed Slecherick to the end of the platform. He was always ready for a challenge. Besides, Slecherick wouldn't survive without him. *Perhaps if the Blazers hear we found a new island, they'll give me a chance to be tested.*

Slecherick leapt into the air, transforming as he disappeared over the edge. A moment later, he reappeared, his glistening white wings carrying him high into the night sky. Rotto was behind him in seconds.

They flew high into the dark sky, their wingtips stretching out as if to touch the stars. Slech looked at them longingly, and Rotto knew that was exactly what his friend was wishing he could do.

His friend was strange. Slech had brought up before that it *was* possible to touch stars! Rotto was still pretty sure that was impossible. Yet the power one could have if they owned the stars...

Slecherick also believed there were realms out there. They apparently lived in a realm that was trapped in the center of them all, in which case, theirs was called the Time Realm.

Now that is just stupid, Rotto thought. *Other realms?* There was something awful about the thought of other realms with more powerful beings.

Once again, the cold night air brushed through his feathers and back toward his long tail. Rotto's bothersome thoughts were forgotten as he was reminded about how much he loved gliding through the air, looking magnificent and bold, to feel as if he were lighter than a leaf caught in a breeze. But mostly, to feel more powerful than the lit-up city below. *I would never give up my wings. I think even if it meant being a Blazer Wing.*

They soared high, gazing down as they crossed over their island. They were nearing the ocean, and after that, who knew? Rotto was surprised to notice his heart thumping with excitement as well as dread, and most of all, doubt.

"What if nothing is out there?" he called to his friend as he looked out across the ocean. "What if we fly for miles until our wings tire?"

"Then I guess it's a good thing you can fly for miles," Slech said. "You're the strongest flyer on the entire island. Even with all the Blazers put together, you would still outfly them. Trust me! You'll make it!"

"I know *I'll* make it," Rotto said, turning in a quick spiral before settling himself into another gentle glide beneath Slecherick. "I'm worried about having to carry you!"

Slech looked down at him before suddenly tucking in his wings and spiraling for the ground. Rotto smiled and mimicked his moves. With all four wings wrapped around himself, he turned rapidly like a screw, heading for the rocky beachline.

He closed his eyes against the rushing air. He felt relieved as if the pressure was pushing away all his troubling thoughts and anxieties. He wanted to believe nothing mattered as long as he could fly forever with his best friend in open skies and over endless seas.

But his dark side knew power was key, and the only way to gain power was to take it from others first. That was why he needed Gossamer to be real.

His eyes shot open, and he saw Slech, inches away from the ground. In marvelous speed, his white wings opened, catching the air and lifting him right before he hit the coastline.

The white blur flew like an arrow, out and over the ocean before stopping a few ways to watch the other Mislea.

Rotto thought about his actions and turned toward the ocean. As soon as he shot over the rocky points, he brought his wings to full extent, catching a strong flash of air.

A large wave grew in front of him, and once more, he tucked in his wings. He tore through the water, upsetting the wave of motion. But with one strong beat from his wings, he was up in the sky, shaking away the liquid between his feathers.

Droplets of water rained down as he flipped in the air before falling on his back and turning once more to fly next to Slecherick.

"Show off," Slech smiled, watching with a gentle grin as he flew in place.

Rotto smirked and pushed himself forward, Slech close behind.

The sound of crashing waves was soothing the further they ventured out. Rotto realized over the countless times they had flown over the waters, they had never gone this far.

Looking back, their island was nothing but a small silhouette in the distance. Their speed made him even more proud to be a Mislea.

The two four-winged raptors flew forward across the endless ocean. They were both silent, listening to nothing but the water below and their own thoughts.

Looking at his friend, Rotto saw a calm happiness on Slecherick's face. It upset him as he remembered Slech wouldn't be able to do what he loved after tomorrow. He would have to take the difficult test that would decide his future. Rotto knew, without a doubt, his friend would pass.

They were tested on many things, including flight, loyalty, leadership, fighting, strength, catching, and focus—everything Rotto knew he himself had.

Even now, he was surprised to see how confident Slech seemed, especially after being told so last minute. Instead of wishing to train himself and prepare, his reckless friend had gone to the library to read legends. And now he was flying across the ocean in search of a fantasy!

"Slech!" Rotto called to him, dipping his left wing down to turn his body closer toward his friend. "If we find Gossamer…would you stay?"

Slecherick released a low sorrowful screech. The sound traveled over the ocean and into the dark sky. Such a sound was rare to be heard, even by a Mislea, and it made Rotto's heart ache.

"I don't know," Slech said after a moment. "I know where loyalty lies, and that is on our island. But I don't think one night is enough to explore Gossamer once we find it."

Rotto knew he was right and quickly pushed away the troubling realization they wouldn't be home for a while. "When you become a Blazer Wing, be sure to put a word in with them about my test, would you?"

"Of course I will," Slech replied. "I wouldn't want to work on my own. Only you have a temper. Promise me that if they don't reply right away, you'll be patient?"

Rotto remained quiet. Slecherick was right. He did have a temper, especially when it came to his leadership and desire for power.

After an hour of flying, the winds began to get stronger. Thankfully, it blew on their backs, helping them fly with an easier glide, so they didn't notice it at first. Automatically, they began to go higher to avoid the ever growing waves.

Soon, the blowing wind and giant restless waves became too hard to ignore, and Rotto looked around anxiously. He called out to his friend, "Are there *Ores* on Gossamer?"

It was getting harder to hear over the crashing waves and blowing wind, but Slecherick's surprised voice rang loudly to Rotto's ears. "Yes, there are. They're what caused the Colossal War. But why do you ask?" He dove sideways as a strong gust of wind took him off course.

"This storm!" Rotto screeched back as a large wave sent a spray of water onto his back. "It behaves like an Ore, doesn't it?"

Slecherick knew he was right. Back on their island, there were special Ores that the Blazer's kept around the island for protection. There were at least fifty surrounding Trailblazer.

Rotto had only seen a few before. They were round and covered with jagged sharp edges. In the center was a crevice that went all the way around. Inside the crevice, if activated, it would glow brightly from the negative energy inside.

Although Slech had claimed that such Ores could grant some races powers, they had never gifted a Mislea. But they knew Ores were special and sacred, and they were treated as such, kept in their sanctuaries and towers.

If an Ore was tampered with, it would be given to the Blazers who would deactivate it before any real harm was caused.

"That one Ore that Markaria found, do you remember? It caused a horrible storm that lasted for weeks!" Rotto yelled. He ducked swiftly as a large wave threatened to overtake him. The wind now seemed to be coming from all directions, threatening to pull them into the horrendous ocean below.

Markaria, a Mislea Raptor who had been born with weak wings and couldn't fly, had found an activated Ore in the eye of a large storm. No one knew who activated it, but everyone was grateful by the flightless girl's courage to find the source of the tempest.

Rotto had spoken with her a few times. He couldn't imagine not being able to fly, but he had to admit Markaria was one of the kindest Mislea he had ever met. To him, he didn't enjoy being around such a caring girl who put everyone's needs before hers when all he searched for was power and his own desires.

But he remembered how strange the storm had acted when the Ore was moved. He also remembered that Briste Blazer, Highest Leader of the Blazer Wings, had deactivated it. The storm had left along with the strange glow inside.

Rotto was tired and was struggling to stay in flight, his wings aching against the powerful wind as it hit them from all sides. Beside him, Slecherick was breathing heavily as he flapped restlessly.

Looking up, a loud screech escaped his throat as he saw a large wave descending on him. The force from the wave dragged him under.

In a moment, his mouth was full of water as he became trapped beneath the waves. He couldn't flap against the pressure as the heavy liquid tried to drown him. His feathers weighed down as they soaked up the water.

Rotto squeezed his eyes as the salty waves stung them and scorched his tongue. His lungs felt as if they were being caged in as he was struck from all sides. He flipped painfully, his large wings drowning him with their weight.

For the brink of a second, he transformed, just to realize that was even worse because now in his smaller form, he had less control.

Transforming back into his Mislea form, he swiped hard with his back wings and flailed with his front, tearing at the water with his talons. He didn't know how to swim, never had a reason to.

His tail felt like an anchor, no longer like a kite in balance.

Suddenly, there was a break in the waves, and with desperate flailing, he lifted himself into the air—weighty, heavy, and miserable.

He fought to stay above the highest waves, his body screaming in protest against their weariness. Once he was high enough, he was faced with a new problem: the horrible winds.

Now being tossed and flipped through the air, it was a fight to stay away from the crazy ocean. Rotto had never felt so confused and lost as he tried to push his powerful wings beyond their limit.

Suddenly, something flashed out of the corner of his eye, and for the briefest moment, his mind cleared. He found his place in the whipping winds. His wings out straight, he glided on the rough draft of air.

Looking around, he remembered with a stab of horror: *Slecherick!* He scanned the sky as far as he could see, but there was no sign of his white-feathered friend. He scanned the water, staring at each wild wave. Nothing. Slech was gone. The sea had swallowed him.

He must've fallen in the water and drowned!

Slech had been right. He wasn't a strong flyer. He couldn't have survived above nor under the waves. He was gone. But...*forever?*

Rotto released a loud mournful screech of agony. "I should have stopped him! We never should've come!" he screamed into the storm.

The current of air he was riding on broke, turning his right wings beneath him, and causing his entire body to flip in a harsh spin. He screeched again, trying to keep his flight. Then in a small break of the large waves, he saw something. A light.

Struggling to focus, to even stay in the air, he stared at the one spot. The waves broke again, and he saw a silhouette shape of something riding the waves. Something large!

His tired aching wings, body, and mind instantly reacted to see something on the water, something he could land on, rest for even a moment!

He flapped harshly against the storm, trying to reach the shape. As he got closer, he saw it was a large wooden ship. It rode the waves like a master, tilting in the harsh winds but staying afloat.

It looked large and strong enough to carry him. He needed to survive, and right now, this ship was the only thing he had. He needed somewhere to land. To rest. He was near quick death if he tried to stay aloft in the air.

Getting closer, he was taken down in a side dive before being able to catch his balance and fly again. He saw characters on the ship. They weren't Mislea Raptors but new creatures that he hadn't ever heard of—or had he? Slech knew almost every breed of creature. Perhaps he had mentioned it? His hurt and sorrow grew more at the thought of Slecherick. His best friend.

Nearing the ship, he saw in the center of it; a soft but bright gray glow. He cried in knowledge as he recognized the glow instantly. It was an Ore! Why did these creatures have an Ore? And out in the middle of the ocean?

That's where this storm is coming from! That's an Ore that controls these waves!

His anger grew at this. The only reason that the storm was there was because of that Ore. The only reason that the Ore was there was because of the character's folly of bringing it out here.

Because of their folly, his best friend was gone. Slech, a future Blazer Wing and adventurer, was gone. Anger replaced his sorrow. Exhaustion mixed with his emotions, and as he reached the ship, he reached out with his back talons, landing on the top of the mast.

He gripped the mast with his talons, keeping his wings stretched for balance. It felt like a wave of relief washed over him to get this small rest. He stretched his wings, then settled them at his sides. He scowled, looking down at the creatures scurrying around on the deck.

The ship pointed up in a sudden movement as it rode atop a large wave. Rotto quickly spread his wings once again, partly balancing the ship as it rocked on the water, his tail swinging like a small flag, helping him keep his balance. He eyed the characters on deck. They grabbed whatever they could to stay on board.

Crates and barrels rolled over the edge and into the ocean. Many of the characters stared at him with wide terrified eyes as they clung to the ship. He partly smiled to himself. He felt power over them, like a leader. He loved it! But his anger was stronger when he saw the Ore, which was secured tightly in the center of the boat.

The wave they were riding crashed down, sending the front of the ship halfway in the air. Rotto, with his wings spread, flapped for a moment, nearly carrying the ship up with him, but they landed roughly back in the water.

Now, steady for the moment, the characters rushed around, quickly panicking it seemed. Rotto screeched loud and long at them before he began yelling, "Fools! Get that Ore away from here! You'll kill us all!" But his voice was drowned out in the storm.

The creatures below were still shouting and running around to one another. All of them were drenched in water. Their skin and short hair soaked. Two long ears covered in fur were pointing up from the back of their heads, and once again, Rotto puzzled for a moment about what they were.

He was struggling to keep his balance as his heavy weight seemed to begin to get to the mast. He thought he heard it crack for a second, but looking down, the mast looked fine. Not that he cared if these creatures drowned anyway.

Rotto considered swooping down and taking the Ore himself, but the storm was rough, and he was tired. He needed this ship to survive. Also, he couldn't help but enjoy the fear that these characters had when they looked at him, but he didn't want to admit that to himself just yet.

For a moment, he turned into his character form, hoping to help himself more than the characters below. But the moment he did, his feet slipped on wet wood beneath him, and he nearly fell. He gripped the structure roughly and turned back into a Mislea Raptor, once more digging his talons into the mast.

Settled again, he watched the characters as they began behaving oddly.

Cocking his head at them below, he saw they were pulling on ropes, bringing a large machine of some sort out from the lower deck. It was wooden and had long multiple pikes attached to it. The pikes had sharp spikes surrounding them. The wood was carved out, so it was ragged and sharp.

It wasn't until one of them began yelling did he realize they were planning on attacking him!

Trying to leap in the air, his wings protested with pain and exhaustion. Right at the same moment, they fired. Rotto screamed in pain as at least ten long spike-covered pikes shredded his right upper wing. He could feel the feathers and muscles being ripped apart as the spikes grabbed his skin and tore through with great momentum.

The pain was intense, and his anger flared dangerously. He tried to get away from the ship and their deadly weapons, but as he did, his large wing failed him. He needed all four to fly, mainly his two front largest wings.

Looking with terror, he saw his injury was worse than he had estimated. Instantly, he knew he wouldn't be able to fly with it, no matter what he tried.

They aimed their large weapon at his other wing, right as the boat went up in another wave. He lost his balance, and a loud crack sounded as the mast snapped beneath his weight. He fell forward, crashing on the deck.

In the few glimpses he got, he saw the boat crack and break from his sudden weight. The boat was breaking apart, and suddenly, water was filling it. He saw where the Ore had been caged in a wooden crate. It was now cracked and broken. In horror and anger, he watched as the Ore disappeared over the edge of the ship. Now it would be lost forever where no one could deactivate it.

Rotto couldn't move. He was tired, too weak, and in too much pain. He was instantly back into his character, feeling delusional for the next few minutes, stuck in a wedge between the cracked wood with water washing over him, the rain pelting him on all sides— or maybe that was a person? He couldn't tell and didn't care at the moment. He was finally getting some rest.

He fell into what seemed to be a deep slumber, only to be awakened by the painful flush of water surrounding him. He was in the ocean, drowning.

He appeared to have been pushed beneath the boat. Feeling the weight of the hull pushing him down deeper, he thrashed wildly, only to find he couldn't move. Anger and hatred for the folly of these creatures engulfed every nerve and emotion in him.

Not only had they killed his best friend, but now he would also die from their foolishness as well. He screamed beneath the water, swallowing a mouthful of the salty liquid.

Large surges of water pushed him upward and against the wild waves. In rare glances, he thought he saw an island. But he couldn't focus long enough or stay above to be sure. Soon, he was less than a mile from land. Mentally, he saw himself fighting to go toward it, but physically, his body refused. A large wave pushed beneath the water, and he felt himself get tangled inside a strong current.

He was being dragged beneath the island by an unseen force.

*****

"Wake up!" a voice hissed.

Rotto tried to move but couldn't. His entire body ached and begged for rest.

"*Wake up!*" the unfriendly voice echoed painfully through his mind.

Rotto forced his eyes to open. He blinked slowly, trying to gain focus. He was lying on his stomach in Character form on hard stone. His neck was turned sideways, his left cheek pressed up against the cold rock.

His vision must have been failing him because it was dark and musty looking wherever he was.

Wait... where am I? What happened?

His mind felt like it was full of a thick fog, and he couldn't break through long enough to focus on his thoughts.

The evil voice didn't wait for him, and it returned with more ferocity than before. *"Get up, I said!"*

It echoed in his mind and through the fog, this time sending ripples of burning pain with it.

Rotto groaned sorrowfully as he tried once more to move. He found he was tangled in some sort of rope. His wings had not detached and were wrapped against his legs in a very uncomfortable position.

Another wave of burns ripped through his head.

"Stop!" Rotto slurred on his words. "Stop, please, I'm trying to get up,"

A low laugh sounded around him in a strange echo that seemed to rumble the ground he was on. A strange sensation tore at his heart, and Rotto realized with terrible horror that he was *afraid.*

The laugh came again, this time much louder. Slowly, it sank into his mind. Rotto winced, trying to shut it out, but it fought back harder.

Stop. stop.

"You can't shut me out."

Who are you?

"I go by many names."

What do you want?

"I want you."

Rotto groaned out loud, struggling once more to fight free of the rope he was tangled in. It had been knotted around his waist and the excess cord had found its way to tangle his limbs. He wasn't sure where the rope had even come from.

The dense fog grew inside his mind, taking over every sense and emotion. Rotto cried out, trying to push away the wretched thoughts that entered his mind.

"You're the answer to helping me escape. But don't worry, you'll get your share. I have an island above me in need of a leader. Someone powerful."

Rotto stopped struggling as the burning fog continued to take over his mind. He opened his eyes. But they were no longer his own, laced with a black curtain of the evil that now controlled his thoughts.

"What do you want me to do?" Rotto asked out loud.

The evil laugh echoed through his ears. *"Now that's what I wanted to hear."*

I

SURVIVORS

Crowley—Year 315; Sixteen Years Later

"This is what we're here for," a gruff voice interrupted the whispered conversation of two boys.

Crowley looked up from his best friend, Malachi, and glanced at what the old captain was pointing at.

They were in the underground scouting tunnels of Smuir, where Captain Ashton led the group of trainees. The older man frowned at them, indicating for them to be silent.

Instantly, Crowley shut his mouth and straightened his shoulders. He wanted to make a good impression on the captain so he could be let out on these missions more often. He was seventeen and believed himself as capable as any other soldier in the group.

He wasn't the youngest there; that was Malachi, the king's son. He was four years younger than Crowley, but the king had raised him as his own and the two boys grew up caring for one another like brothers.

Ashton turned away from them and went back to pointing along the dirt wall, a torch in one hand. Wires lined the earth and had been since they entered these tunnels. Crowley tried not to look as bored as Malachi when the captain began to explain what they were for.

"These cords hold the tunnels together," Ashton continued to explain the science of it all as he pointed out certain colored wires and which ones kept the southern tunnels together and how the eastern ones were getting weaker.

Crowley began to look around at the rest of the group with them. There was one other boy his age, and the other two were twenty. They all knew Ashton had argued with the king about having to teach such a young, rowdy group on how to care for the tunnels.

Crowley didn't want to disappoint him.

Malachi had been brought along because, as he had said, it sounded fun, and if Crowley was going, he could go. Ashton didn't argue with the king but had nodded stiffly while shooting daggers at the boy with his eyes.

Apart from the teenage boys, there was a young woman there. Her name was Trinity, and she served as a medic.

I still think it's stupid to bring a doctor along. Crowley thought stiffly.

Trinity stood out of Ashton's way and listened to the captain with a curious expression.

Crowley glanced over at Malachi who was secretly fingering a few wires closest to him. He watched as the younger boy accidentally twisted a cord from its place, and it disconnected.

Crowley was about to laugh when the ground around them began vibrating, and large clods of dirt fell from the ceiling. After a moment, it stopped.

Ashton's accusing eyes instantly rested on the two boys who stared back with innocent expressions. Another Character nearby reached out to examine the wire.

"Don't," Ashton warned when he saw him. "The cords are very sensitive. It you're not careful, you could make these caves collapse and bury us all alive with them."

Malachi glanced at him from the corner of his eye, and Crowley fought to keep his smile contained.

As Ashton continued to lead them through the tunnels and farther from the safety of Smuir, he stopped occasionally to check wires. Crowley's plan to impress the captain was beginning to die.

He hadn't realized how boring this would be. He thought coming out here would…well, lead outside where they could be confronted with danger and he could show off his fighting skills.

Really, he just wanted to find a reason to put his fighting skills to use. He was told often he was a good fighter when someone stumbled upon his training. He had such a terrible longing to go out and be a warrior that it ached.

Crowley stopped, his ears instantly shooting up at the sound of voices ahead. Ashton and the rest of the group stopped as they heard it too.

Putting a finger to his mouth, the captain turned toward the group. Quietly, he mouthed, "No one else should be in here."

Crowley's heart began racing with excitement. He stepped forward, his fingers curling around the hilt of his short blade. This felt right, unsheathing his short sword and preparing to face danger.

"Wait!" Ashton held out an arm and stopped the boy. He motioned for the group to continue walking as he scanned the tunnels in front of them with a careful gaze. Finally, he said, "Yoel, Crowley, Walt." He jerked his head forward, handing off his torch to a nearby Character.

Giving Malachi's shoulder a comforting squeeze, Crowley and two others followed the captain ahead through the dark passage.

Crowley wasn't the least bit scared. He was only excited to fight someone, kill if it was a stranger.

This is what I've trained for my entire life…ever since Ma and Dad were killed. This is my chance.

After a few moments of silence, Crowley knew, as well as the others, that whoever was there had heard them coming.

The burrows were dark, but ahead was the faint light of a torch beyond the turn. Ashton motioned for them to fall behind more. Crowley was getting anxious. He wanted to jump into a fight, not be backed up.

Then Ashton motioned for them to pick up speed.

Crowley began running, passing Ashton easily. He stayed on the balls of his feet, his boots hitting the earth almost soundlessly.

Ashton didn't try to stop him. It was too late anyway.

A loud shout sounded from the other side of the curve, and Crowley tore around the side, raising his sword in advance. It took him less than a moment to see who and what was in front of him.

A Swiftmaw boy stood there, trying to grip a torch that was sliding from his hands. Crowley surged forward to attack.

Ashton and the two others came around the corner, but the boy didn't attack them. Instead, the Character's quick reactions threw the torch and hightailed it down the dark tunnel.

Crowley hadn't been prepared and tried to push the flying torch away, losing his balance and control over his own blade as the flames engulfed him and he screamed from the burns.

Instantly, Ashton was there, but instead of somehow magically putting out the fire like Crowley's desperate mind hoped he would, the older warrior punched a wire on the wall which snapped perfectly.

Next thing he knew, the ceiling above them fell in, burying him beneath a layer of earth. No longer did he feel the pain from flames; the new pain came from the weight crushing him.

It only took a moment for Ashton, Yoel, and Walt to pull him out. It hadn't been deep, but Crowley stood there for a moment, feeling dazed from the knock.

Still, he refused to sit down and rest, even as he stumbled onto his hands and knees. Walt pulled him to his feet, and Ashton called back for the rest of the group to come and join them.

Before them was a long pile of dirt from the partly collapsed roof. The next eight hours were spent digging and climbing through the ruined tunnel, searching for the Swiftmaw.

They could climb over most of the dirt piles, having to dig through sections where an entire wall had been built up. Bits of air blew in from a few open patches above. Each time they passed one, Ashton would look up and frown.

Once Crowley helped Malachi climb up toward one, where the two of them cautiously looked at the surrounding area above them. The fresh air felt amazing after the last eight hours of digging.

He was surprised to find they were a few miles away from the base of the mountain where their city, Smuir, was beneath. No one ever left the mountain, and Crowley was slightly disappointed to see they were on the wrong side. On the other side of the mountain, he knew, was the ghost town of their outside city.

"Crowley, get Malachi down from there before Ashton sees you," Yoel advised below.

Crowley looked down, his disappointment showing as much as Malachi's. But he knew the teen was right. Carefully, he began to help the smaller boy back down.

Halfway to the ground, he paused. Something was sticking out from the pile below.

"Come on." He helped lower Malachi to the earth, then slid down the pile toward the cloth poking out.

When he reached it, he tried pulling on it. It didn't budge. "Here!" he called. "I found something!"

It wasn't long until the rest of the group were there, helping dig around the cloth. None of them used shovels, not wanting to risk piercing someone, although Crowley felt like it wouldn't be too bad. The Swiftmaw deserved it.

They dug faster as they began to uncover something stiff. A few moments later, they pulled out the body of a young Swiftmaw boy, no older than Malachi.

Crowley wasn't fooled, though. He had read that Swiftmaw were taken at the age of nine and trained to be fierce killers. He didn't pity the young boy either. Malachi hovered by his side, his eyes wide with horror to see the beat-up body.

"He's still breathing," Malachi said quietly.

Crowley glowered at the Swiftmaw. The boy *was* breathing.

"That's impossible. He's been buried for almost eight hours. He should have suffocated," Yoel said. He looked up at their captain. "How is this possible?"

"I'm not sure," Ashton frowned. "Trinity, take a look at this boy."

The doctor came forward, her eyes studying the beat-up body but showing no look of pity from the sight.

Crowley stood and watched curiously as she bent down next to the frail body. But instead of checking the boy's pulse or whatever it was doctors did, her hands went to the boy's side.

"You should take his weapons," she said, her fingers gripping a sheath on the boy's belt.

Crowley frowned. It was a smart idea, which was why he didn't like that a female doctor who didn't have any battle experience had thought of it first.

Ashton almost appeared to be smiling, but Crowley couldn't tell if that's what he was seeing or if the captain was just as annoyed as he was.

"Crowley," the old captain said, "help search the boy."

The words had no sooner left Ashton's mouth when the Swiftmaw suddenly opened his eyes. It took the boy less than a second to realize the situation he was in.

In a blur of action, the Swiftmaw shot to his feet, kicking Trinity in the face and grabbing his short sword with one swift motion. He swung the blade in a circle, forcing the group to step back.

Crowley had grabbed the limp doctor without thinking, but the moment he saw the boy's weapon flashing, he forgot all courtesy.

The blade nicked Walt in the arm, and the teen stumbled back, grabbing at the wound as it began to bleed. Crowley looked frantically for his sword which he had set aside earlier.

He was suddenly struck in the back by the Swiftmaw's boot, and he fell forward. As quickly as he could, he rolled onto his back, clenching his fists, but there wasn't going to be a second attack.

The boy transformed and jumped out of the dirt pile, easily escaping through the patch of air leading outside. Crowley grabbed his blade, ready to chase after the animal with all that was in him.

"He was looking for something," Malachi suddenly said.

Crowley stopped short, quickly glancing at his friend. He had forgotten about the prince in the mad scramble.

He was grateful to see Ashton had grabbed the boy and stood in front of him. Crowley couldn't even begin to imagine what would've happened if the prince had been exposed from where he had been standing before.

Seeing Malachi was okay, Crowley began climbing toward the patch.

"Crowley, don't go after it," Ashton's gruff voice ordered.

Crowley ignored him, but he hadn't realized how fast the old captain was—and strong. Ashton grabbed his arm and yanked him back to the ground.

"I wouldn't care if you were the king's son or not. I am leading this company, and you follow my orders," the old captain whispered harshly.

Crowley bit his tongue to keep from snapping back. "The kid is getting away," he growled under his breath.

"Even if you tried, we never would've caught him. Besides, we can't risk bringing a Swiftmaw into the mountain. He'd call for—"

Ashton was interrupted by Yoel's call. "There's another body!" he cried.

Crowley and Ashton both spun around. Yoel was helping Malachi, who was crouched by the dirt, a few inches away from where they had uncovered the boy.

The other men answered and came to help. Ashton left Crowley and went to the young doctor. She was sitting next to Walt, helping care for his wound. Her own bloody—possibly broken—nose couldn't be ignored, though.

Crowley glowered at the captain's back, then turned to help dig out the rest of the trapped form.

It was a young girl, also around Malachi's age. Crowley scowled with puzzlement. Why were two kids in these caves? It was an even greater shock when Malachi announced she was a Stexphin.

The young prince sat by the girl's head, looking at her intently as he wiped the smudged dirt from her face. Two Stexphin ears were almost hidden in her entangled hair.

Her breathing was much more shallow, and Crowley wondered if she would wake up long enough to at least be questioned. He didn't like that two children had been able to survive eight hours buried beneath a heavy layer of earth.

Crowley began to stand but stopped when a faint purple flash caught his eyes. Crouching back down, he saw a thin chain around the girl's neck. On the end was a crooked smooth circle.

The circle flashed a light purple again. Reaching down, he picked up the charm. He held it close to his face as he studied it. Two musical notes were carved in the light gray metal. Inside each note was a strange course of purple. It almost looked like energy.

What is this?

"Crowley," Ashton's voice came from above.

The teen clutched the charm in his fist and looked up at the captain.

"What'd you find?"

"Nothing." Crowley dropped the charm. "Just a necklace."

Ashton looked past him to the still image of the girl. His stern expression slowly changed as his face filled with a sort of softness.

Crowley smirked and stood as Trinity sat down with her medical bag. Her nose was taken care of, but dried blood still stuck to her face. *Guess bringing a doctor wasn't the worst idea.*

But that wasn't why he was smirking. He found it rather amusing to see this soft side of Ashton. The captain was usually stern and ordering.

"How is she doing?" Ashton asked, the small hint of hope resting in his voice.

"She should live," Trinity said, shaking her head with disbelief. "I've cured soldiers with worse wounds than this. I'm just surprised she hadn't suffocated. Neither one of them."

"Well, you'd best get her to wake up because Ash wants to adopt her," Crowley smirked.

Malachi looked up from where he still sat by the girl's head, a smile forming as he, too, saw the old captain's soft expression.

It didn't last, and Ashton glowered at him with cold eyes. "Why would you say that?" he ordered Crowley.

Everyone knew Ashton's wife and baby daughter had died in an avalanche a few years before Mt. Smuir had been evacuated underground.

"Sorry, sir," Crowley said, really not sorry at all. He put his hands in front of him innocently and stepped back with a shrug. "Just figured you moved on by now and might want—" He quieted and looked away, beginning to realize now wasn't a good time for a crude joke such as this.

"Crowley," Ashton ordered, his stern expression and hard voice returned. "Help carry her back to the mountain. We'll get her to Matthias and question her when she wakes." He turned and yelled at the soldiers standing around to start covering all the opening holes above.

"Walt!" the old captain snapped.

"Yessir?" The wounded boy jumped to his feet, wincing as he did.

"Help Crowley take the girl back. Trinity—" he began.

"I'll stay here," the doctor said firmly. "I've had worse than a broken nose. Besides, you'll need me in case another one of these loafers decide to get themselves hurt."

Crowley was surprised by her boldness and began to wonder if he had underestimated her. He looked at Ashton, whose stern eyes were focused on him.

Suddenly, he realized the captain had meant it when he said he wanted him to carry the girl back.

The city is miles away! He grumbled inwardly.

He waited for Trinity to finish, then bent down next to the girl, forcing his arms beneath her. He stood with a grunt, and Walt came beside him.

"I don't need your help," Crowley said through gritted teeth.

Walt shrugged, knowing that before they walked a mile, the teen would ask him to help.

"Malachi," Ashton said, "go with them. And, Crowley, just because Walt has one arm doesn't mean he can't help you. Malachi too."

The young prince nodded. "I'm pretty strong," he said eagerly.

Crowley ignored all of them and began the long trek back to the underground city.

*****

It started as a dull pain within her ribs, but it soon expanded through her entire body. She felt sick, sweat covering every inch of skin and physique shivering out of control. Her eyes were shut, and she could scarcely think. The pain ebbed at times, only to flare up again and with seemingly heightened intensity.

It had felt like the pain had been there forever, and in a way, she was becoming used to it, but at the same moment, the reality it might stick a little while longer was terrifying.

On any other day, she probably would've gone to bed and rested until she felt better, but not today. Today was a day of pushing the limits.

For a second, she thought she was hearing voices. Familiar voices. She became distracted for a moment, trying to clear her mind and recognize this voice. It sounded like Father. *Mother*. Her family.

Wasn't it just a few months ago when she was back at home, safe and secure? Before the invention and this crazy adventure she never wanted? Where had it all gone wrong?

Was it the day Frazil came home, injured? No, it was before that. It was the day they had gone into the storage room and found those old journals and photographs. She couldn't remember why they went into the room that day. It wasn't very important, just another space in their odd little house.

Home. It felt like a long-lost memory that didn't exist anymore. Nothing but a faint dream. A false hope.

2

A LOST DREAM

Valkyrie—Year 315; A Few Months Earlier

Cautiously, Valkyrie snuck around the side of their oddly built cottage. Lifting her Stexphin ears, she could hear the sound of someone around the corner in front of her. And she was ready.

"Gotcha!" a voice said from behind.

She jumped and spun around to see her twin brother, Virga, standing there with a large clump of mud in one hand.

She stared, eyes wide. "But I heard—"

She never got to finish. Virga, whose arm had been cranked behind his head, now came bursting to life as he propelled it forward, thrusting the ball of mud into the air.

Valkyrie had seen it coming and quickly ducked. The large mudball barely missed the tips of her ears. She began to smile triumphantly when she heard a splat and Virga gasp. She grimaced, somehow knowing what had happened.

Still, when she turned around, it was a shock to see their mother standing there, caked in mud. Brooklyn gaped, then wiped an arm across her face, clearing the muck from her eyes.

Boy, are we in for it now, she thought with a cringe.

"What in the world are you doing?" Brooklyn sputtered, spitting mud.

11

Valkyrie couldn't find the courage to speak, nor could Virga. No excuse would be good enough to say why they were throwing mud at each other. At least none that would satisfy their mother.

Brooklyn wiped her mouth and waited for an answer. When she saw she wasn't going to get one, she shook her head in disappointment.

"All right," she said, her tone serious.

Valkyrie knew she was going to state their punishment. *Please don't say water the garden, please don't make us get water,* she thought desperately.

They grew a large garden, and the main source of water was almost a mile away into the woods: Camino Creek.

Sure, they had running water in the house, but as odd as their house already was, it hadn't been built with an outside pump. Plus, Mother knew the walk to the creek was good for them. It gave them time to think of what they had done…or something like that. Valkyrie couldn't remember her exact words.

*****

"I can't tell if this is better or worse than getting water," Valkyrie grumbled to Virga as he helped her move a large cardboard box to the back of the room.

They hadn't been sent to get water but were sent to clean out and organize the storage room. They hardly went into the storage room, and it *needed* to be organized.

Brooklyn had been planning to do it, but then her children gave her the perfect opportunity to get it started for her. She knew they wouldn't give it their best, but it would be good enough to lighten the load.

Valkyrie set the box down with help from Virga. She sneezed at the unsettled dust, wiping her nose and frowning. Walking back to the door, she soon returned holding a broom.

Virga looked at her and scowled in disgust. "It's disgusting!" he remarked, scrunching his nose.

"I know," she said. "It's why I grabbed the broom."

"I wasn't talking about the floor," Virga said. "Have you seen yourself?"

"You little—" She started bringing the broom around in an arc to hit her twin.

He dodged, inviting a game of chase.

She didn't care that she was covered in filth as she accepted the invitation to race around the cluttered room. It was his fault anyway for starting the war of mud earlier.

Virga laughed as he ran around a pile of boxes. She was right behind him, face set in determination. Bringing the broom around for a second time, she added more strength to her swing to up the momentum, not wanting to miss again.

Virga's laugh was cut short with a yelp as the broom barely missed him, tripping his legs instead. He fell forward, running straight into an old shelf covered with old boxes.

Valkyrie gasped and slid to a stop as Virga collided into the small shelf. There was a loud crack, and together, the shelves collapsed in, crashing down with everything else on top of him.

Valkyrie was quick to pull her brother out from beneath the destroyed shelf. He stood, fazed for a moment as he tried to contemplate what had just happened.

Valkyrie groaned, looking back at the broken shelves. Two large boxes had been knocked from the shelf, and their contents spilled over the floor.

Virga looked down too. "Wow," he said, returning to himself, "that's a lot of pictures for us to pick up."

The wreckage from the shelf was full of scattered photos. Valkyrie frowned. They would never get them organized back to the way they had been. It was going to take forever just to pick them up in general.

"You're such an idiot!" she yelled, turning toward her brother angrily.

"*Me?*" he cried. "You're the one trying to attack me with a broom!"

"Whatever. Just help me clean this up."

It wasn't long before the two of them were sitting on the ground, returning the pictures back inside their crates. It wasn't long until Valkyrie got distracted looking at the images.

"Look how old these are!" she said.

Virga leaned over and peered at the image in her hand.

"Is that Mom?" he asked, pointing at the young girl in the image laughing with two boys.

"I think so. Look how little she was! Do you think those are her brothers?"

"I don't know. Did she have brothers? Mom never talks about her side of the family."

"Nor does Dad. I wonder if *he* had any siblings. I only know a little about the story of our grandfather, Dana," Valkyrie said, reluctantly stacking the image on top of the others inside the box.

"Yeah, the story of how he *drowned*." Virga furrowed his brows. He picked up a few other images and looked at them intently, his frown fading away.

"Let me see." Valkyrie took the picture from him. It was another image of Brooklyn when she was a young teenager. She wasn't looking at the camera but down at a small baby animal in her arms.

"What creature is that?" Valkyrie asked.

"If you let me *look at it*, maybe I'd know!" Virga snapped. He reached over and jerked the image from her hands.

"Careful!" She glared at him. He was so *stubborn* sometimes!

She peeled her eyes away from the pictures and returned to stacking them inside the box. She tried not to get distracted but was soon showing Virga pictures of Frazil when he was a baby.

"Look at him!" she squealed.

Virga gave the picture a weird look. "I wonder where *our* baby pictures are," he mused. They searched all of them but couldn't find any. In fact, there were only two pictures of them, each separate.

Valkyrie frowned at the image of her in the arms of an unfamiliar young girl. The girl was smiling widely, looking sideways as she held the baby proudly. "Valkyrie" was written on the back.

Virga was holding the torn image of him, looking at it sadly. Valkyrie scooted next to his side and looked at the picture. It only showed a newborn baby in someone's arms. She couldn't see who. The rest of the image was torn. Virga flipped the picture over. There were words on the back but only glimpses of them; the rest was torn away.

"Virga…loved like…always…in the dark?" Valkyrie read, nudging him and smirking. She stopped when she saw his sad expression. "I bet Mother knows what happened to the rest," she encouraged.

Virga rolled his eyes. "I really don't care. It's an old picture." He put it in the box and went back to collect the rest.

As they finished picking up the rest of the photographs, they cleaned up the leftover pieces from the shelf and began to pick up the other items that had fallen.

"What was in this one?" Virga asked, picking up a larger box. "No, wait, there's still stuff in here." He looked inside the box and said, "It's a bunch of journals."

Valkyrie looked at the pile of journals they had cleaned up from the shelf wreckage. "Those must have fallen out." She picked them up, stopping as she looked at the top one.

"Wow!" she said, setting the pile inside Virga's box and grabbing the top one. "*292, Dane Kovanee*," she read. "It's Father's!"

15

"Year 292? How old was he then?" Virga asked, looking at the worn leather cover.

"What year are we in now? 315? Father is forty-one now, I think. That means he would have been around twenty, I think." She flipped through the pages of the journal, a smile slowly forming on her lips.

"Look, Virga. This is where all of Father's pictures are." She pointed out a picture glued to the page of their father as a teen. He wasn't smiling nor was he looking at the camera as he stared into the distance.

She flipped through a few other pages and was surprised to find most of her father's pictures were of him in Stexphin form. They hardly ever transformed at home.

Virga was digging through the old journals but stopped as he pulled out one of Mother's. He looked at it, then gave it to Valkyrie. "We should read these sometime," he said.

"I don't know," she said doubtfully. "I'm beginning to feel like we're snooping on personal property."

Virga took the journals from her hands and placed them back in the box. "Fine," he said, sealing the journals inside.

She watched, frowning. "Mother would've told us if she wanted us to read her old journals," Valkyrie said, assuring herself more than her brother.

"True," he said, placing his hands on his hips. "But I'm keeping some of those pictures."

"Virga!" she scolded.

"*What?* They are becoming *dust* here! If Mother ever mentions them, I'll return them. Until then, their mine." He took a small envelope out of his pocket and waved it in her face.

"Let's just hurry and finish, then we can play outside before Mother gives us another chore," Valkyrie said, picking up the broom and tossing it at her brother.

He caught it and nodded in agreement.

*****

After moving around a few more boxes, the twins ran to the woods where they loved to pretend they were adventurers.

"Sneak around to that side so we can cut him off," Valkyrie motioned to the bushes on her left. They had been playing for over an hour and were about to ambush their imaginary villain.

Virga ignored her and jumped out from their hiding spot, raising his stick as if it were a great sword.

"No, Virga!" Valkyrie stood and frowned at her brother.

He stopped swinging his weapon and scowled back.

"You can't just *attack* the man."

"Says who?" Virga challenged.

"We're supposed to sneak up and attack together."

"Crying onions! You're so stubborn," Virga said, rolling his eyes.

Valkyrie tossed her stick aside. "I'm not going to play with you if you're going to act like this."

"What am I doing wrong? Not playing by *your* roles?" he scoffed. "Sorry, Your Majesty. I forgot my place. I am only here to do *your* bidding." He bowed dramatically, flourishing his hand out in front of him.

Valkyrie felt her face go hot with anger, and she jumped at him, shoving him back. Before he hit the ground, he grabbed her arm and pulled her down with him.

They ended in a muddy roll, and without a second thought, Valkyrie transformed into Stexphin form. Virga mimicked her, and they began a new tumble of biting and scratching.

Valkyrie swatted and scratched her brother perfectly down his neck in a break between biting. With a loud hiss, he pinned her to the ground, and they both transformed back into Character form.

He continued to crouch over her, pressing her shoulders into the earth painfully. They were both breathing heavily from their angry lashing.

"Get off," Valkyrie grunted, her eyes beginning to tear up.

Virga glowered at her. "Make me," he huffed.

"You're such a jerk." Her voice cracked, and a few tears spilled down her cheeks. Looking up at him, her eyes went wide to see the claw mark lightly bleeding down his neck.

Virga got off her. "You're an emotional wreck," he said, suddenly looking guilty at her hurt expression. He fingered the scratch. "And mean," he muttered.

"It's not deep," she said stiffly, sitting up and checking her own bruises. "Just cover it with your shirt collar so Mom doesn't see it."

The two of them sat there in silence, their bubbling anger from the earlier dispute disappearing. Valkyrie opened her mouth to apologize, but Virga blurted out, "Sorry," before she had the chance.

"How do you do that?" Valkyrie asked, annoyed. "You always try to beat me by apologizing first. You know that doesn't mean anything."

"What do you mean *try*? I do it each time. Besides, I feel guilty when *you* apologize first."

"What are you apologizing for?" she challenged stubbornly. She watched as his jaw clenched.

"For—" He sighed and threw his hand in the air. "Not playing by '*the rules*.'"

Valkyrie smiled and shook her head at his poor attempt. "I'm sorry, too, for trying to take control over the game, then attacking you."

"What do you *mean try*?" Virga said again, sounding desperate.

Valkyrie playfully shoved him. "What do you want to do then?"

"Finish the ambush," Virga smiled and jumped to his feet. "This time, we can have Tylar *and* Rassel finish off the evildoer together."

Valkyrie smiled and took his hand as he pulled her to her feet. "Let's—" he began, but she held up a hand as her ears pricked up.

"Wait, shh," she listened then said, "Mother's calling for us."

"Ugh," Virga groaned. "She probably saw the storage room, huh?"

Valkyrie sighed. "We'll have to finish this some other time."

"I wish it was real," Virga said desperately. "Then we wouldn't have to be called away."

"I don't think you'd enjoy it if it were real," Valkyrie smirked.

"Yes, I would," Virga smiled, looking up distantly.

Valkyrie knew he was envisioning himself as a great warrior. She took his distraction as an advantage. She jabbed him in the ribs, then took off sprinting. "Race you back!" she called.

3

THE TRUTH

Crowley—Year 317; Two Years Later

It was quiet in the dimly lit library. *How it should always be,* Crowley thought to himself with slight irritation. *Quiet.*

He hated coming here during the day when a group of immature teens used it as their hangout spot. They didn't respect the needed silence unless they were yelled at.

But hardly anyone came in here anymore. Everyone had already read the books.

It was very late, and the only light came from the lamp above. He was sitting at a high desk, leaning over open books showing pictures of maps.

He needed different views on the charts while he tried to calculate where his last scouting party had most likely gone. He knew they should have returned by now, and if they didn't soon, he'd have to send out more groups.

Crowley moved to study a map, and a shadow cast over the graph. Without looking up, he moved the lamp to a different angle. He sighed wearily, rubbing at the heavy bags beneath his eyes.

He missed feeling energetic. Feeling alive. Feeling sunlight soak into his skin. Stexphin weren't created to live inside deep caves underground where windows were considered a crime.

He scowled to himself, pounding his fist on the table, "*Ugh!*" he shouted angrily. Crowley dropped his head into his hands, rubbing his temples stressfully.

It wasn't easy having half the population of Mt. Smuir looking up to you. The other half looked up to their king, King Demoor.

The underground city of Smuir had the largest population of Stexphin.

Demoor had been the king over Mt. Smuir for years. But although he was only forty-seven years of age, Crowley could see he was slowly losing his mind down here.

Crowley was the youngest yet most trusted advisor of the king. At sixteen years old, he was out-grading all the kids in his class. At seventeen, the king's son, and Crowley's best friend, left the mountain with his mother.

At eighteen, the king announced him as his highest-ranked counselor. How Demoor had come to trust him more than anyone else came from years of loyalty to not only the king but also his son as well.

After Demoor's wife and son disappeared, it took months for anyone to rebuild their trust with the king. Even now, he still didn't trust very many people.

Crowley trusted all the men from the guards to the lords. It was their friendships he had lost after his best friend disappeared with the queen.

Even now, three years after the king's son left, he wasn't close to anyone but Demoor. The king and his family had practically raised him.

He had been orphaned after the population of Smuir was pushed into hiding. The beautiful city growing on the side of the mountain was completely abandoned.

Everyone had moved away from the risk of exposure to the Griefolowtros and hidden deep beneath the mountain.

Demoor had led them all here where they lived their lives away from the sun, invisible to anyone from the outside.

The great village Smuir was nothing but a page inside history books. What the outside world thought had become of them, he didn't know.

All he knew were three things, the only things that kept him going every day:

One: Demoor was the only family he had left, and he was loyal to him.

Two: Everyone was counting on him to support and guide the king.

And three: he wished more than anything that his best friend had taken him with them when they left Smuir.

The soft sound of the library door being opened made him sit up and turn around. He didn't know anyone else who would be up at this hour, especially coming into the library.

He was surprised to see a young girl walk in. She instantly saw him and closed the door behind her. She then ignored him, turned on a few small lights, and walked to the bookshelves.

Crowley watched her. She looked familiar.

Smuir's library wasn't big and had very few shelves. As the girl disappeared behind them, he remembered who she was. She was one of the captain's daughters. He didn't know her name but had seen her before. Now he understood why she was here.

Her father had been killed a few months ago, he and a small band of other warriors—the band of warriors *he* had sent out…without the king's permission.

Crowley turned back around in his seat, suddenly feeling guilty. After her father had been killed, the girl had simply disappeared. Sometimes he would see her walking through the halls, staying in the shadows. She stopped all contact with anyone and everyone after her father died.

Crowley bit his tongue, knowing it was his fault the girl was like this. He turned back around, staring hard at the shelf she had gone behind.

I should talk to her. He wasn't sure what he would say, but he owed her a lot. It was his fault she lost everything. *But what do I say? Does she even know it was* me *who gave the order?*

He quietly got to his feet, hesitating before slowly walking to the shelves. He walked around the side and saw the girl standing like a stone as she scanned the books.

Crowley looked at her for a moment. She couldn't be any more than sixteen. She was pretty, though, with long, straight, dark gray hair and a good build of body. She seemed small but was almost his height, and he could see strength inside her.

Walking up behind her, he looked to see what books she was scanning. It was the geography section, which was mostly empty from the books *he* had taken.

Another thing I've taken from her, he silently judged himself.

"Most of them—" he started, but the girl jumped, turning to look at him. "Sorry," he quickly apologized, engrossed by her bright dark green eyes. He quickly looked away, gesturing past the shelf. "I was looking at maps. I probably have what you're looking for."

"I was looking for maps," she said quietly, sounding as if she agreed with him.

He studied her closely. There was something almost *curious* about her.

He led her back to the table and pulled up another chair for her. She didn't sit down but stood over the books for a few minutes as she examined them.

He stood, too, waiting for her to act. She finally did, reaching over to grab a small book opened up to show a map of Gossamer's westward side. She studied the map carefully, keeping it close to her face.

After a moment, she looked up at him. He waited patiently for her to say something as she set the book down on the desk. She looked back down at the map and quietly asked, "Do you know where—" She stopped and swallowed hard.

Crowley took in a sharp breath. She was going to ask him if he knew where her father died.

It was quiet for a long time. The girl closed her eyes, and he knew she was fighting tears.

"What's your name?" he asked her, leaning over to look at her face.

She let out a shaky sigh, then looked up to meet his gaze. He was surprised to see her eyes weren't filled with tears nor red.

"Selah," she said. Her eyes looked shallow, and he knew she was lying. "And you're Crowley, the king's youngest adviser."

He wasn't surprised she knew who he was, but he had hoped she didn't. It would have sounded better if he had introduced himself.

"How old are you?" she asked, her ears flicking backward as if she heard something.

"Twenty," he said, straightening his shoulders and raising his chin higher as he remembered his place. "And you are—"

"Seventeen," she said, turning around to look at the door. Her ears pricked forward, and she waited. "I think—" She hesitated. "King Demoor is here."

"He never comes to the library," Crowley assured her.

The door clicked as someone turned the handle and slowly pushed it open. Crowley instantly straightened himself as Demoor walked in. Looking, he saw Selah had disappeared.

How did she know?

"Crowley." The king's voice sounded more old and tired than it normally was. "I'm glad I found you."

"My king," Crowley said, getting on one knee and bowing his head. He looked up and met Demoor's sad eyes. "Sir, you should have sent a messenger. It's very late to be wandering the kingdom alone."

"Kingdom? Yes…the kingdom." Demoor's eyes went distant, and Crowley knew he was remembering what they used to be. This happened often.

Crowley had learned to guide the king back when this happened. Demoor spent so much time inside his mind. It wasn't healthy.

"My king," he said, standing and walking to his side. "I am here."

"Yes, yes. You are." Demoor looked around. "Are we alone?"

Crowley scanned the library for Selah. Had the young girl left? He was sure she had but couldn't risk it.

"We should go to the central room," Crowley offered.

Demoor hesitated, then nodded slowly.

Crowley led the king away from the library and down the halls. It was dark and quiet as they walked, with only a few torches lighting the dim hallway. They had electricity in most of the underground areas, but some places were unreachable.

"Are you all right, my king?" Crowley asked, looking at the man next to him.

He seemed to be aging more every day or at least more than he should be.

The king's once red hair had been turning an odd gray over the past year. His nicely cut mustache had white hairs throughout it, and his brown, gentle eyes looked drained and ghostly.

No longer was he the strong young man Crowley used to look up to.

"You know I became king after my older brother stepped down," Demoor began, pausing for a moment.

"Yes, of course."

"Did I ever tell you why he stepped down?" he asked, his voice sounding wobbly.

"Yes…no…no, you haven't," Crowley answered, shocked to realize he hadn't actually heard that story before. He realized he had never actually asked the king anything about his past family after his wife and son had disappeared. But hadn't the king told him everything?

He was more than the king's adviser; he was his family and friend, there to always help support and guide him until the war outside passed over.

Then a thought struck him. Would the war ever pass over? How could it when no one was out there to stop the Griefolowtros and their control over the Swiftmaw?

They had to fight if they ever wanted to see the sun again, if he ever wanted to be himself again. The war would only end if they defeated Rotto or he defeated them. It was the only way. They couldn't hide, just hoping.

"*Declan,*" Demoor smiled. "My older brother was a great king for the short time he reigned. I looked up to him, even after he married that Bandit girl."

"Queen Tatyana? She was a Bandit?" Crowley asked, shocked. He had never met the formal queen but had heard beautiful stories of her kindness.

"Yes, she was. They hid it from everyone! Even from me. For the longest time, I didn't know, but one day...one day, they told me. I didn't think badly of them. Tatyana was a beautiful and wonderful queen. I couldn't think bad of her, even if I wanted." Demoor grew quiet and sad.

"But then, one day, they left. They left for Elkhorn Village, simply going to see how the leaders were faring. Declan had taken his entire family, including their three kids."

"Declan had kids?" Crowley asked, frowning in his shock. Why didn't he know this? Did anyone?

"Yes, he did. A daughter and two sons. You were close with them when you and Malachi were children. It was at the village he lost his daughter." Demoor paused, trying to find the right words to explain.

"She was murdered?" Crowley asked, confused who from Elkhorn Village would do such a thing.

"No, she ran away."

They walked on in silence, Demoor waiting patiently for Crowley to process it all. It just didn't make sense.

Why would she run away? What happened to his sons? And was *this* why the former king stepped down?

"Declan's children, they were all half Bandit then, weren't they?" Crowley asked.

"Yes, his oldest daughter, the one who ran away, left with one of the Stexphin from the village. No one knows where they went, but I've been hearing rumors quite recently from our scouting group that returned this afternoon."

"What?" Crowley scowled. "Why wasn't I informed on their return? I've been waiting for word on them for over two weeks!"

"I know," Demoor said.

The two of them stopped, and Crowley opened the door to the central room, holding it open as the king walked through.

26

The room was large, made for holding conferences with all the king's ranked leaders. It was empty now, and Crowley stood impatiently as he waited for Demoor to get a seat.

"As I was saying," Demoor continued once they were both settled down at the wide table. "Tatyana was heartbroken over her daughter's leave, and that became a struggle for Declan. They returned to the village and sent out men to find her, but no one could.

"One night, I was walking through the gardens, thinking of my brother. Do you remember the gardens? They were so beautiful! They're all dead and gone by now, for certain. They were so beautiful." Demoor faded away, and it took Crowley a moment to remind him what he was talking about.

"As I wandered through the gardens, I stopped at the lake in the center, watching the reflection of the moon and stars on the dark waters. I remember wondering what would happen if I were to fall into those waters…if I just let the darkness of them all swallow me up and take me away from this world."

Crowley was listening intently now, still shocked by all the king's words while also deeply offended it had taken the king this long to tell him something of great importance about his brother.

He realized the king had always been a little paranoid, even when he was younger. The last few years had really begun to show ever since his wife and son left.

"And I was going to do it. I am more than ashamed to admit I really was going to fall into those waters. But I was stopped by an unfamiliar messenger. He ran up to me, asking where the king was. I told him, 'In his quarters, where everyone is at this hour.'

"When he learned I was the king's brother, he gave me the message instead. He said, 'King Declan's daughter has been sighted near the shores of Jayside. They say she's been asking for her father. She's in danger.'

"You can imagine how terrified I was at this news. She was in danger? I was confused, but I began to believe she must've never run away! Perhaps she had been kidnapped! I ran through the castle to my brother's sleeping quarters.

"I stood there for a long time, pounding on the door before I finally opened it, just to realize it wasn't locked, which, as you know, is very unusual for a king to just leave his door unlocked. You are most vulnerable when you are asleep."

Crowley knew it was true. He wasn't the king, but even *he* locked his door every night.

Demoor continued, "I ran into his room, just to find it completely empty. The sheets on his bed were unsettled, so I assumed he must have gone to the kitchen or something with Tatyana." Demoor's voice became so quiet Crowley had to strain his ears forward just to hear him.

"It was a horrible night which I remember so clearly. I became desperate when I couldn't find him. I ran through the castle, screaming for my brother. I was joined in my desperate search by the guards and the serfs. But he wasn't there.

"By morning, it was certain the king and his family were all missing. Even his sons were gone. I was advised not to tell anyone that he had disappeared because everyone was already so upset about knowing his daughter had left. It would ruin my brother's name! Everyone would assume *he* ran! And maybe he did. We never found him.

"That day, I was crowned king. I was given the crown I never wanted. But I did my best to own it to care for my brother's people."

4

DECLAN'S GHOST

Demoor's story sent goosebumps throughout Crowley's skin. It didn't make sense. Declan and his family had disappeared. It had to be more than just a coincidence.

They were being targeted. That made sense. Demoor's family had disappeared as well, although they had been believed to have left by choice. But what if they hadn't?

This could only mean Demoor was targeted next. He was the last of the royal bloodline. And if the king was gone, who would take his place?

Would I? I am the king's highest-ranked leader and his most trusted friend. If I took the throne...we could actually end this war.

Demoor must've known his thoughts because he was watching Crowley intently before saying, "I can't let you be next in line to take the throne. I've watched you since you were a little boy. I've seen you grow into the young man you are today. And I know the leave of my son affected you more than it had me.

"You've grown into a young man who has nothing else to live for except to bring death and gain power for yourself. It is your heart's greatest love. I cannot let that replace me on the throne."

Crowley let out a quiet chuckle to hide how offended he was. "My king," he said. "You know I love you more than anything."

"I used to believe that," Demoor said. "Crowley, every passing day, you look at me more different than the last. I see you have lost the respect you once had for me, which is why I wanted to talk to you. I need to have someone ready to replace me, but with my son gone…there is no one left with my blood. It would have to be someone who isn't of royalty. The choice must be perfect."

"Did you have anyone in mind, my king?" Crowley asked, his voice tight. "You seem to know me more than I know myself since I am not worthy enough."

"Crowley," Demoor said seriously, "you know I would choose you, but you must search your heart and understand why I can't."

Crowley remained silent, and his eyes drifted away from the king. Was it true? Did he love power and himself more than this stinking pit in the ground full of mindless drones?

"Then I guess you are right, my king. We cannot let me be next in line for the throne," Crowley replied, trying to keep his voice even.

"You guess," Demoor mused. "Crowley, you must promise me you understand why I am making this decision. I need to know where your loyalty lies."

"I promise," Crowley said, quickly evening out his voice when it still sounded stiff, "I understand. You know my loyalty will always lie with the higher throne. We *will* be a great kingdom again."

Demoor eyed him warily. Was that doubt in the king's eyes? Was he *doubting* him? "I swear, my king, my promise stands true."

"Yes, I know it will," Demoor said quietly. "That's what worries me."

A long silence followed, and Crowley refused to meet the king's eyes. His mind remained focused on what the king had said.

"Demoor—*My king*," he quickly corrected himself. Why had he said Demoor? He had *never* made that mistake before. He continued, pretending he hadn't realized what he just said. "Is this what Declan, your brother, would've wanted?"

"You're wondering why I hid us beneath the mountain." Demoor was silent as his eyes went distant. Crowley wondered if he needed to pull him back when the king said, "I wouldn't have done it, but I *believe* this is what my brother wanted."

"How can you know?" Crowley asked.

"He told me," Demoor paused again. "After my brother disappeared, and I was crowned king, his disappearance seemed to be a forbidden conversation. I tried not to think of him in fear I might go crazy wondering the possibilities of what had happened. I must've gone crazy anyway. A few months into being king, I began to see Declan following me."

"Following you, my king?"

"Yes, only no one else saw him. It was as if I was being haunted by my brother's ghost. I ignored him for as long as I could, but one night, I couldn't take it anymore and asked him why he was haunting me. Of course, I didn't expect him to answer...but he did. As if he was actually there, I heard him clearly."

"What did he say?" Crowley asked, beginning to doubt Demoor's sanity all the more.

"He warned me of hidden threats to the kingdom. He told me I had to bring us beneath the mountain. So I begged him to come back. I told him he needed to return and take the throne because I didn't believe I could do it forever.

"But he said, 'I am limited to how much I can warn you. I can tell you this: I *am* dead. I can never return. I was murdered by a dark force hidden beneath the island. My family... My family still lives, but they are imprisoned in their minds. You must promise me you'll save them! My time is short, but I must say do not keep all your focus on the Griefolowtros but watch for their lord. He will lead you beneath the island. Rotto is nothing but a pawn to—'

"Here I interrupted him. I begged him to tell me the murderer's name and where to find him. And he began shouting at me, saying, 'This man has no name! He lies hidden in the grave of Captain Dana, where he gained control of the entire island! You must find the son of my daughter and a girl who haunts dreams of the future. If this man finds them, he will kill them! All of them. They don't know it yet, but they are still children and don't know the other exists, but only they can stop him. You must find them or I fear he will grip his evil hands around the heart of the girl.'

"'And the son?' I had asked him.

31

"'He will be murdered by his own blood. This man who controls the island; if he ever reveals himself, it can only mean he succeeded in killing these innocent lives.'

"You can guess how terrified I was. I tried to tell him his daughter had been sighted in Elkhorn the night before he had disappeared, apparently murdered. But he screamed not to go to Elkhorn Village. He said by the time I could rally the soldiers and make it to the village, it would be too late. That man with the force of the island would have already wrapped his power throughout the minds of all those who lived there." Demoor stopped and became silent for a long time.

"Then what did he say?" Crowley asked, engrossed by the king's strange story. He wasn't sure if he believed or not just yet.

"He screamed and disintegrated," Demoor finished. "I never saw his ghost again, and I never realized how much I would miss it."

*****

Crowley walked down the halls in silence. He couldn't stop thinking about what the king had said.

On his right hand, he wore a thick ring made from Hidden Rock, which had been given to him by Malachi's mother, Queen Angeline.

When he had first received the gift, he had been disappointed and never wore it, thinking it odd. But ever since they had gone missing, he was never seen without it.

Now, as he walked the halls, he twisted and rubbed the smooth dark metal around his finger anxiously as his thoughts troubled him with Demoor's story.

But why now? Why has he waited until now to tell me? Until now to decide he should anoint someone to be in line after him? Now to tell me he doesn't believe in me?

He scowled to himself angrily. Why didn't the king trust him? He would be a great king, no matter what Demoor said.

The son of my daughter and a girl who haunts dreams of the future, the words repeated in his mind. *If that's what Declan told him, why hasn't he been searching for them all these years? Instead, he's been nothing but a coward hiding inside this mountain of dirt.*

He didn't know anything about Declan's daughter, but what about a girl who haunted dreams? He thought for a few moments. He always had haunting dreams but none he could remember of *girls*.

But that night, he did.

*****

His dreams always started out the same. He was outside in the sun, counting lines in the distance. He never knew what the lines were or why he was counting them, but he enjoyed it.

Then there was the voice. He could never turn around to see who was speaking nor did he know who it was. But, somehow, he knew this voice, and he listened carefully.

Then he would laugh and agree with whatever the voice said before mentioning the lines were ready.

Usually, he would wake after that before falling back asleep and dreaming of fighting a cloaked man with long scars down his face.

But tonight, he didn't wake, and the dream continued.

Through a blur, the dream seemed to have picked up speed, and soon it was almost dark out. He was still on the edge of the hill, watching the lines in the distance.

As he began to count them again, he was penetrated by a jolt of fear. The lines were slowly becoming fewer by the minute. He still didn't know what these streaks were, but somehow, he knew they were dangerous.

He turned around and called, "The lines are attacking!" He didn't even understand what he was saying but stopped, staring with shock at what was before him.

A large raptor of some sort—a Mislea, he guessed—towered over him with death in his eyes. Behind the four-winged bird were armies of Hollowed, all of them armed for war.

As he watched, he saw Swiftmaw, all in Character form, being taken out from pits beneath the earth. They were bound and injured. They were taken to the Mislea who called out dark words.

As he stood there, fire began raining down through the armies, only the fire didn't destroy them. It only killed the Swiftmaw.

"Stop!" he screamed over the noise of pained cries.

The raptor turned toward him and yelled in a deep voice, "Who do you serve?"

"The higher throne!" he trembled.

Suddenly, Demoor was there, only he didn't look like himself. He was younger, wearing beat-up clothes, and crying over a gravestone.

"Who reigns this throne?" the bird bellowed.

"I… I—" Crowley looked around wearily for an answer. Then he saw her. The girl from the library: Selah. She was much older now and was bowing to the wicked raptor. As he watched, he slowly transformed from Mislea to Character. He didn't look any less wicked with his short feathered hair and slightly hooked nose.

Selah looked up from where she was kneeling, turning her head toward him. Her green eyes flashed, almost like a warning.

Then he woke, screaming, and sweat as cold as ice running down his neck.

He looked around his room fervently, gasping and yelling, "Stop!"

It took a moment before he came to his senses, and the vivid details of his hellish nightmare began to fade.

Crowley gasped and fell back, dropping his head on his pillow as he tried to catch his breath. Instantly, he sat back up, throwing the wet pillow to the floor.

He couldn't focus and, swinging his feet over the bed, crossed the room. He yanked his shirt off the chair and pulled it over his head. Then he walked to the bathroom and stood there, staring at himself in the mirror.

Sweat dripped down his face and onto the counter. His eyes looked wild in his reflection, and he held his breath for a moment when the smell of people burning still filled his nostrils.

Quickly, he turned on the sink and stood there, leaning over and splashing water onto his face for almost five minutes.

When he finished, he leaned back against the wall, grabbing a nearby towel as he did.

He wiped his hair and his face dry before going to his closet and changing into fresh clothes. On his way out, he grabbed his scabbard.

He wasn't going back to sleep anytime soon.

5

TERROR AT CAMINO CREEK

Valkyrie—Year 315

The twins cast each other uneasy glances at the sight of their mother standing on the porch with her hands on her hips. Hanging their heads, they approached her, waiting for the scolding.

Instead, she said, "By the looks on your faces, I'm guessing you know why I called you back."

"Yes, ma'am," they said quietly.

Brooklyn sighed heavily, putting a hand over her forehead. "I'm going to finish cleaning the storage room, but—"

Here it comes.

"You two can go get water." She pointed to two buckets on the porch behind her.

Valkyrie inwardly groaned, and Virga stared helplessly.

It wasn't long before the two of them were trekking the worn path through Hickorywood, heading for the creek. Silently, Valkyrie wished she had worn a pair of Virga's trousers. It was nice out, and she would've enjoyed a quick dip in the cool water.

"We'll never get to finish playing," Valkyrie sighed as they neared the sound of running water. "By the time we're done doing this, Mother will have another job for us to do before Father and Frazil get home later tonight."

Their father, Dane, was hardly ever home. He worked at his laboratory hidden at the foothills of the Cliff Shore Peaks. He came home every few weeks. Frazil, their older brother, usually went out to him for a few days before he returned.

When they were younger, the twins would stand on the porch all morning, waiting for him to appear over the hills with Frazil. Then they would race over the meadow to their father before he even got to the house.

But, lately, Dane hadn't been returning until after nightfall. He had been staying longer at his laboratory and only returning home for a few days. Valkyrie didn't understand what it was he invented at his mount but always enjoyed how excited he got whenever he spoke scientifically.

Walking through an opening in the trees, they saw the sparkling creek. Valkyrie closed her eyes and sighed. This was her most favorite spot. The water was beautiful with the brush growing everywhere. A small breeze blew, making the long grass wave.

Camino Creek was flooding after a rough rainstorm from the south last week. The water rose with the current, covering most of the rocks spread throughout the brook. Virga was quick to fill his bucket with the clear water before setting it aside.

"What're you doing?" Valkyrie asked as he sat down and began to untie his shoes.

"Going for a small swim," he stated. Standing, he pulled his shirt off and dropped it at his feet.

Valkyrie glowered at him. She didn't want to have to stand there in the sun, watching him have all the fun. But she knew she couldn't swim in a dress. She'd drown for sure.

"C'mon," Virga pestered her when he saw her scowl. "Mom won't mind. Besides, your filthy from all that dirt."

Valkyrie stiffened. She didn't need to look down to be reminded of the dirt smudges staining her favorite outside dress. "I don't want to get my clothes wet, plus you're not wearing a dress," she huffed.

Virga sighed in exasperation. "You should have told me, and I would've lent you some shorts back home."

Valkyrie felt her face heat up. "How was I supposed to know you wanted to swim?" Her ears fell back with her mood as she scowled at her brother. Why was he so ornery?

"Fine," Virga said, letting out a heavy breath. He leaned over and picked up his bucket. "Let's just get this over with."

Valkyrie stared at him with accusing eyes as she walked past him to fill her own bucket. Not for one moment was she going to trust her pranking brother.

"Go for a swim anyway!"

As the words left Virga's mouth, she knew what he was up to. Spinning around, she dropped the bucket from her hands and barely missed, sidestepping Virga's attempt to push her.

"Don't you dare!" she screamed, shoving him back.

"V!" Virga yelled, looking behind her with wide eyes.

Turning around, she saw her bucket bobbing away with the current. "Why'd you drop it?" Valkyrie turned on him. "I can't believe you tried to push me! What was going through your head?"

"Get the bucket!" Virga screamed. Was he crazy? He must've been because he took a large step and dove into the water behind her. Droplets splashed her, and she gasped. It was cold!

She watched her brother with dread as he fought to stay above the current as he swam after the bucket.

Swimming with the flow, he easily gained speed. Valkyrie bit her lip. The course was strong, and there were many rocks hidden beneath the water. *If he hits a rock—*

Virga snatched the bucket and tried to swim back, now against the current. Valkyrie ran alongside the bank. She stretched out her hand and called, "Give me the bucket! Give it to me!"

Virga fought, too, and was able to thrust the bucket into her hand. The minute she had it, she threw it behind her and away from the water.

"Virga!" she cried. "Get out! Come on!"

Virga looked drastic as he flailed in the water. He almost seemed to be drowning a bit too obviously. Valkyrie saw him jerk, then wince in pain. He hit another rock as he swam toward the shore. Worry began to fill her as she realized he was actually beginning to sink.

Please don't drown, please don't drown, she prayed silently.

"Valky—" Virga's scream was interrupted as he swallowed a mouthful of water.

"Ugghhh!" Valkyrie cried, grabbing the sides of her head. She took a deep breath, kicked off her shoes, then jumped in the freezing water.

It was even colder than she had anticipated. Gasping for air, she swam toward the struggling Virga as fast as she could. The minute she reached him, he grabbed her and dragged her beneath the current. Valkyrie was unprepared for the dunk, and water charged into her lungs as she choked. She came back above and screamed at him, "Stop! You're drowning me!"

Virga drew her under again, and she tried to kick off the bottom of the rocky ground. But her foot got trapped amid two rocks. The current pulled Virga away, and she fought to kick her foot free. She needed oxygen and quickly.

*****

Cooper wandered aimlessly through the trees of Hickorywood. He had a destination but didn't really care to get there just yet. Besides, the others deserved to get worried and come looking for him after making him go by himself to Frazil's borders.

Really, he just wanted to clear his head before returning home. But, oh, how he couldn't stand his family pestering about how much they didn't like him leaving!

I could really use some help, Lord. Maybe even a sign. I don't know if you want me to go back or if I should accept Frazil's challenge to find the Oracle. I know they're my family, and I promised to return. And if I go with the others, I might never return.

Is my family or the lives of others more important? I can only make one choice. If I go home, I might not escape again. Something's taken over Elkhorn, and I fear—well, only you would know if it's a Specter.

Cooper continued his walk, his ears perking toward the sound of running water nearby. *Camino Creek. I've definitely gone further than I should have.* He turned to head back but hesitated.

Finally, he decided to go to the creek first. He wasn't sure why, but he felt like that's where he needed to be. As he neared, he frowned when he heard shouting as well.

Picking up his pace, he soon broke into a run. They weren't battle cries, but they were desperate. Someone was in danger.

Breaking through the tree line, he stopped and scanned the wide flooding creek. He barely glimpsed two Stexphin disappear beneath the waters. Instantly, Cooper threw aside his cloak, jacket, bag, and the weapons attached to his belt.

One Stexphin, a boy, came above the water. He struggled to stay above the rough current and was pulled under again. The water down here was much rougher the closer it neared Hidden Rock River.

In two large bounds, Cooper kicked off his shoes and dove into the water. He was careful to dive shallow, not knowing what lay hidden beneath the waters. With two strong whip kicks, he pulled himself toward the form of the drowning boy.

Grabbing the boy by the waist, Cooper pushed off a rock toward the surface. As soon as they were exposed to air, the Stexphin almost slipped from his grip, and they were both dunked under water again as he tightened his hold.

Cooper swam for the opposite bank which was closer. He kept one hand around the boy's waist who clung to him desperately. Kicking hard and pulling with his free arm, he kept his focus on keeping the youth from submerging.

His feet soon touched the rocky ground as they neared the bank. He grunted as he crawled out of the water, dragging the boy with him. Dropping the Stexphin on the bank, he ran back into the strong current.

He swam against the rough water until he neared the spot where he had originally seen the two Stexphin disappear. Beneath the clear waters, he saw the other. Taking a deep breath, he surface-dived.

He could barely see the girl as her dress tangled around her. He saw her fighting to push herself free from where her foot was stuck between two rocks. She was getting weaker.

Pushing himself down, he grabbed her shoulders until his own feet touched the rocks beneath them. *This is going to hurt.* But he didn't have any time left.

*****

Valkyrie was panicking as a mouthful of water forced itself into her lungs. Suddenly, strong arms caught her and pulled her up hard. Her ankle scraped painfully against the rock but came free.

The moment she was above the surface, she choked and sputtered, trying to cough up the liquid in her lungs and swallow air at the same time. Whoever had her didn't let go as the waves splashed against her face.

She gripped at the arm around her frantically, scared out of her wits this man would let her go. She continued to choke as her weighed-down dress threatened to drown them both.

A moment later, whoever held her was standing in the shallow waters. He hiked forward until they were on shore where Valkyrie was set down. The second her hands and knees touched the pebbly shore beneath her, she crawled forward and gagged.

The water in her lungs was forced out until, at last, she could suck in fresh air. Sitting up, she continued to cough as she tried to catch her breath. Virga was suddenly there, wrapping his bare arms around her.

"You're okay," he said. "I was so scared I actually lost you!"

Tears streamed down her face as she began to calm down. Turning toward her brother, she glowered.

"You," she panted. "You did that...on purpose. You weren't really... d-drowning."

Virga looked guilty as he hugged her shoulders.

"Why would y-you do that?" she nearly screamed at him, but her chattering teeth stopped her.

"Valkyrie," he hissed under his breath, looking past her.

Valkyrie turned and, following his gaze, saw a soaking wet Stexphin standing there, observing them. She felt her heart skip a beat as she looked at him.

The young man had light coffee-colored hair with light gray-blue eyes. He appeared to be about the same age as Frazil. Wearing a thin white shirt and soaked dark gray pants, the stranger looked very strong yet unsettled. Valkyrie trembled just at the sight of him. Virga held her closer.

The Stexphin softly smiled and, in a kind but clear voice, said, "Are you kids all right?" He stepped near them.

Valkyrie felt fazed, bitter, and frightened all at once. Who was this man? She had never seen another Stexphin before besides her family, and she was terrified to see one now.

Looking away from him and at the ground, she saw a long scabbard, a bow, and a quiver of arrows. She felt lost and confused. Why did he have weapons? Was he good or was he evil?

Virga looked as terrorized as she felt as he, too, stared at the weapons. He held her all the tighter and wouldn't let go with one arm over her shoulder and the other hand holding her arm.

A horrible itch started up her throat, and she turned away as deep coughs from her lungs warned a fever coming on.

The man looked at the two frightened Stexphin and tried again. "Please," he said, "I'm Cooper." He nodded his head in a small bow and tried to step closer to them.

But Virga wouldn't have it. "G-Go away!" he cried.

Cooper looked startled and frowned.

Valkyrie felt Virga pat her back, trying to tell her to get up.

She didn't want to get up. She wasn't sure if she could get up. She felt tired, cold, and weak. But Virga wasn't accepting it. He stood, then reached down and pulled her up beside him.

She mentally groaned at having to stand on her legs which felt like jelly. She was certain she'd collapse. Her foot throbbed with pain, and she tried to avoid putting weight on it.

Cooper had bent down and picked up two what may have been coats before standing straight again and examining them before saying, "I don't mean any harm. I fetched you and your friend from the crick. I'm here to help you."

Valkyrie tried to stop, but she couldn't hold it in and started coughing again—rough, sharp, deep coughs. She placed her fist in front of her mouth and turned her head away. Virga looked alarmed as he sat her back down. He gave her a begging look. "Sorry," she said in a rasped whisper. "I'm fine."

"You need to be taken care of," Cooper said to them. "Please, *let me help.*"

Virga shook his head. "N-No, sorry, sir," he said, his teeth chattering.

Cooper looked helpless as he watched the two of them.

Then in a quick movement, the stranger stepped forward and wrapped his cloak around Valkyrie's shoulders. Now Virga looked ready to fight. "Go!" he shouted. "Leave us a-alone!" He pulled Valkyrie back and away from the young man.

Cooper stood and took a few steps back.

The cloak felt warm, dry, and Valkyrie was glad for it.

"Here, boy, please take it," Cooper said as he handed him his jacket.

Virga refused to take it, even as he shivered from the cold.

"Sonny," the young man said sharply, "you're going to get sick!" His voice was stern and authoritative.

Virga slowly responded, reached out, and took the jacket.

Valkyrie knew her brother was thankful for the jacket. He had left his shirt behind, and the cool breeze was no doubt biting at his bare skin. Cooper must've known, too, because a small triumphant smile crossed his face.

Valkyrie closed her eyes, enjoying the warmth from the dry cloak and the sun soaking into her skin. Her teeth had stopped chattering, but the feverish feeling hadn't left. *How are we going to get home?*

Valkyrie kept her mouth sealed as lumps crawled up her throat. She coughed a few times but was too sick to notice. She leaned into Virga and let her exhausted body fall asleep.

She almost didn't even hear Cooper as he asked, "Where do you ki—guys live? I'll take you home, assuming you live around here."

"No, we're fine," Virga said rather roughly as he refused Cooper's offer.

"You don't need to come," she quietly moaned as her brother struggled to his feet. She opened her eyes as he stumbled forward.

Cooper was quick and helped him stand. Then he turned toward Valkyrie and scooped her into his arms. Standing straight, he turned back toward her brother. "Where's your house?" he asked.

She felt grateful when Virga didn't argue this time but instead began to lead him upstream. She couldn't remember a time feeling so exhausted and *miserable*.

As she leaned against Cooper's chest, she closed her eyes and tried to will herself to sleep. She felt warm wrapped in the large bundle. She winced through her tired mind as her ankle moved each time Cooper took a step.

Valkyrie hadn't forgotten the biting pain from where her skin had been brutally peeled away. Her ankle had been turned awkwardly, and silently, she wondered if it was sprained.

She soon dozed off with these thoughts in her mind.

*****

Valkyrie awoke with a start to an unfamiliar sound. Looking up, she saw Cooper, ripping his short sword free from its scabbard, the air around it releasing a noise that could've been a whistle.

She had been placed on the ground, and beside her lay the still form of Virga. He wasn't breathing. *What did he do to him?*

"Are you going to kill us?" Valkyrie asked, staring at the stranger who held the weapon defensively.

Cooper towered over her, his brows furrowing together. "No," he said, sounding perplexed. "Of course not, I—" He was caught off from an aggressive sound across the creek.

Valkyrie jumped at the noise and stared with wide eyes. On the other bank stood a man. He looked sinister with black hair that stuck to his forehead and an evil grin plastering his face.

A loud bark came from the man across the waters, making her shudder at the abnormal sound.

"You have to bring him back!" Cooper snapped at her.

She blinked, then looked at her brother who still lay unconscious beside her. Quickly, she went to his side.

"Virga," she said, shaking his shoulder. *Why isn't he breathing?* "Virga, wake up," She shook him harder. Her voice became more desperate. Why wasn't he waking up? He couldn't be—

Virga's eyes fluttered open, and he sat up, holding his head. Valkyrie sighed with relief, wrapping her arms around his neck. "You scared me," she whispered.

Another loud bark forced their attention. The man had transformed into a large form of a hulking wolf. Valkyrie swallowed a scream as the monster easily leaped across the creek. Virga grabbed her wrist and pulled her to her feet. She bit her tongue as pain shot through her foot.

Looking down, she saw it had swelled bigger than her fist. Virga collapsed the moment he stood. At the same time, she tripped from the pain screaming in her ankle.

She grunted and glanced at Virga's bare feet. She gasped to see they were bleeding with bits of sharp rocks sticking on the bottoms. *It must be from walking barefoot. How did he not notice?*

"Come on," Virga grunted, grabbing her hand and crawling forward. The sounds of combative battle sounded behind them, encouraging speed. The fingers of fear tickled down her spine, sending chills throughout her body.

Ahead was a large thicket resting on the border of the forest. She realized that was Virga's destination and quickly crawled beside him, trying hard to not trip over her dress or the cloak. *I can make it.*

By the time they were inside the thicket, Valkyrie's ankle was throbbing with pain, and her head was swimming. She tried to ignore it and looked back to see Cooper bleeding from several places where the wolf had succeeded in striking him.

The young man was crying through the pain. The bottom of his pants were shredded, revealing his left leg had been torn open with a bite mark. Valkyrie was horrified as she watched. Her heart ached for the young man.

The wolf crouched low, breathing heavily as it examined the injured Cooper. He prepared to leap and finish the distracted warrior when Virga suddenly screamed, "Cooper! Fight!"

Valkyrie's heart squeezed, and she grabbed her brother, pulling him down and planting a firm hand over his mouth. Was he *crazy?*

Then, in more terror then she thought possible, she screamed, watching the wolf jump over the man. It stared at them with death in his eyes.

Cooper managed to strike at the back of his legs, even as the monster trampled over him. But the beast didn't stop. It charged toward the twins' hiding spot, not even slowing for his injuries. Valkyrie struggled to find her feet. Suddenly, her ears shot up, and she heard a short *thwick.*

The wolf tripped and plummeted into the earth, causing pebbles to fly in every direction. It stopped it's slide in front of the thicket. An arrow stuck deep in the monster's bloody fur.

After a moment, Virga whispered, "H-He's dead."

Valkyrie feared she might keel over, but looking past the wolf, her heart swelled with joy. There stood her older brother, Frazil, Cooper's bow in his hands.

6

STRANGERS

With a racing heart, Valkyrie tried to understand what it was that had just happened. She now sat next to the injured Cooper, holding the poor man's head in her lap. His wounds looked fatal.

Virga sat nearby, his shirt back on. Frazil sat with them as well, caring for the Stexphin's injuries. The man was in a lot of pain but wouldn't move.

All was silent, except for the call of nearby birds, the soft breeze, rushing water, and Cooper's occasional grunts as he winced.

Valkyrie tried to calm her racing heart and panicked mind as her adrenaline continued to spike. She felt lost and afraid as flashes of the horrible attack swam through her mind.

Taking a deep breath, she stroked her hand through Cooper's light coffee-colored hair. Mother always played with their hair whenever they felt sick or anxious. It brought comfort in a way that seemed to say, *"You aren't alone, and there are still people who care about you. We understand your pain."*

It was an action Brooklyn once told her was a special touch only women had. Valkyrie had laughed then, but she now realized she was right. Cooper was relaxing.

Valkyrie looked up, wishing someone would say something. She caught Frazil refusing to meet his friend's gaze. Glancing at her twin, she knew Virga had similar questions running through his mind.

Why was Frazil here and not at the mountain with Father? How did he know Cooper? Who was that wolf? But mostly, *What are we going to do now?*

"What was that?" Virga asked as she glanced over at the hulking dead body of the wolf.

"It was a Hollowed," Frazil replied stiffly as he continued to wrap Cooper's leg where he had been bitten. He had already given the wound stitches. "A Character whose heart has been turned black. Hollowed don't think twice about anything. They only have an infinite hunger for blood and dead that they are desperate to fulfill but are *never* satisfied."

"You mean there's more?" Valkyrie asked, her heart picking up speed at the thought. She would never come to the creek again if there were more out there. What if these monsters kept coming?

"Yes," Cooper answered her question when Frazil didn't. "And more will most likely be coming this way."

Frazil shot his friend a warning glance, but he ignored him and continued, "That there"—he nodded back to the dead wolf—"was Antipas. He's a scout, which means there's a camp of Hollowed and Swiftmaw nearby. They won't go on until their scouts return with news."

"And if the scout were to return?" Virga asked. "What would he report?"

"He'd report there are Stexphin living down here, and then they'll—"

Frazil interrupted him, "Which isn't going to be reported." He glared at Cooper. "Because we killed the scout."

A heavy silence fell over the group, and Virga caught Valkyrie's gaze. As Frazil finished dressing the man's wounds, Cooper said, "You need to check their feet. They're pretty beat up too."

Frazil nodded and began to examine the bottom of Virga's cut-up feet. Valkyrie had sat carefully earlier, resting her ankle in an awkward but comfortable angle. It still throbbed, but the pain was going down. *Maybe I didn't sprain it,* she hoped.

But she didn't give herself time to think of her ankle as her thoughts returned to the incident. *A Hollowed.* Even the word made her heart slam against the inside of her chest. For a second, she wondered if she might start having an anxiety problem like her older brother.

An image of the bloodied wolf, his vicious stained teeth and black eyes, pierced her mind, making her shudder. *Why have I never heard of this creature before? Maybe I have. Frazil used to speak of crazed wolves working for that...what was he? Some sort of Griefolowtros. No, wait, he was a Mislea raptor. But those were stories he made up to scare us when we were younger before we went to bed. Weren't they? Maybe they aren't. It would make sense, really. What if Father and Mother are hiding out here, and Rotto's War is a real thing? But then that would mean—*

Her head ached at the thought of war. Silently, she wished she were back where she could curl up in bed and chase this bad dream away.

How much does Frazil know? How much do Mother and Father know? And why won't they tell us?

She needed answers to her questions but wasn't sure which one was proper to ask. Finally, she simply asked, "The Hollowed work for Rotto, don't they?"

Frazil's lips tightened as he didn't glance up from the two stitches he was giving Virga. Medical supplies had been provided by Cooper who had brought them along in his bag.

"Yes," Frazil said stiffly, making Virga cry out as he pulled on the thin needle harder than needed.

Valkyrie watched her twin brother with pity. He was lying on his back, covering his face with his hand. She had no doubt he was crying.

Valkyrie's mind went back to her question, her heart thumping a racing rhythm. Rotto was real. These wolves were real. But most of all, "The war is real." She spoke the statement without a second thought.

Cooper, who had closed his exhausted eyes, opened them and looked up at her. She hoped he couldn't see the fear flowing through her veins.

"Yes," he said, once again ignoring Frazil's scowl, "but I wouldn't call it a war. Rotto isn't here to just kill and destroy. Each time he sends out a secret army to attack, they kidnap more than they kill. A friend of mine likes to say there are a bunch of tiny wars going on, silent wars that no one knows happened. Any survivors are taken."

Valkyrie swallowed hard. The chills she had forgotten about were returning. Her headache intensified, and she fought tears. The thoughts of silent wars were terrifying.

Horrible images of more Hollowed coming and kidnapping them in the middle of the night made her want to scream from terror. She longed to race home, grab Brooklyn around the waist, and tell her all the horrible things that happened today.

"Speaking of your *friend*," Frazil's voice was unforgiving and angry toward Cooper, "I believe he's coming."

Valkyrie looked up and saw three strangers walking toward them along the back. Two of them looked older than Frazil and Cooper.

"Ahoy there!" Frazil called, a smile forming on his lips as he waved them over. No doubt he knew them as well.

The group took less than a moment to scan the scene and realize what had happened. Racing over, one instantly crouched over Cooper, a look of pity on his face.

"Quick," he said "we've got to get rid of this body."

Valkyrie took a moment to realize he was talking about Cooper, not the wolf.

"Throw me in the creek," Cooper agreed, a playful smile as his lips, even as he grunted through the pain. "Some other terrified family will find me in a few days and give me a proper burial."

His friend nodded, smiling at Valkyrie as he took over. She scooted out of the way, wincing as her ankle bit at her.

It wasn't long before Frazil helped the three friends gather enough large sticks to tie their cloaks together and create an awkward-looking hammock to rest their friend in.

Cooper grimaced and held his breath as they lowered him on the makeshift stretcher. Valkyrie had almost forgotten about his cloak. It was still wrapped around her shoulders, fastened in the front.

Cooper looked toward her and smiled, reaching out a friendly hand. Valkyrie took it, and he squeezed. "You can keep the cloak. I'll steal one of Burg's when we get back to camp,"

Valkyrie smiled, her heart swelling at the thought of getting to keep the beautiful cloak.

"Ha!" one of the strangers laughed as they hefted the hammock up. "You even touch one of my jackets, and I'll hang this hammock with you in it from a tree."

"Your welcome to take mine," another offered. "As long as Frazil promises to bring cookies next time. Don't think I can bear another one of your nasty muffins, Cooper."

Frazil rolled his eyes and slapped his friend on the back. "Off with you," he said, annoyed. "Get him back to his family so they can fuss over him."

Cooper sighed before saying, "We'll warn you if there's more. Until then, keep your family close, Frazil. They're not safe if Fang has decided to scout this area."

*****

The three Stexphin hiked through the woods in silence as they followed the broken path. Frazil now carried both of the buckets, each one full with water.

The twins each limped behind their older brother, each one trying not to show how much pain either of them were really in. Valkyrie's ankle had been forgotten and was never examined, but she didn't want to ask if Frazil would check it. *I'll take care of it later. Hopefully, by then, this headache will be gone.*

Her ankle was easier to ignore. She had forced her feet back into her shoes and tightened them to keep her foot sturdy. The growing fever, however, was harder to just brush aside.

Sweat mingled with her wet clothes as she followed close behind Virga. Her head felt light and queasy, chills rushing through her bones every so often.

"Frazil?" Virga suddenly asked. "Why aren't you with Father?"

She saw her older brother tighten his grip on the bucket handles. He continued to walk, not turning to face them. "How did the wolf see you hiding in the thicket?"

Frazil's question confused her. She didn't dare answer, though. The wolf had found them because Virga had been foolish enough to cry out and alert them of their presence. *Is Frazil trying to make him feel guilty? Does he know?*

"Were you scared, Virga?" Frazil pushed on.

Still, the young boy didn't answer. Valkyrie didn't have to see his face to know he was feeling ashamed.

"Frazil," she inquired after a few minutes of silence, "should we tell Mother?"

Frazil didn't answer right away. Finally, he said, "No. I'll tell her what happened. You two stay quiet."

"Why?" Virga piped up.

Frazil stopped and looked down. He sighed heavily. "Listen. I can't give you a reason why just yet, but I need you to trust me. Can you two do that?" He looked back at them, and they nodded.

As they continued their walk, Virga soon asked, "How do you know Cooper?"

"Please," Frazil groaned in annoyance, "let's keep the questions at a minimum."

When they reached the edge of the forest, their older brother refused to exit the trees. Setting the buckets down, he turned toward them and whispered, "Don't tell Mother what happened. Don't tell her you saw me. I'll tell her what happened. That way, you won't get in trouble." His voice went firm. "Do you understand? Don't tell her anything. I'll tell her tonight." He glanced away, finishing with, "I must go find Father now. I will see you later tonight." And with that, he turned back into the trees and disappeared off the trail.

Valkyrie was still shaken over from everything that had happened and stood there for a moment, thinking. "We'd better take these off before we go in," Virga suddenly said from beside her. Glancing over, she smiled at the oversized jacket her brother was wearing.

"You're going to have to grow into it," she said, grabbing the sleeve.

"Same goes for you." Virga nodded at the long cloak that was almost dragging on the ground. "I don't think it's supposed to be that long."

"Thanks for stating the obvious." Valkyrie rolled her eyes, smiling with him. The joy was short-lived as they were once more reminded of the traumatic experience.

"Here," she said quietly, removing the cloak and handing it to her brother.

Virga took it and bundled it with the jacket. "I don't like not telling Mother what happened," she confessed, squeezing her eyes shut for a moment when the dizziness returned.

"Neither do I," Virga sighed. Looking down at Valkyrie's foot, he saw her standing awkwardly. "You should have had Frazil check that for you."

"No," she replied, "he already had enough on his mind. Besides, I can take care of it myself once we're inside." She didn't tell him that she felt like she was going to throw up if she didn't lie down soon.

Virga seemed to sense something more was wrong. Looking down at her foot, then the two buckets of water, he offered, "I'll carry the buckets if you want to hide these clothes in the mudroom."

"I'm not entirely crippled yet," she protested but took the clothes from him anyway. *I may not be crippled, but I can't carry a ten-pound bucket of water on a swollen ankle. Virga's in more pain then he's letting on, but he's too stubborn to admit it.* She inwardly sighed.

It was late past afternoon as the two of them wandered into the house, both trying to hide their limps. By the time Mother was finishing her scolding for coming home so late and scaring her half to death, Valkyrie felt sick and emotional. She just wanted to go to her bed, curl up, and cry over everything that had happened. She could picture Virga teasing her for being so sensitive all the time. Clamping her jaw shut, she walked up the stairs. *I will not cry.*

Once in their room, she went straight to the wardrobe and changed into fresh clothes. This time, she put on shorts, even though it was too late for that now.

Virga hadn't come upstairs yet and was still talking with Brooklyn. Looking into the small mirror on the inside of their wardrobe door, her eyes blurred out. Wincing, she tried to fight the sudden migraine.

Valkyrie walked to her bed and sat down, rubbing her temples. Her ears perked up at the sound of shouting downstairs. Was Mother yelling at Virga? Or was he yelling at her?

Her heart flipped, and she stood, swaying for a moment at the sound of footsteps pounding up the stairs.

Virga came into the room, looking like a hot mess as he shut the door behind him. He didn't stay standing but instead ran to his bed.

Throwing himself on top of it, he buried his head in his pillow. Valkyrie didn't have to see his face to know he was crying. She could hear his muffled sobs.

Suddenly, her migraine didn't seem so important. She stumbled toward her brother's bed, sitting down beside him. She didn't dare ask what had happened. She couldn't even begin to wonder what may have happened.

Valkyrie was quiet and rubbed her hand over his shaking back. He smelled of the creek, and she realized she probably still did too.

After a moment, Virga quieted down, and she knew he felt ashamed of crying. Deciding to leave him alone for a few minutes, she went to sit on her own bed but not before grabbing a clear crate beneath Virga's. Her migraine was disappearing, but the feverish feeling was only growing.

As she sat down, she opened the clear lid and peeked inside. Virga had a habit of collecting all sorts of unwanted and found objects. She knew he had taken some old wrapping tape once after Father brought home extra. He always brought them needed supplies. She figured he made them at the mountain.

Sure enough, she found it. Looking down at her ankle, the swelling had gone down and didn't hurt nearly as bad as before.

By the time she had begun her second attempt to wrap her foot, Virga had gotten up and was changing into clean clothes. As he finished pulling a white shirt over his head, he looked over and watched her for a moment before finally saying, "You're doing it wrong."

"Oh yeah?" she challenged, looking up at him with accusing eyes. Her head already hurt enough. She didn't need Virga's criticism to add to her pains. "When did you become an expert at wrapping feet?" She noticed he hadn't taken off his shoes since Frazil had put them back on, warning him to be careful.

"When Frazil showed me how," her smart-aleck brother said hotly. His old self was returning. Virga walked to her bed and sat on his knees. Taking her foot, he began to rewrap her sloppy job. Valkyrie watched him with a scowl, occasionally wincing.

"Is it sprained?" she finally asked, her anger disappearing.

Virga had always been more talented when it came to first aid. She didn't really care for it. As long as Virga was with her when someone got hurt, she doubted she really needed to learn it.

"Sort of looks like one. We'll say it is. Just a minor one, though." Virga shrugged as he finished the wrapping job.

"Do you think I can shower with this on?" she asked, lifting her foot and inspecting the wrapping.

Virga stood and gave her a helpless look. "Seriously?"

7

THE BANISTER

Valkyrie tried to ignore the light streaming outside her eyelids, waking her from sleep. Loud voices forced her to open her eyes. She watched Virga's silhouette against the light of the open door as he snuck out.

Glancing over at a nearby clock, she counted the numbers on the side before inwardly groaning. *What is Virga doing up? It's midnight.* She hated her curiosity as it forced her out of bed.

Throwing aside the covers, she lowered her bare feet onto the cold wooden floor. Walking across the room, she looked down at her foot and smiled. It was still tightly wrapped but kept her from limping too much. *Maybe I* should *learn how to aid people better.*

She took a deep breath as she tried to forget her fever. But the continuous feeling she might suddenly throw up wouldn't leave her.

Valkyrie reached the door and silently crept out. She spotted Virga sitting a few steps down the stairs, staring through the banister railing.

"What are you doing?" she whispered as she joined him.

Virga jumped, then turned to scowl at her. "You nearly gave me a heart attack!" he hissed.

She smirked. *Honestly. He's so dramatic sometimes.*

She opened her mouth to ask again, but Virga held up a hand to silence her. Valkyrie frowned at him, then listened to the voices downstairs. She recognized them to be Mother and Father. They were talking about Frazil.

"Where's Frazil?" she asked quietly, grabbing Virga's arm anxiously.

He shot her another scowl, then shrugged as he went back to eavesdropping.

"You know it's not nice to eavesdrop," she whispered to Virga after a moment passed.

"Would you just shut up?" Virga shot back in a harsh whisper.

"Sorry," she mumbled, silently glad she had succeeded in getting under his skin. Valkyrie listened to what her parents were arguing about, and it wasn't long until she caught on to what they were saying. She gasped as she put it together. They were arguing about Frazil. Apparently, he hadn't been at the mountain with Father all week like he claimed. Father said that he had met him at the mountain that evening and said a Hollowed wasn't too far from their home. Frazil had left before he could talk with him more.

It didn't take long for Dane and Brooklyn to put it together that whenever Frazil claimed to be going to the laboratory, he never really did. Father said he only came once a month or so. Mother sounded scared at how long Frazil had been lying to them, which alarmed Valkyrie. Her mother never sounded frightened.

Valkyrie was also confused. If Frazil wasn't going to Father's cave, then where was he going? She tried to think of an answer but couldn't. She and Virga were not allowed to go to Father's laboratory, and they never really bothered to ask why.

Valkyrie squeezed Virga's arm harder as she heard Brooklyn sniff and cover a hand over her face. *She's crying? This is bad.*

The sound of the front door opening and shutting made Valkyrie want to cry out. Frazil looked shocked to see his parents waiting for him in the dining room.

"Mother. Father," Frazil said, nodding to them both.

Her anxious heart hammered out of control. She dug her nails into Virga's arm. This wasn't going to end well. She squeezed her eyes shut as another sickening rush flooded her. *Don't throw up,* she ordered herself.

Opening her eyes, she tried to ignore the horrible sensations in her stomach and head and focus on the conversation below.

"Let's not waste any time now, son. Where have you been?" Father's stern voice ordered. He was very upset.

"Father, I—" Frazil began.

"No! No excuses and no more lies. You tell me right now where you've been, you hear?" Father said harshly. He took a step toward Frazil who was still standing by the door. He had a hand on the handle, and Valkyrie wondered if he would try to make a run for it outside.

"Father, I've been doing no harm with leaving," he said in a reassuring voice.

He didn't answer their question, Valkyrie realized.

"I'll decide your harm once you tell me where you've been going!" Father's dark voice sent a wave of chills to add to her already shaking feverish form.

"Stop trying to stall, Frazil," Mother said, sounding heartbroken, "and answer the question." She paused. "Have you seen *him?*"

"Are you accusing me of betraying my own family?" Frazil asked, horrified.

Valkyrie quickly glanced at Virga. Were they talking about Rotto, the Mislea?

"Yes!" Mother was close to shouting. "Yes, we are. Until you tell us the truth, then yes, we *are* accusing you."

"I can't tell you where I've been! I can't say what I've been doing!" Frazil sounded desperate now.

"Why!" Mother cried.

Frazil closed his eyes and put out his hands in reassurance, but his voice shook. "I promise you, I am doing what I can just to keep you safe. To keep the family safe! It's the only option I had—"

"What?" Father cried angrily. "What are you doing?"

"I can't say, you'll make me stop! You'll make me give it up! You'll lead us all deeper into our graves *you* dug if you pull me away now. I am doing all I can to *fix your* mistake!" Frazil screamed furiously.

Father cried out as he jumped forward, grabbing Frazil by the shoulders and throwing him onto the ground. Valkyrie trembled, and tears filled her eyes. Virga quickly clammed a hand over her mouth, pulling her closer. "Shh," He whispered.

Valkyrie squeezed her eyes shut, terrified to watch. She couldn't believe this was happening. Her heart raced with sickening lurches. Why was her family *fighting?*

She heard Brooklyn's desperate cries to stop the struggle. Tears streamed down Valkyrie's cheeks, but she couldn't stop them. Opening her eyes, she saw Father over Frazil, holding a clenched fist behind his head.

Her horrified gasp was muffled beneath Virga's firmly clasped hand. Father was shaking vigorously over the top of Frazil. Their older brother didn't try to fight back. Instead, he turned his face away, squeezing his eyes shut as if he knew he deserved what was coming for him.

Virga quickly grabbed her and pulled her up the stairs. Valkyrie tried to pull away. She wasn't ready to go, not yet. But his grip was firm, and he wouldn't let go as he dragged her along.

As he reached their bedroom door, they both stopped at the sound of someone sobbing. Valkyrie wanted to collapse but instead squeezed her eyes shut. She was almost scared to know who was crying.

Opening her eyes, she saw Virga looking at her. He squeezed her hand as the words *Whatever happens, we're in this together* echoed through her mind.

Then he left her and peered over the top banister, careful not to be seen. Trembling, she went to his side and looked down as well.

It was Father. Dane was the one who was sobbing as he sat on the ground beside a relieved looking Frazil. "I'm such a horrible father!" he cried, burying his head in his hands.

Slowly, Frazil got to his feet. "No," he whispered. "You're not."

Brooklyn went to Dane's side and rested a loving hand on his shaking shoulder.

"Father," Frazil's voice cracked, "I am so sorry. You're not horrible. You didn't bring me up this way. I... I chose this." The light reflected a tear running down Brooklyn's face as she smiled at her son.

Valkyrie grabbed Virga's arms for support as she felt exhausted with relief. At the same time, another rush of pain shot through her head. Virga didn't even seem to notice, but he reached over and steadied her to the ground to sit beside him as they continued to watch out the banister.

"You're right. though, my mistakes are going to kill us all if not the entire world someday," Father said soberly. "He will find me, and after he's finished with all of you, he *will* kill me."

"He's already found you," Frazil said, his voice choked as he looked down. A mask of guilt covered his face.

Father looked up, and Mother fell to her knees. "No," she whispered.

Valkyrie felt her throat closing up. She closed her eyes as wave after wave drowned her in fear. She trembled. Had *Rotto* found them?

Brooklyn patted Dane's back and motioned for him to return to the table. Soon, the three of them were sitting there in a grievous silence. All of them in their own thoughts.

Finally, Father said, "If he's coming, then I must have *Misericordia* running at once. You know I have to have somebody."

Mother let out a shaky sigh and stared at the table. "Virga…and Valkyrie…it's why *they* lived."

Valkyrie's eyes shot open. *What does she mean it's why we lived? Father has to have us? For what?*

"What? No!" Frazil cried. "You can't use the twins." He turned toward Dane. "Use *me*, Father. Use me first. If I don't work, *then* ask the twins. You need to start slow at first, you know that! You tell me that all the time—"

"Frazil," Mother began, but he interrupted.

"No, sorry, Mother, but you've raised them, they're your own, you feel that. You can't just throw them away. Besides, they've done nothing to deserve it."

Valkyrie looked through the banister and saw the horror on Frazil's face.

"Virga's been acting up lately," Mother said quietly. She covered her face with a hand. "I don't know what it is with that boy, but he's not content here. He's just like your grandfather. I can see it in his eyes, the longing for adventure."

Valkyrie frowned. What was she talking about? *Acting up? Longing for adventure like Grandfather?*

"If you don't do it soon, he's going to leave on his own either way," Mother finished quietly. She sounded stressed.

Valkyrie struggled to swallow. Was that true? Virga was going to leave?

"He'll never leave Valkyrie, though," Frazil objected. "The only reason he's staying is that she's here. We both know that."

Valkyrie stared at her twin with hurt, confused eyes. Virga looked like he was inwardly struggling with something. When he saw her eyes on him, he shook his head in denial.

How do I know if he's lying?

"Then he'll take her with him," Father said. "If I don't do it soon, they both are going to end up *somewhere* either way, and I'd rather have them alive."

Valkyrie moved close to ask Virga what he meant when suddenly, Dane asked, "How'd he find us?"

Valkyrie only listened with one ear as Frazil explained the attack on the creek that afternoon. She leaned against Virga and closed her eyes. Her brother seemed engrossed in the retelling of the story while she shook with feverish chills.

She squeezed her eyes shut and buried the hurt and confusion pulling her under. *Just don't listen to them. Go to sleep.* Her body was tempted, and she soon dozed off, leaning against her brother's shoulder.

*****

Valkyrie woke up early that morning, confused to find herself in bed. Sitting up, she stretched her arms over her head and yawned. She didn't remember a lot from last night and didn't want to remember.

Just get up and pretend nothing happened, she thought to herself as she slid from bed. She winced as she was reminded of her fever.

She closed her eyes and sat there for five minutes, trying to clear her head. *I won't be able to hide this from Mother.*

Standing on her feet, she swayed for a moment before stumbling to the wardrobe. She shivered as she pulled on a new outfit. Leaning against the door, she closed her eyes and let herself have a few minutes of rest.

Opening her eyes. she glanced across the room where Virga laid sleeping in his own bed. Their one-bedroom window showed the beginning of a coming sunrise.

She slowly walked toward her brother and began shaking his shoulder. "C'mon, Virga, you better wake up before it's too late."

His only response was a grunt as he pulled his pillow over his head.

"Fine," Valkyrie said stubbornly. "But don't go blaming me when Mother comes hollering up the stairs for you to wake up."

He grunted again.

Valkyrie walked toward the door, taking a deep breath before heading out. She just wanted to lie down and sleep the rest of the day. She also didn't enjoy Virga acting ornery to her.

"Do you think Frazil is on good terms with Father then?" she asked quietly, waiting for a response from her brother.

Virga sat up. "I think so," he said, then scowled at her victorious expression. "I was planning on getting up anyway," he mumbled.

Valkyrie smirked and shook her head. *No you weren't.* Then she slipped through the door and headed toward the stairs. Silently, she wondered if she might suddenly black out while attempting these steps.

She struggled down them. The end of the steps entered into the kitchen. She hadn't even gone two steps when Brooklyn's voice rose from the stove. "Valkyrie! Are you sick?"

"Yes," Valkyrie grunted, dropping to sit on the last step. She closed her eyes. Brooklyn walked over and sat next to her, placing a hand on her forehead.

"A fever." She sighed. "You're lucky your Father brought home some more antibiotics just last night."

"Oh, Father's home?" Valkyrie asked, pretending to be oblivious as she leaned into Mother's shoulder, her eyes still closed.

Brooklyn kissed the top of her head and rubbed her back. "Let me get you some pills."

Valkyrie opened her eyes and sat up. She watched her mother as she opened a few cupboards before finally pulling out a small container. She stopped at the sink and grabbed a glass of water before returning. "Here you go. Take three. These should work amazing for a few hours."

Valkyrie accepted the pills and glass of water, swallowing them quickly.

Brooklyn returned to the pancakes, and a moment later, Valkyrie stood. Her head was cleared, and the hot feverish feeling had left. *Nice.*

Walking over to a cupboard, she grabbed a mug and took her time filling it with coffee. Without a backward glance, she walked into the mudroom, grabbing a folded blanket before going outside.

She set her mug aside and wrapped the blanket around her shoulders as the cold morning air nipped at her bare arms. Settling down on the front steps, Valkyrie watched the sky change colors while sipping her warm drink.

The sky streaked with pinks and yellows. The grass was still covered in dew as the cold morning breeze rustled Valkyrie's messy hair in front of her eyes. She smiled and leaned against the porch railing.

She came out here whenever she felt troubled. She had learned a while ago that early cold mornings cleared her head. Although she was too tired to empty her mind and think straight, she still enjoyed the sunrise. She no longer felt sick while the pills did their effect. She was still exhausted. *How late did we stay up last night?*

Her ears flipped back at the sound of the front door opening. She ignored it, guessing it was Virga. She closed her eyes, waiting to hear her brother whine about being woken up.

But as strong arms circled her in a bear hug, she knew it wasn't her brother. Opening her eyes, she turned her head back to see Father, his kind green eyes smiling down at her.

"Good morning, sweetie," he said, kissing the top of her head as he sat next to her.

Valkyrie leaned into him. She hadn't enjoyed a morning like this with him for years. "I missed you," she replied. "Where were you this morning?"

"I was in the living room with your brother."

"Frazil?"

He nodded, and Valkyrie had to bite her tongue to keep from blurting out what happened last night.

"You seem tired." Dane put an arm around her shoulders.

"Couldn't sleep," she said without thinking. She felt him stiffen beside her. "A half sleep really. Mother gave me some of those pills you brought back this morning."

"I heard you two talking. Are you sick?"

"A little." She closed her eyes, not wanting to remember why she was sick. She shuddered when she couldn't stop the image of being trapped beneath the waters and drowning.

Father seemed to notice, and he rubbed her arm, pulling her closer. "You get so big each time I return," he said, laughing quietly.

"You don't have to leave," Valkyrie suggested. "You could stay."

Father didn't respond, and when she looked up at him, she saw his eyes were filled with tears. "If only I could," he whispered.

8

A NEW INSTRUCTOR

Crowley—Year 317

Crowley thrust his blade through the air in quick lethal swipes. Sweat ran down his face as he continued to repeatedly kill the unseen enemies in front of him.

Flashes from his nightmare only encouraged his adrenaline. All fear was replaced with a mask of anger as he continued to swing his blade.

He was the only known soldier to train on the mountain, and he did so in a small empty room. The walls were mostly formed by the underground dirt. It was originally supposed to be a room meant for medical supplies but had been forgotten about.

Malachi had found it years ago, and the two friends had claimed it as their own.

Now that Malachi was gone, Crowley used it as his own training room. It wasn't private, and once in a while, younger teens would come in who had also claimed this as their hangout spot.

Whenever they came, and if he was in the middle of training, it depended on his mood if he'd either leave or make them go. Sometimes people would stumble upon it, then apologize and quickly leave when they saw him.

It was late now, and he doubted anyone would bother him. After his nightmare, he didn't dare go back to sleep. Instead, he used it to fuel his determination.

His lungs began to give up on him, and he stopped, breathing heavily and wheezing. Clutching the hilt to his sword, Crowley gritted his jaw together. He wanted to fight someone. He wanted to attack with real competition. He was tired of his talent being wasted away because Demoor was their paranoid king!

Crowley yelled angrily and threw his blade across the room as hard as he could. It sailed smoothly and sank into the dirt wall, stopping at the hilt. He wanted to kill someone.

Sensing a presence, he spun around, eyes flashing dangerously. It was a young girl standing at the door, watching him.

He prepared himself to scream at the teen to leave but stopped himself when he met the two green eyes staring back at him.

"I didn't mean to come here," Selah said, slightly frowning as if she sensed his oncoming outburst.

"Then why did you?" Crowley growled, turning and walking back to the wall to pull his short sword free.

"Because I couldn't sleep. Clearly, you can't either," she said in a tight voice.

Why was she mad? Crowley hadn't done anything to her.

Gripping his fingers around the hilt of his sword, he pulled it free from its grip in the wall. He began to wipe the murk along the blade with the end of his shirt when something soft hit him in the head.

Turning around, he glowered at Selah. Looking down, he saw she had thrown a rag at him. Picking it up, he began to wipe his sword clean.

He finished in silence and sheathed the blade. Using the rag, he then wiped the sweat from his face, not caring if it was dirty. "What are *you* doing, carrying around a rag?" he asked out of curiosity.

"In case I needed to clean my own blades," she said quietly, closing her eyes as if the thought of weapons brought bad memories.

Crowley frowned, even more confused than before. "You—" he began but was interrupted.

"You're not the only one who trains beneath the mountain," Selah said. Her voice went soft, and she opened her eyes. "I was on my way there now," she hesitated before offering, "It's an old cellar. No one goes in there. It's full of weapons and a nicer place to train than in here." Looking around, she sniffed. "Kind of murky in here."

Crowley surprised himself when he smiled. "Are you assuming I have never heard of this room? I am the youngest adviser and know even more than the king."

"Oh, I don't doubt it," Selah said, turning to go. "But not even the king's youngest adviser has a head big enough to know everything." She quickly left to escape Crowley's scowl.

She treats me as if I were her brother and not of importance. No one, not even Demoor, would dare treat me like that. She's too young and doesn't understand. How old is she? Seventeen? Hmm...only three years younger than me. Maybe she does understand but enjoys seeing me squirm.

He wasn't sure if he should smirk or scowl at the thought. Walking out the door, he jogged to catch up to the retreating girl.

Crowley was surprised when they went to the highest floor closest to the surface, upset when she led him to a metal door he didn't recognize. He didn't let her notice his confusion and kept a shielded mask over his expression.

When they entered the room, he was impressed by the cement walls and floor. Lights running on electricity ran along the ceiling, and as she had promised, weapons lined the barrier.

There weren't many choices but a fair amount of small daggers and blunt short swords.

Selah turned to leave.

"Wait, I thought you said you train?" Crowley said, hoping she didn't hint the challenge in his voice.

Selah glanced at him, suddenly looking embarrassed. "I-I don't train with people."

"I believe you do train, but if you're inclining you taught yourself, I don't believe *that*." He raised his brows accusingly.

Crowley had always been known for his skill to fight and observant eyes. Selah had muscle, and it wasn't from regular daily work.

"Yes, well, I don't have a teacher anymore. He disappeared a while back, and no one knows why," she said dismissively.

"Who was your teacher?"

"I won't say his name. But he taught many of the younger Stexphin here. No one else would."

"We didn't think we had any good teachers," Crowley said in defense.

"I think the real reason is because King Demoor didn't want to prepare for something that won't ever happen. He's afraid that training soldiers will only bring the fight closer."

"Don't speak ill of the king," Crowley snapped firmly.

Selah blushed and looked down. "I should be going then," she said and slipped out the door before he could say anything.

Crowley stood there for a moment, trying to clear his thoughts before he began to inspect the room. *Who is she really? She's too blunt to actually be from here.... She couldn't be the girl who haunts dreams, could she? And a secret instructor in Smuir? I don't recall any men who supposedly just disappeared. He must have been a part of the survivors from Hickorywood Forest. It would make sense, but her father was never fond of them. Why would he let one of them train her? Unless they waited until he passed. No because they left before I sent out that scouting group.* Crowley fingered at one of the short knives hanging from the wall. He sighed.

I don't dwell on the past, he reminded himself as he took out his own blade and once again began sword drills.

*****

It was almost a week later until Crowley ran into the strange girl again. He had tried searching for her many times before, but she seemed to know the mountain more than him and would disappear faster than he saw her.

He saw her walking down one of the more darker halls. Staying close to the wall, she was almost a shadow. But he glimpsed her green eyes reflecting from a nearby torch, and immediately, he sprinted toward her before she could disappear again.

There were a few other Characters in the hall, and she was nearing a turn. "Selah," he whispered harshly as he neared. He instantly regretted it when she jumped.

Turning on him with wide eyes, she hissed, "You scared me!"

"Sorry," he said, slowing as he neared, "I didn't want to lose you again. Have you been hiding from me?"

"No." She frowned. "I don't hide from anyone."

"Really? Because the fact you only come out when the halls are mostly empty and stick to the shadows," he whispered roughly as he challenged her, "kind of gives off the wrong impression."

"I'm not hiding," she said innocently. "Just staying out of the way."

"The way of what?" Crowley asked, looking up as the last man who had been walking down the hall disappeared into a nearby room.

"The way of people and their nagging questions!" she huffed impatiently.

Crowley glared, though silently, he knew he deserved that.

Selah looked him over, then in a softer voice, asked, "Have you not been getting any sleep lately? You look awful."

"Thank you." He breathed as if it had been a compliment. "Here, walk with me."

Selah hesitantly followed him.

"To answer your question, no, I haven't been getting much sleep," he said, pointing his voice at her.

"You're making it sound like I should know why," Selah said, raising a brow.

Crowley studied her for a moment with suspicious eyes. "It's because of you," he finally said, looking away. Selah didn't respond, so he continued, "I find myself waking up in terrible fits every night from horrible nightmares. In each one, I see who I believe is the source of the war going on outside."

"Rotto," the girl breathed. Slowly, she met his gaze. "You said you haven't been getting any sleep *because* of me. Where do I play out in these dreams?"

"It's always different," Crowley said, shaking his head as they turned down another hall. "Sometimes I see you bowing before the

Mislea. Other times, you are in the distance among lines of which I know not of what they are." He was quiet, trying to debate how much he should tell her.

The reason he was telling her anything at all was because of his theory she could possibly be the girl who haunts dreams of the future that Demoor had spoken of.

"I would never bow," Selah began, sounding mortified.

"I know," Crowley assured her, though silently, he was still debating. "It's just what I see."

"Why are you telling me this?" Selah looked at him with distrustful eyes.

I have to earn her trust or she'll never tell me anything. He thought for a moment, then confessed his thoughts. "Because I want to earn your trust."

Selah let out what may have been a scoff. She stopped walking and turned to face him. "I don't trust people," she stated, putting her hands on her hips. "How are you proposing to earn mine?"

"I want to train you," Crowley forced out before he could change his mind. "Like your old instructor."

Selah's hands dropped to her sides, and she gaped. For a moment, she just stared at him, looking shocked. Finally, she closed her mouth and frowned.

"Let me try," Crowley urged. "I'm the only soldier here who isn't retired. You can't improve without challenge, and you can't challenge yourself without any competition."

Selah looked down at the hem of her gray dress. When she looked back up at him, she was still frowning. "Why do you train, Crowley?" she asked, no curiosity in her voice, only durability.

"Because I—" He stopped and returned the frown. Why was she asking such a giddy question? "Because I am skilled and serve the higher throne. The king needs a defender."

Selah stared hard into his eyes, almost as if she was searching his mind. He feared he was pouring his soul out and she was seeing all his dark thoughts.

"Who is the higher throne?" Selah asked without blinking.

"King D—" Crowley paused, his mind wandering to his nightmare. "I serve King Demoor."

Selah blinked, and the strange trance-like image in her eyes disappeared. She looked down the hall where a young girl, about her own age, was turning around the corner.

Crowley recognized the other girl but couldn't place a name. She had short curly brown hair with beautiful dark eyes and a cute broad-tip nose.

Selah's eyes went wide. "You can train me," she said quickly, looking back at him.

Noticing her hurry to get away, Crowley said, "We'll start tomorrow, 7:00 a.m. at your training room."

With a short nod, Selah disappeared.

Walking down the hall, Crowley passed the brown-haired girl. Suddenly, her name came to him. *Yes, I know who you are. You and the rest of your friends…a troublesome group when they were younger. She appears to have changed over the years.*

"Miss Jolee Parry," he said politely, nodding his chin.

The girl looked at him and smiled, returning a respectful bow of her head.

"King's adviser, Crowley Price," she said. The two passed and continued on their way.

Why can't Selah have her manners? he thought with a shake of his head. *Years have changed her…but being alone for so long hasn't in a good way, I fear. I hope this isn't a mistake. I've never trained anyone before. I've attempted with Malachi, but that was years ago. We were both younger. It can't be that hard as long as she does what I tell her to. But this is Selah. Not Miss Parry. I think I'm beginning to realize that this is going to be much harder than it sounds.*

9

SECOND ATTACK

Valkyrie—Year 315

It's been three weeks since the Hollowed scout attacked Cooper at the creek. I haven't seen him nor any other wolf since. I don't want to believe Father, Mother, and Frazil are hiding stuff from us, but after that night Virga and I eavesdropped—

Valkyrie frowned and scratched out the last word. She sighed, resting her head against the back of her bed. Looking back down at her journal, she continued to write.

Virga and I heard them talking and learned that Frazil has been sneaking out. They haven't shown any clues or hints about what they spoke of that night.

I'm just confused why all of this is suddenly happening. Or even why we're being kept out of this. We haven't gone back to the creek since, and no one mentions what happened.

Father took Frazil—actually took him this
time—to his mountain two weeks ago. They had
spoken of going to work on a grand invention
that could change everything. What does everything mean? The war? Turns out that's real.

Valkyrie frowned and shut her journal. Closing her eyes, she
pondered the events. *I'm so sick of being treated like a child. Why do
adults get to know everything? Frazil's eighteen, but he's been treated as
an adult since he was sixteen. Why can't we be like that?*

As she began to stuff her journal back inside Virga's clear crate,
she froze when she saw the yellow envelope he had stashed all the
pictures inside of from the storage room. *Hmm.*

Throwing the crate beneath her brother's bed, she skipped
down the stairs two at a time and into the living room where Virga
loudly banged on the piano keys. His back was facing her, and he
groaned loudly before taking a deep breath, turning the pages of his
song, and starting over.

Valkyrie marveled at the speed of his long fingers. Where she
preferred the violin, her brother could play the piano as if it were a
part of him. She closed her eyes and smiled to the fast sobering tune.

Turning toward Brooklyn who sat on the couch, folding laundry, she asked, "Mother, why don't you have any pictures of Virga
and I when we were younger?"

Brooklyn looked up in surprise. Virga stopped playing and
turned to face them.

"I lost them," her mother replied simply. "In our old house."

"I remember that house," Virga said. "It was destroyed, wasn't
it?"

Brooklyn looked at him with wide eyes. Quickly, she blinked,
and instantly, a mask of calm covered her shock. "What *do* you
remember, Virga?" she asked curiously.

"Hardly anything," Virga said, eyeing Brooklyn suspiciously. He
closed his eyes for a moment as if lost in thought. Finally, he opened
them with a look of disappointment before saying, "I remember

somewhere dark…and crying. I saw you leaving moments before the lights went out."

Valkyrie raised her brows. She was impressed by her brother's memory.

"It might have been a dream." Virga shrugged carelessly when he saw them both staring at him.

"*Was* our older house destroyed?" Valkyrie asked.

Brooklyn hesitated. "A lot was happening during that time. I'm impressed Virga can remember anything. He was only an infant at the time." She paused, looking uncomfortable.

"What year was that?" Valkyrie urged the subject on.

"The year 305," Brooklyn said. Suddenly, her expression changed. "Why don't you two go outside and play until supper?"

*****

"Honestly, Virga!" Valkyrie shouted half an hour later as she landed in the grass. "You throw like a tortoise!"

"Well, you jump like a kangaroo rat!" Virga hollered back from his place near the edge of the woods. "You and your long legs!"

"At least I *have* long legs!" Valkyrie laughed at her brother's offended expression. Virga hated the fact that she was getting taller than him.

The twins were throwing their small medium-sized ball to each other in turns. They challenged each other by stretching out farther and farther while also testing who could jump the highest, catching the sphere midair.

Stexphin had amazing special springs in their legs and could jump incredible heights when forced.

Valkyrie chucked the ball far overhead, watching Virga frown, knowing he wouldn't reach it. She was surprised when he coiled his legs and leaped to attempt the catch anyway.

He barely missed as it skimmed over the top of his fingertips. Valkyrie stood with wide eyes. For being shorter, she silently envied her twin had just jumped almost nine feet.

"Ugh!" Virga shouted at her angrily, not seeming to realize the height he had just accomplished. "We'll never find it now! *Valkyrie!*"

Looking past him, she realized the ball had disappeared into the woods beyond. Closing her eyes, she sighed heavily as Virga began to taunt her.

"I told you we shouldn't have played so close to the woods, but what did you say? You said, '*No, Virga,* let's just play here, that way we—'" He continued mimicking her voice in a high pitch as she crossed the distance between them.

"Shut it," she said harshly, pushing him in the back of the head. "Let's just go get it." Valkyrie ignored the lingering thought of Hollowed wolves waiting for them in the woods as they searched through the trees.

Virga glanced upward and shielded his eyes from the rays of sun shining through the treetops. "There," he said, pointing up at the large elm. "It's in that tree." He sighed and dropped his hand. "Forget it. We'll never get it from up there." He turned to walk away.

Valkyrie grabbed his arm to stop him, never taking her eyes off the sphere stuck in the high branches overhead. "No," she said firmly. "We are not leaving without that ball."

"And how do you propose we do that?" Virga challenged.

"You can boost me up into the tree," she said, rolling her eyes as if it were just too obvious.

Virga stopped her as she edged near the trunk. "*Puh-lease,*" he warned with a blank stare. "You know what happened *last* time you tried to climb a tree this height?"

"I'll do it quickly. Besides, this tree is sturdy. I was only *five* when I fell. I'll be careful," Valkyrie stated, but she couldn't ignore the doubt she heard in her own voice. She remembered spraining her wrist from that fall. It wasn't something she wanted to do again.

Virga shook his head as if he read her thoughts. "No way am I going to let you break your neck when I have the chance to do it before you. I'll do it," he stated firmly. "Besides, I'm a better climber than you."

"What? How do you know?" Valkyrie asked, sounding hurt.

"I don't know, it's just kind of obvious," he said, patting her shoulder affectionately.

Valkyrie smirked and tousled the white hair between his black ears. "You're delusional," she replied.

Virga scowled and quickly brushed his ears back until they were hidden behind his hair. "Just boost me up," he said.

Valkyrie smiled victoriously. "Admit it," she said. "You couldn't lift me, even if you tried. That's the real reason you didn't—" She was caught off guard, and a loud squeal escaped her mouth as Virga grabbed her around the waist and lifted her off the ground. For a moment, she thought he was going to throw her over his shoulder, and she screamed, "Put me down right now! You've proven your point!"

Stexphin were unusually light creatures, but Virga still grunted as he set her down. He smiled at her, but she knew he had still struggled.

Shaking her head, she clasped her hands together and bent down. Virga stepped, and she quickly thrust him up.

Reaching for the branches, he succeeded in pulling himself on top of them. Valkyrie watched from the ground as her brother continued to climb up the large limbs.

Halfway up, he glanced down at her. "Another thing!" he called. "You're scared of heights!"

"You are being very critical today, aren't you?" she shouted back. She saw him smile and couldn't help but smirk herself.

Virga was soon making his way back down, much slower now that he held the ball beneath one arm. When he reached the lowest branch, he sat and looked down at Valkyrie.

His feet nearly touched the tips of her ears. "If I were your height, I think I'd kick you right now," he said, giving her a ruthless smile.

Valkyrie forced a gasp and pulled her ears down. "Toss it down." she smiled, rolling her eyes as he dropped the sphere.

She caught it and looked back up. "Good job," she stated. "I guess I can agree that you are a better tree climber than me."

Virga jumped from the branch, but instead of landing nicely, he lost his balance and tumbled onto the ground.

Valkyrie stood over him with wide eyes. "Are you all right?" she asked. "You didn't roll your ankle, did you? Because I won't help you back if you did."

Virga scrambled to his feet with a groan. "Yeah, I'm fine. It was just a small fall," he stated.

"Your clothes." Valkyrie shook her head at his white shirt which was now covered in dark brown smudges. "Mother is going to have a fit. She said to try not to get muddy for once, remember?"

"Here," Virga said, stooping down and scooping a handful of murk. "Join the uprising." And with that, he rubbed the mud onto her shoulder.

Valkyrie shrieked, threw the ball down, and began attacking at her dress. "I've been infected, like you!"

"You're so stupid sometimes," Virga said, shoving her. "We got the ball, let's head back and finish our game."

"Such a pushover," Valkyrie replied, tripping her brother as he leaned over to grab the ball.

A minute later, as they were exiting the tree line, Virga suddenly grabbed her arm. "Look!" he cried. "There's Frazil!"

Valkyrie instantly looked to where he was pointing and was overjoyed to see her older brother just barely coming over the hill past their oddly shaped cottage.

"But where's Father?" she asked, looking past him.

"Valkyrie," Virga's voice dropped to a low whisper, "he looks hurt."

He was right. Even from the distance, she could see Frazil holding his head and limping as he stumbled down the sheer hill.

"Valkyrie, he's been attacked!" Virga said under his breath.

"Go get Mother!" Valkyrie ordered as she took off for her older brother. For once, Virga didn't argue and ran for the house.

Valkyrie passed him on the way and sprinted the distance quickly between her older brother and house. As soon as she reached him, she saw it was much worse.

Blood steadily flowed down the side of Frazil's head, and his left ear was sagging backward as if broken. His once dirty blond hair looked mostly gray as if someone had dumped soot on his head.

Bruises covered his arms, and Valkyrie struggled to find her words as she stopped at his side. "Frazil?" she choked. It took him a moment to realize she was there.

When he finally glanced at her, he stopped walking and smiled weakly. "Jaylee," he breathed. At the same moment, he fell forward on his knees. He groaned and crouched over.

Jaylee had been an old nickname her brother had given her when she was younger. She wasn't sure where it had come from, but Frazil never dropped it.

"Frazil, what happened?" Valkyrie asked desperately as she sat beside him. Hesitantly, she touched his blood-covered shoulder. Blood leaked from his head and dripped down the front of his sweater. She feared she might suddenly faint at the sight.

Forcing herself to focus on her brother's pained green eyes that matched her own from Dane, she asked, "Where's Father?" But after starting, she couldn't stop, and more tumbled out.

"Are you okay? Were you attacked? Is there more Hollowed? Please, won't you talk?" She let the questions spill over one after the other without even giving him a chance to answer.

Frazil looked up at her with such a weak smile it forced the air from her lungs. She had never seen her brother like this. "Father will be here soon… I think. He had to simmer down his inventions. Where's Mother?" His voice was so shaky and hoarse it scared her.

Glancing back toward the house, she spotted Virga and Brooklyn running toward them. "She's coming," she encouraged her brother while also waving for the others to hurry.

The moment they reached them, Brooklyn asked, "Where's your father?" while also opening the bag she had brought along full of medical supplies.

"He's… He's at the mountain," Frazil grunted.

"Virga, take Valkyrie back to the house," Brooklyn ordered.

Valkyrie stared at her older brother with tears running down her cheeks. What was going to happen to him? Why did Mother want them to leave? Was he going to die?

"V," Virga said, clasping her hand, "let's go. You should change into clean clothes."

She tried to pull away, but he kept a firm grip and gave her a stern look that meant to listen. Halfway back to the house, Valkyrie began running. Virga stayed close.

Flying through the house and pounding up the stairs, the two of them didn't stop until they were in their room. Valkyrie went straight to her bed, but Virga stayed at the door. *I can't cry. Not now,* she ordered herself, although she was tempted to throw herself onto the bed and burst into scared sobs for her brother.

"V," Virga said, "change into something else."

She stopped and stood there for a moment, her back facing him. She knew he was trying to make her do something else so she wouldn't start crying.

Slowly, she walked to the wardrobe and pulled out a clean light dress. She stopped and looked at him. "Don't you need to change?" she asked, eyeing his own filthy clothes which were worse than hers.

"No," he said, his voice softer. "You go first. I'll change later. When you're done, go downstairs and fix a bed for Frazil in the living room. That way, he doesn't have to be carried up the stairs to his room."

"Don't leave me by myself!" she cried. Suddenly, the nightmares of Hollowed coming through the window and kidnapping them flooded her mind. She felt scared.

"I'm just going to help Mother with Frazil. I'll be back. Just change, then take some pillows and blankets downstairs." He walked through the door, then stopped. He poked his head back in the room. "Can you do that?"

"Yeah," she whispered, tears spilling down her face. "Yeah, of course I can do that," she added a little more stiffly. *I'm not helpless. At least... I don't want to be.*

Virga walked into the room and pulled her into a quick embrace. "Hey, he's going to be all right. Father too. You'll see. Everything is always all right in the end. Just give it time. Things will cool down," he said gently.

"Yeah," she replied quietly, closing her eyes. Virga soon left her standing by herself. Taking a deep breath, she quickly reminded herself, *Don't cry. Stay focused on helping.*

It didn't take long to clear the couch from folded laundry and replace it with a few blankets and pillows. She closed her eyes, refusing once again to let the tears return. Finally, she decided she would go back to the room and wait for Virga to come and get her.

As she began to go, she stopped. She looked at the framed picture of their family on the bookshelf in the room. It was from two years ago. It reminded her of their earlier discussion.

Without giving it a second thought, she soon found herself in the storage room. It took her a while to find the old box that had been full of the journals and photos, but when she did, she only removed one thing.

Back in her room, she sat on her bed and studied the thick old leather journal. Opening it, she read on the inside "Brooklyn, Year's 296–305."

She sighed, feeling a little guilty for taking it, but she wanted answers. Tucking the journal beneath her pillow, she retreated back downstairs at the sound of the others entering the living room.

10

BEAST

Valkyrie's breath was caught in her throat as she and Virga stood at the living room door. She didn't have to go any further to know something terrible had happened to their brother.

Holding her breath, she approached Frazil who was lying on his back on the couch. He looked up at her as she neared, and her eyes went wide.

His eyes, ears, hair—everything about him looked different, almost as if a disease was slowly engulfing him. It was much worse than the other day when she had seen him on the hill.

His hair was almost fully developed into a dark charcoal gray with only a few streaks of blond left. She realized it wasn't soot but actually his hair color.

His bright green eyes looked more vivid than ever. Above his iris, a large white glare had cut through, interrupting his hourglass pupils.

His ears had also changed color to match his hair. Lightning streaks of blond grew throughout the gray. But that wasn't what bothered her most. It was that his ears had also changed shape. No longer were they tall and pointy like a Stexphin. Instead, they had been pulled forward to be on top of his head, short and wider than usual as well.

Valkyrie reached out with a tender hand and stroked her brother's hair. She had to be sure this was actually him and not some sort of dust clinging to him. It wasn't.

"Frazil?" she questioned, staring into his strange eyes.

"It's all right, Jaylee," he said, sounding strained as if he was holding his breath. His voice sounded hoarse. No longer did the firm kindness linger. "I'm still me."

Valkyrie smiled softly. She moved a few strands of his ratty hair from his face. "I think you need to take a bath and comb," she said.

Frazil looked away, letting out a breath. It almost seemed to choke him, and he flinched as he did. Yet, he looked relieved.

"I was so scared you'd hate me," he said, taking in a few short breaths. He closed his eyes and held his breath.

"I could never hate you," Valkyrie said, grabbing his hand and stroking the top of it to calm him down. She noticed it seemed bigger.

Frazil took another deep breath and opened his breath. He glanced over at Virga who still stood at the door, staring at them with suspicious eyes.

Hesitantly, he approached. "Why?" he asked in a hard tone.

"Like Father says," Frazil grunted as he tried to pull himself into a sitting position, "sometimes it takes risk to try something new, but that doesn't ever not make it worth it."

"Will you ever be normal again?" Virga asked.

Valkyrie was quiet, trying to ignore her twin's resentment in his voice.

"Just give it time," Father's voice came from behind them as he entered the room. He placed a hand on their shoulders, but Virga flinched away.

"He'll recover in time," Father continued.

Valkyrie stared at her twin brother with questioning eyes. Why had he flinched away as if Dane were diseased?

Looking back at Frazil who had finally settled into a sitting position, she asked, "What happened? Were you attacked?"

Frazil sighed and closed his eyes. "No," he said. He opened them and glanced at Father with eyes that almost seemed to be begging.

"Frazil was helping test a new invention," Dane said, slightly rubbing Valkyrie's shoulder. His gesture made her calm down. *So he wasn't attacked. Good.*

"The machine got out of control." Father shook his head with disappointment. Valkyrie knew how much his inventing meant to him and was sad herself to know one of his new contraptions had been a fail.

"Was that the one that could change everything?" Valkyrie asked, looking up at her father's matching green eyes. He tried to smile but faltered.

"Yes," he said. "Frazil was standing the closest to it when he began to lose control."

"But what happened? Why does he look like *that*? Like this?" She looked back at her brother, giving him an apologetic look to say she meant no offense.

Dane was quiet before saying, "You would have to understand what the machine is for to know why."

"When will we know?" Valkyrie asked.

"Soon," Father said quietly. "Hopefully very soon"

*****

And he was right. A few days later, the family sat at the table for a warm breakfast of eggs and toast. Halfway through the meal, Dane announced he was taking the twins to his laboratory for the first time since Frazil could no longer join him due to his injuries.

Valkyrie gasped at the sudden news. They were going to his laboratory? To help him with his new invention? *Today?*

She wasn't sure how to feel. Excited? Overwhelmed? Nervous? As the twins scurried to pack bags with belongings, she felt all three.

I wonder how long we'll be staying. Weeks like he usually does? Or just a few days? Or is it undecided?

She packed a few dresses along with slacks and a few sweaters. She didn't have the slightest clue what she should be prepared for.

Glancing over at Virga, she noticed he seemed excited to finally be leaving. Her thoughts drifted to the night they had said Virga wanted to leave but wouldn't because of her.

She closed her eyes in a pained expression as she was reminded of the other night. Virga had asked her if she would ever leave. Then he had tried begging her to leave with him.

Why are you so desperate to leave? She opened her eyes and stared at her twin's back.

Virga stiffened and stood up straight as if he had heard her thoughts. His ears flipped backward toward her, showing he was listening.

He turned around. Looked at her, his brows scrunched up and his eyes searching. Valkyrie's stomach tied into knots. Had she said that out loud or had Virga actually heard her thoughts? *That's impossible. He would have to be gifted; he's not.*

"Do you hear that?" Virga asked, tilting his head in a curious way.

Valkyrie blinked a few times. Then listened. Yes, she did hear it.

Groans, loud and pained, were coming from downstairs. "Frazil?" she guessed. But why was he groaning as if in pain?

"Twins!" Father's voice suddenly called up the stairs. "Are you ready to go?"

*****

In a few moments, after saying goodbye to Brooklyn, they were walking over the hills of Magsay and heading toward the distant Cliff Shore Peaks.

Valkyrie silently wished she hadn't packed such a big bag for the trip. On top of her backpack was the cloak from Cooper. She had tied it together in a bundle and strapped it to the top. Inside the clump was her mother's journal. She hadn't read it yet and hoped she'd have time to at the mountain. *As long as Father doesn't notice it.*

Glancing over, she saw Virga was wearing the leather jacket. It was large on him, but she smiled as she silently admitted it looked good on him. *Just wait until you grow into it.* She imagined what he would look like.

It was a beautiful morning as the sun shone pleasantly and the grass swayed under the soft breeze. Wildflowers splashed the meadows with color here and there.

They walked on in silence most of the way, her legs slowly feeling weaker and weaker as they climbed small hills, one after another. The mountain didn't seem to get any closer than it was ten minutes ago.

Virga tried a few times to start a conversation, but after asking a few questions about Frazil and why he was so distant lately, Father got unsettled and suspicious. Valkyrie knew Virga was only trying to get some answers, but he only seemed to be making Father upset.

As they kept walking, Valkyrie began to realize she had never noticed how far the mountain really was. She had never felt so tempted to whine, "Are we there yet?" but she kept her mouth shut.

"Don't worry, children, we'll be there soon," Father said as if he could read their minds.

But after a few more minutes passed, Valkyrie was really beginning to wonder if they would ever reach Father's laboratory. And was her bag getting heavier or was she just getting weaker?

Walking with her head down, she hadn't realized the others had stopped until she bumped into Virga. She quickly apologized, then looked up to see the worry on Dane's expression. He stood stiff like a board with his head slightly turned and his ears pricking side to side.

She was about to ask why they had stopped when a loud doleful shriek sliced through the air, making Virga yelp. Fear cut through her like a blade, and she screamed.

A hundred nightmares of the Hollowed flooded her mind.

"Run!" Father cried, jumping sideways. He transformed an inch before he hit the ground. He took off for the mountain in Stexphin form.

Valkyrie was too scared to follow. Every thought screamed at her to transform and follow him, but she couldn't move. Fear kept her trapped in place. What had made that noise?

It's not a Hollowed, not a Hollowed. She tried to calm her racing heart, but nothing worked. *It was too painful to be a Hollowed. It's something else…something worse than a scout?*

She scanned the hills behind them, searching the hills for any sign of movement. Then she saw it. With a horrified gasp, she clenched Virga's arm and stared.

In the distance, a large creature climbed over one of the hills. Stopping on top of the mount, it released another wild shriek, this time sounding more like a howl.

The monster was large, much larger than the Hollowed scout. But it had ears, legs, and a tail matching the creature. It appeared to be some sort of deadly wolf. Something worse than a Hollowed scout.

"He's seen us." Virga's voice was quiet and ghostly.

Valkyrie squeezed her eyes shut, fighting the urge to suddenly fall over and faint.

"Go!" Virga suddenly screamed.

She saw in horror the monster disappear behind another hill as it ran in their direction.

Her brother transformed into his Stexphin form and took off. Valkyrie quickly followed suit, suddenly more afraid of being left behind.

In the shape of what looked like a small cat with long legs and thin body, it only took a matter of seconds to race forward.

Valkyrie saw the distance they still had to reach the mountain and automatically began to pace herself to the speed she knew she needed to make it without collapsing before they reached the safety of Father's laboratory.

"C'mon, V!" Virga's desperate hiss reached her ears. "Push yourself!"

Valkyrie squeezed her eyes shut, knowing he was right. *But I can't sprint that distance. I won't make it!* The ground vibrated beneath them, warning the monster's approach.

Opening her eyes with a new determination, she took longer strides. *I have to make it.* She didn't have to look back to know the wolf was six feet larger than them in Stexphin form.

Her adrenaline spiked, and she picked up speed, silently encouraging herself. *You can make it. Just keep one foot in front of the other. You have to make it. Breathe. Go faster!*

Ahead of her, she saw Virga glance back. *No!* She realized what was happening and instantly transformed back into her Character form.

Virga tripped, which instantly led into a series of painful somersaults.

Running in Character form instantly slowed her down a few paces, but she wasn't about to abandon her brother. Stretching her legs into long bounds, she pushed her burning body even faster.

She could feel the hot breath of the monster nearing.

She grabbed the Stexphin as she passed him. It was like holding a cat, only this one was taller and thinner.

Spittle landed on the back of her neck, and she knew the wolf was preparing to bite into them.

Act now!

She thrust Virga forward, giving him the momentum he needed to find his footing and continue his race to the mountain.

Forcing her eyes to stay open, she jumped up and transformed into her Stexphin form.

The wolf was right there, deadly jaws open and ready to swallow her in one bite. Arching upward, she barely missed the slavering jaws.

Unsheathing her claws, she dug them into the wolf's face.

II

LABORATORY

The pain must have shocked the monster, and Valkyrie barely hung on while massive claws threatened to rip her away. The deadly stroke missed as the wolf tripped.

She felt the beast lurch forward, and quickly, she jumped off, transforming into her Character form as she did. She hit the ground painfully, her knees buckling.

She gasped as she crumbled into the long grass, but she knew they weren't safe yet. Staggering to her feet, she saw Virga at the base of the mountain.

She sprinted toward him, panting desperately for air. *I can't believe I just did that and didn't die.* Virga stood between two large boulders, leaning against each other, forming an arch.

"Where's the door?" Valkyrie cried when she reached him. She felt the hard stone with a sweaty hand, hoping to feel a hidden handle.

"I don't know!" Virga cried, turning toward the sound of a loud ferocious bark. Their enemy was getting back to his feet, looking even more angry than before.

Valkyrie couldn't breathe, still fighting for the air she had lost in her desperate scramble to save her brother. Now as the large wolf bounded toward them, her shortness of breath was only encouraged through fear.

Suddenly, Virga grabbed her in what could have been an embrace if they weren't about to die and turned his back to face the monster.

Helplessness engulfed Valkyrie, and black dots surrounded her vision. She squeezed her eyes shut, waiting for the horrible feeling of Virga being yanked away from her moments before the monster would sink his teeth into her own flesh.

She yelped as strong hands grabbed her shoulders and ripped her back from her brother. She wouldn't let go, and they were both pulled through the stone wall.

Valkyrie tripped on her own feet and fell on her back, Virga landing on top of her painfully. If she wasn't struggling to breathe, she may have been shocked by the reality they had both just gone through stone.

Now the air came, sweet and fresh, as she gasped loudly, jolting with a desperate attempt to take in more air then she could swallow.

Tears filled her eyes at the horrible trauma of everything that had just happened. *I want to go home.*

"Father?" she heard Virga gasp above her. Loud ferocious growls made her shove her twin aside so she could see where the wolf was.

"Don't worry," Dane chuckled nervously. "He can't see nor hear us."

Beyond them, where the twins had just been pulled through the stone wall, was what appeared to be a screen. On the other side was the large wolf.

The monster growled ferociously as it paced the wall. Valkyrie trembled all over to see how close the beast still was. Now she could define its appearance. Dark, ugly, gray with scarred streaks covering its body, dangerous eyes and muscles bulging from beneath its coat of fur.

For once, she didn't have to fight off tears. They didn't come. "Are you okay?" Virga asked, glancing at her with concerned eyes.

"I'm… I'm still in shock, I think," she replied in a shaky voice. Glancing fretfully over at the noise of metal cranking, she watched Dane as he pulled a large lever.

The screen in front of them disappeared, replaced with what looked like solid stone, hiding the monster outside from view.

Valkyrie collapsed, lying on her back as she tried to contemplate what just happened. She wasn't given a moment of rest as Virga grabbed her arm and pulled her up.

He followed Father through the mountain, looking excited to learn more. Valkyrie removed the annoying pack from her back and set it aside as she followed the others.

Walking through the large caverns inside the mountain, Dane showed them all sorts of machines scattered around. Virga enjoyed asking many questions, but Valkyrie remained quiet. How easily they could forget what just happened.

Her mind, too, soon drifted to other subjects as she studied a few of the strange inventions herself.

She had to admit, though, that when Father led them to a couch, that was definitely the best contraption in the entire mountain.

She sat down heavily, glad to finally be given the break her body longed for. All the earlier exhaustion came rushing back. *I wouldn't be surprised if I fell asleep right here.*

Instead, she found herself waking up when Dane gave them glasses of milk and cookies. *Mmm, Mother makes the best oatmeal cookies in the world!*

"Now I think it's time I explain to you kids what I've been working on," Father began as he sat on a separate recliner.

Finally! Valkyrie thought with excitement.

"Years ago, before either of you were even born, I had a 'friend' of mine who challenged me to try this invention. At first, I was hesitant, but I haven't given up on it since. Especially after—" He stopped and cleared his throat. "This coming year, I've finally found the key to get it to work. I need your help to keep it going, though."

"Is this the same invention you tested Frazil on?" Virga asked stiffly.

Tested Frazil on? What does he mean by tested?

"Yes and no. I have it under control. It has improved, and—" Dane began, but Virga interrupted him.

"I'm *sorry*, but you saw what *you* did to Frazil. I still don't know *what* you did to him, but you've scared him! You've all been keeping secrets from us. You can't just expect us to let you use us as bait when we still don't know why!"

Valkyrie shot her brother a warning glance. Why was he acting up? *Just do as he says, Virga!* she wanted to yell.

"Virga," Dane said, his voice firm. "I have my reasons. *We* have reasons, and the sooner you help me, the sooner these secrets will be revealed to you. After this invention, I hope to tell you everything. Then you will see why I need your help so much. You have no idea what has been happening in the world around and among you."

Valkyrie looked at him hopefully. Were they finally going to get some answers? Virga saw it differently, and she saw him heating up.

"What do you mean we have no idea?" her brother yelled. "We know so much more than you think! Do you think we can't hear you when you whisper at night? Do you think we couldn't hear your *rage* when you attacked Frazil? We're not gone, just invisible when you *don't want* us!"

Valkyrie gasped beside him. His words shocked her. *He's been keeping this from me for a while. Why is he so angry? Why didn't he tell me how he felt? I thought we shared everything with each other.*

"I expected more from *you*," Father said, punctuating he wasn't only referring to Virga. Valkyrie felt as if her heart had just been punctured by his words. *What did I do?*

"Where I come from, children do not *disrespect* their elders. Especially not the ones who raised them. Listen, I understand how you feel, and I will tell you everything, but first, I must make sure you can go through with this invention. I must know that you trust me," Dane said.

"Haven't you *seen* Frazil?" Virga said desperately. "He's a monster! You've ruined my brother—*our* brother! Did you give *him* a choice?"

Father scowled angrily. "All I was asking for was a little help," he said through gritted teeth. "If you can't do that, all you had to say was no with the respect you owe to your elders. All I needed to know was that you kids still trust me! And if you will not help, I see no reason for you to be here!" With that, he turned and walked away.

Valkyrie couldn't find any words for the sudden outburst that had just happened. She couldn't believe it. Virga hadn't meant any harm, but nor had Father. What was happening that she couldn't see?

What did I do wrong? Why has it all come to this? Tears filled her eyes, and she looked down. She had never felt this despised and defenseless in her life.

"I-I'm sorry," Virga said. "I should have listened to you. I just... Do you think we should help him? Do you...*want* to help him?"

"I don't want to disappoint him," she said quietly.

"I already have," Virga whispered. "It's only that... I mean, you saw what he did to Frazil. I don't want that to happen to you."

"But do you remember what Frazil told us? Sometimes it takes a risk to try something new, but that doesn't ever not make it not worth it." Valkyrie looked at him earnestly. She was beginning to realize what Virga had said was true. Father wanted to invent something on them like he had on Frazil.

As much as she felt frightened to do something that could change her into something like Frazil, she wanted even more to prove herself. "Will you take this risk with me?"

Virga remained silent before asking, "So you think we should do it? Whatever *it* is."

Valkyrie searched his eyes for a moment. He looked hesitant but not exactly afraid. "Yes, I do. And I think you should be the one to tell him."

Virga flinched. *You know he needs to know you didn't mean what you said. Even if you did at the moment.* Valkyrie thought, conceptualizing Virga could read her thoughts through her eyes. *I'm afraid. But I can be brave and do this. It will be new, and we may turn out like Frazil, but we have each other. Like you said. As long as we have each other.*

"You're right," Virga said, a small smile forming on his lips as if he heard her thoughts. "I'll do it."

She watched her brother leave the cavern and into a narrow small corridor. She decided to wait until he returned before going after them.

Father would know Virga was only apologizing because she told him to if she went along. He'd also guess he was only agreeing to do this experiment because of her.

And although that was true, she felt like Father needed better support than what they were giving him.

While she waited, she found herself wandering through the caves. She passed a strange violin hanging on the wall and smiled. Father had shown it to them earlier.

Dane had all sorts of strange machines everywhere.

Valkyrie spotted a small desk across the cave and walked toward it. It had all sorts of papers and sketches on it. She began going through the drawings and picked up an unfinished one. It looked like a wolf.

She frowned. "Why would Father need this?" she asked aloud.

A loud crash sounded from behind, and she spun around. It didn't look as if anything fell. Loud scratching followed the sound of the crash. It was coming from the wall.

Placing the side of her head against the cold stone, she listened. She heard shuffling noises and small grunting on the other side.

"Valkyrie?"

She jumped at the sound of Father's voice. Scolding herself, she ran back to another open cavern.

This room was more empty than the others but held large machines and scraps of metal and other disowned objects scattered on the floor.

Father was standing by one of these large machines. Virga was nowhere in sight.

"Where's Virga?" she questioned as she glanced around. Father smiled, which seemed forced as he pointed at the machine in front of him.

Frowning, Valkyrie strode over. She gasped. The front of the contraption was made of clear blue glass. On the other side of the container laid Virga. His eyes were closed, and he wasn't moving.

"W-What's wrong with him?" she asked, her hand near her mouth. He looked dead.

"Nothing! Nothing at all. It's moving along very smoothly. He's just been put to sleep. Are you ready?" he then asked, looking at her.

"Uh, I don't know," she said, hesitating. She had hoped this invention only included a small shot or…well, she wasn't sure what she had been expecting, but it definitely wasn't this.

"Come now, it's perfectly safe," Father said as he went to the second glass box and opened it. He held out his hand to her.

Valkyrie wanted to remind him about what had happened to Frazil but didn't when she remembered how upset he had gotten the last time that was mentioned.

Slowly, she took Father's hand as he helped her step up and into the box. He gave her an assuring smile as she laid back on the cushioned mat and began to close the large clear blue glass lid.

She tried to relax but couldn't stop her racing heart. *Calm down, it's nothing,* she assured herself. *You're fine, Father knows what he's doing. I hope.* She peered out the glass to see Dane fiddling with a small remote.

Faint crashing sounded through the glass, and Valkyrie's breath got caught in her throat. Father jumped at the noise and turned toward his left. His eyes went wide, and he gasped. How she wished she could see what was going on!

Father jumped into action and snatched a large sort of gun off a messy table. All sorts of things clattered to the ground as he took the rifle in such a hurry. His eyes went up along with his gun, and he shot.

It wasn't a bullet that left the strange contraption but something that appeared to be warped energy almost.

Valkyrie hadn't noticed that the glass tube had filled with a thick mist, which slowly began to fog the glass. She began hyperventilating.

The last thing she saw was something large leaping onto Dane. She cried out, but her voice drifted away. Her eyes began to feel heavy, and she willingly closed them.

****

Everything hurt. Where was she? What happened?

Still half asleep, Valkyrie struggled to come fully awake. Her eyelids felt heavy and refused to open, keeping her concealed to darkness. Everything felt weird. *She* felt different.

Valkyrie tried to move or even speak but couldn't do either. She tried to remember what had happened but only felt sick. Soon, she fell back asleep.

12

DELTA'S REPORT

Crowley—Year 317

When Crowley had first begun training Selah, he wasn't sure what to think. But over the past few weeks, she turned out to be a rather good trainee.

She listened well but wasn't very good at keeping her thoughts to herself when she didn't want to do something. He had found she had a skill with the smaller throwing knives, so they worked on those the most.

Not only did they train in combat, but he also tested her on escape plans, fighting techniques, and quick reaction time.

Today, he took her to the library where he told her to find books on old wars. Then he wanted her to take notes on the written escapes and weapons.

He named off a few certain books she could find before letting her go. She complained about having to write everything down but did as she was told.

Although she was a quick learner and a skilled fighter, she had weaknesses. Smart with books and names, Crowley had quickly learned she had horrible vision memory.

For him, all he had to see was the object, human, or location, and instantly, all his knowledge of that would come flooding to him.

Selah, however, was the opposite. She had to have a specific name to everything before she remembered what or who it was and their appearance.

"Why did you grab that book?" Crowley asked as Selah laid her pile on the table. He picked up the small cover and read the title out loud. "*Ruins of Old*. I doubt this speaks of fighting techniques."

"Yes, but it does speak quite a bit about the Colossal Wars," she said.

"Sometimes I forget you've read the entire library," Crowley replied as he returned the binder.

"Not yet, but I plan to," she said under her breath as she flipped through pages.

As Selah sat down and began to write notes while scanning through her first book, Crowley began to inspect her other choices. He was surprised to find a fantasy story.

He picked it up and began to flip through the pages. He laughed as he read the desperate attempts the writer had for fight moves.

Selah looked up and said, "I haven't personally finished that book yet."

"Really?"

"It's kind of predictable." She shrugged. "Haven't been able to get myself to fall in love."

"Predictable? In what way?" Crowley asked, stopping to scan a few pages. Silently, he decided he would read this later.

"It's just another battle story," she said, sounding bored as she went back to writing notes. "Important characters are going to die, no one will remember the ones who were never named, and in the end, everyone is going to live happily ever after."

Crowley eyed her. "Have you ever read an interesting story, one you fell in love with that didn't end happily?"

"Well, no." She closed her book and looked up at him. "I think everyone has a happy ending, though."

"Even those who died unnamed?"

"Yes. They had joy in their lives. They didn't live without ever smiling or forgetting their memories."

"You confuse me," Crowley confessed, closing the book with one hand and eyeing her.

"We're all going to struggle through something horrible, but in the end, we look back and realize life wasn't too bad."

"And your life. After what happened to you, do you consider yours a happy ending?"

Selah went quiet, her eyes flitting down.

"Not everyone sees life the way you do, Selah," Crowley went on. "I think even if you don't agree with yourself, you want to believe everyone will have a happy ending because that's all you've ever read. But life is more than a book. It's a wild journey full of thorns and thistles, yet there *is* light. But that doesn't mean we *live* happily ever after. We're not given the privilege to read our ending."

"Have you ever met someone with a 'sad ending?'" Selah demanded. She hated losing debates with him.

"No. But that doesn't mean they were happy when they were stabbed in the back," Crowley snapped. Selah went back to her books, clearly set on her notion of life being predictable.

"I have a short meeting. I'll come back in an hour," Crowley said, turning to go.

Before he left, he heard Selah whisper under her breath, "You're predictable."

*****

As Crowley walked through the dark halls of Smuir, he shook his head as he thought about Selah. She had become even more rambunctious the more they saw each other.

He realized she looked to him as if he were her older brother. *But I'm not. I'm much more. I am the closest adviser, strongest warrior, and have more knowledge than the king. I deserve to be respected as such. But how to make that stick in a mind like Selah's?* He sighed and shook his head. *And yet here I am, stepping way out of my league for her.*

Crowley freed his thoughts of the abrupt girl. He had to have a clear mind for the meeting he was about to have.

At last, he reached the room where they had agreed to meet. Opening the door, he saw his respondent was already there. Locking the gate behind them, he approached the man.

"Delta," Crowley said, "scout of the destruction of Illicit Group."

"Yes," the older man's voice groveled, throwing off his friendly features. "That is me. I know who you are. Is what I don't know why you wanted to meet?"

"Your report," Crowley replied, "from 316 on the Illicit Group."

"I gave my report. To the king. Last year," Delta responded.

"And I am asking you to report it again," Crowley said, his voice tight.

Delta eyed him sharply. Realizing he wasn't going to get to leave without giving the report, he stated, "I followed the trail of Illicit and was stopped near the edge of Moonglow Reservoir. There I found what was left of the band."

"Blood and disregarded weapons," Crowley said quietly.

"Sir," Delta said, taking a deep annoyed breath. "I know you've heard the report before, from the king himself, no doubt. Why are you asking to hear it again?"

"I know we're missing something. I'm trying to find it."

"Adviser."

Crowley looked up at the sudden change in Delta's voice. He sounded younger, almost concerned.

"Is there any doubt about what happened to them? They were attacked by Rotto," Delta finished.

"That part of the report was not given to the king, I take it?"

"His Highness doesn't like *his* name spoken," Delta said, eyeing Crowley.

"What were the weapons?" Crowley asked, ignoring the gleam in the man's eyes.

"Swords," Delta replied. "Still sheathed."

"Sheathed swords…and among them? There was more, I can tell."

"A gun," Delta said, a small smile turning at his lips.

Crowley turned his head to eye him. "Rotto doesn't use guns," he stated plainly.

"You're right, he doesn't. But clearly, someone does." Delta's smile never left.

"Then how do you know Rotto was the culprit?" Crowley questioned firmly.

Delta stared at him for a long moment before saying, "Because there was someone else there. A victim of the gun. He told me what happened."

Crowley stared at him, trying to find if there was any truth in his words. He saw no sign the man was lying. "Who?"

"His name is Walt." Delta smiled mischievously when Crowley's mask dropped and recognition showed. "Yes, you know him."

"But Walt was—he wasn't in the band I sent. What did he tell you?" Crowley demanded.

"Some very interesting things," Delta nodded, his smile disappearing.

"Does King Demoor know any of this?"

"Every word. Of course, he wouldn't have told you. Although you are his adviser, he has no reason to trust you with such matters." Delta's gravelly voice was slick.

Crowley could feel his blood boiling beneath his skin. How dare Demoor not tell him! And no reason to trust him? No *reason to trust him? I have over fifty reasons he can trust me! Is he blind?*

He took a deep breath and closed his eyes. Opening them slowly, he studied the respondent before him. "And what of the captain? Did Walt have any word on him?"

"Yes." Delta's face turned grim. "It was he who shot him, moments before he turned."

"You're lying,"

"Do I *look* like I'm lying?" Delta said firmly. He furrowed his brows. When Crowley didn't answer, he continued, "Walt claims that Rotto *respected* him." He said the word smoother than honey.

Crowley bristled. *Something's not right.*

"And what of Walt? Was he dead when you left him?"

"Yes and no." Delta laughed deep in his throat. "He was almost dead, so I left him, of course. I couldn't afford to haul a carcass back with me."

"What do you mean yes *and* no?" Crowley demanded, glowering at the scout.

"I saw him a few days ago on a scouting mission ordered by the king. Another one you didn't know of?" he guessed when Crowley's frown increased.

"Tell me about Walt," he demanded. "I'm not here on the king's behalf."

"Yes, but you never are, are you?"

"You said you saw Walt a few days ago," Crowley growled. "How was he?"

"He was very much alive," Delta smiled wickedly. "And I am going to see him again very soon."

13

INVENTION

Valkyrie—Year 315

Valkyrie woke up from her deep sleep to find a glare blinding her eyes. She moaned and put her hand in front of her to block the light. Something definitely seemed different, but she wasn't sure what it was.

The light moved away, and she moved her hand to see a familiar face peeking through the blue glass in front of her. What was going on?

It took her a few moments to remember what had happened. Father's invention, falling asleep, waking up every once in a while to find herself in pain.

The glass lid in front of her opened, and someone helped her up. She sat there blinking for a second. She felt sore but at the same time stronger, energetic, and all jittery.

Valkyrie took the offered hand and climbed out of the invention. She took a step, and immediately, her head felt dizzy, and she lost her balance and stumbled.

Someone caught her by her arm, and she glanced up to see a dark, ugly kind of gray-haired Stexphin with odd golden brown streaks throughout it. She couldn't tell who it was, but for some reason, she felt a little connected to him.

"Who are you?" she demanded as the young man helped her to her feet. She pulled away from his grasp and looked the Character over. He looked so familiar.

"Jaylee," the Stexphin character said with a wounded look. "It's me, Frazil."

Valkyrie gaped and looked him over once more. She had almost forgotten her brother's new look.

Frazil's kind smile looked to Valkyrie the way it always did. She opened her mouth to say something but then stopped and shook her head. What was she supposed to say? Her beloved brother had changed completely from his friendly golden brown to a dark and menacing look. She missed the old Frazil.

105

Valkyrie heard a slight shift behind her and turned to see Father standing there. He still wore his long white lab coat, and he looked at her with troubled but excited eyes.

She was actually surprised she had heard Father behind her. He had only slightly moved, and yet her ears seemed to automatically move backward, and she had heard him.

Valkyrie glanced around to realize the workshop seemed to have changed a bit. A few machines had been moved to different spots, and three or four desks were all lined up beside each other covered in all sorts of papers.

Another thing she noticed was a black-haired boy sitting on a small stool a little ways away from them. His back faced her, and Valkyrie felt a strong connection to him.

Before she could say anything, Father walked toward his desks which brought her to attention. It slightly bothered her how every movement made attracted her awareness.

"Children, come here," Father said, motioning to them as he bent over his desk.

Valkyrie followed Frazil to the desks. "Virga, you too," Father said, motioning to the boy without glancing up from his papers.

Wait. Virga?

Valkyrie raised her brows as the boy responded and got up slowly. He walked over, looking at the ground, refusing to meet her eyes.

"Virga?" she asked when he reached them.

He slowly looked up, and for a moment, she wasn't sure that it was her brother.

Not a trace of white was left on top of his hair, and his eyes were a faint silvery color. This new black color looked dull and no longer silky like his old strands. He also seemed a few inches taller and stronger.

She met his sad eyes to realize he had been staring at her the whole time. His eyes slowly seemed to be coming back to purple, and Valkyrie knew that this was, in fact, her brother.

She smiled and threw her arms around his neck. "You look so different!" she exclaimed.

106

He nodded as he hugged her back.

"You do too," was his heartbroken reply.

Valkyrie glanced down to see that she was different. Slowly, she untangled her arms and grabbed a few strands of hair. Her once beautiful light gray color was gone. It had changed into a darker gray, nearly matching the same shade as Frazil. She frowned.

Father finally looked up from his desk and grabbed something. He turned toward them and grabbed Valkyrie's arm.

Virga instantly reacted and pulled her away, putting himself between her and Father. Dane just smiled and let out a small laugh.

"You've certainly changed, son," he said. "You've become quite defensive and great at reacting! That's good. But you need to trust me. I'm not going to hurt her."

Virga moved away, but Valkyrie could sense he was hesitant. He clearly didn't trust Dane.

Father took her hand and slowly pricked something in her arm. She winced. "Just need to run a few more tests," he explained. He did the same to Virga, then returned to his desk.

Virga scowled at him, and Valkyrie felt discouraged by her brother's attitude.

Frazil came up between them and put a hand on each of their shoulders. Virga shifted away, and Frazil moved his hand. He gave him an apologetic look, then turned toward Valkyrie.

"I'm glad to see you did all right." He turned to Virga. "Both of you."

Valkyrie nodded but was still confused. "I'm not even sure what's going on," she confessed. "No one's told me anything. What is this invention?"

"I've been wanting to know the same," Virga frowned. "This invention had better have more to it than changing our color."

Frazil nodded an understanding look to Virga. "Father will tell you soon enough, but you must understand this: he has good reasons for it. He will not be able to tell you straight away, but you must not react with anger."

Valkyrie noticed he was mainly speaking to Virga.

*****

It wasn't until the next day when Dane led his three children through the mountain, finally going to explain what his invention was. Frazil walked next to him, whispering quietly.

Although they were whispering, Valkyrie could still hear them easily as if they were speaking to her. She wondered if Virga could, too, as that was who they were whispering about.

"Is this the best choice of plan, Father?" Frazil was saying.

"I'm not sure how else to break it to them. Might as well get it over with," Father replied with a resentful grunt.

"True, yes, but you know as well as I do that this may affect Virga. I mean, he has a lot of anger in him."

"Yes, I know. But if he hasn't hurt anyone yet, then I believe he may not have the same side effect as you."

Frazil nodded in agreement, and they went on in low whispers.

Hurt anyone? Valkyrie frowned. She glanced at her twin who had his head hanging and his ears back. Perhaps he hadn't overheard what Frazil and Father had said.

They were soon at the exit, and Valkyrie became excited as she realized they were finally leaving the laboratory.

Father pulled the lever, which made the exit change from solid rock to more of a screen. She could see outside, the large open meadow, the sun shining, the grass waving beneath the wind.

The second they were out, Valkyrie took a deep breath and let the sun sink into her skin. She sighed with satisfaction as a strong wind blew all around them.

The wind was very powerful today, and Valkyrie felt almost sure that it could blow her away if she let it. Virga also had a small smile on his face as he looked around at the beautiful view. Valkyrie laughed and joined him.

She had never realized how much she would rather be out here than in a stuffy old cave full of machinery.

*****

A little while later, Dane was ready to show them what the invention really was.

He nodded to Frazil who had a small nervous smile on his face. "All right," he said as he transformed into Stexphin form and began to race across the meadow.

Valkyrie was confused. Frazil was just running, nothing special about that. He was going a little faster than usual, but still.

She glanced at Dane who had a large smile on his face. Then at Virga, whose expression looked rather terrified.

Frazil had gone quite a distance and now stopped. He faced them and began to run back. Now Valkyrie was really confused and a little disappointed.

Frazil was picking up speed every second, and Valkyrie began to wonder if he was looking different because of his speed and distance or if it was just her?

He got closer, and as he did, the fur on the back of his neck seemed to grow, and his paws got bigger. His face narrowed, and his ears shrunk. A long tail followed from behind. Before she knew it, a very large wolf was racing for them.

Her ears sank back, her hands went to her mouth, and she cowered. How was this possible?

The wolf, or her brother, trotted over. He was quite large and seemed to tower above them. His fur was rough and a dark gray with lightning streaks of blond.

"Y-You're a wolf!" she stammered.

Father let out a triumphant laugh, and she turned to Virga, only to realize he was fuming. He did not look happy about this at all.

"You're the monster who tried attacking us!" Virga yelled angrily. Suddenly, realization dawned on her. *Frazil was the wolf who chased us to Father's mount!*

"And you attacked Father on the mountain," she exclaimed. *That's what he had been pointing his gun at before I fell unconscious.*

"You have to be careful." Dane stepped forward. "An unintentional effect is how your emotions affect the transformations. That day Frazil chased us to the mountain he was grieved about. You can't let your emotions get too complicated.

"Frazil said he had no control over himself that day. The DNA offered of the wolves was not any calm-going creature. Swiftmaw aren't normally angry creatures, but because of Hollowed, well, I hadn't realized it would affect the fusion with you three." He paused, glancing at her. "Lately, it's only affected the two of you."

Valkyrie knew he was right. Frazil and Virga had acted like fragile bombs since she woke up. They had especially been biting at each other's necks. She closed her eyes painfully at the thought. Last night was not enjoyable.

Father continued, "Frazil was much worse, being tested on first and everything. I hadn't even fused him with all the planned DNA. The twins, however, had a stronger chance and were merged with Griefolowtros as Swiftmaw—"

Valkyrie wasn't even given a chance to understand what his words meant when Virga suddenly screamed, "You've ruined us! You've turned us into the *enemy! I* am so *ashamed* to be in this family!"

Father's expression filled with surprise. He hadn't expected them to know about the dispute over Stexphin and Rotto. "Son," he said carefully.

"No!" Virga screamed. "You should have given us a choice! Instead, you kept us locked up in a glass tube for weeks!"

Valkyrie gasped. *Weeks?* She hadn't realized it could've possibly been that long.

She backed up nervously as she realized Virga was changing. Father glanced at her, his expression telling her she needed to calm her brother down.

"Virga," she said in a soothing tone, trying to control her shaky voice. "Calm down. Father has his reasons. He needed something to keep us safe from the dangers in the outside world. We need to be able to keep ourselves safe," Valkyrie said, trying to recite most of the things she had heard the night before.

But it was too late.

A large black wolf soon staggered before them.

"He won't be able to control himself. He's too angry," Frazil whispered who was now in Character again. The wolf crouched down and let out a terrible growl.

"Run," Father whispered. "*Run!* Quick! Go!" he yelled, grabbing Frazil's arm when he tried to object. "We have to get you out of here. You'll kill each other if you transform as well,"

Valkyrie hesitated for a moment too soon, and the wolf came crashing down on her. But she was quick and ran through his legs.

Instantly, she was off in a dead sprint across the meadow. Pricking her ear's backward, she could hear the wolf close behind her. She tried to run faster, transforming into her Stexphin from as she did.

I'll never outrun him. We barely escaped Frazil. But the mountain was behind her. She'd have to get around the beast her brother had become.

Virga had always been the sprinter between the two of them. He was much faster than Frazil. Even worse, his Stexphin blood was still a part of him, giving him much more speed than an average wolf would normally have.

What if I transformed? I could easily outrun him that size.

The wolf was on her heels, and she could feel his hot breath on the back of her neck. She needed to do something and fast. Looking out of the corner of her eye, the wolf got ready to take a bite of her.

So she stopped. Planting her small paws into the ground so hard she nearly sat down and flipped forward.

The wolf, who was running too fast to realize what had even happened, ran right over her. Quickly, Valkyrie turned to go the other direction, glad she hadn't been stepped on.

A loud heart-stopping shriek went through the air. It sounded like a howl mixed with the angry scream of a young boy. The wolf was mad.

Valkyrie knew she only had a few options left. Was she to die by her brother murdering her? *No, that's not my brother. I need to transform, but how? What was it that Father said about emotions?* Right then, her main emotion was definitely fear.

Valkyrie tried using her fear to picture a wolf. She felt stupid, thinking, *I'm probably doing this wrong.* But then she began to feel *different.*

Suddenly, she felt much stronger than ever before as her legs began to take longer leaps by the second. Looking down, she saw her wolf-like paws. She smiled.

Valkyrie continued to run toward the mountain. She reached her father's secret entrance, transforming back into Character. Feeling the wall, it was hard stone.

Just as she was about to pound her fist against the invisible door, she fell through the stone and landed inside Dane's laboratory. Frazil hurried over and helped her up.

"Thank you," she said, breathing heavily.

Father was also standing there, smiling. "You transformed!" he praised. "How did you do it?"

"I am not entirely sure. But I know I was thinking of emotions like you said," she replied, still trying to catch her breath.

"Emotions? What were you feeling?" he questioned.

"Fear," Valkyrie replied, a little embarrassed.

"What about Virga, Father?" Frazil asked.

"Yes, of course," Father said as he disappeared into another cavern. He soon came back, holding the big gun Valkyrie had seen him with before.

"What is that?" she asked, ears pricked forward in concern.

"This is a weapon I made. It contains special bullets filled with a formula I created to help with your transformations. Like when Frazil attacked me, I shot him with it, and he calmed down in an instant and turned back to a Stexphin. It helps simmer you down and control your emotions," Father said looking proud. "Frazil, show Valkyrie the darts while I take care of Virga," Dane finished as he disappeared through the mountain's hidden entrance.

Frazil took her hand and led her through the cave. He stopped at a table with a weird box and papers all over it. The papers, Valkyrie noticed, had all sorts of writings, drawings, and sketches covering them.

But Frazil was more concerned about the box. He slowly opened it and revealed strange dart-like things. They weren't too large but were sharp, she could tell, and filled with some sort of fluid.

"What are they for?" she asked.

"To help control ourselves. When you begin to boil up or anything of the sort, stab one into yourself to calm you down. Or you may end up like Virga and hurt innocent Characters."

Frazil's words stuck to her. This was really happening. She could actually transform into another creature.

But hurt innocents? Virga didn't do that. And I know he wouldn't.

Frazil grabbed a small gray pouch next to the box and filled it with a few darts.

"What if I run out?" she asked as she took the small pouch.

"Don't worry, just make more," he replied.

"But I don't know how," she whined.

"It's not that hard, Jaylee," Frazil said. "All you do is get the Althea plant and—"

*****

Later on, Virga was struggling.

Father had shot him, and he was transformed back into his Stexphin Character, but he remembered everything, mainly how he had nearly killed his best friend.

Virga was weeping while Father held him in his arms. He tried to stop the tears from flowing, but he felt like a fool. What would've he done if he had, in fact, killed Valkyrie?

"Virga," Dane said, "come now, Valkyrie will be worrying about you."

"I-I can't. I can't ever face her again. What if I had killed her? What then?" Virga sobbed.

"But you didn't kill her, and if you never face her again, it *will* kill her. It won't make a difference unless you see her. Come on, I'm sure all is already forgiven." Father took Virga, and together, they walked back to the mountain.

When they entered the laboratory, Valkyrie was standing there, waiting. "Virga!" she cried as she ran and hugged him. "Virga, what's the matter?"

"I-I'm so sorry, V. I never meant to hurt you," Virga cried.

Valkyrie firmly looked him in the eye. "You didn't hurt me. You could *never* hurt me. I love you," she said, embracing him again.

Virga smiled.

For the rest of the day, Valkyrie was sure to stay by her brother's side.

She couldn't help but notice Virga was hiding much more than he let on. She couldn't stop thinking about what Frazil had said about Virga leaving.

He wouldn't actually leave, though, she thought to herself as she sat on the couch, scanning through Mother's journal. Brooklyn had written something about meeting a woman named Sastruga whom she suspected was close with wolves.

She looked up at her twin who stood over a counter nearby. He had been building something for a while now. She was shocked when she saw what it was—a beautiful pendant, shaped in a crooked circle, with two musical notes in it.

Virga gave it to her as a gift, and she stared at it in wonder. The notes weren't parallel, but one was higher than the other. They were a bright purple and almost seemed to glow against the silver colored metal.

She looked up at her twin brother with hopeful eyes. *You wouldn't leave me...right?*

14

RUN

Five days later, Dane announced he had done enough research and tests that they could go home for a few days to put Brooklyn's most likely anxious mind to rest.

They left early that morning and were surprised with the fog that covered the lonely hills of Magsay with a layer so thick they couldn't see more than six feet in front of them.

Halfway there, Valkyrie and Virga talked Frazil into letting them ride on the back of his large wolf form. The twins held their breath while the beast swayed as he stood.

Frazil was the largest of the three in wolf form. Dane had compared him to a bear standing on its hind legs. Valkyrie had never seen a bear personally as they lived farther down north in Hickorywood Forest, but she had seen pictures.

Dane said Virga stood six feet, which was two feet smaller than Frazil. Valkyrie was upset to learn she was the smallest until Father said she was the only one who was the perfect size of a wolf at four and a half feet.

Being so large, it wasn't long until they were far ahead of Dane who had insisted he didn't care to try and keep up with them. Looking back, Valkyrie couldn't even see their father as he was swallowed in the thick mist.

She clung to Virga's waist and looked around, wondering why they hadn't reached the cottage yet. It wasn't until Virga asked, "Why are we slowing down?" She realized they had already arrived.

"I can't find the house."

Hearing Frazil speak from his wolf form sent shivers down her spine. His voice was so low and gravelly that she could feel him vibrating beneath them.

"Maybe we still have a ways to go?" Valkyrie suggested, trying to keep her voice even. Who knew how long it would take until this smog cleared up? *I just want to go home. I'm not ready to be lost on our own property,* she thought with slight annoyance.

She glanced at the ground, then back ahead, trying to peer through the fog. *Shouldn't the house be right there?*

Frazil began to walk a few more steps forward.

Valkyrie felt her brother begin to slide in front of her. Virga had lost grip completely and sagged to the side.

"Frazil!" Valkyrie cried when she felt herself slipping as well. She let go of Virga and clutched the wolf's fur in front of her.

A loud thump followed as her brother disappeared over the wolf's side. Instantly, Valkyrie jumped from Frazil's back, transforming midair, and landing on all fours of her larger form.

She silently loved the harmony she had in her Swiftmaw. She had always considered wolves large unbalanced creatures, especially after the Hollowed had attacked Cooper.

She had been wrong. They were rather graceful. *At least Swiftmaw are,* she thought to herself.

As soon as she landed and was next to Virga's groaning form, she transformed back into Character. "Are you okay?" she asked, leaning over him.

Frazil was back into his own Character form as well and got down on his knees next to their hurt brother.

"Ah," Virga winced, "what happened?"

"You slid right off my back," Frazil said, shaking his head as he and Valkyrie helped him sit up. Instantly, Virga twisted back to look where they knew the house should be.

Valkyrie looked as well, ignoring the rest of Frazil's words as she tried to peer through the fog. Nothing was there.

Turning back to her twin, she asked, "What happened? Did you faint?"

Virga looked up at them, his eyes full of fear. Valkyrie's heart began racing. She didn't like that look, especially not on her brother.

"What is it?" Frazil asked as he, too, noticed the angst etched in Virga's expression.

"I can hear her," Virga said.

Valkyrie didn't have to ask to know who he meant. Her heart continued to race. As Frazil helped her brother up, she stared into the thick mist.

"She's in trouble," Virga continued, walking forward as he, too, tried to see past the thick veil. "But nothing's here,"

Valkyrie and Frazil joined him at his side. *Where are you, Mother? Where's the house? Why can't I hear you?*

In the ground before them was a shallow dent, the same size as the foundation of their cottage. Their house truly was gone. "*Mother!*" Valkyrie cried. *Please, still be here.*

Suddenly, a strong current of wind began to blow, causing her loose strands to blow in her face. Another thick layer of fog covered the large dent in the ground.

And then, there was a break, and the curtain cleared to reveal an oddly shaped cottage before them. Beside her, Virga gasped.

It's back. Valkyrie stared in disbelief, reaching up to pull her hair back from her eyes as the wind continued to blow. She began to go forward when Frazil grabbed her arm.

"Stay away from the house," he warned. "We need to stay together."

But what about Mother?

"Virga!" Valkyrie screamed as her twin ran forward. He jumped the porch steps easily and was through the front door before any of them could stop him.

The door slammed shut, and he was gone.

"Virga!" she screamed, trying to pull free from Frazil's grip.

"Jaylee, don't!" he cried, grabbing her around the waist and jerking her away from the direction of the house.

The wind around them began to increase, pushing in a new veil of smog. Her hair whipped around her face, but she ignored it as she continued to fight him.

"Frazil, he—" she began, taking a breath of air. She was cut short and gasped painfully which instantly turned into a choked desperate noise.

Frazil wasn't given the chance to ask what was wrong as he took in a breath of the burning fog. He doubled over, releasing his grip, but no longer were Valkyrie's concerns on Virga.

She tried to gasp for fresh air but each time only received a mouthful of this new fog. It burned. It burned her throat, her lungs, and her eyes.

Squinting against tears, she looked around, trying to understand. Was there somehow a poisonous toxin in the air?

Frazil grabbed her again, this time as if to protect her as he hovered around her. She squeezed her eyes shut and leaned into him, grabbing his shirt to hide her face from the noxious smog.

Her ears shot up, and she trembled in her older brother's arms as the familiar sound of wolves howling filled her mind. Rough barks and angry voices screamed inside her head.

She let go of Frazil and pulled her ears down, trying to shut out the nearby noises of her nightmares. *This can't be happening.*

"Hollowed," Frazil's strained voice hissed in her ear. "Jaylee, you have to go." His voice turned desperate. "Run!"

"What?" She tried not to choke and look at her brother clearly. It was impossible as the unwanted tears streamed down her face from the pain burning her eyes.

"Go! They're here for you, you have to go!" he yelled as he tried to push her away.

"Go? Go where?" she cried as she stumbled back. Her hands fled to her eyes, and she covered them, desperately trying to keep the smog away.

"Go to the city, Smuir. Northeast, you'll find it. I know you can, you've seen my maps," Frazil said, stepping back into the fog to where he was almost hidden. "Don't tell anyone who you are."

"Frazil, don't leave me!" her voice trembled.

"I'll hold them off!" were his last words before the noxious smog swallowed him. Through burning eyes and flooding tears, she saw the shapes of wolves fighting.

Turning, she fled. She wasn't sure where she was running, but she needed to get out of this fog. She couldn't even keep her eyes open as she ran blindly.

A mad bark close behind only encouraged her speed.

Something grabbed her foot, and she fell forward with a loud grunt. Scrambling and kicking away from the grip, she opened her eyes to realize she had tripped over a tree root.

I'm in the woods. She realized the fog wasn't nearly as thick here. Looking back, she saw a silhouette nearing. It was an unfriendly shape, and she knew it wasn't one of her brothers.

Transforming into her Swiftmaw, she jumped to her feet and took off, this time keeping her eyes open as she dodged around trees and brush. The fog was becoming thinner the farther she went.

Whoever was following her seemed to be falling behind as she could no longer hear the pounding footfalls of her pursuer.

A loud trembling shriek split the air. *Frazil.* But she didn't stop. She couldn't. Leaping over brush in long bounds, she continued her flight.

Valkyrie didn't even know where she was running. She didn't see their trail that led to Camino Creek anywhere. *How am I supposed to find the northeast?* she thought desperately. *What am I supposed to do even if I find Smuir?*

Frazil had been right when he said she'd seen his maps. She wasn't sure how he knew about her and Virga's secret break into his room. He hadn't been home at the time.

They had found many maps, many of which were marked wherever Stexphin villages were. *If those wolves find his maps, they'll know where to attack next.*

119

Valkyrie was finally forced to stop when the screams of her burning legs were no longer bearable. She had never run that fast for so long before.

Transforming back into Character, her chest heaved as she tried to catch her breath. *I should've paced myself. I was just so scared.* The air was fresh here, and she took it in with gratitude as she leaned her head against a nearby tree.

Once she was breathing easily again, the tears threatened to come. She stared up at the branches overhead. *I've lost everyone. But I can't go to Smuir. After the fog and wolves leave, they'll be searching for me.*

I have to go back. But not now. If I stay out here for the night, what will I survive on? I'll freeze to death long before I starve.

One thing for certain, she wasn't going to the city of Smuir. She didn't want to believe her entire family had just been slaughtered. *They're alive. I know they are. Everything will soon be back to normal. I just have to wait until the wolves leave. I can't fight them off. Frazil can. I know he can.*

Taking in a shaky breath, she once more told herself it was going to be okay. Before she could decide what she was going to do next, the sound of heavy footfalls jerked her attention.

For once, she was thankful her ears could now pick up every sound going on around her. Even the vibrations in the earth from the nearing character got her attention.

They were too heavy to be Virga, but maybe it was Frazil, already coming to get her to tell her everything was going to be all right.

She pushed herself from the tree and walked a few steps away, watching the spot where the character would suddenly appear.

They were getting closer.

"Frazil?" she questioned.

An unfamiliar character burst into view. He didn't even take a second as he transformed into a light brown wolf. *A Swiftmaw. Not Hollowed.*

Instantly, the Swiftmaw leaped forward, straight into her. The force from the beast knocked her back and into the ground where they both tumbled in a roll.

Valkyrie was shocked by the impact, but her mind was more agile since the invention. She had glimpsed the boy's soldier attire before he had transformed.

Without even having to think about it, her gray dress and Cooper's long cloak, which she had been originally wearing, transformed. Her outfit matched the soldiers.

Dane had taught them this trick at the mountain. He had explained the atoms surrounding them were constantly being torn apart and built back together so fast it wasn't noticeable.

Valkyrie had tried to understand, and Virga later explained to her that Father had used an Ore as a part of the machine. The negative energy inside was connected to them.

"In other words," he had said, "you can change the shape of the atoms before they recreate themselves in their endless loop. You can change what your clothes look like."

In less than a moment, the Swiftmaw was once again in his Character form where he stopped on top of Valkyrie, pointing the edge of his weapon against her neck.

Valkyrie stared with wide eyes at the long sword. She was certain the Character could hear her racing heart upon seeing the naked blade inches from killing her.

"Who gave you orders to retreat?" the boy growled.

15

DEADLY FRIEND

Valkyrie trembled beneath the weight of the Character hovering over her. She had laid her ears so far back that they were hidden beneath her hair. If she didn't keep them like that, this boy would know she wasn't really a Swiftmaw.

He must have seen me transformed. He thinks I'm a part of his group. Best to play along with that.

Her eyes widened to see the boy's eyes were completely white. No pupils, no iris. It was rather terrifying.

"I should kill you on the spot if you don't answer," the Character threatened. Valkyrie had to think of something. And fast.

"I-I wasn't retreating. I was chasing," she stammered.

"Chasing? Chasing what?" the Character barked.

Valkyrie was terrified. This boy couldn't be much older than her. But he was strong. And scary.

"S-Stexphin, sir," she forced the words out.

The boy relaxed and slowly got to his feet. He sheathed his sword, which had to be a good sign. Still, she didn't dare move.

"Then where are these Stexphin?" The boy taunted, looking pleased to see how scared she was.

His attitude reminded her of Virga. "If you hadn't attacked me, they wouldn't have gotten away," she snapped, her fire returning as she propped herself onto her elbows. No one gave her attitude, *especially* not this boy. Who did he think he was? *If he was Virga, I would've pinned him down by now.*

But he's not! a voice snapped with a purple flash in her mind. She blinked, coming to her senses. Although stubborn and clearly in need of a good pounding to put him in place, he was also much stronger and skilled than Virga. *Plus, he's the one with the long sword.*

"Then why did you stop?" the boy barked angrily, clearly hating Valkyrie's stubbornness as much as she hated his.

"I didn't!" she cried, sitting up, her brows furrowed. "I was *this close* to catching them. And unlike you, I tend to approach with a secret ambush rather than just leaping into them." She waved an angry hand at him.

The boy now looked amused. "What's your name, soldier?" he asked, seeming satisfied with her answer and holding out a hand to help her up.

Valkyrie brushed it aside and got up herself. *No way can you just start pretending we're friends. Wait, name? What's a wolf name?* Frazil's words echoed in her mind. *Don't tell anyone who you are.*

"Sastruga," she said when the only name that came to mind was one Brooklyn had written about.

"Sastruga?" the boy mused, his white eyes beginning to fade away. "Well, *Sastruga*, I'm Gavin."

Valkyrie began to calm down. *He told me his name. That's a good sign, isn't it?* "Well, I had better be on my way then, sir," she said, hoping he didn't notice the vain in her voice.

"On your way? Oh, no, we had better head back to the site. Runyan will be furious, and don't call me sir. I'm a soldier, just like you," Gavin replied, turning to go.

"B-But the Stexphin," Valkyrie said, beginning to feel desperate. She couldn't go to a Swiftmaw site! What if Frazil came looking for her? Or Virga?

"Leave them, let's go," Gavin said sharply, motioning for her to come. Silently, she began to follow him. *I'll have to wait for a chance to escape. Now isn't that time.*

"Hurry up, Sastruga," Gavin said.

Valkyrie hurried to walk by his side.

"You have a long name for a wolf," he said.

"You have a simple name for a wolf," she replied. *I wonder if their names change once they've transformed into Hollowed? I know Cooper said that scout's name...and it definitely wasn't John.* She glanced backward. *Where is he taking me? How close is the Swiftmaw's site to our house?*

"What's wrong?" Gavin asked.

"What?" her voice croaked.

"Why are you so jumpy?" Gavin asked again, looking annoyed.

Valkyrie fidgeted uncomfortably. "We might get in trouble for not catching the Stexphin?" It sounded more like a suggestion than an answer.

Gavin scoffed. "It'll be fine."

After a few miles of walking, they came to a large clearing. Valkyrie gasped at the sight. Swiftmaw Characters filled the entire area. They all wore matching uniforms of peacock green, slate gray, and chiffon white.

Valkyrie named the colors in her head. Virga had stolen—no, wait, borrowed the book from Frazil's room. It showed millions of palettes of color. They had studied the page that was marked.

Is this why Frazil had that bookmarked? He was studying the colors of Swiftmaw?

As Gavin continued to lead her through the site, she found herself edging closer to him with her head down. She didn't dare make any eye contact with another Swiftmaw.

What if they recognize my hourglass pupils? They'll instantly know I'm Stexphin. Although a white glare had formed above her eyes, like it had on Frazil, indicating the Swiftmaw in them, if one were to study her eyes long enough, they'd see the hourglass shape as well.

Hadn't she played similar scenarios like this with Virga countless times? Her body knew the movements, and her mind knew fabricated words she could improvise long enough, so why? Why was fear consuming her to a point of hesitancy?

Gavin seemed to notice her uneasiness and elbowed her in the ribs. "Stop looking so cowardly," he snapped in a harsh whisper. "No one's going to hurt you, I think. But you're making the Younger League look bad."

The Younger League? She wasn't given a chance to ask what that was as they approached a tall angry Character. This *wasn't* a Swiftmaw. She knew right away.

His long hair that almost looked like feathers instantly gave away the presence of the Griefolowtros. She struggled to match Gavin's confident stride.

She realized with confusion the boy's eyes were no longer white but looked like a normal Swiftmaw's should. His eyes were a deep chocolate brown. *Kind of handsome.*

They stopped once they reached the Grief Character who didn't notice them as he was too busy screaming orders at nearby Swiftmaw.

Valkyrie's hands began to tremble like never before, and it took all her strength to keep it from spreading over her entire body. She hid her hands behind her back and stared at the ground, repeating over and over to herself that she was a regular Swiftmaw soldier. She was used to this treatment and wasn't scared.

I'm not scared. I'm not scared. This is so normal.

Gavin was tall with a strong build, but not even he matched the enormous character before them. Valkyrie stared with wide eyes. She had never realized how tall Griefs were. Nor how buff. She realized that must come from their front half being part lion. Huge muscles bulged beneath the man's uniform. She was certain he could kill them both with one punch.

His legs were very long and skinny, giving his height a terrifying and intimidating look. She couldn't understand how his legs even managed to keep up the upper half of his body. They were slender, but as he took a step, Valkyrie's eyes widened to realize that they were indeed very muscular.

"*What?*" the Grief suddenly shrieked as he spun on them.

Gavin didn't even flinch. Valkyrie nearly fainted.

"We've just returned from the attack outside of HickoryWood Forest," Gavin cleared his throat.

Attack? Valkyrie slightly trembled at the word.

"What are your identities?" The Grief stood up straight, the veins in his neck calming as his anger began to fade.

"Captain, I am Gavin, and this is Sastruga," he replied confidently.

Valkyrie was grateful she didn't have to say her name. She wasn't even sure she could if she tried.

"Gavin, the troops from the attack reported back to me almost fifteen minutes ago. Why weren't you with them?" His voice was gruff and slick.

"Sorry, Captain Runyan. We were chasing Stexphin," Gavin continued.

We? We? Valkyrie bristled as her mind silently screamed it's rebuttal. *Only I was chasing—no, wait, no, I wasn't.*

"And where are these Stexphin now?" Captain Runyan sounded annoyed with Gavin's confidence.

"Gone, sir, I'm afraid Sastruga lost them,"

Valkyrie clenched her jaw to keep from shouting, "I wouldn't have lost anything if it weren't for your stupid stunt!" but her eyes shone with fire.

Runyan noticed. He stared at her with his slit pupils, and instantly, her anger diminished.

Once again, she was reminded that she hadn't been chasing anything at all but fleeing herself. *I can't believe I'm here. What am I doing in a Swiftmaw camp?* she suddenly realized with alarm.

"Is this true?" the captain hissed.

Valkyrie couldn't move. She couldn't speak. It took all of her power not to start trembling or to break into terrified sobs. She lowered her gaze to Runyan's feet.

The strange Character was barefoot. His feet looked as if they had scales along them, and long hooked claws replaced where his nails should have been. She felt disgusted at the sight but not nearly as much as she was terrified.

"Why doesn't this one ever talk?" Runyan demanded.

Valkyrie ignored Gavin's warning glance. No one could make her speak. Her mind was set on terrified silence.

Runyan must've known her thoughts. "Just go away and find your group," he growled irritably.

Gavin saluted and began to walk away, Valkyrie close on his heels. As soon as they were out of earshot, he turned on her, fire in his eyes.

"What was *that*? Do you know how hard it is to get respect around here? You've just flushed all my work down the river!" he snapped. Gavin huffed angrily and grabbed her arm, pulling her close. "Runyan hates Rotto for giving him Swiftmaw soldiers that started at a young age. He's already sent the rest away but hasn't found any fault in me yet because I won't let him." He squeezed Valkyrie's arm and gave her a helpless look. "Are you even a soldier? You've hardly got any muscle on you! Are they sending weak Swiftmaw down here just to get rid of you?"

Valkyrie ripped her arm free, her face heating up at his cruel words. Still, she wouldn't say anything. Gavin turned on his heels and stormed away. This time, she didn't follow him.

I need to get out of here. But how? She turned toward the woods. *All I need to do is get there, then find northeast. Clearly, I'm not going back home anytime soon.*

The thought made her insides feel sick. *No time to cry. I have to get out of here first before anything.* Glancing around, she began to walk casually toward the trees, developing a plan in her mind in case someone else wanted to scrap at her.

Thankfully, no one paid her any attention, and she began to think she'd actually escape without any trouble.

She was wrong.

A large Swiftmaw wearing heavy armor stepped in front of her. She stopped and straightened her shoulders, copying Gavin's act of confidence as she eyed the man. Inwardly, she was sobbing screams of terror. Carefully, she mentally concealed her eyes, refusing to let any of her thoughts leak through.

This man stood almost as tall as the Grief but was even scarier. His white hair was shaved close to his head, and strange markings lined his scalp.

His Swiftmaw ears stuck out plainly against his short hair. They were scarred with rough fur and slits cut throughout them. His eyes were a mixture of white and black.

In his hands. He held a Greatsword, which was beautifully fashioned, making her slightly envious, along with a shield stained with dried black blood. *Only Hollowed bleed black.*

"What are you doing?" the man barked.

She frowned. Hadn't he noticed she was heading for the woods? Or why was he asking so randomly?

"S-Sorry, sir." *Don't stammer!* "But I believe I misplaced my sword somewhere," she said briskly, once more eyeing his magnificent blade. *I didn't realize Swiftmaw cared to have beautiful anything. Especially not a sword. Not like that.*

"Misplaced?" He looked at her with such an ugly expression she was forced to close her eyes. "Rascal, once you find it, come to me, and I'll teach you a lesson about misplacing things!" he threatened.

"Yes, sir." Valkyrie opened her eyes and pretended not to hear the warning in his voice. The Character wandered off, muttering his wicked thoughts.

Now she was so close to the woods she didn't want to be stopped by anyone else. Quickening her pace, she was soon in the trees. The moment she knew she was out of sight, she began running.

She was beginning to think she didn't like Swiftmaw at all. *Cruel creatures.* Valkyrie quickened her pace as she hurried through the thick woods. She didn't recognize anything.

After jogging a mile, she stopped and listened, her ears perking up and into view. She was far enough from the Swiftmaw camp now. For caution, she climbed into a nearby thicket before transforming into Stexphin form.

Now much smaller, she could easily climb through the large vegetation. *The brush here is huge!* she thought to herself as she crept deeper through the branches. *I need to find the northeast. How do I do that? Smuir... I have to cross the Hidden Rock River to be on the right track.* She closed her eyes and listened. In the far distance ahead, she could hear rushing water. She smiled at the fact that she could hear it.

Behind her, she could hear the far off camp. *Snap!* Valkyrie jumped and her eyes shot open at the sound of a nearby branch snapping. She had been so distracted listening to the distance she had forgotten to listen to her own surroundings. She quickly quieted her breathing and listened again.

Someone was here. Just outside the thicket she was hiding in. Then a voice spoke, one that filled her with dread.

"Sastruga?" Gavin said.

No! I'll never get out of here with a Swiftmaw on my tail! And if I transform, he'll make me go back. But if I don't and he finds me—

"Sastruga, I know you're here! I saw you!"

Gavin was getting closer. Valkyrie needed air but continued to hold her breath, although she knew it wasn't Swiftmaw's hearing she needed to worry about. It was the scent.

He can't get into this thicket. But he can still destroy it enough to reach me. Should I make a run for it? No, not yet.

Carefully, Valkyrie began to creep away in the brush, watching her step and dodging under the thin branches that threatened to snap if she pushed against them.

"Sastruga! Come on. You can't run away. The Griefs will torture me once they account for us. If you're missing...they'll stop letting Swiftmaw my age—" Gavin's voice faded. His words filled her with pity, but her mind was set, and she wasn't going to stay behind to get killed because one boy was bullied.

"Listen, I followed you after I saw you get in trouble with Fang. If he promised a lesson, don't go! No one ever returns after that, especially Swiftmaw. Rumor is he turns them into Hollowed if he doesn't kill them." Gavin's voice trailed off once again, and she realized he was afraid of the black-blooded wolves.

"You probably can't even hear me," Gavin muttered to himself. "Ran off and I didn't see you. I'm just here, yelling at the trees like an idiot."

Valkyrie looked back toward the direction Gavin's voice was coming from. *I'm sorry. But I can't stay.* She felt guilty. Even though he had ratted her out earlier, she kind of considered him a friend. Her first friend she had ever had outside of Virga. *What would he say if he learned I made friends with a Swiftmaw?*

She hadn't been paying attention, and suddenly, a loud crack broke into the silent woods as she stepped on a branch. She froze.

She didn't have to see Gavin to know the tension in the air they both were feeling. The sound was practically echoing through the woods.

Valkyrie held her breath, listening for the slightest sound Gavin might make if he planned to attack. She felt petrified. *Should I call out and pretend to be Sastruga? No because then I'll have to transform, and if I do that, I'll be stuck in this brush.*

"I know you're there," a deep voice growled, followed by another sound. Gavin had transformed. "I can smell you, *Stexphin*."

Valkyrie was terrified by how quickly he could change from friendly to deadly. Footfalls so quiet, she almost didn't catch them, even with her excellent hearing.

A leaf crunched beneath Gavin's foot. The noise was exactly what she needed to be brought back to life. She bolted through the thicket, dodging roots and rocks on the ground, but freely crashing through thin branches.

Gavin was after her in an instant, tearing through the brush with fury. She knew the thicket slowed him down, but she also knew that it wouldn't last forever.

16

UNDERGROUND

A few more leaps, and Valkyrie would be out of the thicket. She needed a plan, but nothing came to mind.

She hated to admit it now, but Gavin was a friend, no matter how difficult he was and how short they knew each other. And he was about to kill her.

Valkyrie's back legs coiled and sprang. Jumping out of the thicket and into the small clearing, her feet hit the trembling earth.

At the same moment, the ground caved in. She stumbled, releasing a desperate yowl as the dirt beneath her fell, bringing her down with it. *What's happening!?*

She flipped once in the air, flailing like crazy as she fell into the deep pit. A scream arose in her throat when she hit the ground below, and pain shot through her front leg like electricity.

Dirt continued to rain down, and she quickly rolled away, crying out as she did.

She could hardly see anything in the hole except for the light from far above. Fear of whatever else might be in there swelled inside her faster than she could measure.

But a frenzied howl made her blood freeze. The form of a wolf came over the edge of the hole, and she scrambled as far back into the pit as she could.

The moment Gavin hit the ground, he transformed back into his Character. But he didn't get back up.

Creeping back even farther from the still form, her back end suddenly hit the wall of the pit, and she transformed into her Character form.

Sitting against the dirt, her knees curled up and clutching her broken arm, she stared at Gavin with wide eyes. The light from above easily shone on him like a spotlight.

He wasn't moving.

Breathing heavily, she squeezed her eyes shut against the pain. A short sob escaped her throat, and she ducked her head, this time letting the tears come willingly.

Everything is so horrible. So horrible! How did it come to this? She wept louder, curled against the earth behind her and pain weaving through her arm like fluid.

Where are my brothers? What happened to Mother? To Father? What was that fog? And why was the house gone? How did the wolves find us? Did they kill Frazil?

Valkyrie continued to bawl, choking on her own sobs and shaking so hard it made her head hurt. She was so sick of living in the dark. And now because of it, she was trapped down here.

Hunger pangs and dehydration began to gnaw at her. She hadn't noticed them earlier in the panic of everything.

Where's Virga? I can't believe he left me. He ran into the house and left me. He promised whatever happened, we'd have each other, and he left. They've all been keeping secrets. Even him. Mother won't say anything, Frazil's terrified of something but can't admit it. And Father doesn't even care. I know he doesn't. No one does.

Her stomach twisted, and her heart lurched. She had never felt this way before. So unloved. So unwanted. Abandoned. *Even if I did return home, would there be a point to it all?*

A moan made her look up to see Gavin was waking up. Quickly, she gained control of herself, pinning her ears back so they wouldn't be seen.

Taking in long shaky breaths, she waited for Gavin to get up. He never did. Instead, he lay there, seeming to have gone unconscious again. *My blubbering must've brought him around.*

Sniffing and wiping a dirty hand across her tear-streaked face, she forced herself to stand, wincing as she did. Slowly. she walked over to the form.

Bending over Gavin's stiff body. she saw with gratitude he was still breathing. A large bump on his head proved he had landed much rougher than she.

Doesn't look like you broke anything, though.

Looking up, Valkyrie could barely see the treetops way, *way* overhead. She realized it was far past noon. *I need to do something. But what? What would Virga do if he were here?* She looked around the dark pit for ideas but couldn't see anything. She blinked, waiting for her eyes to get adjusted to the dark. *He would think ahead. It's going to be a cold night, I'm sure, and I'm not leaving Gavin to die. A fire. I wonder if there's roots along the dirt.* Walking over with her right arm cradled against her, she felt the walls with her left.

She felt *something* along the walls. But it definitely wasn't tree roots. *What are these? Wires?* She pulled on one, and the ground began to tremble.

She fell against the wall for balance, her eyes wide with terror. The sound of dirt falling caught her attention. Overhead, their only light began to close up. "No!" she cried.

Instantly, she pushed the wire back in place, and the earthquake stopped. But it was too late. The hole overhead had covered itself once again, leaving only a crack for light to stream through.

We need that fire more than ever now, she thought as her eyes began to adjust to the dark. She continued to search the pit to find that it was a small circle.

Wires covered most of the walls, but this time, she didn't dare touch them. As she continued to feel around the cave, she noticed a break had formed in the dirt, leading through a tunnel with more cords lined along it.

She wanted to walk down it, hoping it would lead out, but there was no light, and she didn't want to leave Gavin. And she definitely wasn't strong enough to carry him with or without her broken arm.

Valkyrie shivered. Now without the sunlight, it was getting colder from the moist earth surrounding them. *What if Gavin doesn't make it? I'm no medic, that's for sure. If Virga was here, he would have that boy up in no time. Virga. Surely, he didn't die. But he didn't try to come back either.*

Valkyrie's heart ached terribly for her family. But another moan from Gavin kept her from drifting off again. Stumbling through the dark, she found his form.

She could barely even see him. Feeling around, she silently rejoiced as her hands found sticks that had fallen down the pit with them.

Making a small pile, she crossed her legs and sat down. Even if she had the tools to start a flame, this wasn't nearly enough. Her body trembled from the cold, and she knew Gavin was shivering as well.

Closing her eyes, she concentrated on Cooper's cloak. Slowly, it appeared, and she sighed shakily from the warmth. *Gavin needs it more than you do,* the voice with a purple flash reminded her.

She frowned but knew it was right. Gavin had landed on his head pretty bad. His body was probably fighting enough as it was.

With shaking fingers, she took off the cloak and laid it over the boy. Pity rushed through her heart. *He's young. I wonder how long he's been a soldier. Does he have a family? Were they separated? Was he left behind like I was?*

After a moment, exhaustion took its toll, and she became too tired to even think anymore. It was impossible to lie down comfortably with her hurt arm and shivering physique, but it didn't take long to fall asleep.

*****

Someone was calling her name. Valkyrie sat up in the dark and looked around. It was Brooklyn! *Oh no! I didn't sleep in, did I? She'll be so upset.*

Valkyrie reached to throw back her covers, only to realize they weren't there. *Odd.* Still, she leaped out of bed.

The minute her feet hit the ground, everything lit in flames.

The room was no longer cold and dark but hot and bright. She could hear her mother downstairs screaming for help. But Valkyrie couldn't even escape her room! The flames were edging closer.

She heard Virga yelling for her to wake up. *Virga?* No, that voice was deeper than his. Perhaps Father.

Then everything began shaking.

Valkyrie's mind came awake, and she realized it had all been a dream. But someone *was* shaking her. She moaned.

"C'mon, get up," said the voice. But she didn't want to. She was finally feeling well from her nap, and the warmth from the fire finished off the great feeling.

Wait, fire? Then the person shaking her grabbed at her arm, her bad arm. "C'mon, Struga! Get up!" he snapped.

Valkyrie cried out in pain and pulled her arm free from the grasp. With a powerful leg, she kicked the Swiftmaw away. Then she came to her senses.

They were still in the pit, and Gavin was awake. She frowned at the boy who stared at her with shock from the kick. It was terribly strong for her being Stexphin.

"It's about time you woke up. But you didn't need to be so mean about it," Gavin said, frowning at her while he rubbed his shoulder where she had kicked him.

135

"Well, you don't need to be grabbing my arm like that!" she shot back.

Gavin just rolled his eyes and sat by the fire, poking at it with a larger branch.

Valkyrie was boiling. *Did he really just roll his eyes at me?*

But one more glance around the pit reminded her of the situation they were in, and her anger calmed. "How did you start the fire?" she asked, watching the orange flames.

Gavin was quiet for a long time before looking up at her. "Oh, you're serious?" he asked.

Valkyrie glared but stopped when she noticed that most of the bottom of his uniform had been torn away. *I should have thought of that.*

"Struga, you have got to be the weirdest *dumbest* Swiftmaw I've ever met. I'd say a lot more, but I'm sure you already know," Gavin said, smiling as if he thought what he had said was funny.

Valkyrie was tempted to reply with her own rude remark but kept quiet. She knew that Gavin was different. He could turn friendly to deadly almost too quickly.

She wasn't sure if she would call it a temper; he just knew when it was time to be serious and, well, he actually wasn't very friendly.

Valkyrie finally spoke into the silence. "Are you hurt?"

Gavin gave her another one of his puzzled expressions.

"I mean when you fell."

Gavin's face suddenly went wide, and he jumped up. "There was a Stexphin!" he said.

"What?" Valkyrie replied, trying to sound like she didn't believe him.

"There was! It fell down here," Gavin said. Then his face turned into a frown. "Wait, how did *you* get down here?" he asked.

"Um, I fell?" she said.

"No, how did you *really* get down here?" he demanded.

"I went on a walk, then I thought *I* saw a Stexphin, and I, uh, you know, fell into the pit," Valkyrie's voice trailed off. She absolutely hated saying that she was chasing Stexphin. *I don't want to encourage this behavior, I'd like to stop it!*

Gavin shook his head. "We need to get out of here," he said. He turned and walked off into the darkness.

Valkyrie slowly stood. "Gavin?" she whispered, afraid he had just left her. But he returned, this time holding a torch. He held the end into the flames, then handed it to her.

Valkyrie took it with her left, then watched him stomp on the fire until it went out. She raised her brows to see his shoes hadn't melted. *I have a lot to learn.*

Gavin, taking the torch, led her to the passage she had found earlier. He wasn't much of a communicator about his plan, she realized, and followed him in silence.

Valkyrie tried to stay close, not wanting to be left alone in these unknown underground tunnels. As they walked, she realized there were many unlit torches hanging on the wall as well as wires.

A couple of times, there was more than one choice of passage, and she could tell Gavin was getting frustrated. He groaned loudly when they came to another bend separating into three different tunnels.

"There's no way out of here!" he said hopelessly.

Valkyrie felt defeated. She didn't want to be stuck underground with Gavin forever, that was for sure.

Her stomach growled painfully, and Gavin spun around, thrusting the torch toward her. "You try and find the way," he said.

Valkyrie hesitated, then nodded, and followed the path to her right. Whenever they came to more than one passage, she continued to always take the one to their right.

"This is probably just leading us in circles," Gavin told her. But she ignored him. After a while, she stopped, and Gavin, who wasn't paying attention, bumped into her.

"Watch it!" he snapped.

"Shush," she said, frowning.

Gavin was about to give it to her, she could tell, but then he paused and listened. "What is it?" he asked quietly.

"I don't know, but someone's coming," she whispered back.

"Friend or foe?"

"I don't know." She was hearing footsteps, but it was a little harder to tell with her ears back beneath her hair. As the footsteps got closer, she could tell there was more than one. "I think we should go," she said, turning to face Gavin.

He didn't budge.

The footsteps were speeding up and just around the corner. "Go!" she yelled. Shoving the torch into his hands, she pushed past him and took off running into the darkness.

Her hurt arm, still cradled against her body without a sling, begged for attention. But she didn't stop until the angry voices were far behind. But someone was coming—fast. She turned around but couldn't see anything. Whoever it was, they didn't have the torch.

A Character plowed into her, and Valkyrie tumbled back, crying out in pain. Her broken arm was twisted back, and she didn't have to see to know more bruises were lining her skin.

"I'm so sorry! I didn't see you! We've got to go!" Gavin sounded scared. He helped her up, then, grabbing her left arm, he began pulling her along the dark tunnels.

"Where's the torch?" Valkyrie managed to say through gasps and tears.

"I ditched it! We'll be harder to chase if they aren't following our light," Gavin panted.

"*Who?*" she asked.

"Four of them, we have to *go!*" he said as he ran faster, pulling on her arm even harder.

After a while of running, they both stopped and stood in the dark, panting.

"Are...you okay?" Gavin asked through gasps.

"No, I'm *not*," Valkyrie said, biting her lip to keep her tears under control.

Gavin was suddenly at her side. He put his hand on her shoulder. "What is it?" he asked. She could barely see the white glare above his eyes in the dark.

"My arm," was all she said. Gavin bent down, and she covered her mouth to keep from crying out as he felt along her broken arm.

"It's bad," He confessed. "Was it me? Did I hurt you?"

"No, it happened when we fell," she said, trying her best to keep a brave face on, even though he couldn't see her.

"Why didn't you tell me?" Gavin asked.

Because I didn't think you'd care.

Shouts echoed through the cave.

"We gotta get out of here," Gavin said, stepping away from her. Suddenly, a loud explosion split through the air. The ground trembled, and Valkyrie could hear the tunnels crashing.

"*Now!*" Gavin yelled. But it was too late. They both felt that the vibrations of the explosion had reached them.

Gavin leaped for her, but the roof crumbled before he could. Valkyrie reached out and barely grabbed his hand before the dirt roof collapsed on them.

A bright flash of purple. Then everything went black.

17

A SILENT CITY

Crowley—Year 317

It was easy to tell neither of them were in the mood for strength training when Crowley walked into the cement room. Large dark circles beneath Selah's eyes matched his own. She sat on a crate, elbows on knees and head in hands.

"Couldn't sleep?" he guessed.

She nodded, putting a hand over her mouth as she yawned, which easily spread to him.

It had been almost five months now, and Crowley always had something different for them to do. It wasn't exactly training anymore but more of a practice which kept them in shape for when a battle did come. He had come to realize they had both improved, which surprised him. He hadn't realized he had anything to improve on. He was wrong.

Crowley had learned a lot from this girl just by watching her. He knew they had both opened up more than usual.

He noticed Selah didn't mind letting him know when she wasn't in the mood to train, but if he forced her, she would do whatever workout or routine he had planned.

She respected him more but still enjoyed pricking his nerves every once in a while. Sometimes he found he rather enjoyed their moments of playful stabbing with words.

Mostly, he had noticed just how much she had matured over the past months, not only in skill and knowledge but also beauty as well.

"Let's do something different today," he suggested. Selah looked at him as if he was crazy. "Take it or leave it. It's probably the only time I'll spoil you like this."

"I'll take it," she said. Getting to her feet, her beige-colored dress swept around her legs at the sudden movement. Her hair had been pulled back into a ponytail, which threatened to fall loose.

In a few moments, they had walked to the top floor of Smuir's tunnels. Crowley led her down a dimly lit hall lined with a few cupboards. At one of these shelves, they stopped. He grabbed the case and pushed it aside.

On the other side was another hidden tunnel. Selah smiled. More of a mischievous grin than the shock he had suspected.

Eagerly, she followed him inside. After grabbing a torch and pulling the shelf as much as he could back into place, they followed the path.

"Where does it lead?" she asked as he led her down a few turns.

"To be honest? I'm not sure," he said. "Malachi, an old friend of mine, found this when we were younger. We got lost in here for hours. I never came back, but he did. He told me that if I ever came here to follow his trail."

"What's that?"

"Right here," Crowley pointed at the small crevice along the dirt wall. "That's what we're following. He made this with a spoon, I think he said it was. Said if I ever want to do something exciting for a change to come here." He laughed, which turned into guilt. "I wish I came here sooner. With him. Even after he disappeared, I couldn't bring myself to do it on my own."

"He was the king's son, wasn't he?"

"Yes," Crowley said. Before anything else could be said, he saw something up ahead. He held the torch higher, squinting into the dark. "What is that?" They neared the strange object hanging from the ceiling.

"It's a ladder," Selah said, and he could tell she was smiling.

They both stared at the rope. Above it was a hole, something covering it on the other side.

Selah was up the wobbly ladder in an instant. "Wait," Crowley began but stopped when light shone in.

He squinted and saw the girl disappear out the trap door. Looking around anxiously, Crowley found a sconce and left the torch. He climbed up the ladder quickly.

He squinted as he looked over the top of the hole. They were in an open stone building. Sunlight streamed in where a wall should have been.

"Is this," he said, disbelief in his voice. He crawled out of the hole and looked around. Selah stood nearby, staring out. He turned back and shut the trapdoor, then went and joined her.

The building they were standing in held a large anvil near an unlit furnace. Tongs, buckets, and hammers littered the floor. A nearby faucet showed the shop had access to running water.

Hesitantly, the two Stexphin walked out of the building and into a street made from cobblestone. Crowley turned in a slow circle. "It's Smuir!" he breathed. "I don't believe it!"

Houses and buildings lined the street, overgrown with vines and a few falling apart. Weeds grew anywhere they could find a break in the stones and beside buildings.

"It's marvelous," Selah said. She began walking down the street, and Crowley followed her.

"It's a ghost town," he said after a moment. "Do you hear how silent it is?"

"I don't think silence makes a sound," Selah turned. Two laughing eyes at him, her lips parting as she smiled.

At the end of the street was a large area with a dry fountain in the center. Several streets connected from this range.

"It's the town square," Selah said. "I read about it once."

"Yes, I remember," Crowley said, taking a few steps as he looked around. "And east of it is—" He trailed off, staring.

Selah came and stood beside him. "The castle," she whispered.

The stone building looked over the town like a mother guarding her children. It was beautiful and frightfully large.

Soon, the two of them found themselves in front of the castle. They paused at the doors. Selah stretched her neck to look up at the incredible height.

Finally, Crowley said, "Come on," and he pushed against the large doors. They opened with ease, and he led her inside.

Walking in was a large stone-colored room with rays of sunlight streaming in from windows, lining the wall. A large violet carpet with an emerald green fringe covered the ground.

Declan's colors, Crowley thought with amazement.

Selah tried to stop and take in a breath as she looked around the room, but Crowley urged her along, smiling at her face.

Walking up a beautiful marble staircase, dust floated around them with each step.

Crowley stopped when something glinted from the corner of his eye. He bent down to pick up a small chain caught on the banister.

"What is it?" Selah asked, turning her head as she studied it.

Crowley stood and examined the chain in his hand. He blew on it, letting dust fly. The chain was thin with small patterns engraved along it.

"Just a chain," he encouraged, dropping the silver into his pocket as they continued their hike. Silently, he knew it wasn't just a chain. The patterns he recognized as Queen Tatyana's mark.

They went up four floors before finding the large balcony that hung off the castle.

"This is where the kings would address the town," Crowley said, smiling as the two of them walked to the edge and looked down at the large courtyard below.

The sun was slowly crawling down the sky, and a small chill of a breeze began blowing. Crowley's thoughts went back to his most recent dream. He had been standing in such a place beside a high ruler. He was the most respected warrior there, more than just an adviser.

He wanted answers to these strange dreams. If Selah would confess who she was, then maybe she could give him answers.

Crowley glanced at the beautiful girl standing beside him as she gazed out over the empty town. He trusted her. But did she trust him in turn?

After a few moments of silence and debating how he should bring the subject up, he asked, "Selah, I mentioned once what King Demoor said on the two children that needed to be found to stop this war. The son of Declan's daughter—"

"And a girl who haunts dreams of the future," Selah finished. She turned toward him and studied him with her piercing eyes.

"Are you her?" Crowley asked hesitantly.

"No," Selah answered, shaking her head and staring at him with wide eyes. "Why would you believe that?"

Crowley folded his arms and leaned against the balcony edge, staring down at the quiet city below. "My nightmares haven't stopped." He glanced at her. "You're in every one."

Now that he said it out loud, he began to realize that perhaps he was foolish to listen to the paranoid king's story. When Selah didn't say anything, he said, "You must think me an idiot to have been chasing a ghost story."

"No, but I think it unwise. I understand you were desperate, though. You want this war to end as much as I do," Selah said, leaning on her arms over the balcony as she gazed across the sunset.

"I fear we are the only ones who hope for that," Crowley said stiffly.

"I don't think that's true."

"It feels like it is."

"Crowley," Selah looked at him with concerned eyes, "what do you hope to get out of war?"

He was confused by her question and answered hesitantly, "To prove myself and be promoted. For respect."

"Are you willing to do anything for respect?"

"I don't think I understand, but yes, I would. If you're asking what I want from respect, I want to serve the highest throne and offer my allegiance. And from there, earn my place as second best," Crowley confessed.

"Not first?" she mused.

"No, I believe it's in my blood to serve beneath someone,"

"But you don't know who that someone is," Selah eyed him.

Crowley didn't answer. Normally, he would have said King Demoor, but with Selah, he felt he could be himself. And being honest with himself, he didn't believe it was Demoor.

They stood there in silence, watching the sun slowly disappear over the ghost town below and beyond.

Crowley turned toward his friend as a small breeze began. The bottom of her dress floated in front of her with the wind, her hair slowly untangling from its ponytail.

Selah turned toward him, and they looked at each other for a moment before she said, "I think you're going to have a happy ending."

"What?"

"Our debate, a rather foolish one now that I look back, about life being easy to foretell. I still won't take back what I said about *you* being predictable. You really are, Crowley."

"Predictable?" He smirked. "I've outsmarted you more than I can count. I can count pretty high."

"To ten?" she teased.

"That's the highest number *you* know," he pushed back.

"You remind me so much of my brother." She shook her head and looked back through the town square. "It's beautiful out here," she whispered under her breath.

Crowley looked at her and said, "Yes, it is."

An annoying thought reminded him of a conference he had with the king that night. *Just a little longer.* But he knew they couldn't stay.

"Selah, we have to go. I have a conference, and—"

"Please, let's not leave just yet," she said, looking at him with sad eyes. Her longing to stay affected him, but he knew he couldn't miss this conference. "I want to enjoy this while we still can," Selah finished. The sun was almost gone and seemed to bring a small sadness over the castle.

"We can always come back," Crowley said. "This castle is abandoned. We could call it ours if we wanted." Reaching into his pocket he pulled out the royal chain. Uncinching at the end, he then pulled off his ring from Malachi's mother. Carefully, he slid it onto the chain before putting it back together. Selah watched him curiously.

"Here," he said, putting in on the balcony railing in front of her.

"But this is—" she began.

"I know, but I want you to keep it. To remember this moment. When we leave, you can always remember this castle is ours," he said, emotion touching his words.

Selah's eyes lit up, and she stared out with a sort of eager expression. "We should stay here," she said, turning toward Crowley with excitement. "We don't have to go back. I don't want to go back. Even you said that the king—" She stopped when he frowned.

"I have a meeting with the king tonight," Crowley said adamantly. "I can't miss that." He saw Selah's sad expression and said again, "We can always come back."

He reached out to touch her shoulder, but she shied away. His heart felt as if someone had squeezed it. From everything they'd done together, he had never once physically touched her. He felt a desperation to do so now. She looked at him with her green eyes, and he stepped back.

"We have to go," he said firmly. "I can't neglect my duties as the king's adviser for one girl."

Selah simply nodded in understanding, her old mask covering her face. He felt a pang in his heart, knowing he hurt her, but pushed it away.

I have commitments. Still, he felt a glimmer of hope when she gingerly grabbed the chain and put it around her neck before hiding the ring beneath her dress collar.

As they walked back through the castle, it was dark without the sun shining through the windows. It took a moment to find the stairs. By the time they walked out the front doors, the sky had darkened to a pale blue.

"You'll do anything for respect," Selah suddenly whispered as they walked, "won't you?"

Crowley didn't hesitate to answer this time. "Yes," he said, clenching his jaw.

"It's not too late to go back," she said even more quietly than before.

Crowley ignored her and led the way back into the blacksmith's shop. He went to the trapdoor, moved it aside, and crawled through. He looked back up at Selah and, for a moment, lost his breath.

She was looking away, her body tense. He feared she was going to run back to the castle. "Selah," he said, his voice softer.

She blinked a few times and looked down at him before crawling down the makeshift ladder.

18

SMUIR

Valkyrie—Year 315

Pain. Everywhere. That's all she felt. It's all she could think of. The pain. *Please, make it go away,* her mind begged.

It started as a dull pain within her ribs, but it soon expanded through her entire body. She felt sick. Sweat covered every inch of her skin as she shivered out of control.

The pain ebbed at times, only to flare up again and with seemingly heightened intensity.

It had felt like the pain had been there forever, and in a way, she was becoming used to it, but at the same moment, the reality it might stick a little while longer was terrifying.

On any other day, Valkyrie knew she probably would've gone to bed and rested until she felt better, but not today. Today was a day of pushing the limits. She could feel herself fading. But the purple flash encouraged her to fight.

For a second, she thought she was hearing voices. *Familiar* voices. *Did they find me?* She tried to clear her head to focus on whoever was speaking, but slowly, her body shut down again.

When she came back around, someone was still talking to her. But who? Who was she? *Where* was she? Valkyrie weakly forced her eyes to open, but everything was a blur.

Blinking twice, she still couldn't make anything out. The voice wasn't even very clear. They sounded muffled as if they were trying to speak through a blanket.

Valkyrie tried to move, but her body hurt too much. She tried to speak, but nothing came out. She closed her eyes.

When she came around for the third time, Valkyrie kept her eyes shut, listening to her surroundings.

"Yes, she's doing much better," a man said. His voice was kind and low. Valkyrie twitched her ears around, trying to listen for any clues where she might be.

Whoever had been speaking must have noticed her movement. "Hello, lassie," he said. "It's okay to get up, but you're still very weak."

Valkyrie did not recognize that voice, and she didn't have a clue where she was or what was going on. Instead of coming fully awake, she stopped moving and slowed her breathing.

The man sighed before saying, "She's taking her time to come around. I don't blame her, though. It's a miracle she survived at all,"

"How did this happen?" a woman's sweet and gentle voice asked.

"Captain Ashton found her buried in the tunnels while training the rookies. A Swiftmaw wasn't too far from her. They think he was trying to snag her before the collapse," the man replied.

"That's horrible," the woman said. "How do you think a Swiftmaw even got in the tunnels?"

"Captain Ashton says someone must have messed with the wires. Most likely, it opened a passage from the outside in Hickory." The man's voice dropped lower. "But that's not even Ashton's biggest concern. He's worried about this young lass because she's not even from the mountain. He even asked King Demoor to come see her,"

"He didn't recognize her?"

"No one does. Trinity thinks she came through the same passage as the Swiftmaw boy."

Swiftmaw? Suddenly, Valkyrie remembered what happened. She remembered everything. *Gavin!* Her eyes shot open. Her vision was still blurry, but she could make out the shapes of two Stexphin standing on each side of the bed she was lying in.

Valkyrie tried to sit up, her heart racing, but her body screamed at her. The two Stexphin were quick to help her lie back down.

"Calm down, lassie," the man said, "you've been through a lot."

She stared at the blurry form on her left with wide eyes. A gray mop was on top of his head with two ears to match. But she couldn't make out his eyes, nose—nothing but a dark tan skin color.

On her right stood the woman. She could barely glimpse the long brown hair pulled back. Both of the characters wore white clothing.

"It's okay, just relax," the man said, placing a hand on her shoulder to keep her down. Eyes watering and breathing heavily, she tried to calm her racing heart.

"I'm Doctor Matthias, and this here is Nurse Alania," the man continued.

Valkyrie nodded, taking a deep shaky breath as she finally began to unwind.

Matthias leaned over to the nurse and whispered, "Send word to Captain Ashton. Tell him she's awake. He was hoping to hear some answers from her." Alania left.

Valkyrie tried to look around the room, but it was all a gray blur. She opened her mouth to ask where she was, but her throat scratched hoarsely.

The doctor left and returned a second later with a cup of water. Valkyrie drank it quickly, thankful as the cool liquid ran down her throat. She hadn't realized how thirsty and hungry she was. After receiving some food and more water, she felt much more refreshed.

Looking toward the doctor's blurry shape, she asked in a raspy voice, "Where's Gavin?"

"Was there another Stexphin with you in the tunnels?" Matthias asked, his voice giving away the fear if it were true.

"No," she said quietly as she closed her exhausted eyes.

"Who's Gavin? What happened to him?" Matthias asked.

Valkyrie kept her eyes shut and whispered, "He's my friend. Did you kill him?" She felt so tired and fell into a half sleep.

Footsteps neared the bed, and she recognized Alania's voice. Someone else was with her. Another man.

"Captain Ashton," Matthias addressed him, "I'm afraid you've just barely missed her."

"Did she give you anything?" Ashton asked. His voice was low like Dane's. She liked it.

"Yes, she said her friend, Gavin, was with her," Matthias hesitated. "Then she asked if we killed him."

"The Swiftmaw boy?" Ashton grunted.

"Oh no, surely not," Alania defended. It was easy to tell she was frowning.

"I'm afraid we have other patients to attend to," Matthias said, clearly not liking where the conversation was going. "Walker got knocked down by Deirdre. She gave him a sprained ankle."

"And the twins cut their brother, throwing those sharp stones again," Alania added under her breath as they walked away.

After they left, Valkyrie dozed off into a deeper sleep. It must not have lasted long because when she opened her eyes, there was a dark form standing over her bed.

It was too late to pretend to go back to sleep. "Who are you?" Captain Ashton's voice asked calmly.

Valkyrie blinked. Lifting her left hand with slight strain, she rubbed at her eyes before blinking again. Her vision was slowly coming back. Was Ashton frowning at her?

Right! He had asked her a question. *Who am I? I can't say Sastruga. That's the name of my wolf form. Frazil said to not tell anyone who I was.*

"My name is Jaylee," she said, rubbing her eyes again.

"Do you have something in your eyes, Jaylee?" Ashton asked.

"No. Maybe. I don't know. But I can't see you," she said, blinking a few times as she lowered her exhausted hand.

Captain Ashton leaned forward. He was close enough she could make out enough details to distinguish features. He had dark blue eyes and blond hair with bits of white, almost like Frazil's before the invention. *The invention!*

"Hm," Ashton moved back and sat down in a chair near the bed. "I'm no doctor, but your eyes do look a little messed up. Your pupils are broken at the top by a white glare."

Valkyrie's stomach tied in knots. *That's from the Swiftmaw inside me, not what's affecting my vision.* She hoped he wouldn't recognize the mark.

"I'm really here because I wanted to ask why you were in those tunnels last week," Ashton said. He seemed to be folding his arms.

Valkyrie stared at him with bewilderment. "Week? Have I really been out that long?"

"I'm afraid so," Ashton nodded. "I want to know how this all happened."

"I fell into one of your pits," she said, blinking again as her vision was almost back. She could see the captain but nothing past him.

Ashton leaned forward and rested his elbows on his knees as he peered at her with deep blue eyes. "We don't have any pits," he said.

Valkyrie's ears went down, and she turned her head away from him. "Then I don't know what happened," she said stubbornly. "I was running from a Swiftmaw then I fell." She gasped and sat up.

Her head pounded with pain, and she grabbed her left temple, wincing as she tried to steady herself. Ashton was suddenly by her side, grabbing her shoulder to direct her back down, but she shrugged him off.

"Where is he?" she asked, staring at him with wide eyes.

"Gavin?" Ashton questioned.

Her heart sank. She couldn't tell them they were friends. "No, the Swiftmaw," she said, shifting uncomfortably.

Ashton frowned. "He's gone."

Valkyrie felt as if she'd been stabbed. She lay back down, inwardly demanding she wouldn't cry.

"I'm sorry, he got away before we could catch him," Ashton finished.

Relief flooded her, and she turned away to hide her smile. *At least I know the Stexphin didn't kill him.*

Looking down at the rest of her body, she noticed for the first time her right arm had been wrapped tightly against her. She could feel other bandages on her legs and abdomen, but they were hidden beneath the sheets.

"Where am I?" she asked, glancing up at Ashton. The old captain sat on the edge of her bed, and she was surprised at how comfortable he was here.

"Jaylee—if that is, in fact, your real name—you are in Smuir, a city hidden beneath the ground of a mountain. You are in one of our largest and cleanest rooms, the hospital." He studied her eyes before saying, "It took my men eight hours until we found your body. There was a Swiftmaw boy inches away from you. Once we had him out, he awoke and injured some of my men before taking off."

"Was he hurt?" she asked.

"No. Not a scratch." He watched her confused expression.

How did Gavin escape unharmed and I've been in the hospital for a week?

"Tell me, Jaylee, did the Swiftmaw get your friend, Gavin?"

Valkyrie was quiet and glanced away before saying, "I don't know."

"Little one," Ashton said softly. "What happened before you found the caves? Where's your family?"

Valkyrie squeezed her eyes shut. *Don't choke up!* She opened her mouth, but no words came out. With her left hand, she covered her eyes. She didn't want Captain Ashton to see she couldn't stop the tears from coming. Now that he had asked, it really seemed to settle on her that her family was, in fact, gone.

Frazil's probably dead. I heard his howl of pain. Virga ran into the house even after he was told not to. Mother and him probably got trapped. The cottage disappeared with them. And Father? He probably came during the attack and was kidnapped or he ran away to save himself. My entire family's gone. They're not coming to get me. I've been left behind.

Valkyrie hadn't noticed that Ashton was holding her in an embrace, and she clung to him, crying into his jacket that smelled like earth.

She had thought she already cried for her family and no more tears would be spent on their thoughts. *I was wrong. It hurts so much to think of what I've lost.*

After a moment, Valkyrie's tears turned into small whimpers as her physique trembled, but she wouldn't let go of Ashton. This captain seemed to understand her pain, and even just his embrace was as comforting as one from Dane would have been.

"Shh, it's okay, little one," Ashton said, stroking her hair the way Brooklyn would have done. Silently, she wondered if he had his own children and family. *He's a good father.*

"Captain," Matthias's voice turned their attention. A glance passed between the two men, and Ashton nodded. He let go of Valkyrie, and the doctor laid her back down.

"I'll come again soon, little one." Ashton took his leave.

*****

"If I catch you walking around one more time, then you're in for it," Matthias scolded.

"I'm sorry, sir," Valkyrie apologized as the doctor carried her back to her hospital bed. She had learned quickly not to underestimate the man's strength.

"And what have I said about calling me *sir*? It's either Doctor or Matthias." He shook his head.

"Yes, sir. I mean, Doctor, sorry. It's just that my mother always taught me and my brothers to call older characters *sir*." Valkyrie looked at him with desperation. "I guess it's turned into a habit."

Matthias tilted his head as he laid her back in the bed and raised a brow. Valkyrie quickly shut her mouth.

It had been two weeks since she had woken up to find herself beneath Mt. Smuir, and Matthias treated her as if she was paralyzed!

He insisted that she needed more rest and that her body should still be healing. *Should.* That word bothered her.

Her eyesight was still a little fuzzy, but she could always make out enough to see where she was going. She was very frail-looking, and she longed to get up and run around to rebuild her muscles.

Valkyrie hadn't talked about her family at all during this time, so she was surprised herself that she had even spoken of Mother and her brothers.

"I mean," she went on to insist, "it's just that I feel like I'm so full of energy. I have never stayed in bed this long. *Ever.*"

Matthias chuckled, and she frowned. *No way I can just lie here for another week! I'm fine!* She needed fresh air, to go outside and stretch.

Yesterday, she had felt such a terrible urge to transform that she had slid from the bed and ran for the hospital doors. A doctor named Trinity, with a cast over her nose, had stopped her before she got out.

With so much time to herself, Valkyrie spent most of it thinking. She had come to the conclusion that her body was healing so fast from the invention.

She also thought about Gavin a lot. How was he not injured after the tunnel collapse? Matthias had shown her the x-rays of her broken ribs and legs. She shuddered.

"I'm getting so bored," she told Matthias. "I can walk perfectly fine. What if you went *with* me on a walk? We could go outside," she encouraged. "Or even to Ashton's place!"

Over the last weeks, the captain visited her frequently. He seemed to sense she was bored and would come and sit with her for hours, teaching her card games.

She had come to realize the captain acted how she always wished her father would have. He came every day and spent time with her. They laughed and played together.

"Jaylee," Matthias shook his head, "Smuir is completely underground. We're beneath a mountain. King Demoor doesn't let anyone go outside."

"What? Why?" she asked, horrified. *Never go outside? I used to practically live outside. Even just staying in Father's mount was miserable without the sun and wind and—*

"Don't you see? Beneath Smuir, we are protected from Rotto. Here, we are hidden beneath his radar. Here, we don't have to worry about Hollowed."

19

NEW JOURNAL

Valkyrie was sitting up in her hospital bed, propped up against some pillows, writing in a journal Alania had given her upon request. She was recording everything that had happened since the invention. With so much time on her hands, she was easily caught up to the present.

> I don't know what's going to happen to me after I'm released. Will I live by myself? I don't have a family to stay with. This must be my new life.
> It's really happening. I'm not going back home anytime soon.

She sighed heavily.

Valkyrie set aside her journal onto a nearby table. She replaced it with a long piece of string. She began to interweave her fingers along the thread as she thought.

She looked down at the string she had attempted to coil around her fingers. Slowly, she began the difficult task of untangling them. After a few moments of struggle, she began to realize it wasn't coming off.

I'll have to ask Alania to cut it again, she realized with embarrassment. Looking up, she tried to see if she could spot the nurse.

Instead, she saw three young boys with their mother walking past. She recognized the group. It was their second time in the hospital.

She had come to learn the hospital was a large oval room lined with many beds and certain areas for more injured Stexphin. Hardly anyone was ever in there.

Valkyrie had learned the boys were all brothers; two were twins. The older one had dark chocolate brown shaggy hair that grew around his face. On one side was a white strip that almost looked like a stretched-out teardrop.

The twins also had extraordinary hair. Theirs was pure white with splotches of black tips. Both had pale blue eyes. They smiled and waved at her as they passed, and she returned the gesture.

One of the twins was leaving this time with a pair of crutches. Last time, the older one had left with bandages around his arm where he had been hit with a sharp stone that split his skin open.

What do they do? she wondered, and not for the first time. She longed to go with them. *It must be exciting if they keep injuring each other. They are boys, though. Virga would have been good friends with them.*

Before she could be pulled into another depressing state at the thought of her twin brother, she heard the others talking as they walked away.

Her ears picked up every noise in the hospital, and she had become used to the low chatter of doctors, the occasional clinking of a needle being dropped by one of the newer attendants, and always Matthias's muttering to Alania about how her body was healing very unusually.

"She's been here for almost three weeks now," one of the twins was saying under his breath. "Doesn't even look hurt,"

"She's probably sick," their mother said sharply, indicating for their whispers to stop. Three heads turned her direction, and she looked away.

"Doesn't look very sick."

"She is rather bony, though."

Valkyrie frowned as the large hospital doors shut behind them. *Bony?* She looked down at herself. It was true. The gray nightgown she wore that had fit her perfectly two weeks ago almost seemed too big on her now. *Why is everything getting better except for my physique? That only seems to be getting worse.* Another worried mutter she had heard Matthias talking about.

She panicked, thinking this must be about the invention. Was it failing? Was she getting weaker? Would she keep getting smaller until she looked like nothing but a skeleton?

I eat plenty. I've been walking a lot, sometimes with or without Matthias's permission. I think he knows I need to move around to strengthen my body.

She glanced up as a nurse approached her. She smiled at Alania's disappointed frown to see her hands tied together again. "I don't understand why Captain Ashton even considered bringing you a string." She shook her head as she grabbed nearby scissors.

"He taught me how to tie all sorts of knots. I've been practicing." She held up her hands.

"Clearly," Alania huffed. The string fell away, and Valkyrie rubbed her sore skin.

"Ms. Alania, when am I allowed to go?"

Alania looked puzzled. "I'm sorry, Jaylee, but Dr. Matthias thinks you had better stay in the hospital a few more weeks until we figure out what's happening to your body."

"She looks fine to me," Came a voice from behind.

Alaina spun. "Captain Ashton," she addressed him.

A wide smile appeared on Valkyrie's face when she saw him.

"I've just finished talking to Matthias. He said she's good to go with me," Ashton said.

"All right, I'll go grab her belongings," Alania said as she walked off.

What? Belongings? Go with him? I don't understand. Valkyrie glanced at Ashton with a confused look. "What's going on?" she asked.

The old captain smiled. "Matthias said you need a family to care for you, and he's agreed you can live with me,"

Valkyrie wasn't sure how to feel. "You're *adopting* me?" she asked.

Ashton's face turned serious. "Jaylee, unless you tell us what happened to you and your family, we can't get you home. Until then, I'm afraid that makes you an orphan. So, yes, I am adopting you."

Valkyrie was a little shocked how straightforward he was. *An orphan? I don't want to be an orphan. My family could still be alive. But how am I supposed to know? I could tell Ashton. Maybe he would take me back home. But they wouldn't be there. Nor would the cottage.*

Valkyrie's mind filled with questions and very few answers. She finally nodded. "But I don't own any belongings. I left all of them at home." *Where they were all destroyed, most likely.* She thought about all her old journals, filled with the penmanship of her and Virga's grand days. *Don't think about it!*

"You did come with something, something Matthias has been trying to figure out what it is," Ashton said. "It's an odd thing for a little one like you to be carrying around."

Valkyrie was confused. She didn't remember having anything at all.

Alania soon returned, and Valkyrie looked earnestly for what she might be holding. In her hands were nicely folded clothes as well as Cooper's cloak. Her mind spun as she remembered Mother's journal.

When Alania handed her a small gray bundle, Valkyrie gasped in horror. She quickly took the pouch and looked inside. It was empty. It was the sack that Frazil had given to her, the one that he had filled with the darts.

"Where are they?" Valkyrie asked anxiously.

Alania frowned. "Matthias has them. He'd also like to know what *they* are. Would you care to tell him?"

Valkyrie was sure she looked as scared as she felt. *I need those. If Matthias figures out what they are, I'm done for.*

"No, and he can't have them. I need them back. They're mine," Valkyrie said quickly.

Alania still frowned.

Valkyrie realized she *wasn't* going to return them. Looking wildly around the room, she tried to find Matthias. She spotted him. *I need those darts back, and now! Who knows what might happen if I were to transform here? I could hurt so many before they even got the chance to kill me. I haven't transformed in so long. It might be too hard to resist without those darts.*

Valkyrie threw back the sheets and leaped out of bed. Alania tried to block her, but she dodged around the nurse. She sprinted for Matthias.

Her legs slightly quaked beneath her, and she was shocked at how weak she felt. She hadn't felt like this at all yesterday. Suddenly, a thought struck her. *I need those darts. Father said they help with transforming. Maybe my body also physically needs them to heal properly.*

She had almost reached the doctor when someone grabbed her around the waist. She struggled roughly to break free.

"Stop! Jaylee, stop!" Ashton said as he tried to keep her under control.

"*No!* Matthias! I need those! Give my darts back. *Please!*" she shrieked. She didn't care if she was causing a scene. She needed those darts.

Matthias frowned as he ran over to them. "*Please!* Give them back! I *need* those!" she cried. Her emotions were rising quicker than she could calculate. She needed a dart before she went out of control.

She was still struggling to break through from Ashton's grasp, but the Stexphin was not about to give in, and he held all the tighter. Matthias didn't know what to do.

"Jaylee, You need to stop," he whispered in a stern tone.

Valkyrie noticed that she had the attention of almost everyone in the room. She stopped struggling as Matthias quickly led them away but this time couldn't stop the tears. *I need those darts or I'm going to die. Why? Why did this happen? How am I supposed to live with these transformations?*

Matthias was glowering the whole way as they left the hospital. He led them down a hall made of dirt and into a small room that was kind of like their old living space back home.

Valkyrie now had her tears under control and tried to calm down. But she felt this small fire inside of her, the same feeling she got when she had transformed for the first time.

Matthias sat in a chair at a small table while Valkyrie and Ashton sat across from him. He reached in his pocket and took out the darts. Valkyrie looked at them with wide eyes. *Should I grab them and run?*

"Now, Jaylee, can you kindly tell me what these are?" Matthias asked with a tone of authority.

Valkyrie shook. They weren't going to let her hide anymore. They were forcing her to say what happened. *What should I say? The truth? That's not safe. Just return them! Please!*

Valkyrie felt a hand on her shoulder. It was Ashton. She had been trembling the whole time, and the old Captain looked intently at her with kind eyes. He was worried about her.

I wouldn't mind him being my father at all. But it still feels wrong because I already have a father, and he could still be alive.

She looked up at Matthias who had a stern look on his face. "I don't understand why you must know," she whispered.

He frowned. "Jaylee, it's not every day a young lassie will show up out of nowhere carrying around these...these weapons," Matthias stammered to find the correct word.

"But they're not weapons!" Valkyrie cried. *And please stop calling me Jaylee! I know that's the name I gave you to call me, but I don't like it! I miss my real name. I miss my mother who gave me my name. I miss my brothers. I miss Virga. He would know what to do and say. Jaylee is a name Frazil calls me, not these men.*

"If they are not weapons, why can't you tell me what they are?" Matthias questioned, sounding annoyed.

"Why, though? Why must you absolutely know? Can't I be allowed to have secrets?" Valkyrie said, the fire inside of her growing.

"Lassie! Your whole life is a secret to us!" Matthias snapped.

Valkyrie could tell he was frustrated, and she was getting angry as well. It was taking all her strength to not transform. By now, she was now shaking terribly. She stretched her neck from side to side, trying to loosen up.

"Jaylee," Ashton began gently.

161

But Valkyrie had enough! She stood up so fast her chair fell over. "It's not Jaylee! All right! I lied, that's not my name. And I'm getting sick of hearing that. And those are mine! Father gave them to me, and I am not going to let you claim them!" Valkyrie was boiling. She felt an awful feeling crawling over her. Her body tingled horribly. She tried to calm herself but couldn't. Her skin was getting rougher.

Thoughts flooded to her brothers. *Isn't this what happened to them before they had transformed and gone out of control? It's happening to me. I can't stop it.*

"What's wrong?" Ashton said. "Little one, what's happening?"

Valkyrie was breathing heavily, and she stared at the darts on the table.

As quick as lightning, she grabbed one before Matthias could stop her. Then she dropped to the ground and ducked beneath the table. Trembling, she quickly uncovered the end of the dart and stabbed it in her leg. It was painful, and she squeezed her eyes shut, swallowing a scream.

Instantly, she began to feel much better than she had in a long time. Matthias reached under the table and grabbed her by the arm and pulled her out. "What did you do?" he ordered.

*****

Valkyrie later left that room feeling guilty. She had eventually been able to make something up for Matthias to believe. She told him she had a disease, and her Father was the only one who knew how to control it. She hated lying. She hated the fact that her whole life seemed to be a lie.

Now with her darts back, she was solemnly following Ashton through the dark hallway carved underground with only a few torches for light.

Matthias had left to return for the hospital. Valkyrie couldn't even keep track of how many times she had apologized to him. *This whole transformation thing has really changed me. But I don't like it. I can't control my temper, and half the time, I feel delusional. Matthias will be wanting more answers. I don't know what to tell them. I can't trust anyone with this secret.*

Ashton slowly led her through a few more hallways before turning to a door. She wasn't entirely paying attention while he showed her where to find things and the sort.

After he showed her to her new room, he left so she could settle in.

Valkyrie looked around the small bedroom. *It's not as big as my old room back at the cottage, but it's nicer than the hospital.* She glanced around the room one more time before sitting on the bed with an exasperated sigh. She clutched the gray pouch close to her heart as she thought of home.

The room was small with a bed in the corner. There was a small chest at the end of the cot and a small bookshelf on the wall along with a desk and a big shelf of drawers.

She walked over and opened a drawer to realize they were all empty, except one. The top one had a book inside.

Grabbing the thick copy, she took it out and read the top. "*The Scriptures. Holy and Sacred Writings.* I think I've heard of this before. Frazil had one in his room."

The Binder was a smooth chocolate brown color. *Almost like Gavin's eyes.* She was surprised that was her first thought. Lifting the book, she smelled the leather and smiled.

Their room used to smell the exact same after Virga tried to build a leather case. He had given up after a while and stuffed the remains beneath his bed.

Valkyrie wondered if Ashton meant to leave this for her. Returning the beautiful binder, she placed her new journal beside it. Then she went to the bedroom door and checked if it had a lock. It did.

Reaching into a deep pocket of the cloak, she pulled out her mother's old journal and placed it on top of hers in the drawer.

Virga had helped her transform the cloak to fit her size and look less like a man's. She had added only two pockets on the inside where she had stuffed Brooklyn's journal.

Sitting on the bed, she inspected her arms and legs. Already, her health seemed to be returning. Her normal skin color was back, and her bones weren't sticking out as much.

After changing back into her original clothes, the necklace from Virga, and tying the pouch to the belt around her waist, she glanced around the room once more.

So this is my new life?

A small knock sounded on the door. Valkyrie quickly jumped up and opened it. It was Ashton. "We need to talk," he said.

Her stomach flipped.

Ashton went to the desk and sat on the chair while Valkyrie sat on the bed. "First, if your name isn't Jaylee, then what is it?" he asked with a questioning glance.

Valkyrie was relieved to hear he wasn't angry. He only wanted some answers. "It's... It's Valkyrie," she said, face down.

Ashton nodded.

"My brother told me not to tell anyone," she added quietly. "And I don't *want* to tell anyone else."

"Little one, listen. I don't know what has happened to you, and I don't know why you don't trust us. I will let you know that if you don't want to be exposed to other Stexphin, it's fine. But I need you to trust me. Can you do that?"

Valkyrie nodded, remembering when Frazil had said those exact words.

"Now, would you like to tell me what happened to you?"

Biting her lip she looked down. "No," Valkyrie whispered, "but I will." She took a deep breath. *Where do I start? Should I tell him about transforming? No, I'd better leave that out.*

She went on to tell Ashton that she and her brothers had gone to their Father's mount, and when they returned home, the cottage was gone, and fog was burning them.

"Burning you?" he asked.

"I don't know why or what it was," she said. Tears starting at the edges of her eyes. *No. No tears.* "But my twin went into the cottage before it disappeared again, and my older brother suddenly started

164

telling me to run." She let out a shaky sigh. *I've mourned enough for my family. I'm stronger than this. Don't lament anymore.*

"He told me to go northeast to the city Smuir. He said Hollowed were in the fog, so I ran. I could hear him—" She closed her eyes and forced herself to continue. "I could hear him crying out in pain behind me."

Ashton got up and went to sit next to her, placing a loving arm around her shoulders.

"But I... I couldn't help him." She went on to explain shortly that a Swiftmaw had chased her in the woods moments before the ground had suddenly collapsed in. She finished her story and stared numbly at her hands. Two tears dropped from her eyes. Stubbornly, she wiped them away.

Ashton pulled her close into a fatherly embrace. "It's a horrible thing for little ones to lose their family. But it's happening everywhere all the time." He looked down at her.

"Am I supposed to *pretend* it never happened and move on?" Valkyrie asked, trembling. She squeezed her eyes shut. Tears escaped.

"No, you'll never forget them," Ashton said. "But you must learn to live without them."

"*How?*" she cried. "I feel like they left me behind."

"I can't bring them back, but I'm here to stand by you the whole way," Ashton encouraged. "We aren't made to go through it alone. Everyone needs someone who they can be completely open and honest to. You don't have to tell everyone, but you need to be sincere with someone. The only way to move on is to first overcome your fear of being honest," he finished.

But I can't be honest. No one can know what I can do. Not even you. She took a deep breath. *Virga's right. I am an emotional wreck.*

20

HER SECOND LIFE

Two Months Later

Valkyrie sat down heavily at the campfire, grateful for a break. After moving in with Ashton, she had been afraid of many things living beneath the mountain; boredom had been at the top of her list. But she had been wrong.

As Captain of the king's guard, Ashton was sent every once in a while to lead a quick scouting party outside Smuir. He had explained it was their job to make sure Rotto's armies weren't approaching.

At first, she had been worried he was saying he was going to leave her behind like her last family. Instead, he had invited her to come, assuring her these trips were usually fun with campfires and stories.

They had left at sunset and didn't stop until midnight. By then, Valkyrie was tired. She had struggled to stay caught up but forced herself to go on, not wanting to slow the group down.

Ashton came and sat beside her. "I hope that trip wasn't too rough for you, little one," he said.

"No, it was fun." She forced a weak smile, and Ashton laughed. "Just tired. It's late."

"Get some sleep. We have more walking tomorrow." Seeing the disappointment on her face, he added, "Don't worry, these always start out slow. I usually stop and let the boys *be boys*. Some of them are only a few years older than you."

"Because you're training them, right?" she asked.

"Yes. But, usually, while they climb trees, hunt squirrels, and try to find bears, Dr. Trinity—I believe you two were introduced—can take you to the Riverforge Rampage."

"Riverforge Rampage?"

"Guess you'll find out tomorrow." He smiled at her, his dark blue eyes dancing in the firelight. "The first night, everyone is tired. By tomorrow, we'll have some meat hunted from the boys to cook over the fire, and I'm sure Yoel will have a few songs to sing."

Valkyrie fell asleep with these reassuring images in her head. *Tomorrow will be a better day,* she told her aching feet. *I can stick through it.*

*****

"Wake up. Little one, come on," Ashton's voice aroused her from her peaceful dream.

Valkyrie opened her eyes to see the captain's worried face hovering over her.

"What is it?" she asked, accepting Ashton's hand as he pulled her up to her feet.

"Packard just returned from night duty," Ashton began.

Looking around, Valkyrie noticed the fire had been put out and the others all stood defensively, weapons out. Her heart began racing at the old captain's next words. "A scouting group of Swiftmaw are on their way."

"I thought you said—" she began.

"These Swiftmaw are exposed to becoming Hollowed or else they never would have been sent out this far. Stay by me no matter what happens."

She could hear the fear in his voice and nodded firmly, although the rest of her trembled.

"There!" the young warrior named Yoel suddenly called. Instantly, four large wolves tore through the trees. Valkyrie screamed

167

as they fell on Dr. Trinity with a desperate fury. Ashton was there in a moment.

Three more Swiftmaw in their animal forms broke the clearing, one leaping onto the old captain and throwing him off balance.

Immediately, all the warriors were in combat, except for one. She couldn't remember this young man's name, but he ran toward her. Swinging his short sword in a large arch, he ended a wolf that had nearly slammed into her.

Valkyrie stumbled to the ground, shocked that she hadn't even noticed the charging beast.

The Swiftmaw's lifeless eyes were completely white as they stared at her, and she scrambled to her feet. *Swiftmaw aren't supposed to have white eyes! It's just like Gavin had!*

"Get behind me!" the soldier snapped.

Quickly, she obeyed as another white-eyed Swiftmaw charged them.

Valkyrie felt terrified. Her old nightmares of being kidnapped by Hollowed filled her.

For the moment, Ashton's group had the upper hand as they pushed the Swiftmaw back. Many of them began to retreat as the order was barked at by their leader.

Staying beside this warrior, a few times, she feared he was going to hit her with his dangerous blade. *I wish I knew how to fight or at least had a weapon to protect myself.*

Glancing back toward Ashton's direction, Valkyrie gasped in horror to see Trinity lying nearby in a heap. She wasn't dead, but blood seeped through the front of the doctor's dress. Another warrior nearby fell with his own mortal wounds.

The soldier beside her put an arm out to pull her closer behind him as he watched for the next enemy to approach. Valkyrie clung to the hem of his shirt, eyes wide with terror.

"Walt!" Ashton cried. "Get her out of here!" The desperation in his voice was frightening.

I can't lose him.

"Let's go!" Walt cried, grabbing her arm and pulling.

A loud cry from Yoel sounded behind them. "Find cover! Ragged arrows!"

"Ragged arrows, what's that?" Valkyrie cried as Walt grabbed her shoulders and threw them both behind a tree. A moment later, a thousand sounds of swishing passed them. "What is that?" she asked again, terrified.

Walt grabbed her shoulders and stared her in the eye. "It's what they use for kidnappings. The fluid inside each little splinter knocks you out, almost dead before they call in the Griefs and drag you away," he looked back. "This is no ordinary scouting group. It's a Grief camp turning Swiftmaw into Hollowed."

Turning back to her, he said, "They're coming. If I fall behind, leave me and keep going. I'll send Ashton to find you later."

Large jaws snapped around the tree, sinking into the bark, inches away from Walt. Valkyrie didn't have to be told twice to run. She was gone before the white-eyed Swiftmaw even saw her.

Running through the trees, she transformed into Stexphin form. Her tired legs came alive with adrenaline, and the attack was soon far behind.

She went on, not sure where she was or where she was even going. But then she stopped to listen. Her ears pricked at the noise of leaves crunching beneath someone's footfalls. Quickly, she ducked behind a brush, getting as low as she could. A soft growl sounded.

Her breathing increased as a new fear of bears entered her.

But after a long silence, she began to wonder if she had just imagined it. *My mind must be playing tricks on me.*

Slowly edging forward, Valkyrie soon neared a small clearing in the woods. *I wonder how much ground I've covered.*

Standing on the edge of the tree line, she glanced up at the sky. The black night was beginning to turn a dark shade of blue, proving the nearing of sunrise in the next few hours.

Valkyrie crouched down and transformed into her Swiftmaw form. She couldn't help it and smiled.

A sudden strange noise intercepted her wolf ears, and she blinked a few times, trying to clear her head. She couldn't describe what she was processing. She had never heard such a sound.

Without words, it whispered for her to go forward, to keep going. And, somehow, she knew it was Gavin. *Gavin is out here? He's looking for me. I need to find him and let him know I'm still alive.*

In a quick bound, she sprinted across the clearing, taking large leaps. She loved how much faster she was in Swiftmaw form. Her legs were still long like a Stexphin but strong as a wolf.

Her Stexphin was affected almost the same as her Character form and was rather skinny. But her Swiftmaw was still as strong as the day it was when she first transformed.

Thwick!

Before she reached the end of the clearing, she heard the small noise, and without a chance to act, the speeding arrow pierced the back of her left shoulder.

Her eyes bulged from the incredible pain, and she stumbled forward, skidding into a thicket with a howl of strain. The pain was agonizing!

Transforming back into Character, Valkyrie squeezed her eyes shut and pulled the arrow out. She couldn't believe she had actually been shot. Thankfully, it didn't appear deep.

Breathing heavily, she glanced around, trying to see the archer. She barely glimpsed light fur running away between trees. *Is that a wolf? Why would a Swiftmaw shoot me in this form?*

Another series of pain rippled through her, and she struggled to swallow her cries. Chills raced down her back, and taking deep shaky breaths, she tried to feel her wound.

Something wet stuck to her fingers, and she stared at her trembling hands covered in blood. The sight made her head pound.

You have to stop the bleeding. Purple flashed before her eyes.

Reaching back, she pressed her right hand over the wound. *I have to find Gavin. I can't take care of this myself.*

Struggling to her feet, she began to stumble through the woods, trying to stay close to trees and out of clear shot.

Valkyrie wasn't even sure how long she had been walking for. Her head throbbed, and taking a deep breath, she told herself it'd be over soon. Whether it was true or not was irrelevant as it gave her the necessary strength to deal with it nonetheless.

She never liked blood. She never wanted anything to do with blood. *I'm scared of blood. I think that's what it is.* It made her feel weak, and she hated it.

Valkyrie's thoughts drifted to the rest of the scouting group. *I'll be back before Ashton even realizes I'm gone. Please don't get kidnapped.* The thought of being left behind again bothered her.

Once again, trying to listen, she stopped. In character form, she couldn't perceive the sound that had told her where to go. Closing her eyes, she found she didn't need to hear it. A strange connection seemed to be pulling her conscience in the direction.

I must keep going. Gavin is close. I can feel it.

Why do you keep fighting to reach him? Go home, the purple flash whispered.

Because he's my only friend, and I'm not going to disappear to him like Virga did to me. I want to know he's all right, how he survived, and let him know I'm alive.

Closing her eyes and letting out a pained shaky breath, she transformed back into her Swiftmaw form and continued a painful jogging limp through the trees.

He's here.

The sound warned her a moment too late as something slammed straight into her and sent her flying. She sprawled out across the ground and cried out in pain as her shoulder began to bleed once again.

Turning over, she looked to see who her attacker was as black dots began to engulf her vision.

Her attacker was a Swiftmaw wolf, and he crouched down, ready to pounce and kill her. "Gavin—" she choked. But her vision blurred. She groaned and turned back over. She was losing too much blood. A sharp pain in her head forced her to realize her shoulder was no longer the only bleeding injury.

Gavin raced toward her in his Character form, but her vision completely blacked out, and her mind shut down before he reached her.

*****

Valkyrie groaned. *Why does my head hurt?* Opening her eyes, she jumped. She almost screamed to see the Swiftmaw character in front of her, and quickly, she stopped herself.

It was Gavin.

She was in Character form; somehow, her ears seemed to have learned to go back automatically in the presence of Swiftmaw.

"Struga!" Gavin said, hovering over her, his face slightly showing he was amused by her jump.

"Yes?" she whispered, squinting up at him.

He smiled, but it disappeared as soon as it came. "I hurt you," he said quietly, glaring.

"What? *No.* You didn't hurt me," she said quickly as she tried to sit up, but her head told her no. *Yup, he hurt me. He's got a problem with doing that.* She glanced around to see they were in some sort of dark cavern. "Where are we?" she asked.

Gavin glanced around. "A cave?" he said.

"Well, yeah, I got that part," Valkyrie remarked as she tried once more to sit up. Gavin helped her.

"We're on one side of the hill grade. But, what happened to you, Sastruga?" Gavin asked aggressively. His tone featured a concern that he didn't seem to know how to express.

Good, he's friendly, not deadly. "I don't remember," Valkyrie said, glancing around once more to realize they weren't alone.

There were two other Swiftmaw in there, a boy and a girl.

The girl, one look, and she obviously meant business. A section of dark blond bangs went across her forehead and covered the top of her left eye; the rest of her hair pulled back into a ponytail. Her long hair was full of braided beads and long, dark silky strands.

She leaned against the cave wall opposite of them, fiddling with a knife and chunk of bark.

The second was lying on his back near the girl, his hand beneath his head as if sleeping. Even from here, she could see the boy's beige-colored hair sticking up in all directions. *He needs a brush,* she thought with a small smile.

The girl glanced up and met her stare. Quickly, Valkyrie looked down, not liking the way those deep purple eyes bore into her soul.

Gavin noticed her gaze at the others and said in a quiet whisper, "These are my...old acquaintances. That's Courtney." He nodded toward the girl. "And that's Diesel. He's pretty friendly, but Courtney is, well, let's just say she doesn't really like people anymore."

Valkyrie slowly nodded.

"What happened to your uniform?"

Valkyrie stared at him blankly. *Uniform?* Then she realized all three Swiftmaw wore matching outfits. They all had on slate gray pants, but only Courtney wore a peacock green shirt. The boy wore chiffon white.

"Under my cloak," she lied, grateful Cooper's gift covered her completely like a dress. Silently, she changed her black dress beneath to match Courtney's outfit, just without Rotto's symbol. *I don't dare wear it.*

She sat against the hard stone wall and watched as Gavin walked over to his friends and started a quiet conversation. Courtney cast a scowl toward her while Diesel continued to lie with his eyes closed.

Gavin noticed and scowled at him.

Valkyrie's eyes widened as she watched Gavin kick his friend with such force that it sent Diesel rolling.

Instantly, the boy jumped up and struck Gavin with a well-aimed punch. Transforming, the two Swiftmaw wolves began to fight each other that sent them both crashing to the ground in a growling tumble.

Valkyrie gaped.

Gavin was now over Diesel in Character form where he struck him in the face repeatedly. Not dangerous punches, but hard enough to say he meant business.

Diesel, after trying to struggle free from his captor's grasp but failed, put his legs between him and Gavin, then kicked hard, sending his opponent to fly back.

He then lay down on the ground, laughing hard as Gavin tried to get up, clutching his stomach.

But Gavin wasn't done getting his revenge yet. Valkyrie watched with a small gasp as he stood tall, then leaped for his friend.

Diesel had stopped laughing and was now trying to escape Gavin's fury. The two fought for what seemed like an endless battle. Courtney rolled her eyes and walked over to sit next to her. "You look as if you've never seen a fight before," she remarked.

"No, I'm just surprised at how quick they are to get back at each other," Valkyrie replied as she watched the two fight on. Diesel sent another kick for Gavin's middle, but this time, he dodged, then leaped for his opponents legs, tripping him.

"Those two never know when to quit," Courtney said, her voice still low.

If I can get her to smile, that would be a good sign.

Valkyrie realized her shoulder was all stiff. Moving aside her cloak, she saw it had been wrapped with tight bandaging.

She fingered the wrapping, then finally glanced up at Courtney. The Swiftmaw girl looked stern and fierce, but looking into her eyes, Valkyrie felt like she seemed pretty compassionate.

"Okay! Stop! I surrender!" came a call from Diesel.

Turning her attention back toward the fight, she was surprised to see Gavin had pinned Diesel up against the cave wall. Releasing his grip, the beige-haired boy fell to the ground with a thud.

This time, he laughed with a joy on his face that proved he was the happiest boy in the realm. *Isn't he the one that just lost the fight?*

"Aww, Gavin," Diesel whined playfully as he felt his face. "You made me bleed again." It was true. A small gash from a well-aimed claw ran down the side of his face.

"*Please!*" Courtney called. "All the more scars to help hide your ugly face!"

As Diesel laughed, Valkyrie noticed his face was indeed covered in scars. *He's actually pretty good-looking.*

But where do you think he got those scars? the purple flash made her frown. She closed her eyes, trying to shut out the image of Stexphin fighting to escape the young warrior.

"You have a knack for hurting people, Gavin," Diesel commented, making his friend frown.

He didn't appear to enjoy hurting people.

"Are you the medic here?" she asked Courtney.

"No," the girl replied, a smile appearing, "Diesel is. He's always getting hurt. If it wasn't for him *being* a medic, he probably wouldn't even be here right now." Courtney said the last part in a low whisper for only her to hear.

"Oh," Valkyrie blinked. She watched Diesel go to a large brown satchel with two straps and buckles down the front. He reached inside and was soon caring for his small gash. Courtney got up and left Valkyrie to go join him. *At least I got her to smile.* She smiled to herself. *I like these Swiftmaw.*

They almost reminded her of Virga. The all too familiar hurt returned. *Stop,* she ordered herself, but the desperation of feeling unloved returned.

Gavin came over and knelt beside her. "Are you doing okay?" he asked.

"Of course!" Valkyrie replied, plastering a smile.

Gavin sighed and sat next to her.

"But why aren't you happy?"

"I don't know. It's hard not to—I mean, do you ever feel guilty hurting people? Diesel and I do it in all good fun, but I mean, actually...*hurting* someone," he asked as he watched Courtney and Diesel.

"I've never really hurt someone," she said hesitantly. "You shouldn't feel so guilty, though. I mean, you're pretty good at it," Valkyrie stated, but then she realized what she had just said and quickly covered her mouth.

Gavin chuckled at her reaction. "I didn't mean to hurt you. I didn't know it *was* you," he said. His face going grave again.

"Of course I know that!" Valkyrie snapped. *I'm surprised you didn't actually kill me.*

Diesel walked over. "Hello!" he said brightly.

Valkyrie smiled back. Gavin got up and moved as Diesel kneeled down next to her. "Mind if I check your wound?" he asked.

"Not at all," Valkyrie replied. She winced as he moved her cloak and slowly undid the wrappings around her shoulder.

Courtney stood nearby. "She's really skinny," she commented.

Valkyrie nodded, ignoring that she hadn't been speaking directly to her. "It's a disease," she said, going with the lie she had told Matthias.

"I've never heard of a disease like this," Diesel said.

"Nor did I until I got it."

"I think that's an excuse," Courtney said, eyeing her.

"It kind of is," Valkyrie confessed. "I haven't been able to move for almost three weeks."

"Why?"

Valkyrie realized now was the right time to ask Gavin how he had escaped the tunnels unharmed. He looked puzzled at her question, but then his eyes opened in recognition.

"The moment the ceiling collapsed," he began. "You're going to think I'm crazy, but I saw a bright purple force of some sort stretch out and try to cover us like a shield. I couldn't move or else I would have helped you. The shield hadn't reached you in time. It barely protected your head after you had already been hit. I think the rest broke before it covered your body. I was scared to even touch the force. So I waited.

"Hours later, something overhead struck the shield, and it broke, letting all the dirt fall on me. I couldn't breathe and went unconscious. Thankfully, less than a minute later, I woke up to find Characters around me. I tried to fight and find you but couldn't, so I ran."

"No one was there when I woke up," Valkyrie lied.

"How'd you even get this?" Diesel asked, changing the subject as he examined her wound while reaching into his satchel for an ointment.

"I was shot," Valkyrie replied, wincing as she watched him add the ointment.

"Were you with Fang's camp?" Gavin asked, frowning.

Suddenly, Valkyrie realized they had been a part of the attack on Smuir's scouting group. *They must've retreated.*

"No," she sighed. "I haven't seen anyone in the last months."

"Who shot you then?" Diesel asked.

Who knew two lives could be so confusing? "I think it was a Swiftmaw." As soon as she said it, Valkyrie's eyes grew wide. *Ashton, I forgot! I can't stay here. He's probably out there looking for me.*

"A Swiftmaw?" Courtney sounded doubtful.

"I was confused as well." She shrugged, and Diesel winced with her at the movement of her shoulder. But then a new thought came to mind. "Maybe it was Fang," she suggested. "He wanted to give me a lesson a few months ago."

Diesel gasped, and Courtney grimaced. "No one—"

"Ever survives, so I've heard," Valkyrie nodded.

"Did he retreat as well? What would Fang be doing out here?" Gavin frowned.

"Looking for us, I hope," Courtney said.

"Doubtful," Diesel replied with a shake of his head. "Besides, *I* don't want to be his next victim."

"Why would he be looking for you?" Valkyrie asked.

"A recent attack," Gavin replied, his eyes shining as he remembered it. "We retreated after the order was given out, but Fang didn't say where to go. We were still on the trail. We didn't even have a return to site."

"Basically, he's saying we're lost." Courtney shook her head.

21

ALLRED

Crowley—Year 317

It had been four days since they had found the ghost town of Smuir. Crowley hadn't seen Selah since, and he began to worry she might've gone back to the castle. *But she wouldn't have left without me. Would she?*

Crowley walked through the halls, silently fuming as the lights flickered on and off. Finally, the electricity gave in and shut down completely.

"Stupid piece of junk. We're never going to survive down here. How much longer does Demoor expect us to wait before going above ground again?" he muttered to himself.

Reaching into his back pocket, he pulled out a small lighter. Holding it up to a nearby torch hanging from the wall, he lit it. Leaving that one, he grabbed another.

Lifting his lighter to set another flame, he was shocked to realize it was gone. He frowned and began to look around. Checking all his pockets and the ground, he finally gave up.

"I swear I just had it." He scowled at the disappearance of his lighter and instead held up the torch to the other flame.

As he began to walk down the hall, he carried the spare torch, occasionally lighting another on the wall when he felt like it. It wasn't his job to keep the torches lit, but he figured he'd light a few for anyone else who planned to walk down these halls today.

Crowley wasn't surprised when he found himself in the hall full of the shelves. His eyes instantly eyed the one that he knew hid the secret passage. *I wonder.*

He began to walk toward it, frowning to see the shelf hadn't been put back properly. *Most likely, someone had used it recently. But Selah wouldn't be so careless to leave it like this. Anyone could see it. Maybe she would've a few months ago, but not today. She's...changed.*

With one arm, Crowley moved back the shelf so he could fit through the passage. Turning back, he pulled it back in place, this time not leaving any space for someone to see it on the outside.

Holding his torch in front of him, he walked forward, eyes constantly searching for the rope ladder ahead. *There it is.* As he began to near the ladder, his torch suddenly went out as if a strong breeze had been there.

"What the? *Ah!*" Crowley dropped the torch as something burned his hand. Ripping his short sword free, he stared into the shadows with wide eyes. But he couldn't see anything. The darkness had swallowed him completely.

Carefully, he began to walk forward, keeping his blade poised and ready at his side. With his free hand, he tried to find the rope ladder. He hadn't been that far from it. *It should be right here.*

His hand bumped something, and he inwardly smiled as his fingers curled around the rough rope. Suddenly, a light shone from behind, and he spun around. Someone was there, holding a torch in front of their face so he couldn't identify them.

"Who's there?" he demanded.

"Adviser," the familiar gravelly voice said. At the same time, Delta moved the torch away from his face. "Odd finding you here."

"What are you doing here?" Crowley ordered.

"Don't you know?" Delta questioned, his old eyes looking confused. "I am going to see Walt from above. Are you here to join me?"

Crowley was quiet as he debated the scout's words. Walt was above? *Waiting to meet with Delta...* "Yes," he replied stiffly.

"Good," Delta stated. "He is bringing some friends that I would like you to meet." He approached the ladder but then stepped aside and motioned for Crowley to go first.

Ignoring the warning in his mind, he sheathed his sword, grabbed the coarse rope, and began to hike up. When he reached the top, he pushed the trapdoor aside. Light streamed down, and he squinted.

Climbing out, he looked around. No one was there.

The young warrior held the trapdoor open as he waited for Delta to put out his torch and climb up. When the scout reached the top, he simply nodded and began to lead the way through the empty city.

It was around ten in the morning, and dark clouds littered the sky, casting a long shadow over the ghost town. Crowley followed the old scout by three feet, keeping his distance. His boots splashed in puddles along the cobblestone road.

It must have been raining pretty hard earlier. How I miss stormy days. A small drizzle began, and he quickly pushed his thoughts away from the weather. Walking with his shoulders straight and head high, he kept a wary eye for any movement in the quiet city.

Even Delta, the oldest scout under the mountain, around sixty, walked with long strides. He could see the man watching for any signs of betrayal as well.

The two of them were a strange sight as their boots sloshed through the lonely streets.

Two men, one old, the other young, both armed and walking as if they owned the place and yet looking like outlaws, strode through a city that had been abandoned for years.

Suddenly, Crowley realized Delta was leading him to the town square. Ahead, he saw four other men, three standing, while another sat on the edge of the fountain. As they approached, this man stood. No one was smiling.

"Delta," a familiar voice said. "Who is this? You said you were coming alone."

"Good to see you, too, Walt," Crowley said, glowering at the young soldier who should've been dead.

"The king's adviser?" a nearby Stexphin by the name of Packard said, his brows raised and shock laced in his voice.

Crowley stopped six feet apart from them. He examined each man, memorizing every detail about them. Three of the men wore long coats fashioned from fine leather with a thin waterproof layer to protect them from the rain. Two of them kept the hoods on. The one who didn't was Walt.

The fourth man, the one who had originally been sitting on the fountain, wore a simple raincoat and jeans. Crowley tilted his head as he eyed the gun sticking out from beneath the jacket. He examined the man once more and frowned harder. *He's a Bandit. No wonder he has a gun. Fallacious creature,* he cursed.

The other three were Stexphin, all of whom were a part of the king's guard. Crowley didn't speak with them much, but they had all been trained together by Captain Ashton to take care of the tunnels below. *Yoel and Packard are in on this too? What's going on?* On the outside, he refused to show his confusion.

Walt folded his arms and studied Crowley with accusing eyes. "How did you know? Delta wouldn't have ratted us out, I know that much. Are you here to *arrest* us?" he mocked.

Crowley didn't blink as he stared his old friend down. Delta stepped in before he could say anything.

"No," the old scout said. "I told him willingly. He's here to learn what happened." Something else hinted in his voice, and the other two smiled eagerly.

"I want to know how you survived a gunshot. And who shot you," Crowley ordered Walt, glancing at the Bandit who stepped forward.

"I shot him," the man confessed freely. "Three bullets in his right leg and two in the back." He said all this without revealing anything. His face remained expressionless and his voice stiff.

"And how did you come by a gun?"

Now the Bandit smiled and let out a short laugh. "You've been living under the mountain for too long, young boy," he said.

"Allred, that's enough," Walt snapped. "This isn't a young boy. He is the king's closest adviser. I will not let you stand there and not treat him as such." No hint of sarcasm touched his words as he glowered at the Bandit.

"My apologies," Allred replied stiffly, one brow cocking as he glanced at Crowley. He folded his arms and shifted his weight to one leg. "All Bandits carry guns," he said. "They don't last over three years before they disappear. You may have heard our realm doesn't accept such machinery."

"Our *realm?*" Crowley questioned.

The Bandit's arms dropped to his sides, and he gave Walt a helpless look. "The kid's been living beneath a rock!" he exclaimed, pointing a finger at Crowley. Warning glances came from the others, and he corrected himself. "The king's adviser is much more uninformed than I presumed," he said, once more folding his arms.

"Walt, tell me what this man won't," Crowley demanded, turning all his attention to the warrior.

"The Bandit's race has been threatened by Rotto's army's," Walt began. Crowley noticed Allred look down at this. "Your band, the one you sent out years ago, the first to be attacked by Rotto, was found because Allred lead them straight to the army."

Crowley stiffened and shot daggers at the Bandit with his eyes. "Why would you do that?" he said between gritted teeth.

"It's a new operation," Walt went on to explain. "If Rotto can stay busy keeping Stexphin, he won't have any need to go after their race."

"So you will sacrifice another kind to save your own?" Crowley asked, his scowl deepening.

"You would do the same," Walt said sharply.

"I'm speaking to the Bandit!" Crowley snapped. He spun on Allred. "How do you know so much about Rotto to know where to lead *my* band?"

"I have friends on the inside," Allred said. He fingered one of his pockets. "They gave me a map, but I never meant for your band to be slaughtered."

"How can you say that?"

Packard spoke up, "We have intelligence Rotto doesn't kill them unless they fight back. If we can help, no more blood has to be shed."

"What are you saying?" Crowley asked, folding his arms as he eyed each Stexphin once more.

"We have a treaty," Walt said, lowering his voice. "Rotto needs a captain, someone who is skilled and knows his directions, someone to be secondhand. Delta promised me names, but it seems he found who we're looking for."

Crowley remained quiet. He didn't have to pretend not to understand. They knew he did. "You want me to turn on the king?" he finally asked.

"No, we want you to help the king," Yoel spoke for the first time. "Everyone knows he's paranoid. He didn't know the difference between leadership and fear when he forced the city to evacuate beneath the mountain. He never has. He doesn't even know now."

For once, Selah came to mind. *What would she say?* "I won't. I *can't* just walk out on the king behind his back and break his trust."

"He has done that to you. How would this be any different?" Delta asked quietly.

Crowley shook his head and looked down.

"I won't have any witnesses," Allred's voice was followed by the sound of a gun cock.

Crowley's head snapped up. How did he let them get to him? Why had he dropped his guard? Even if he pulled out his sword now, he couldn't stop a well-aimed bullet this close.

"Allred, don't!" Walt snapped, turning toward the Bandit. "You can't kill him!"

Allred didn't drop his deadly gaze as he stared Crowley down. "Delta?" the man asked.

"Don't," the old scout said calmly.

Flipping his pistol, he caught it by the handle and stuffed it back inside its holster. Crowley hadn't even flinched during the entire ordeal, and he was thankful they couldn't hear his racing heart at coming so close to death. *Selah would've argued I had just read my ending right there. I knew what was going to happen. But it didn't. Would I count that as a happy or sad end? Probably sad if I hadn't met Selah. She's right. I still have joy in my life.* His heart gave a small lurch at the thought of being shot right then. Suddenly, he realized he needed Selah as much as she needed him. He had always felt that way, but only now was he actually confessing it to himself and letting his feelings come to the light.

I need to find her and apologize. I can't deny my love for her anymore. I've been afraid it would be a sign of weakness, but if I were to lose her like I did Malachi—

He turned his head to focus his gaze on the old scout standing three feet away. Delta nodded, knowing he was expressing gratitude beneath his stern mask.

Looking back at the others, he knew this secret meeting was over for his part. "Gentlemen," he said, indicating his courtesy as he turned on his heel to leave. There was nothing else for him to say, and he doubted they were in the mood to answer any more questions.

"Adviser Crowley," Walt's voice rang out as he walked down the street.

He turned back to face them.

"If you ever change your mind, you know where to find us."

Crowley only stared at him before turning back and continuing his walk. Lightning flashed overhead, and heavy rain began pouring from the sky, hitting the cobblestone street with a satisfying sound.

Reaching behind him, Crowley pulled his hood over his head and made his way back to the old blacksmith's shop, his long coat drifting out behind him with each stride.

*****

The others watched him go. No one spoke until he disappeared onto another distant street.

"You're just going to let him go?" Allred turned on them. His face contorted with anger. "What will we do if he tells your king? He knows our names! He'll—"

"Enough," Walt said calmly, still staring at the spot where the young adviser had turned. "We know Crowley. He won't utter a word about this morning."

"How? How can you trust him not to say anything? You realize what you just confessed to him, don't you?" Allred asked desperately.

184

"He's…how will I say this?" Delta began. "*Predictable.* Even the king knows it. Already, Adviser Crowley doubts his place here beneath the mountain. I've seen it. He hides only behind a thin mask. His eyes, however, scream out words."

"That's why you brought him," Yoel said, looking at the old scout. "You knew this meeting was exactly what he needed to push him in our direction."

"Plant a seed, something is sure to grow." Packard's lips curved left in a side smile.

"Something's still holding him back, though," Delta said curiously. "I was certain we'd be leaving with him today. Surely, it's not the king that holds him back. Crowley doesn't respect him the way he used to since Prince Malachi and the queen left."

"The girl," Yoel said quietly.

"What girl?" Walt questioned, turning toward his comrade.

"I forget you haven't been inside the mountain for a few years," Yoel commented. "But, yes, there is a girl. The daughter of the captain who led the band he sent a year ago."

Delta smiled widely. "That's why he came to me in the first place. He wouldn't be stepping out for this young lady unless she meant something to him."

"Then get rid of her," Allred cut in impatiently. "I can't wait another month. If Crowley doesn't show up in less than ten days, you better have somebody else stepping in for him."

Walt turned toward Packard. "You know her?" he asked.

"I know everyone," Packard smiled wickedly.

"If we can get rid of the girl, then I'll find Crowley and bring him back," Delta said.

"Leave it to me," Packard said, eyeing Allred's holster. "She'll just be another small obstacle to take down. We'll be leaving this ghost town with Crowley in less than five days. *Trust* me."

22

LEFT

Valkyrie—Year 315

Valkyrie woke up with a small grunt from her aching shoulder. Pushing herself up into a sitting position against the cave wall, she looked around to see the other Swiftmaw lying in different spots.

Wait, where's Courtney? Carefully getting up, she ignored the knot in her shoulder. Surprisingly, it no longer burned the way it had yesterday.

Valkyrie slowly walked toward a passage leading outside the large rounded cave. Following it outside, she was shocked to see how dark it was. *No! Ashton. I know he's still alive, but he doesn't know that about me.* She looked around the shadowed forest, trying to figure out where she was.

Thick trees grew everywhere. A silent cold breeze blew through the air, once more reminding her of the fast approaching winter. She shivered and pulled her cloak on tighter.

Her ears perked up at the sound of footfalls. *Courtney,* she realized while also reaching up to quickly brush her ears back beneath her hair again.

The Swiftmaw girl was standing in the shadows of the trees, looking up through an opening in the branches at the full moon overhead. Her wolf ears turned back, indicating she heard her approaching.

Valkyrie went and stood next to her, glancing up at the beautiful night sky above.

"Sastruga, right?" Courtney looked at her.

"Yes," Valkyrie smiled back.

Courtney didn't return the kind gesture. Instead she stared at her with accusing purple eyes.

"How does Gavin know you?" Courtney asked. "He hasn't spoken about you very much."

"We met a few months ago at Runyan's army," Valkyrie replied. "Where I also met Fang." She looked away with a guilty expression.

"Diesel and I were recently transported there," Courtney went on, looking back up at the night sky. "It was easy to become friends with him. Gavin's hard skin, but he's a pretty good friend for having gone through Rotto's camp led by the Griefs in Wingspread."

"Did you and Diesel not do the same camp?" *And what camp are we talking about exactly?*

"I did. Diesel didn't. Somehow, he escaped the Griefs and was trained by a Swiftmaw named Van Dyk. He was friends with Gavin when we lived back on Dawn Shadows before the Griefolowtros came, and I think they're glad just to be back together." Courtney smiled sadly, her eyes sparkling like the stars overhead. "I think even if Diesel went through the camps, he would've come out the same. He's hard to break."

"And you?" Valkyrie asked quietly. "Did they break you and Gavin?"

Courtney's eyes clouded over, and she turned her head to look at her. "I can see Diesel is hurt by how much I've changed. Gavin has enough life left in him to remember who he once was. I never told anyone this, but"—her ears fell back, and she lowered her head shamefully—"I almost joined the Hollowed."

Valkyrie was quiet. *She's hurting so much more than she's letting on. But Ashton was right—You can't live alone. We all need to tell someone our pains eventually.*

"It's easy to tell Gavin is scared to lose us," Courtney said, the cloud in her eyes disappearing as she turned the subject of conversation. "I understand now that he was scarred after leaving you behind and doesn't want to do that again."

"That's why I came out. To find him," Valkyrie said. It was partly true.

"What made you think you *could* find him?" Courtney asked.

"I can't explain it, but in a way, I felt like I could hear him, which led me here," Valkyrie confessed, embarrassed.

Courtney eyed her curiously before saying, "Sorrowcrest."

"What?"

"Please, you've never heard of the legends?"

"No, what legend?"

"It's the legend of Sorrowcrest. It was told on Dawn Shadows to all the younger Swiftmaw. It used to be very...*common,* you could say. But after Rotto happened, it *stopped* happening," Courtney said, folding her arms as her eyes glowed with a sort of excitement.

"Yes, but what is it?" Valkyrie questioned.

"Swiftmaw who have connected minds. You're not born with it, but it grows into you over time."

"I haven't even known Gavin for a year. We only knew each other for almost two days," Valkyrie argued.

"And yet you came out here to look for him. Why?" Courtney pressed.

"Well, I guess because he's my friend."

"That you only knew for two days." Courtney raised a brow. "It's because of Sorrowcrest, don't you understand? It's why you care about each other. I knew Gavin before...before we were herded by Rotto for training. He was friendly but a very closed-up boy. He doesn't remember me, but I've never forgotten a face in my life."

"How is that? I mean, why me?" Valkyrie asked.

Courtney shrugged. "I'm not sure, but we'd best head back. The boys are most likely up by now."

"Wait, does Gavin know? About this Sorrowcrest?" Valkyrie asked, heat rising in her face.

"No." Courtney smiled at her reaction. "I don't think he understands just yet why he cares about you so much. But that's boys." She paused. "Don't repeat anything I said today. No one else knows. I don't know why I even told you."

"I think we both just needed to have a girl talk." Valkyrie smiled, realizing she'd never had a girlfriend before.

This time, Courtney returned the smile. "I'm glad I'm not the only female here anymore," she said. "But before we head back, I have to ask, if you weren't sent to Rotto's Grief camp, where have you been?"

"What makes you think I wasn't at his camp?" Valkyrie's throat tightened. *I don't even know what a Grief camp is.*

"Your hands." Courtney smirked. When Valkyrie showed no sign of recognition, she reached out and grabbed her right one. "Look," she said, pointing at her palm. "Soft skin. You haven't done a day of work in your life."

"That's not true," Valkyrie frowned. She did plenty of work back home. Carrying buckets of water was not an easy job.

"You were a serf, weren't you?" Courtney guessed. "You don't have fighting hands. Yes, tough skin, but only a layer. That's why you were sent to Runyan's camp, I'm guessing."

"*Why?*" Valkyrie asked, still frowning. *A serf? For what?*

"Runyan, the Grief. It's his job to turn Swiftmaw into Hollowed. Gavin confessed he was almost gone until he met you." Courtney smiled again as the word *Sorrowcrest* danced across her eyes.

*****

When they made it back to the cave, they went in to find Gavin and Diesel awake.

"Where'd you go?" Diesel questioned while he checked his satchel. Gavin was leaning against the wall, cleaning his longsword.

"A walk," Courtney and Valkyrie said at the same time.

"Alrighty then," Diesel said as he began to buckle his satchel.

"Are we moving out?" Courtney asked.

"Yes. Gotta start somewhere," Gavin said without looking up from his sword.

Valkyrie felt uncomfortable as she thought about what Courtney had said about Sorrowcrest. *What does it even mean? I'm not even Swiftmaw born.*

Valkyrie stood there as she watched them clean their weapons and put together a few of their belongings in sacks. *Belongings.* She quickly felt at her side and sighed with relief. Her gray pouch was still there.

Diesel approached her, eyed her wrapped shoulder, then asked, "Why didn't *you* have a weapon when Gavin found you?"

You mean attacked me. "I've honestly never used a weapon before," Valkyrie replied.

Diesel gave her a doubted look, a playful smile crawling up his face. "You really must have hit your head when those caves collapsed on you. I don't know any Swiftmaw that has never used a weapon before."

Don't think I've ever even touched a weapon before.

"Guess I did hit my head," she said quietly.

"Well, you're going to need one. Never know what might be out there," he said.

Like what? Bears? I don't even know how to use a weapon, plus I don't have one.

As if reading her mind, Diesel pulled two daggers from his belt. He handed them to her. "They aren't much, but at least you'll have something, am I right?" he said, smiling.

"Thank you." *But what would I need to protect myself from? Stexphin? I could never—*

"Let's go," Gavin said, heading for the passage.

*****

Gavin led the way with Diesel at his side, Courtney and Valkyrie trailing behind them. "Earlier, you said we were lost, so where are we going then?" Valkyrie asked in a hushed tone.

Courtney frowned. "We're going to have to trust Gavin. He has amazing tracking skills."

Glancing ahead at the boy, he looked confident, striding through the woods. It was still dark, and she could barely make out his brown-colored hair.

They walked through the trees aimlessly for a while, and pretty soon, the sun began to rise. Valkyrie was feeling exhausted. She didn't have nearly as much energy as the others. She wasn't trained to be a warrior and have strength like them.

It didn't take long for her to start trailing farther and farther behind.

She didn't want to call out and ask them to wait for her. She didn't want to sound weak. *Wait for me! Please!*

Valkyrie stumbled but quickly caught her balance. Looking up, the rest were so far ahead she doubted she could ever catch up.

I literally just met them. Please don't tell me I'm just going to lose them again. Valkyrie wheezed as she tried to carry on. Then something made her stop, something she had forgotten about.

Leaning against a tree, she looked at her wrapped shoulder. Red was beginning to seep through. *Maybe Diesel can rewrap it.* She looked up to faintly see the others about to disappear into the trees.

What is this? Every man for themselves or something? Do they even remember I exist? Valkyrie began walking again, but her head was spinning, and her shoulder ached terribly. She stumbled again but this time didn't have the energy to catch herself. She fell to the ground with an "*Oof!*"

Looking back up, the others were gone. *You have to be kidding me.* She slowly got up, trying not to put pressure on her hurt shoulder. She sat against a tree and rested.

I'll just wait for them to realize I'm gone. They'll come back for me eventually. But maybe this is for the best. Hopefully, Ashton can find me first. Yes, this is for the best. Ashton's...coming. She dozed off.

*****

"Valkyrie! *Valkyrie!*" a voice came. A voice she knew. She opened her eyes to see Virga standing over her. "Let's *go*," he said, holding out his hand to help her up.

"V-Virga? Did… W-What happened to you? Is Mother okay? I thought you were dead!" Valkyrie said, taking his hand and standing.

"What are you talking about?" he questioned. Then he turned and darted into the trees. Valkyrie quickly followed. She felt as if she had renewed strength and hurried after her brother.

Virga disappeared into a nearby brush, and Valkyrie leaped in after him. She came to a frightening stop to see a cliff before her.

She looked around, then stooped over the rock. "*Virga?*" she screamed. She tried to catch even the tiniest glimpse of him over the edge but couldn't.

With a cry, a large Mislea Raptor emerged from the fog below the cliff. Valkyrie stifled a scream. She was petrified from fear and couldn't get her legs to move.

Kind purple eyes stared at her. "*Virga?*" she gasped.

"Virga's dead," the Mislea screeched. "I killed him."

*****

Suddenly, Valkyrie sat up. Cold sweat ran down her skin as she tried to catch her breath. *It was just a dream! Just a dream!*

Glancing around, it was still dark in the dense woods. *No one came back for me.* Her heart broke. *Maybe they never cared. No one does.*

Don't think that. Purple flashed inside her head. *You need to transform into your Swiftmaw form.*

She grunted and crawled onto her hands and knees. Wincing, she transformed into her Swiftmaw. Instantly, the strange sound from earlier returned. This time, a voice came with it.

Sastruga? Struga! I couldn't find you! I thought you died!

Gavin?

Yes, it's me. I didn't realize you fell behind. I'm so sorry. Where are you?

I honestly have no idea.

Are you hurt? You sound hurt.

No, it's just my shoulder. It's fine, though. Gavin, how is this possible?

We were just attacked when we realized we couldn't find you, and then Courtney told me about the Sorrowcrest.

Oh.

Can you try to figure out where you are? We'll come back and try to find you.

A sound from the woods interrupted Valkyrie's thoughts, and she froze. *What was that?*

What was what?

N-Nothing. Gavin, I'm really far back. Don't try to come back for me. I'm fine, don't worry.

You want us to leave you?

She could hear his pain.

Please, Gavin, I'll try to find you again sometime, but I have to go.

Wait, Sastruga? What's there? Are you in danger? We're going to—

His voice disappeared as she transformed back into Character form.

She froze and pricked her long ears forward, trying to listen. There was that sound again. *What is it?* It sounded like someone's footfalls, only instead of pounding on the earth, they were dragging slowly. *Not a bear. Please don't be a bear.*

Valkyrie grabbed a tree for support as she slowly stood. Fingering the daggers on her belt, she carefully transformed her clothes into the simple black dress beneath Cooper's gray cloak. Her emerald green eyes darted back and forth as she tried to find what the source of the noise was.

Suddenly, the sound of dragging leaves stopped, followed by a *thump.*

Valkyrie froze and shot all her attention to the thicket where she had heard the noise. Her breaths became ragged as she tried to control her racing heart. *What should I do?* Slowly, she pulled a dagger from her belt and crept toward the thicket. Her hand twitched nervously by her side.

What am I thinking!? I can't kill a bear!

It's not a bear. Now go. The sensation of purple.

Taking a deep breath, she began to go around the thicket, staying as alert as possible. With the dagger up, she readied herself for a sudden attack.

Instead, a gasp escaped, and she dropped the dagger, her hand flying to her mouth.

A dead—or at least seemed to be—Stexphin Character was lying face down on the ground. His streaked brown hair was barely visible as red liquid matted most of it down on the side of his head. His leg was split open and covered in blood.

Valkyrie grabbed her dagger and put it back on her belt before kneeling down next to the character. "Sir," she said in a quick, hushed tone. "Excuse me, sir? Please don't be dead!"

Turning the Stexphin over, she bit her lip to keep from crying out. The poor man had a long gash across his face, which was bleeding freely. He wasn't breathing.

Valkyrie didn't know what to do. But if this Stexphin were to die, she wasn't sure what she would do with herself. *That is if you aren't already dead.*

She went on, talking in low tones to the Character as she pressed her ear against his chest. A faint heartbeat sounded. *He's still alive! What would Virga do? Well... First, I better do something about this deep gash.*

Tearing a strip of cloth from her dress, she pressed it alongside the Character's face. Where the hem had ripped, it slowly came back.

Valkyrie tried to be as delicate as possible as she wrapped the cloth around the man's head. Her thoughts went to her own wrapping around her shoulder. She glanced at it.

If only I could use my wrapping for him. But I don't believe it would help him too much. It is stained with my own blood.

But as the fear of losing the Stexphin grew, her thoughts kept going back to her own wrappings. *They could help so much better!* She finally decided that just because they were stained with her blood didn't mean they were soaked. Slowly, she began to unwrap her shoulder, wincing as she did.

When she got the bandages off, they were dry. Her shoulder had stopped bleeding long ago. Yes, they were stained red, but no longer were they wet with blood.

Only stained. She hoped there was a difference. Wrapping the Stexphin's head, she ignored the pain her shoulder was now inviting without the bandages.

Valkyrie looked at the man's leg. It was really bad. *I need to do something, but what?* She took the cloth from her dress but couldn't bring herself to touch the man's limb. It had been torn open completely with marrow showing. She had to look away from the gruesome sight with a gag, and for a moment, she panicked, thinking she might vomit.

Seeing the Stexphin was wearing a uniform, she realized he was a soldier. His attire was peach, light yellow, with a faded blue—or at least should've been—but it was now covered with splotches of dirt.

She tried to tell what his symbol was but couldn't see it clearly through the blotches of blood.

The soldier shifted.

Valkyrie's eyes widened. "Hello?" she said. "Please wake up! Sir?"

The soldier let out a low groan and slightly moved again. His hands went to his head, yet his eyes never opened, and he never said a word. He felt the wrappings, then his hand went limp, and it fell to the ground.

"No, no, no," Valkyrie said as she moved around to his head. She slowly rested his head on her lap as she tried to make him comfortable. She rested her hand on his cheek and spoke softly to him.

The soldier seemed to be more relaxed and was breathing small steady breaths. Valkyrie sighed. She felt proud of herself for being able to care for him but also disappointed that she couldn't have done *more* for him. *Bandages aren't enough to help his leg.*

"Come on, soldier, fight through this! You can make it. You *have* to make it," Valkyrie whispered. *Where could he have come from? I don't understand why he would be out here by himself. Unless he isn't by himself.* She twitched her ears and glanced around. She didn't hear anything besides the soldier's heavy breathing with her own.

195

A cold breeze went through the air, shaking the branches of trees and causing a few leaves to fall. Valkyrie was cold but felt quite calm. She stroked the soldier's head as she went on silently whispering to him. Her back was feeling sore, and she longed to lean against a tree or something, but she was scared to move the man.

Her fingers began to feel numb, and a new fear began to rise in her. *What if this soldier freezes to death? Maybe someone will find us. No, I doubt that. Who would be out here on a night like this? But then, why would this soldier be out here? I hope Gavin doesn't try to come back for me.*

Valkyrie soon caught herself dozing off when the soldier suddenly moved. She quickly straightened up and looked at him.

The agony in her back was becoming unbearable! How she longed to lie down and stretch. But she would bear through it. She couldn't let this soldier die just because she was uncomfortable.

Come on, please show me a sign that you might make it.

And he did. Groaning softly, he barely opened his eye. He couldn't open his left as the wrappings covered it.

His eye was a very dark color that nearly looked red. *That's amazing. They're almost like Mother's.*

At first, he just looked at Valkyrie before it clicked in his mind. His eyes widened, and he tried to speak. A pained rasp came out instead.

"It's all right, soldier," Valkyrie said quietly.

His hands went to his throat as he tried to talk once again.

"What's happened?" he asked in a raspy voice.

"I'm not sure. But I found you hurt. I've done my best to care for you." She tried not to show how scared she really was. *What if he uses all his strength to talk that he doesn't have any left to live?* All sorts of possibilities were going through her mind as to how he may not make it.

The soldier slowly gazed around, then he reached and felt the bandages on his face. He still seemed fazed and couldn't remember what had happened to him.

"What's your name, soldier?" Valkyrie asked.

He tried to get up but failed to do so. It took him a moment before he said, "Carter, missy."

Carter. The man's eyes soon shut, and he fell back into a deep sleep. Valkyrie smiled weakly. Her body was aching with exhaustion.

I can make it. I can make it for Carter. But she didn't make it and fell over, asleep.

23

STORM

"Valkyrie! *Valkyrie!*"

There was that voice again. But she couldn't see anything. Everything was a gray blur. Valkyrie rubbed at her eyes, but before she was even given the chance to look around, a young Stexphin jumped on her. His violet eyes glowed, and his white patch of hair stuck out among the silky black.

"Knock it off, Virga," Valkyrie said, kicking him away with her feet. Her brother flew back and hit the floor. He sat there looking stumped, one ear hanging lopsided.

Instantly, his expression changed to a wide grin. "Better wake up! Mother's going to be angry if you don't."

Valkyrie quickly sat up and threw off the covers.

Virga began to roll on the floor, laughing hysterically at her reaction.

"What?" Valkyrie snapped. But then she realized what was so funny. Glancing at their bedroom window, it was still dark out.

Fuming, she grabbed a pillow and hurled it at her twin who quickly dodged. As Virga opened his mouth to protest, everything turned gray and blurred out.

Rubbing at her eyes again, she found they were now on the front porch. "Look, there's Father!" Virga cried.

Spotting Father and Frazil walking back from the mountain, the two of them transformed into Stexphin form and raced across the meadow.

But as they were running, the ground began to shake. "*Virga?*" she shouted for her twin. But he was gone.

Suddenly, the ground opened up, and she fell. She didn't stop but continued to flail through pitch black nothingness. There was nothing to grab, nothing to catch her.

"Virga!" she screamed. But wherever he was, he didn't answer.

She came awake with a terrified cry.

Tears pooled in her eyes as she reassured herself it was nothing but another dream. *Where are you, Virga?*

*****

Shivering and numb, Valkyrie rubbed her eyes and sat up off the cold hard ground. She glanced around wearily.

The sun was just barely beginning to rise, and there was a small sheet of snow covering what ground it could. Her ears picked up in alarm as she remembered Carter.

Quickly turning to her side, she saw the soldier lying stiff like a board. She felt his face. It was cold.

Valkyrie quickly took off Cooper's cloak and put it over the soldier. *I can't let him freeze to death!*

She looked at his leg to see it had stopped bleeding. Still, she couldn't bring herself anywhere near the sight.

Around Carter was frozen blood staining the earth. It only reminded her how she didn't help his leg just because she was scared of blood. *You don't think it stopped bleeding because it's frozen, right?*

The soldier's limb didn't look any better than it had earlier. Torn open, she had to guess it was a Swiftmaw's doing. *I wonder if it was Gavin and the rest of them. I most certainly hope not. Maybe this man ran into a bear?*

Clearing her head of any bear notions, she said aloud, "How are we going to get out of here?"

199

Standing up, she stretched her sore muscles. It felt amazing to move around! Glancing back down at Carter, who still lay motionless, she crawled away from the thicket. In the open, she stood there for a second, ears twitching and eyes darting.

Nothing.

It was a beautiful morning with the sun shining across the blue sky; white clouds lingered everywhere; snow covered the ground and trees. Dark clouds could be seen in the distance.

Valkyrie smiled at the view, even as she shivered from the crisp morning air. She walked along the trees for a minute, not sure what she was looking for. *A sign. I guess. A sign that someone might be out here to help Carter. Right. Carter.* She turned and quickly began to head back. A few times, she was scared she had lost her way, but she found the thicket.

Once there, she realized Carter was awake. He was still lying on the ground; his eye was open, and his attention was drawn toward her as she approached.

He was trying to get up but was failing. Valkyrie rushed to his side. Propping himself on his elbows, he eyed her as if trying to figure out if she were an enemy or not.

"Who are you?" he demanded.

Valkyrie hesitated a moment, Frazil's words once more coming to mind. "I don't just give strangers my name," she finally said.

Carter groaned and lay back down. "You're an ornery little girl, missy," he said while wincing.

Valkyrie's ears went back. "Are you okay?" she asked, watching him as he fingered the wrappings on his face.

He scoffed. "I don't know, girl. You tell me, what did you do?"

Valkyrie scowled. "I didn't do anything to you. I helped you." *At least I think I did.*

Carter shifted and let out a painful groan. He looked at his leg in horror. "What happened to my leg?" His voice became desperate, and his eye widened at the horrific sight.

Valkyrie's ears pricked forward, and her face changed to concern. "I'm sorry, sir. I don't know what happened to you. I found you like this last night."

Carter looked as if he was going to say something, but then he stopped. He stared at his leg for a few seconds, looking dazed. Then he whispered to himself, "I remember."

Valkyrie tilted her head. "What?"

His voice sounded sorrowful as he spoke. "I remember now. I remember what happened." He groaned and hung his head back, closing his eye in frustration.

Valkyrie scooted closer to him. "What happened?" she asked eagerly.

Carter's brows furrowed. "We need to get out of here," he said, opening his eyes.

Valkyrie's face showed her disappointment. *I wanted to hear his side of the story.*

Carter noticed. His scowl didn't change as he said: "Why are you out here? You're not alone, are you?" he questioned.

I'm friends with Swiftmaw, but they left me behind.

"I was with a group of scouts, but we were attacked and separated," Valkyrie said, glancing around.

"Where are you from, missy?" Carter asked.

"Smuir," she replied.

"Smuir? Why were you—" Stopping, he eyed her. She wasn't listening, he could tell, as she sat there looking around. Her ears kept pricking from side to side. Carter lifted his own but heard nothing. "What is it?" he asked.

"What *really* happened to you?" Valkyrie said without looking at him. She kept her attention on the woods surrounding them. Carter was bothered by her actions.

"I was with my own company. A few friends of mine and I were sent ahead to scout our path when we were attacked by Swiftmaw. I believe it was three—no, four, I think—wolves. There were only a few of us. We were easily outnumbered.

"I barely escaped. One snatched my leg and dragged me through the forest, but something or *someone* scared it off. It left me to die. I tried to find my way back to my company, but it's hard to do anything with an injured leg." He glanced at his torn limb. "I'm not

201

remembering that much, but I believe you fit yourself somewhere in the story after that."

Valkyrie finally stood up and began to walk away. "I'll be back," she said. "I need to check something out."

Carter was left, bewildered. He couldn't believe she would've just left. He knew there was no way he could defend himself if something were to happen, but at the same time, what could that young girl do to protect him?

Valkyrie walked away from the thicket, keeping her ears at alert. *Did he ever say how big his company was?* She wasn't sure what she was hearing, but it was faint, and whatever it was, it would be a while before it reached them.

Still, it could be Swiftmaw. And what about Carter's story? Could it have been Gavin? But there's not four of them. I'm so confused. Valkyrie shivered. *We need to find a place to go before it gets worse. It's going to keep getting colder.*

She looked down at the slushy snow. It was getting warmer as the sun continued to rise. A faint thundering noise sounded in the distance, and Valkyrie quickly returned to the thicket. Carter was now sitting up. He was already looking healthier.

"What is it?" the soldier asked.

"A storm is coming and fast. There was also something else." She hesitated.

"Something else?" he questioned.

"I'm not sure," Valkyrie replied. She frowned at Carter's leg. *We need to go, but he can't move. I could leave him. No, that's out of the question. But if we stay, we're going to either die in the storm or by something worse. Like bears. I will not leave him! Not like my family did to me. I'll never leave anyone behind.*

Carter seemed to be reading her mind as he asked, "We need to leave. Don't we?"

"Yes. Yes, we do," she said, looking down.

Carter nodded. A determination set on his face as he tried to stand.

Valkyrie ran to his side to help him.

With help, he could stand, but Valkyrie knew they would never get anywhere if she were to have to stay at his side the whole time, helping him walk. Carter sat back down with a heavy sigh.

Valkyrie stood there with her hands over her face. *I've got to think of something.* She ran off, and Carter thought for a moment that she might have left him for good.

*****

When the young girl didn't come back, he looked at his leg and knew something had to be done. Pulling out a nearby frozen cloth, he bent it so it wouldn't be as stiff. Then, taking the torn gray cloth, he wrapped it around his leg tightly.

That should help at least a little bit. He felt his side where his scabbard used to be. *Must have lost it when the wolf had hold of me.*

He decided he needed to try to do something, but what? *I can't believe that girl just left me.* He tried not to feel angry by this. *She's young, and if she stays to help me, I'll just kill us both.* Then his face turned glum. *I'm not going to make it, am I?*

Then the brush in front of him rustled as the young girl appeared. She was holding a pile of long sticks in her arms.

"I found these," she said. Valkyrie dropped the small pile, first lifting a strong sturdy branch, nearly the same size as herself.

Carter took the branch and used it to balance himself as he stood up. *A crutch.* "Good thinking, missy," he said.

Her face beamed.

Carter knew it was bad when he couldn't feel anything in his leg. The young girl turned back to the pile. "Missy, what *is* your name—" he stopped. "That's my scabbard!"

"I was thinking it might be. I found it a little ways from here," she replied as she handed it to him. He kept his balance on the stick as he reached for it. His short sword was inside. He attached his scabbard back on his belt, then took the sword out. It was wet and dirty.

"I'm afraid I didn't find it in the scabbard. It was a few feet away buried in the snow," Valkyrie said.

Carter nodded and wiped it off on his sleeve. It didn't help much, his clothes also being dirty. He placed his sword back in his scabbard.

*****

Valkyrie had left to find a sturdy stick for Carter. But it was harder than she thought it would be. Most sticks she found were either too big or too short or wouldn't be strong enough.

But at least now Carter has something to help him walk. And with his sword, he can defend himself if something bad happens. But she silently doubted he could fight off anything with his injuries.

When another distant thundering crack was heard, Valkyrie knew it was time for them to leave.

They left the thicket with Valkyrie leading. Every once in a while, she would stop and twitch her ears before heading on.

"Do you know where you are going?" Carter asked after a few minutes.

She paused. "Away from the storm, but other than that, no." She twitched her ears again. The thundering noise was behind them. *Good, we're going the right way then.*

It wasn't long before they had to stop for a break. Valkyrie was sure she could've kept going, but Carter had it harder than her. He didn't have a lot of energy, and his injuries slowed him down.

While he rested against a tree, Valkyrie focused on listening for sounds. Silently, she hoped she might hear Ashton. *He's still alive. I know it.*

"You use your ears a lot, missy," Carter interrupted her focus.

"Yes, I do," she replied hesitantly. *What kind of statement was that?* "Don't you?"

"No, at least not nearly as much as you," he said.

"Well, I can hear very well."

"And what about your name? Why won't you tell me?"

Valkyrie shrugged. *I don't know why, but Frazil said not to. And do you really need to know my name?* She felt that small urge inside her again that warned her to keep her identity a secret.

"Well, if you won't tell me, I'm going to give you a name," Carter said.

Great, another nickname. "I'll call you"—he paused and looked her over—"Spade."

Valkyrie raised a brow. "Spade?" she questioned.

"Well, if you don't like it, you can tell me your real name," Carter said stubbornly.

"No, it's fine, but *Spade?*"

"Yes, your hair color makes me think of Spade."

Valkyrie looked at her gray strands. *It used to be prettier,* she thought to herself, still not liking the new dark gray color.

Her stomach churned, and her thoughts went to food. She had eaten in the caves with the Swiftmaw, but that was hours ago.

"Do you have food?" she asked the soldier.

"I might," he said as he began digging into his pockets. "I believe I snatched a few rolls back with my company, but they may have fallen out." He pulled out a small wrapped napkin. "I'm afraid they won't be fresh at all after all I've been through," he said.

Unwrapping the rolls, he gazed at them as if checking to see if they were safe or not.

He handed one to her, then began on the other. Valkyrie took a small bite. The roll was actually pretty good. But she began to worry about how much they had. Who knew how much longer they might be in these woods?

And Carter's condition needed serious care, no matter how good he was at hiding it. She could tell how exhausted he really was and that his injuries were causing him a lot of pain, and yet he bore through them anyway. He was suffering a lot, though, just to be sure that they could keep moving.

Maybe I should save this. I'm not that *hungry, and Carter will—*

You need your own strength if you plan to help him, the purple flashed.

Hesitantly, she finished the roll.

It was getting darker the closer the black storm clouds neared. The sounds of thunder were getting louder. Most of the snow had melted into slush, making the ground slippery with mud.

Carter was struggling terribly to go on. Valkyrie's shoulder began to throb with each step.

Soon, the storm was right on top of them, and they struggled to find a safe path to travel. Carter was beginning to lag behind, but Valkyrie made sure to keep track of him, not wanting to lose him as Gavin and the others had lost her.

She was forced to stop as she waited for Carter to catch up. It was raining hard as the storm continued, making the ground slippery with deep mud.

A splash followed by a loud groan sounded behind her. Turning around, Carter had slipped into the murk. She ran to his side and tried to help him up. He winced as she helped him. "Should we stop?" she asked.

"No, it's fine, I can make it," he replied through gritted teeth.

No, you can't make it. You're just too stubborn to say so. Valkyrie helped him stand and felt heartbroken at his condition. He was covered in mud from head to toe, his hair was matted, and he was soaking wet. His leg was once more bleeding freely through the cloth. And the wrapping on his face was coming undone. He was breathing heavily and shivering uncontrollably.

"We should stop and rest. I'm tired. I need the break," Valkyrie lied. She took off her gray cloak and put it around Carter's shoulders. It was the only thing she had for warmth, but she wasn't nearly as cold as the soldier.

He refused to wear it earlier, not wanting her to freeze. But he knew she could survive the cold or at least better than him. She was barely even shivering.

"Spade," he started, but he began coughing roughly. "You're... you're bleeding," he finished.

Valkyrie looked horrified, but then one glance at her shoulder told her it wasn't that bad. Her dress was stained red around her wound, but she ignored it. "Come on," she began.

Lighting split across the sky. She froze, as did Carter.

They had both seen the same thing: a silhouette shape standing between two trees a little ways ahead of them.

"Was that—" Valkyrie began to whisper, and a loud howl answered her question.

24

SLIDE

Petrified, Valkyrie held her breath, never taking her eyes off the spot where they had seen the Swiftmaw.

The rain continued to pour, hitting her in the face and drenching her clothes. Her cloak had helped keep off most of the rain, but she had now given it to Carter.

The soldier stood there as well, frozen, leaning on his stick with one arm while the other was still around Valkyrie for when she was helping him get up.

Maybe he didn't see us? The sound of splashing footfalls told her wrong. "Go!" Carter demanded.

"*What?* And leave you?" she replied. *Not happening.* They were running out of time.

She finally turned and ran, pulling Carter behind her. Keeping hold of his wrist, she refused to let go. *There's no way I could possibly leave him behind.*

Valkyrie glanced behind her and nearly stumbled to see a large beige Swiftmaw bounding after them. *Diesel? This is bad. Very, very bad. He can't recognize me.*

*****

Carter couldn't keep up with Spade as his feet threatened to trip over each other. *Why won't she just leave me?*

He tried to break free of her grasp, hoping she would let go and leave him so she could save herself, but before he even had the chance, she pulled him roughly into a brush.

They fell in, landing roughly on their stomachs. Neither one of them dared move, let alone breathe.

Carter tried to ignore the pain stinging through his head. The numbness in his calf was slowly growing up to his thigh.

Valkyrie lifted her head, and he quickly put a hand over it to pull her back down. *We can't take any chances.*

They waited in the murk until he couldn't tell what was sweat and what was rain running down his neck. He tried to steady his breathing, but it all felt shallow as if his lungs were closing in, bit by bit.

His head throbbing, he glanced at Valkyrie who had her left ear up and turning from side to side, her right resting over the side of her head where Carter still had his hand over her.

He moved his hand away, and Spade's ear shot up like a bullet at the same time. Even he heard the faint whizzing sound.

He tried to pull her head back down, but it was too late. Valkyrie cried out in pain and ducked, pressing her head against the muddy ground as she held her ears.

Carter forced her hands to move and was relieved the arrow had only sliced through the top of her ear, leaving a terrible long slit straight through the middle starting at the top of her left.

Blood flowed freely, but he knew there was nothing they could do. At least it wasn't her face. *We need to go. They know we're here.* Feeling at his side for his walking stick, he nudged Valkyrie. She looked at him, and he jerked his head back.

She nodded, a brave face replacing her pain as they both began to crawl away from the brush. Grabbing his arm, Valkyrie helped him to his feet.

The two Stexphin walked hastily through the trees. *We need to get out of here. We should be running.* But Valkyrie stopped and listened. Carter frowned. "They're coming," her voice choked.

She reached for his wrist, but he pulled away. "I'll slow you down, just go," he ordered.

"I'm not leaving you," she said, her face showing hurt and determination.

Carter was about to argue back, but a howl stopped him. Exchanging quick glances, the young girl grabbed his wrist, and they ran.

Carter struggled to keep up, but she dragged him along, his feet slipping on the mud while his body screamed at him to stop. Wild barks were behind them.

Dread began to rise. The more he struggled, his body began failing him. It was a horrible feeling, a feeling that he wasn't going to make it. He felt like he was leading on this poor girl and that she was going to die trying to save him. He knew *he* wasn't going to make it. *But Spade might actually have a chance. If she would just leave me.*

*****

Valkyrie was also beginning to feel it was hopeless. She glanced behind her to see Diesel was nearly on top of them. But she wouldn't give up. She couldn't. *Where are the others? Why is it just Diesel?*

Whiz! An arrow sped past. *Of course Diesel is chasing. Courtney is most likely in the trees with her crossbow. But what about Gavin?*

*****

Carter had seen the arrow fly past and feared it would hit Valkyrie, but it didn't. *This is it.* He just couldn't do it anymore. His body was ready to collapse, and he could hardly breathe.

Turning to look behind them, his body gave in. His right leg buckled, and he lost his grasp with Valkyrie as he slipped sideways.

He hit the ground and slid through the mud like a helpless heap. He lost his stick somewhere in the slide and looked up, only to see the wolf descending on him.

*****

210

Valkyrie was about to consider transforming when Carter had slipped and jerked away. Her hand was slick, and she let go of him. She tried to turn, but her own feet slid out from under her, and she fell forward.

The next thing she knew, she found herself tumbling downhill, head over heels. She hit a rock, and her body flared with pain.

When she landed at the bottom, it seemed to be a large mud swamp. She slipped through the murk and finally stopped.

Breathing heavily, she tried to catch her breath, spitting mud, and trying to clear her head when she heard a howl above the hill.

Valkyrie looked up frantically through the darkness and rain. She couldn't see anything. *Carter!* Her hands flew to her mouth as her eyes filled with tears. *He didn't make it.*

Her ears pricked in an instant, and she froze. Still sitting in an awkward position, she had wet clay in her mouth and eyes and was covered in it head to toe.

She listened again, trying to find what the noise might be. *What if it's Carter? What if he* did *make it?* She peered into the dark and slowly stood. There was a faint noise of heavy footfalls in the mud heading for her.

She bolted.

Valkyrie wasn't sure where she was going. The only thing she knew was where she *wasn't* going, and that was toward the wolves. *Why can't they leave me alone? Should I transform? Should I just let them get me? They already took Carter, wasn't that enough?* But thinking of that only reminded her that she had failed to save the soldier. That wasn't even the main thing that weighed her down. It was really just the fact that she had lost a friend. He was left behind.

Valkyrie dashed through the mud, doing her best to keep from crying and slipping. She felt as if an arrow had just been shot through her heart. The loss of Carter was beating her up.

She couldn't see where she was going. The tears in her eyes blurred her vision, and the rain continued to pour. She tried to wipe her eyes, knowing it was useless. What did crying ever do to help anyway? It didn't. It only made her blind and distracted.

Valkyrie looked from side to side, transforming into her Stexphin form as she tried to find somewhere to go. There was the steep hill she had fallen down on her left, and on her right was what looked like a drop-off.

She ran a bit closer to the edge and glanced over the best she could. It was about seventeen feet down before going out into more of the Hickorywood Forest. But there were many rocks and stumps that Valkyrie didn't want to risk hitting, so she ran away from the edge and kept going forward.

The hill on her left was a mudslide, and she doubted she would ever be able to climb up it. But what was in front of her? She couldn't tell.

Ferocious barking came from her left as a dark shape ran straight at her. It jumped down the hill and dove, teeth bared. But right before the Swiftmaw was about to collide into her, she realized that she didn't recognize this wolf.

Open jaws reached for the back of her neck. *Whiz!* And before she knew what was happening, the arrow sank into the beast's side.

But the Swiftmaw wasn't about to let an arrow stop him, and he still snagged the scruff of her neck. *Whiz!* Another arrow came. This time, the wolf jumped and sent them both spilling down the steep hill.

Valkyrie screamed as she fell. The Swiftmaw released her and fell away. But she didn't have any time to think of the wolf as she was in her own trouble. As soon as the grip on her scruff was gone, she transformed back into her Character.

Sliding forward at an uncontrollable speed, rocks and stumps threatened to end her. She tried to grip anything to stop her mad slide when she felt herself in the air.

Suddenly, strong arms grabbed her. She clung desperately to the character who had snatched her. Looking up with wide eyes, she saw it was a Stexphin. He had deep dark brown eyes with light gray hair. A rope was tied around his waist, and he hung on with one arm while the other wrapped around her. She noticed that his uniform matched Carter's, only cleaner. *His company!*

The Stexphin landed on a large stone cropping sticking from the side of the hill grade. He took a few stumbling steps before stopping.

Valkyrie crumbled weakly to the ground as the young man quickly untied the rope from his waist. With one sharp pull, he yanked it from the nearby tree growing from the side of the slope, and a large grappling hook jerked from the branches. He caught the hook and placed it on a belt strapped across his back. "Help is coming," the man said, bending down beside her, placing an encouraging hand on her back.

She looked up through rain and mud to see ten more Stexphin at the bottom of the hill. They couldn't climb the steep slope.

"Little one," a familiar voice said as two hands grabbed her shoulders.

She spun her head to look up. *Ashton!* Instantly, she wrapped her arms around the Character's neck.

Ashton returned the hug, circling his arms around her. "You're hurt," he said, fingering her ear and glancing at her blood-stained shoulder.

She was painfully reminded her cloak had been with Carter before Diesel got to him. *How am I supposed to tell his company he's dead because of me?*

A loud crashing noise behind them caused many of the Stexphin below to flee into the woods or up trees. Only two or three stood their ground.

"Captain," the stranger breathed.

Valkyrie feared to look behind her, but her curiosity got the best of her. Releasing Ashton, they both looked back to see a large avalanche of muddy water, trees, and dangerous shapes hurling toward them with a sliding speed.

The gray-haired Stexphin was quick to act. *We'll never make it to the bottom of the hill in time.* But instead of trying to climb down the hill, he jumped off the rock, calling, "Hurry!"

"Quick, little one," Ashton said, grabbing her hand. He disappeared over the stone, barely catching the edge of the cropping. Valkyrie fell over with him, clinging to his arm.

Looking down, her air came in quick gasps. One fall could be deadly. Her fear of heights drowned her. "Hey!" Ashton snapped, and she looked up at him. "Look at me!" he demanded.

The gray-haired Stexphin grunted as he found grip beneath the stone. "Come on, hand her to me!" he said, reaching out with one arm.

Ashton held out Valkyrie's hand to the soldier, and she panicked. With one hand refusing to let go of her adopted father, she slipped to grip the other Stexphin's.

"Come on!" the stranger encouraged with his trusting eyes. "You have to let go!"

She did, and her heart dropped as she almost missed the man's slippery hands.

Gripping her firmly, the Stexphin pulled her close as Ashton gripped the rugged edges beneath the stone. He swung his legs to help move himself forward.

Hanging beneath the stone, Ashton reached out and grabbed her wrist. Together, the two Stexphin lifted her hands to the rugged stone so she could find a grip under the rock.

As soon as Valkyrie found a hold, the stone began to tremble as the avalanche reached them and began flooding over the top of the cropping with incredible force.

Mud and branches began to swarm beneath the rock, and the Stexphin lifted his legs to dodge it. Ashton followed suit. Valkyrie tried but wasn't strong enough.

A loud crack sounded, and the rock slowly began to slide forward.

"That's unfortunate," the gray-haired Stexphin said as he glanced up at the stone.

"We need to get back on top now," Ashton said. "The mud will slide over the edge the more the rock tips, so we'll have room, but if we stay here, we'll be submerged."

Mud began to rise higher as the rock slid forward, and soon, Valkyrie was in it to her waist. The current was strong, and she struggled to keep her grasp.

Something under the mud snagged her foot, and she lost hold of the rock, disappearing into the sliding murk without even a chance to cry out.

Submerged beneath the clay, she couldn't breathe as she kicked furiously to free her foot. The mud caked her vision, and it was impossible to swim in the thick current.

Finally, her foot was free, and she flailed her arms in the runny thickness. She hit her head on something right as hands grabbed her and pulled her above into the air.

She coughed and sputtered, rubbing her eyes furiously. When she finally opened them, the gray Stexphin had her. Ashton was pushing large sticks and clumps of mud away from the edge of the rock they were now on top of.

With one final tilt, the stone fell forward and began sliding down the hill of mud. Ashton quickly grabbed her, using his body to shield her from flying mud and sticks as they flew forward.

Valkyrie wrapped her arms around the old captain's waist to keep from flying off. The gray-haired Stexphin grabbed the front of the rock for grip then Ashton's forearm.

The Stexphin character was almost standing, his ears pointed back as he squinted against flying mud. Valkyrie looked ahead to see they were hurtling toward the line of trees. A scream rose in her throat but didn't escape her lips.

"In the trees!" the man cried. His earlier uniform which had been clean was now caked in mud as was Ashton's. Valkyrie didn't know what he meant, but the captain did.

The rock surged forward, taking air as it aimed for a tree. Her eyes widened in horror as her life flashed before her.

A branch struck the Stexphin character in the head, and he released Ashton and stone, falling backward, limp as a sack.

Ashton kept an arm around her waist and pushed off the rock, jumping backward as the stone crashed into the tree. She was horrified as the air whipped at them.

Then she saw them. Carter's company in the trees with ropes. One jumped and grabbed the fallen Stexphin character. She felt someone grab Ashton as their fall was abruptly stopped.

The sudden change of momentum made them jerk roughly, and Valkyrie lost her grip as Ashton's hands slipped. He dropped her.

Another hand instantly grabbed her, and after a moment of swinging momentum, the rope which was tied to this new Stexphin character lost its swing.

They hung over the swirling wreck beneath them, the man keeping a firm grip under her arms while she held onto him tightly, refusing to lose grip this time.

"That was so scary!" she whispered, closing her eyes.

"You're safe now," the man said. "Just hold on. Help is coming."

Slowly, they began to be pulled upward as other Stexphin grabbed the man's rope from above.

Valkyrie looked up at this Character and was a little upset to see his clean uniform was now stained with mud from herself.

The man hesitantly smiled down at her as they neared the overhead branches. Looking into his golden-yellow eyes, she saw many secrets and regrets.

Around his right eye, his skin was darker, shaped as a symbol of an ace. She silently wondered if it were a scar or a birthmark.

Hands reached down to pull her up as they reached the branch. She was grateful as her feet were finally set on firm ground, but her legs shook, and she collapsed to her knees.

Her entire body was trembling, and she took in deep grateful breaths.

That was too close.

25

SECOND IN COMMAND

Crowley—Year 317

Crowley stormed out of the king's central room, his anger dangerously consuming him. He fled through the halls, trying to understand what had just happened—not to the king but to himself.

He had screamed at Demoor with all the rage he had been holding in for months. The king's calm attitude toward it all upset him more than ever.

He demanded to be told the truth, and Demoor had said he was too easy to foretell and therefore didn't trust him.

Doesn't trust me? He doesn't trust *me?*

Ahead, Crowley spotted Delta. The old scout saw him and called, "Adviser, wait!"

Crowley wasn't in the mood to talk and ignored him, turning down a separate hall. Delta easily caught up.

They walked in silence for a moment when Crowley saw something in his hands from the corner of his eyes. Turning his head, he saw the man holding a long thin silver chain. There was a ring on the end.

"Where did you get that?" Crowley ordered. He stopped, grabbing the man by his shoulders and shoving him against the wall.

"The girl gave it to me," Delta said, glowering at him, "as well as a message."

"I haven't seen Selah for days. Why would she go to you?" Crowley growled under his breath. His heart panged with stabs of jealousy and hurt.

"She left," Delta said calmly, his stern expression unwavering. "She's no longer inside Smuir. She asked me to return this to you."

Crowley's heart felt as if it had been split in two. *She left?* He stepped back, releasing the scout. Delta dropped the chain in his hand.

"You're lying," Crowley whispered as he inspected the necklace to be sure it really was the same one. He fingered the ring. It was the one he had given Selah.

"Crowley," Delta said in a low guttural voice, "I *don't* lie."

Crowley looked up at him. He never cried and didn't now, but the pain he felt showed clearly on his face. "Why would she leave?" he asked, his voice full of grief.

"It's time for *us* to leave as well," the scout whispered.

"What do they plan to do?" Crowley asked, fighting to keep his voice firm as the subject was changed to a more serious matter.

"We're going to Wingspread. From there, you will become Rotto's second man, and Mt. Smuir will be cleared out by his armies," Delta said.

Crowley didn't answer. He didn't feel any emotion toward Mt. Smuir anymore.

*****

In less than twenty minutes, he found himself once more in the empty town of Smuir, standing beside the fountain in the courtyard. He was quiet most of the way, still not able to wrap his mind around the fact that Selah had left.

She's really gone. He had never felt so abandoned in his life.

Allred and Yoel weren't there. And this time, he didn't care about keeping a distance and willingly stood less than a foot from the others.

Packard stood in front of the fountain with a black eye, several cuts, and over a dozen bruises covering his skin.

"What happened to you?" Crowley asked carelessly.

The young man spat angrily before declaring, "Your stupid girl-friend was tougher than she looked."

With horror, Crowley suddenly realized what happened.

"You murdered her!" he breathed as shock grabbed at his heart with its cold fingers and prepared to squeeze.

Walt shot Packard a dangerous look, then turned back to him. "We didn't *murder* her. He *did* what had to be done," he said calmly. "There's no time to think about it now. Allred gave us directions to Rotto's nearest camp. We'll go there, tell them Mt. Smuir's locations, and—"

Without thinking of his next actions, Crowley's short sword was ripped free in one quick movement. He thrust it forward into Walt's middle. Pulling the red-stained blade free, he found his next victim in less than a second.

Delta crumpled soundlessly to the ground.

"Don't...move," Packard's icy cold voice warned from behind. He felt the sharp point of the young man's sword slowly pushing into his back. "Drop your weapon."

Crowley did as he was told, and his sword clattered against the cobblestone.

"Now——" Packard began.

But Crowley spun sideways, barely missing the sharp point as it stabbed forward.

In one swift movement, he kicked Packard's wrist, sending his blade to fly across the courtyard. Stepping into a stronger momentum, he slammed his fist into the Stexphin's chin, causing the man's neck to snap to the side as he fell backward in a heap.

Crowley didn't stop. Grabbing a handful of Packard's hair, he ripped the man's head back to look up at him. "What did you do to her?" he growled dangerously.

"Why should I tell you?" Packard grunted, spitting in his face as blood began to drip from his mouth. "You'll kill me either way."

Crowley didn't bother to wipe the red saliva from his cheek. He pushed his face close to Packard's. "You're right." In one swift movement, he snapped the man's neck and let the body drop.

He stood there, over dead bodies, breathing heavily as he wiped his face. A dangerous rage seeped through his veins.

"What," a weak voice coughed. "What will you do without us?"

Crowley turned on Walt who laid curled in a ball on the ground as he gripped his stomach.

"I'll go to Wingspread myself. I don't need a stupid camp to escort me," he snapped.

Walt grunted. "I survived wounds worse than this before. I'll survive again." He turned toward Delta weakly. "You didn't have to kill the king's best scout."

Crowley ignored him. He did have to kill Delta. The old scout was the only one who knew by heart where Rotto's fortress was. He would have left instantly and alerted them of Mt. Smuir's location.

Bending over the fallen form, Crowley dug through the dead man's jacket until he found a small sheet. Taking one glance at it, he instantly knew what it was. Stuffing the paper back into his own pocket, he stood and walked to Walt.

Crowley leaned over and gripped a calloused hand over the man's arms. Pulling him to his feet, Walt cried out in pain.

Putting an arm over his shoulders. Crowley began to haul the man with him across the courtyard. Walt grunted the entire time as he tried to limp along while also being tender on his wound.

On the other side of the square, standing in one of the streets, were Yoel and Allred. They watched Crowley approach with steady unmoving eyes. As soon as he reached them, he dropped the injured man at their feet.

Ignoring Walt's cry of pain, he stared hard at Allred. "Give me the map," he ordered. With slightly trembling fingers, the Bandit reached into his deep pocket and pulled out a rolled-up piece of parchment. He tossed it to Crowley who caught it and opened it to be sure that it was the real thing. Satisfied, he pushed it into his own pocket. He turned to leave.

"Wait!" Allred called, sounding bewildered. "How are we supposed to find the camp without that?"

"Ask your friends for another," he said without stopping.

"That was a one-time opportunity! I don't know where to find them *without* that map!"

Still not stopping, Crowley removed the chart. Piece by piece, he tore it apart, keeping some so they couldn't put it back together once he left.

Allred cried in dismay. "How do you expect to find the camp now?" he screamed angrily.

Crowley spun on his heel and shot the man a dangerous look. Yoel was leaning over his friend, Walt, trying to keep him still while he checked his mortal wound.

"I'm not going to the camp!" Crowley bellowed. "I'm going straight to Wingspread, and from there, I am marching into Rotto's fortress and giving him my allegiance!" Saying it out loud made it feel more official, and he straightened his shoulders.

"He'll kill you! That map was the only proof to get you through!" Allred screamed after him as he disappeared into the ghost town.

"No, he won't," Crowley whispered to himself. Reaching into his left pocket, he pulled out a small image of a young boy. He had taken the parchment from Delta's jacket.

The scout has been going many places for a king who is supposedly paranoid to leave the mountain. He studied the detailed sketch of the boy's face. *Rotto will want to know where to find the son of King Declan's daughter.*

Strange shadows came out from behind the boy, large open jaws growling on one half. The boy wore a sweater with small words and a symbol.

"Drakewood. A Bandit School of Music," Crowley read writings on the shirt aloud. *All that's left now is to find the girl who haunts dreams of the future.*

His heart broke at the thought of Selah. *She's not dead. But she did leave the mountain like Delta told me. Like he said, he's not a liar.*

The only place she could've gone is to Rotto, just like in my dreams. After Packard failed to kill her, Delta must've told her a lie to somehow leave the mountain. I was wrong about her being the girl who haunts dreams, but she is still of value to me.

He was coming near the old walls surrounding the solid city of Smuir. The stones were crumbling, and a large section of the wall had been blown apart, proving Rotto had sent an army here once to attack. *He must have left after realizing it was empty.*

Climbing up the crumbled wall, he found his footing and stared out across the large land of Gossamer. It was beautiful. *I'll find you again, Selah. Until then, my skill is needed to serve the higher throne.*

*****

It took Crowley three days until he reached Wingspread Woods. By then, he had cooled down, but the determination in his mind had only grown.

Delta had spoken of telling the location of the survivors from Smuir so that Rotto could clear out the mountain, but after two days, he had decided not even he could do that.

He no longer felt emotion toward the mountain nor respect for the king. He wouldn't mind at all if the community was cleared out.

But then he thought of Malachi and Selah. What would they say if they knew he had betrayed them? Besides, he had been raised there and made good memories, even if the bad outweighed them.

Walking through the woods, he was amazed by the difference here than in Hickorywood Forest. The trees were huge, open, and wide, but the tops were so thick it was almost impossible for the sun to pour through.

He felt right at home. It was also very green whereas Hickorywood was always more brown.

As Crowley went deeper into the trees, he was a little disappointed that he hadn't been attacked yet. *I thought these woods would be flooded with Griefolowtros.*

The smallest noise of the leaves rustling overhead made him whip out his sword. Two large lion-faced creatures dropped heavily from the trees.

Silently, he had never realized how big these beasts were. *At least eight feet. I thought Hollowed were big.*

One of the creatures spread his large wings, and Crowley calculated they had to at least be ten feet long on each side. *They say Rotto's wings are bigger than the Griefs.* A small feeling of excitement mixed with the magnificence of these being's stirred inside him.

One of the Griefs transformed into Character form, his hair falling over his shoulders like a mane of long feathers. "Who are you that would dare come inside these woods?" the man questioned.

Crowley stood straight, no emotion showing on his face. "I'm here as Rotto's second-in-command," he said.

The other Griefolowtros opened his mouth, showing his large teeth as he growled. His wings flapped once before folding back into his sides.

"Second-in-command?" the Grief frowned. "Slecherick holds that position!"

"Not anymore," Crowley said darkly.

The second Griefolowtros swept his tail over the ground, an almost curious sort of expression on the lion's face. Finally, he transformed.

Crowley was surprised to see this man's character form. With short feathered hair, the sides of his head were shaved with marks along his neck.

His eyes were deep sea-blue, an unusual color for a Grief. He stood taller than Crowley and wore an outfit of leather. "I like him," he said in a honeyed voice. "Let's take him."

Instantly, they both transformed, the second man looking up as he did. In Griefolowtros form, his wings were once more spread, and his large mouth opened threateningly.

The first Grief flapped his tremendous wings, causing a current of air that forced Crowley to step back to keep his balance.

The second scratched the ground with his back taloned hands, leaving marks throughout the earth. Finally, he lowered his left wing to rest on the ground and stared at Crowley with his deep blue eyes.

Sheathing his sword, Crowley stepped forward, walking up the wing like a ramp, silently amazed at how strong it was. He set himself onto the creature's back, careful to keep his legs over the wing joint.

Inwardly, his heart leapt to his throat as the beast flapped his wings and leapt into the air. He clutched the mane of hair with a mix of long feathers as they dodged around trees.

In a few moments, Crowley slightly smiled at the coming view. All around them, in the large trees, were open buildings of wood with entrance ramps, many of them built at the base of trunks and opening up inside the timber.

Past the housing was what appeared to be half a mountain. All around the large section of stone were outcroppings and wooden platforms. Together, he could see it was one large barrier, halfway built into the rock and into the woods.

Rotto's fortress. The Grief turned his wings with incredible speed and ducked into the largest platform. His front padded feet hit the ground first before being followed by the sound of his talons smacking the wood.

Before the Grief even stopped, he transformed into his Character form. Crowley wasn't taken off guard for even a second and landed straight up on his feet as the man appeared beside him.

He eyed Crowley with what may have been a side smile. He looked almost impressed that he had landed surefooted. His eyes told the countless stories of characters who had fallen and made fools of themselves.

The ease was instantly forgotten as Crowley looked around. His eyes easily went over the Stexphin and Swiftmaw slaves standing in the shadows along the walls.

His attention was drawn to the large throne created out of thick woven branches three feet off the ground. On the chair sat a large Mislea Raptor.

Even more magnificent than a Griefolowtros!

Crowley walked forward before bowing on one knee. The Mislea in his raptor form had only three wings. The largest one on his right was tucked in and held there by a few straps. But Crowley had seen the missing feathers and bare bones.

What happened? he wondered. The Mislea transformed into Character, and Crowley instantly absorbed the man's physique.

He had short brown hair, the sides shaved, with cunning sharp eyes. His diamond-shaped pupils thinned as they inspected him carefully. But what stuck out the most was the man's missing right forearm. Only a shoulder to the elbow was left, which was terribly scarred all the way up.

Still, he looked strong and muscular, nothing like the bulky Griefolowtros, but no doubt just as powerful. His jaw was sharp with a Grecian-shaped nose.

But not even Crowley could ignore the large bags beneath his eyes, proving the man's restless nights. He almost looked sick. Still, his added features didn't diminish any of the man's agile sharp eyes and working mind.

"Who is this?" Rotto's leisurely voice surprised him.

Not letting himself be announced, Crowley stood, head still bowed with respect. "Crowley Price," he said clearly.

"He claims he's here to become second-in-command," the first Grief from earlier said, his voice smiling as if the thought was humorous.

Use him.

Crowley frowned at the words echoing inside his mind. By the looks on everyone else's uncomfortable faces, he wasn't the only one who had heard the disembodied voice.

His mind felt foggy after the words, and he couldn't think straight. Watching the Mislea Character before him, Rotto nodded firmly.

Crowley smiled wickedly, his eyes turning black as he accepted the burning fog.

26

HALF OF ORACLE

Valkyrie—Year 315

Valkyrie opened her eyes to find she was midair, wind blowing across her face and tossing her hair in every direction.

The sky was blue, and white clouds lingered everywhere she looked. Looking down, she found she was sitting on the back of a large bird of some sort.

Examining the black-feathered creature, she realized the two sets of wings proved this to be a Mislea Raptor.

Her cloak had been returned to her shoulders, and no longer were her clothes heavy with caked mud but instead dry and airy.

Looking at the raptor's head, she questioned, "Virga?"

The Mislea cocked his head back, his eyes flashing purple. Valkyrie smiled and hugged her feather-covered brother as the wind pleasantly blew through her hair.

"But why are you a Mislea?" she asked, sitting back up. "What does this mean?"

The Mislea ducked, and she squealed at the sudden change, grabbing a handful of feathers.

Her joy was instantly stripped away at what she saw next.

Inside the canyon, trees were burning, and war raged everywhere. Stexphin began shooting at them as Virga tried to dodge their flying spikes.

"Traitors!" voices screamed. At the same moment, a well-aimed spear impaled her brother straight through his middle.

"No!" she cried as they crashed to the ground. The impact knocked her off, and she rolled painfully.

As soon as she stopped, she was quick to recover, and she ran back to her brother who was now in Character form.

The long spear stuck from his gut, keeping him partly off the ground as he struggled to lift himself. "Valkyrie," he said weakly as blood ran from the side of his mouth.

Then he slumped lifeless, his head falling back, stretching his neck.

"No, no, no," Valkyrie muttered as sobs began to crawl up her throat. She tried to grab him, at least touch him, but her hands went through him as if he were nothing. He began to fade until nothing but a bloodstained spear sticking from the ground was left.

Valkyrie spun around at the sound of rhythmic marching. Stexphin soldiers began to surround her, all bearing weapons and scowls full of hatred. She cried out when she recognized a few of them to be Mother, Father, Ashton, Dr. Matthias, and Frazil.

"You're a traitor!" they screamed at her.

"No, no!" she sobbed. "I'm not. I'm not a traitor, I promise!"

Suddenly, she came awake with a jolt. Cold sweat ran down her skin, and tears flooded her eyes. Her body ached as her head pounded. The only sound she heard was a shrill pitch.

Where? Everything came back to her, and she remembered the avalanche. Quickly sitting up, she looked around, even as her head flared with pain.

She was in what appeared to be a small tent. Few lanterns were lit, causing a dim glow. Looking down, she saw she had been lying on sheets.

Throwing off her blanket, she quickly stood. Instantly, pain shot through her stiff muscles, and she stumbled. *No, stop. I need to get out of here.* She glanced around for the flap.

229

For the first time, Valkyrie realized she wasn't the only one there. In the corner of the tent, where no lanterns hung, two green eyes reflected a close resemblance to an emerald.

She squinted at the figure before whispering, "Hi."

The Character said nothing, so she hesitantly walked to the tent flap.

"I would stay here," the Character said in a monotonous voice.

Valkyrie frowned. "Who are you? And where am I?"

The Stexphin stepped into the light, his ears lifting to show he was listening. His hair was a light brownish red, but his left ear was completely white.

"You're from Carter's company," she said as she recognized the uniform. Only now could she actually see the symbol. It showed four brown wings. Only one stood out white.

The Character raised his head with concern. "Carter?" he asked.

How do I tell them he's dead? "Yes, sir," she said quietly, looking down. "I knew him."

The man straightened up and walked toward her. He stuck out a hand and said, "I'm Verrader, Carter's brother."

His brother! Dread filled her as she shook the strong man's hand. *How do I tell his brother he's dead?*

"I-I'm… Call me Spade," she said quietly.

"Spade?" Verrader mused, his eyes going distant for a moment. Finally, he blinked and asked, "What happened to Carter?"

Valkyrie looked up and blinked stubbornly against tears. "The Swiftmaw got him, a-and—" She choked and looked down. "It's all my fault. He's dead because of me,"

At first, Verrader looked alarmed, but then his face relaxed into understanding. "No, little one," he said. "You haven't heard, have you?"

"Heard what?" she asked, looking up into the green eyes that closely resembled her own.

"Carter isn't dead."

She almost didn't even hear the rest as tremendous relief flooded her.

"Ace retrieved him before the wolf got to him. The Swiftmaw is most likely dead now. He tried to run away with several arrows sticking from him. We made sure he fell before it was too late."

Valkyrie's face filled with shock. Carter had lived, but Diesel hadn't. *This will destroy Courtney and Gavin.* She blinked several times to shake away the disruptive image.

"So Carter is alive?" she asked, feeling she needed more clarification.

"Yes, he's alive. But barely," Verrader said. His monotonous voice almost made it seem like he didn't really care. "But what happened to him? How did you get into this mess?"

"I found him hurt after being separated from Smuir's scouting party." She stopped as the first real emotion entered Verrader's voice.

"Smuir," he said, looking almost pleased. "I've always wanted to find the abandoned city."

Something in his voice made her say no more. She didn't like the way he showed such interest for the most boring place ever.

Verrader seemed to sense her new train of emotion and left the tent without a word. Valkyrie stood there, stunned. *What am I going to do? Where's Ashton?* Her head spun, and her eyes began to blur.

Quickly, she stumbled back to her "bed" and sat down, grasping her head as the screams of those in her nightmare echoed through her mind.

Her ears lifted to the sound of someone once more entering the tent flap, and she looked up. But her vision had clouded over completely.

Matthias had said her vision would be permanently damaged, but she had found her eyes usually fogged when she became worked up.

Traitor! Your entire family is full of them!

Valkyrie pulled her ears down, hoping to shut out the monotonous voice of Verrader screaming inside her head.

Suddenly, the voice left. She touched her ears, and her eyes came back into focus. The long slit from where she had been shot by Courtney was still there.

*My ear. I can't believe this. This is too much. I just want to go home!
I can't live like this anymore!* Tears pooled, but she pushed them back
as she was reminded of the Stexphin who had entered.

Looking up, her eyes focused on the young man, and she was
surprised to see it was the same gray-haired Stexphin who had saved
her from the avalanche with Ashton.

"Are you doing okay?" he asked kindly.

She nodded, not sure what to say.

"That sure was something, wasn't it?" he beamed.

Valkyrie couldn't help but smile. She liked this Character. He
didn't seem to mind that they had almost died. *He just thinks it is
another normal adventure, I'm sure.*

"So I heard your name is Spade?" he asked.

Again, she didn't say anything. "That isn't your name is it? I'm
guessing Carter gave you that name," he said, still smiling.

Valkyrie nodded.

"Spade was Carter's sister," the man continued, looking distant
as he spoke. "She looked a lot like you. I can see why he would call
you that."

"What happened to his sister?" She was almost scared to ask.

"Gone," was all he said. Shaking his head, his eyes came back
into focus as he looked at her. "I'm Caleb."

"Thanks for saving me, Caleb," she said.

"You're welcome. I've got to be honest with you, it was fun." His
smile was rather charming with his two rows of straight white teeth.

"I thought it was terrifying," Valkyrie confessed plainly.

Caleb laughed.

"How long ago did our *'adventure'* happen?" she asked.

"Just the other night, not too long ago," Caleb said.

Good, I haven't been gone that long. "What is this place?" she
asked.

"We are in Oracle," Caleb replied, walking over and setting
himself down next to her. He rested his arms over his knees as he
continued. "At least half of it. We've been living near the base of
Fontana Cliffs, staying well away from Gloriole." His eyes laughed.

"What are you doing way down here?" she questioned.

"Meeting up with the second half of our company. The Oracle down here has a barricade hidden in the forest. It's kind of near Jayside Coast, which I'm sure you knew where that is."

"No, sorry, I don't, actually," Valkyrie confessed.

"Oh," Caleb looked surprised. "Anyway, we're coming down to meet up with our second half and make plans on what to do about Rotto." He shook his head sadly.

"Him I do know about," Valkyrie said quietly.

"It's a good thing we found Captain Ashton when we did. He explained to us what had happened to his scouting group. He told us he needed help finding you. I can't lie, I thought he was crazy thinking you'd still be out here. I was certain you had been taken." Caleb smiled at her. "I was wrong."

"Where is Ashton now?" Valkyrie asked earnestly.

"He went back to his base with the other survivors from his group. Said to keep you with us until he returns in a few days. Explained he had to report back."

"Was Dr. Trinity with them?" Valkyrie asked, not sure why she was anxious to know if the female Stexphin had made it.

"No, I'm afraid it was only three others," Caleb said, and Valkyrie's heart dropped. *Only three? Out of eight?*

"I have to say," Caleb leaned down to whisper, "Captain Ashton is excellent at keeping secrets, but I know my history. Your group"— Caleb shook his head, a smile playing at his lips—"I instantly recognized the colors. How did your city survive?"

Knowing she wasn't going to say anything, he said, "Well, I had better leave you to rest. I just wanted to check on you and be sure you survived." He smiled and got up to leave. "Wait," he said, stopping at the entrance. "I nearly forgot." He reached into his pocket and pulled out Valkyrie's gray pouch. Her hands flew to her waist as if checking to be sure that really was *hers*. She felt nothing and stared at the gray bag Caleb held.

He tossed it, and she caught it. She looked inside and counted the darts. They were all still there.

"Odd thing for a little girl like you to have. But they're not mine, so I won't bother you about them," he said.

Valkyrie was thankful. *What would I say anyway?*

"And these," Caleb cleared his throat. He looked ready to toss something but then stopped and walked over, handing her the two daggers from Diesel. "I'd better not throw those," Caleb said, winking.

Valkyrie took them in her hands. "Thank you, but why did you have all my stuff?" she asked.

"I didn't. Verrader did. He doesn't trust you at all. Took a bit of convincing to reclaim them. I believe that your property and your own story is yours to keep. Unless, that is, you are willing to share?" he questioned.

"No, not yet," Valkyrie whispered. *I don't know if I'll ever be ready to share my story. And clearly, Mt. Smuir is much more secretive than I ever realized. I wonder how Frazil knew.*

Caleb left her to her thoughts.

I can't believe Carter is alive! I want to see him. Maybe I can? Valkyrie slowly stood. She pressed her hand on the side of her head. It helped it not spin so much.

Edging toward the tent flap, she peeked out. It was dark. Few campfires and talking Stexphin were littered through the trees. Staying close to the tent, she snuck around the back.

I'm guessing Carter's in one of these tents, but which one? There weren't very many tents as most of the Stexphin Characters were sleeping on mats around campfires.

Walking to a tent, she stopped and listened through the canvas, not wanting to just barge in. Loud chatter told her Carter wasn't inside.

There were only four tents, including the one she had been in. After checking the second tent, she looked to see the last two were a little bit away. She wasn't sure how to get to them unseen, realizing there were at least three campfires between them.

Taking a deep breath, Valkyrie slowly began walking by the edge of the brush. She walked casually, knowing she was in sight of all the Stexphin and that they weren't dumb enough to not hear or see her, even if she tried sneaking past.

There were too many of them. Many of the Stexphin characters glanced her way but didn't seem to mind that she was wandering around.

A few did, though. They cast her wary glances while others frowned. Three even stood up and looked ready to go over and talk to her.

Valkyrie didn't look at them and kept walking calmly, even as her heart raced. The Stexphin began talking and soon sat back down. She sighed with relief and finally made it to the tents.

She heard gruff voices in one and sat down behind it, out of sight, and listened. She heard Verrader's voice. He sounded frustrated, no longer monotonous.

"We can't trust her! You're not going to find young girls wandering around in the woods with weapons every day," he said.

They're talking about me. Then she heard another voice. *Caleb.* "If she didn't have weapons, then how do you think she would defend herself? Besides, Captain Ashton explained she was a part of the scouting group." Valkyrie was happy that Caleb was defending them.

"And you think Stexphin just happened to be wandering around and at the same time we happen to see a Swiftmaw camp? I'm sure they're with them," Verrader said. "Why else would the captain—if he even is a captain! He refused to tell us where he's from!"

Valkyrie was sad because what Verrader said was partly true. She was, in fact, with the Swiftmaw, but she wasn't actually *with* them. She would never turn traitor.

"What evidence do you have that the girl is with the Swiftmaw?" another voice asked, one she didn't recognize.

"I don't need any. She was even muttering in her sleep about traitors and Mislea," Verrader snapped back.

Valkyrie didn't want to hear anymore. *I came out to find Carter, that's all.* She went to the second tent and slowly peeked in. To her success, she found Carter there.

He was lying on blankets the way she had been. Valkyrie slowly walked in, this time checking twice to be sure no one else was there.

"Carter?" she whispered, kneeling down beside him. He was cleaned up now with fresh bandages. He looked much better, but she could still hear his shallow breathing, and his skin was wet with sweat.

She saw her cloak, washed and dry, folded nicely nearby. She took it, returning the warm cloth around her shoulders.

"Hey, Carter?" she said again, slowly reaching out and touching his head softly. He was hot, no doubt fighting a fever.

He groaned and opened his right eye slowly. His left eye was covered with bandages around his face. "Spade?" He blinked a few times as if to be sure he was seeing right. "I thought you were gone," he whispered.

"And I you. I'm so glad you're okay. I thought... I thought I had killed you."

Carter smiled weakly and, with one hand, reached up and held Valkyrie's face. "You never killed me. You helped me...saved me," he said.

Valkyrie smiled, and tears lingered at the edge of her eyes. "Carter, thank you so much." She held his hand against her cheek.

He smiled, closing his eyes, and let out a tired sigh. Valkyrie laid his hand down and looked at him with kind eyes.

Opening his eye, Carter glanced at his leg, which was wrapped tightly. "I'm afraid they said they're going to cut it off," he said. His voice wobbled.

After a moment, he seemed to have dozed off.

"Carter?"

He had his eyes closed but nodded to let her know he was listening.

"I'm afraid I have to go, and by that, I mean actually leave," she said.

Carter opened his eyes. "I understand, missy," he said.

Valkyrie nodded, happy he understood. *If I stay, they'll only cause trouble for Ashton when he returns to get me. I know how to get inside of Smuir now. I just need direction.*

"I'll miss you," Carter said.

"I'll miss you too," Valkyrie said with a smile, glad to know the man cared. "They don't trust me enough to stay, and it'll just cause trouble."

Carter nodded. Then his face went grave. "Don't trust Verrader with where you're from. He can't know Smuir is out there," he said plainly.

"What?" she asked, eyes wide with surprise. *He knows.*

"He's my brother, yes. But I'm afraid you can't trust him." Carter sounded hurt by his own words.

Voices sounded outside the tent. "I have to go, Carter," she said quickly.

He nodded a sad smile. "Head northeast. Mt. Smuir is that direction, past the hill grade."

She nodded her thanks, going to the tent entrance. She turned toward him one last time. Carter nodded to her. "Thank you, Spade. Thank you for saving me. Thank you for not giving up."

Valkyrie's heart broke as she disappeared outside of the tent. *Will I ever see him again?*

She had left almost a moment too late. Behind the tent, she hid in the shadows as a few Characters entered the canvas-laid structure.

As they began a quiet conversation with Carter, she turned and quickly ran into the woods, staying low and ducking from brush to tree.

Transforming into her Stexphin form for speed, she stayed in the shadows as best as she could. Silently, she wished she could transform into her Swiftmaw form which was much faster combined with her Stexphin blood.

After a while, she sighed with relief, believing she was far enough from the campsite.

Transforming back into her Character, she looked around. *Now to find the northeast.* Her ears shot back at the sound of approaching footsteps. But she had heard them too late.

27

TRAITOR

Valkyrie lost vision completely as a hard punch hit her in the back of the head. She fell forward, feeling as if her skull had just been split open.

Blinking rapidly, she turned on her back to see who her attacker was but wasn't given a chance as another fist planted itself into her face.

Fazed, dizzy, and in pain, she couldn't even find the tears that would normally be coming. Her nose began to bleed, but she didn't notice from her spinning head.

For less than a second, her mind cleared, and she barely glimpsed who it was before a soundless punch landed on her sore shoulder. This time, she screamed.

She kicked as hard as she could to get Verrader away from her. She tried to scramble to her feet, but the crazy man was quick, and he sent another crushing blow to her middle, causing her to stumble backward.

She gasped for air, which felt impossible, as if her lungs had been crushed and her very life was being sucked away.

She didn't have a moment to think of a plan or even wonder why Carter's brother was attacking her. Verrader jumped at her with a dagger in his hand. So she did the only thing she knew she could do. She transformed.

Valkyrie transformed into her Swiftmaw form where the pain was still agonizing, but she felt stronger.

She turned on the maniac who didn't look shocked at all but rather pleased. "I knew it!" he laughed wickedly. "Rotto sent me to find you, you little scum!"

Valkyrie didn't have time to let this evil Stexphin get away with her secret. *Rotto?* Verrader was enraged as he dove at her again, blade bared.

She dodged away from him, her own anger rising. *This is Carter's brother!* "You're a traitor!" she screamed at him, which came out sounding more like a wild bark.

With one strike, she shoved the man away, leaving four long red marks across his stomach, tearing through his shirt.

Verrader didn't seem to notice. "I believe you are referring to yourself!" he shouted.

Valkyrie was taken aback, and her hesitation was all the skilled Stexphin needed as his knife found her.

She had seen it coming too late and put her arm in front of her to block it. She cried out in pain as the sharp edge cut deep into her forearm, splitting her skin open.

Her mind had never felt so active before, and she kicked the man away, transforming once again into Character. She grabbed one of Diesel's daggers and threw it at the Stexphin. Verrader wasn't fast enough, and the blade found him.

He screamed more from anger than pain as he ripped the blood-stained dagger from his side and dropped it on the ground.

Valkyrie knew his wound was mortal, and he knew it too. He stared at it, then turned and ran into the darkness, limping as he went.

Valkyrie was too weak as her head once again started to spin. For the first time, she tasted the blood running down her face. She could hardly believe what had just happened.

Her legs collapsed beneath her, and she fell to the ground with a thud. Her ear pressed against the earth, she could hear the vibrations of someone coming toward her.

She feared it was Verrader. He was coming back to finish her. But everything was a raging blur. All she could hear was a loud shrill.

*****

Caleb left the tent in a rage. Verrader had managed to make everyone believe Spade was a Kovanee and they should be rid of her. He even claimed to have seen her transform.

Caleb needed to do something. But what? *Verrader has always been overenthusiastic to stir up trouble inside camp. I don't believe Spade is a Kovanee.*

He walked to Carter's tent with Ace by his side. Before he entered, he saw Verrader standing outside the meeting tent, fuming as he stared in their direction.

Caleb didn't have time for him. He needed to talk to Carter. *If he's awake, then perhaps he can give me answers about Spade. Perhaps he knows if she was just a close relative to that doctor she had spoken of or something. Maybe she even told him enough about herself to prove she's not a traitor.*

He still had some time to save her before Ashton got back. The old captain had asked that he take care of her until she woke up. *But if Carter doesn't have anything? What then? They'll tie her up in chains and treat her like a prisoner if Verrader doesn't kill her first.*

Silently, he was still considering joining the other half of Oracle. Their leaders, Challis and Kaden, were some of the kindest people he had ever met. *They wouldn't even question Spade.*

Caleb entered the tent with Ace at his heels. Carter was lying there, awake. He looked tired and sad. Going to the man's side, he put a hand on his shoulder while Ace stood at the entrance.

Ace was a strong blond-haired Stexphin with yellow eyes and a special symbol around his right that was shaped like an ace. It was where he had received the nickname.

Carter turned his attention towards Caleb. "Where's Verrader?" he asked, his voice sounding tired.

"Verrader? He just left the meeting tent. Fuming, he was," Caleb replied. His voice still had a hint of energy as he spoke these words solemnly.

A look of fear flashed over Carter's eyes. "You came to ask me about Spade, didn't you?" he said.

"Sure did," Caleb said, his casual smile appearing. "I need something to throw in her defense. Nobody trusts her."

"It's hard to trust people these days," Carter said weakly. Carter looked wary.

Caleb knew that he trusted him, but did he trust him enough?

Caleb nodded. "Carter, you can trust me."

"I know I can," Carter replied, and Caleb noticed he was eyeing Ace.

Looking back at his friend, Caleb jerked his head back for Ace to leave. He looked offended but nodded and left the tent.

"She's gone," Carter said.

"What?"

"She left seconds before you guys came in."

"*What?* Where is she heading?" Caleb asked, panic rising in his voice.

"Northeast," Carter said. His voice was getting weaker the more his energy drained.

"Mt. Smuir," Caleb mused. "It really is true. Do you know where it is?"

"I know where everything is. Smuir, accordingly, is beneath the mountain. You'll find an entrance to their tunnels near a large boulder with strange carvings in it," Carter said with a grunt as he tried to lift his head. "But why doesn't anyone trust her?"

"Your brother claims he saw her transform. He says she's Kovanee."

Carter became quiet and he looked down, deep in thought. "That can't be true," he said, looking back up to meet his eyes. "I trust her. She's proven I can trust her with my life even. If she really was what Verrader claims, she would've left me."

"That's good. It is indeed hard to find good trust these days," Caleb replied. "But sending her out there to find the city of Smuir by herself?"

Carter's eyes shut, and for a moment, Caleb thought he had fallen asleep. He sighed and got up to leave. Carter needed the rest, and he didn't want to keep that from him.

"Verrader."

Caleb turned back to see Carter's eyes wide. He cocked his head.

"Verrader, you can't trust him. You need to find Spade. Verrader will kill her."

"What are you talking about, Carter?"

He tried to answer but was taken over with a coughing fit. "Find her," he forced out. "Caleb, find Spade."

The fear in his voice scared him. Nodding firmly, he turned and left the tent.

Outside, he found Ace waiting. "Were you listening?" he asked, knowing his friend well.

Ace nodded, no guilt playing in his eyes. Caleb shook his head, then smiled. "I had a feeling you might. You've always been quite the eavesdropper." He chuckled.

"Where to?" Ace asked.

"We have to find the girl. She might be in danger," Caleb said, getting serious.

"What if Carter's fever is getting to his head?" Ace shared his concerns. "He could be saying things."

"I promised him we'd find her," Caleb replied. "Let's go." Going into the trees, he grabbed a low hanging branch and pulled himself up with Ace close behind.

They were fastest by trees, skilled to remain silent yet swift jumping from one limb to the other.

After a few minutes, Caleb slowed to a stop, holding up a hand for Ace to follow suit. He twitched his ears. "Listen."

A small scream was heard in the distance. "That was close," Ace said. "Do you think it was her?"

"We'll find out soon. Let's go down." The two of them dropped to the ground and took off toward the sounds of struggle.

"No!" Ace cried as they rounded a large brush to see the motionless body of a young Stexphin. Caleb ran to the girl's side, dropping to his knees.

"Is she—" Ace began.

"She's about to be if we don't do something about it," Caleb snapped. Putting his arms beneath the girl's frail body, he lifted her.

"But we can't go back to the company," Ace said. "They won't accept her. Not after what Verrader said."

Caleb glowered. "Verrader. He did this to her!"

"But if Verrader did it, where is he? And why wouldn't he have finished her off completely?" Ace asked.

Caleb looked troubled. "I'm not sure," he said as he turned his head and listened to Valkyrie's breathing. "But if we don't do something fast, she's not going to make it. Ace, do you have any sort of 'medic' training?"

Ace looked taken aback. "No, I'm afraid I never wanted anything to do with blood."

Caleb frowned. "Well, I don't either." He looked around the dark woods. "We should return her to Smuir," he said.

"Mt. Smuir? Do you know the way?" Ace asked.

Caleb nodded, and he looked around for a minute before heading the direction he was sure was northeast.

Ace was about to say something but stopped. Something glistened on the ground. He went over and picked up a dagger. It was covered in blood.

Caleb eyed the knife. "That's hers! She must have injured him. I'm sure she put up quite the fight."

Ace nodded as he frowned at the blade.

"Ace, we need to go," Caleb said. He started walking through the woods while Ace trailed behind, frowning while he pondered on his own ways. After a long silence, Caleb asked, "Ace, what's troubling you? I can tell you're upset."

Ace hesitated. Caleb could always tell when he was upset without even looking at him he always seemed to just know. "It's this blade," Ace finally said walking up beside him. "It's, well, it's not a Stexphin's blade. I know this craftwork. It's Swiftmaw."

Caleb slowly nodded. Ace was very good when it came to weapons. He had grown up helping Rotto's blacksmiths. Nearly his whole family worked for the Mislea.

He had been trained and raised to fight for Rotto. But he was troubled by it and afterward escaped. Only Caleb and a few others knew this secret.

Ace tried hard to forget his past and help stop the wicked Mislea, but it was hard for him. The guilt was too great.

"Perhaps she found it or stole it?" Caleb suggested, trying to find the best ideas on how she could've come to own such a blade.

"Caleb, Verrader might be right," Ace said.

Caleb fumed but took a deep breath and sighed. "I don't want to believe she's a traitor. But I can't deny the evidence. What we are accusing her of is very serious."

Ace nodded in agreement. The two Stexphin walked for a while without saying anything.

Finally, Caleb broke the silence. "Carter trusts her," he said. "Once we get to Mt. Smuir, we can find somebody and ask. She must have family or someone there. If they don't know who she is, then we have every right to suspect her." Caleb was huffing as he spoke.

Ace knew that carrying Spade was using his energy. "Let's take a break," he suggested.

"No," Caleb said with determination. "I have to bear through it if we want her to make it." He looked at the still face of Valkyrie. Sorrow filled his heart.

"Here," Ace said. He held out his arms to take her. Caleb hesitated, then passed off the motionless form of Valkyrie.

Ace took her with ease, and they resumed their walk. Caleb stretched his arms as they went, glad to move his stiff muscles.

Ace realized Valkyrie was lighter than he had suspected. But, also, holding her made him feel sick inside. He hated pain. Whether it was on him or another Stexphin, he couldn't stand it. Valkyrie had a long gash down the front of her arm. *That's going to leave a horrid scar*, Ace thought to himself.

She was also covered in bruises, and blood ran down the front of her face and soaked the back of her head. He pitied the young girl and began to fear she wouldn't make it. Her breathing was shallow and was coming in short ragged breaths.

"How much farther, Caleb?" Ace asked.

"We should nearly be there. Just hold on a few more minutes," Caleb said, casting Valkyrie a wary glance.

They considered themselves lucky as they walked the dark tunnels of Smuir and were met by a soldier named Joaquin who quickly led them to the hospital.

There, a doctor named Matthias took over, and soon, the two young men found themselves standing in the shadowed dark tunnels of a place they hadn't even known existed a few hours before.

"I can't believe it," Caleb whispered as they walked through the dim passages. "The entire community of Smuir isn't just a ghost story told at campfires"

"I want to know how they've survived down here for so many years. What do they eat?" Ace smiled, his growling stomach giving him away.

Before Caleb could reply, an older Stexphin came sprinting around the corner, running into him. Caleb tripped back into Ace, and all three of them ended in a groaning heap on the ground.

"I'm sorry," the Stexphin character grunted. "I'm not used to people using this passage."

Caleb propped himself on his elbows and looked at the man. "Captain Ashton?" he questioned.

Ashton looked back at him, and recognition flashed between them. Getting to his feet, the captain was quick to help them up.

"Caleb," he addressed him, confusion clear on his face. He turned toward Ace, then stopped and stared hard, frowning.

"Ashton," Caleb said, turning the captain's attention back.

"What are you doing here?" Ashton asked before he could say anything else. "How did you find us?"

"Carter, our friend, you saw him," Caleb replied. "He told us how to get in through a secret passage."

Ashton frowned before hesitantly saying, "I knew I recognized him. I just don't remember what unit he may have come from. We've had a few groups of soldiers stopping in here. All of them are led by a former Character from Smuir who left after the queen."

"Where were you going before we stopped you?" Ace asked, reminding the captain.

Ashton's eyes widened as he remembered. "Right, sorry, I have to go. I got word of my daughter in the hospital."

Caleb hesitated, suddenly seeming to piece it all together. "Wait, your Spade's *father?*" Caleb asked.

"Spade?" Ashton questioned as he walked past them. "I can't thank you enough for bringing her back. She means the world to me. Please excuse me, I'll find you two later." And with that, the Captain resumed his run but not before casting Ace another wary glance.

"We can stick around. I have a few questions to ask him anyway," Caleb smiled, slapping Ace's shoulder, encouraging him to follow him through the unknown tunnels.

*****

Ashton nearly ran into Matthias as the hospital doors opened. "Doctor," Ashton breathed, looking at his friend with questioning eyes.

Matthias shook his head and pulled him away from the entrance. "Ashton," he started quietly. "I can't promise she's going to make it. She's really bad off."

"But she's survived before!" Ashton urged gruffly.

"This was a full-on attack, Captain," Matthias frowned before going soft again. "I have to go."

As he was left alone in the tunnel, the all too familiar hurt from when he lost his wife and daughter years ago returned. *An attack? Who would have done this to her? I need to find Caleb.*

246

28

A NEW DISCOVERY

Wandering through the tunnels of Smuir, Caleb and Ace met a young Stexphin named Jamin and a group of his older friends.

With a strong accent, blond hair, silver eyes, and long legs, the boy seemed nothing like a warrior. They were even more shocked to hear he was nineteen.

Jamin was quite the talker, and repeatedly, Caleb asked him, "Come again?" The boy's accent was nothing he had ever heard before.

Jamin went on to explain to them he was the youngest fighter in his group and also the only one who wasn't from Elkhorn.

They were led deeper underground until they came to a large open cave. Caleb gasped at the view.

A large lake underground with all sorts of vegetation grew everywhere. Most of the plants he had never heard of before, and some glowed multiple colors, lighting the cavern with beauty.

"I know, righ'?" Jamin smiled. "I was jest as sur'prised as y'all when I saw this place. It's a'mazing this is wha' they survive off."

"Wow," was his only response.

It wasn't long before they were back to lively chatter as Joaquin showed them how to eat most of the plants. Caleb enjoyed every minute of it while Ace stood at a distance.

Caleb loved meeting new people and getting out, Ace, however, didn't enjoy it nearly as much. Sometimes, he felt as if strangers could read his mind and instantly know his deepest secret.

Half the time, Ace guarded his thoughts, distracting himself with their surroundings because he was so afraid characters actually could read his past.

He examined the beautiful underground cave but soon turned his attention back to his friend as Jamin asked how they got here which soon led to Caleb explaining their recent "adventure."

"Our company was travelling through Hickorywood Forest," Caleb began. "When we stopped for the night and sent scouts ahead, we sent a man named Carter, his brother, and a few others. We waited for hours, but they didn't come back.

"Verrader, Carter's brother, finally returned, injured. He claimed they were attacked by Swiftmaw, and the others had been lost. Hearts heavy, we knew we couldn't stay there, so we packed up to move out.

"When we sent out more scouts, Ace and I went as well. A storm moved in, and we found a Swiftmaw, so we trailed him from the trees. He didn't appear to be a threat but soon met up with another.

"After the two Swiftmaw split up, our group was separated as well. Ace, Verrader, and I followed a white wolf. That's when we ran into a few Smuir scouts who had survived a recent ambush. Captain Ashton was a part of the group. Anyway, he joined us in our trailing, saying he was still looking for survivors from his band. When we caught back up to the Swiftmaw, he was trying to chase Stexphin characters below.

"We were shocked to see it was our friend, Carter, with a young girl who the Captain claimed was from his band. It was amazing watching them push through, and we would have jumped straight down to help if it weren't for another Swiftmaw in the trees.

"She was feisty and sent one of our friends crashing to the ground before making her own retreat. With only a little time left to save the others, we made a quick plan, and I was sent to go ahead.

"Carter and the girl were separated, and Ace was quick to save our friend and stick the Swiftmaw a few times. So while Carter was taken by Verrader and another, Ace, Ashton, and I continued.

"Now, a black wolf—almost thought he was Hollowed, but he wasn't—bearing no symbol tried jumping the young girl. I was on the hill grade but couldn't reach her. Thankfully, Ace shot a few arrows before jumping down trees to the bottom where he met with the other half of our scouting party and the few survivors of Smuir's band.

"The storm, however, had caused large mud to slide down the hill grade. Ashton had slid down ahead of it and got to the girl and me, but we were trapped on an outcropping in the middle of the slope." Caleb paused, and Jamin waited with wide eyes as he hung on every word.

"To sum it all up, we went back to our campsite and cared for our injured friends while Ashton had to return. The young girl tried to leave for Smuir on her own, but"—Caleb bristled—"Verrader betrayed us. By the time we found her, she was almost dead. Ace and I knew we had to return her to Smuir, and therefore, we ended up here."

Ace slightly smiled. This was definitely going to be one of the main stories told at their next campfire. Caleb was great at telling stories, and everyone always enjoyed to listen.

"That's one load of a story," Jamin smiled. "Joaquin tell them a'bout the time y'all and I found the blue wolvers carcass down near Shall-gar-ee—"

Ace missed the rest of the boy trying to pronounce the word as his skin tingled with the familiar feeling of someone watching him.

Then he locked eyes with Ashton. The captain stood near the cave entrance, leaning against the wall with his arms folded across his chest.

"Caleb," he hissed, getting his friend's attention.

Jamin noticed the captain as well and seemed to understand. "Ashton's fun," he said. "I used tah be scared of hem' but he's become on by less gruff since he's adoptive-ed daughter."

"Adopted?" Ace asked, stopping with a frown.

Jamin nodded.

Caleb nodded his thanks, then said farewell to his new friends as he and Ace walked toward the captain.

Ashton's ears were back, and he looked upset. Caleb and Ace exchanged glances. They both thought the same thing. When they reached him, he said in a low gruff tone, "I need to talk to you."

They nodded and followed him out. He led them down a hall, then up some stairs. When he reached the top of the stone stairs, he turned down another hall and finally led them into a small library.

They sat at a small table, Ashton put his hands over his head before finally glancing at them with a sad expression. "Thank you, again, for saving her," he said. "I'm grateful that you brought her back to me. Even though I'm afraid Dr. Matthias said she won't make it." His voice cracked.

"Captain," Caleb started carefully, "we heard Spade is your adopted daughter."

"That's true," Ashton affirmed.

"How long have you had her?" Ace asked.

"I adopted her only a few months ago. Her own family was killed, and she was found half-dead in the tunnels of Mt. Smuir."

Caleb and Ace nodded. They were both thinking the same thing.

If she was adopted only a few months ago, she still had plenty of time to be a traitor. Neither of them wanted to believe it. They weren't sure if they should.

After a small silence, Caleb stood, pulling Ace up with him, saying, "Thank you for letting us talk to you, Ashton."

Ace nodded.

Ashton looked at Ace and began to say something, but then stopped. Finally, he stood and said in a low whisper. "I heard the end of your story. This man, Verrader, where is he now?"

"He escaped in the woods." Caleb shook his head shamefully. Ashton nodded.

"Before you leave the mountain, King Demoor speaks with everyone," Ashton changed the subject.

"We understand," Caleb replied.

"I'll send a messenger before morning." With one more questioning glance at Ace, he turned and left the room.

"Have you met him before?" Caleb asked his friend.

"No," Ace said quietly.

"He seems very uncomfortable with you. He wouldn't know. I mean, you don't think he suspects you, do you?"

Ace sighed deeply, and his face contorted with sorrow. "I most certainly hope not. That was my past, and I regret every single moment of it."

Caleb placed an encouraging hand on his shoulder. "It's not your fault you were brought up that way. We don't get to choose what family we're born into, but we do choose our actions on how we live with it. You, my friend, have chosen this path, which, in my opinion, is the right one."

Ace smiled and slowly nodded.

*****

Caleb and Ace had left Smuir, returning to the Oracle, and Ashton visited Valkyrie every day in the hospital. She still wasn't conscious, and Matthias said her chances were very low.

After a few days, nothing changed. Matthias allowed her to be moved to her room. It broke Ashton's heart to see her scars and bandages.

He sat there in her room one day, listening to her shallow breathing. He was about ready to get up and leave when she began moaning. He quickly returned to her side.

"Valkyrie?" he asked.

Her low moans soon left, and she began to sweat as her breathing quickened.

Ashton knew he should get Matthias, but he was scared to leave her. He held her hand and whispered soft words. She began to calm. He sighed.

Matthias will want to hear this. She hasn't moved at all since Caleb brought her back. And it was true. Valkyrie had been in the same condition for the past week. Her breathing was always shallow, and she never moved. Until now.

"Please wake up," Ashton whispered. When nothing happened, he decided to go talk to Matthias. He went to the door and was about to exit when Valkyrie began screaming in pain.

Her eyes were still shut, but she tossed and turned in the covers. Ashton was about to rush to her when he stopped and gasped.

As she tossed and turned, she was beginning to look different. Feathers grew along her arms, and before Ashton could react, a Griefolowtros had replaced his daughter.

The Grief stretched it's long wings in the small room, and one of them found Ashton. He hit the ground with a thud. There was a cracking noise, and the dresser standing against the wall was hit and fell forward, landing on top of the captain.

He groaned as a large number of pains filled him. Glancing back up, the Grief was gone, and Valkyrie was back on her bed, panting and moaning.

Ashton crawled out from the dresser and coughed. Quickly, he stood and stared at Valkyrie. *Did that really just happen? I must be dreaming.* But one glance around the wrecked room told him he wasn't. *What just happened? That's impossible.* Ashton stood there, stunned, trying to think of every capable way how that was possible. *I can't tell anyone this, not that they would believe me anyway. She would be killed on the spot. Who else knows? Does she know? She has Stexphin ears, but I've never seen her transform. A hybrid perhaps? Does this mean she works for Rotto?*

He stood there with so many questions and very few answers swarming his mind. How long did he stand there? Now he wasn't sure, but when he finally left, night was falling.

29

NO MORE SECRETS

Valkyrie groaned softly. *Sore, so sore.* She heard chatter and tried to regain consciousness. *Okay, where am I? What's happened?* She let the questions swarm and tried to answer them. Then she heard a voice.

"Father?" she asked quietly. She slowly opened her eyes to see Ashton and Matthias standing at the end of her bed.

"This is impossible," Matthias said, shaking his head.

Valkyrie was a little disappointed. She had been so sure she had heard Father's voice.

"Valkyrie," Matthias asked. "How are you feeling?"

Her eyes were drooping. She was still tired. It took her a few moments to really understand what Matthias had asked her.

"Tired," she said. "Really, really tired."

He nodded, then turned back to Ashton. She realized he was holding one of her darts. It was empty.

"I'd be careful," he whispered. "I'm not sure how she's awake, but she is. I have a few other patients to attend to. I'll send Alania over if there's any trouble." Matthias walked away, and Valkyrie realized she was in the hospital.

She groaned. *I'm always here. Always! Can I ever have a break from this nightmare of a room?*

253

Ashton turned toward Valkyrie as a weak smile appeared on his face. He still hadn't told anyone what had happened a few weeks ago. He also felt a small resentment toward her now.

"Valkyrie," he said quietly. She turned a tired face toward him. "I want you to know that—" He stopped. Maybe now wasn't the best time to talk to her. *I should wait until she's feeling better and more awake.*

He looked back at Valkyrie to realize she had fallen asleep again. He sighed. *What am I supposed to do? I can't bear to live with this secret. I need to at least be able to talk to her.*

He bent down and softly kissed the top of her head, then began to walk toward the exit. But then he stopped. Valkyrie had been moved back to the hospital that day.

She had been moaning and groaning a lot, and he had insisted that she be brought back where Matthias could keep an eye on her. The doctor had asked permission to use one of her strange darts. A few minutes later, she woke up.

But what if she goes crazy again? Then what? Her secret will be revealed. Ashton hesitated. He feared to leave her but had other duties he needed to attend.

He began briefly walking toward Matthias but then stopped, changed his mind, and left the hospital. *She'll be fine, I'm sure of it!* But doubt crept into his heart.

*****

Valkyrie awoke with a memory of Virga, and she sat up. It was dark in the hospital, and she wondered how late it was. She checked herself over and realized she wasn't in pain.

Her head felt fine, no more bruises and cuts. But a large ugly scar bore across her arm. *No!*

She panicked as she remembered all that had happened. *Verrader, he tried to kill me! I actually thought he had succeeded. How did I get back here. A-And Carter and Caleb? What happened to them? I need to get out of here and find Ashton. I can't wait a moment longer. But what do I tell him? The truth? No, that will absolutely ruin him, and—*

Her thoughts were interrupted when she heard someone. She looked around the dark room, then spotted Alania entering the hospital with a small lantern. She watched as she checked on the patients.

The nurse was nearly at her bed, so Valkyrie quietly lay down and pretended to be asleep. She was not ready to talk, especially not to Alania.

She saw the light from the lantern glow on her eyelids and knew the nurse had stopped by her. She thought she heard a sigh before Alania walked away.

Valkyrie opened her eyes. *I need to find Ashton.* She felt healthy again, and she wanted to be sure the captain was all right himself. She looked to see Alania on the other side of the hospital and quietly slid from her bed.

She walked toward the two doors and opened one, freezing as it creaked. She could feel the nurse's eyes on her, but to her surprise, Alania let her be.

Sliding through the door, she began to walk down the hall. She scurried through a few tunnels and finally came across a familiar door.

She entered slowly and walked into the small room. She recognized the door that led to her own bedroom but walked toward Ashton's.

Valkyrie opened the door and peeked into the dark room. She could barely see a form in the bed. "Ashton?" she whispered. She slowly crawled onto his bed and shook him. "Ashton," she said again.

He let out a small groan and opened his eyes. He peered at her, and she noticed he had tears in his eyes. "Valkyrie?" he questioned, blinking as he came to himself.

"Yes, it's me," she said, smiling.

"You're awake." Ashton embraced her, and Valkyrie felt joy surge through her. She hadn't ever realized how much she truly did love him.

Dane had never treated any of his children with such love the way this captain did. *Why didn't Father love me? Why didn't any of them? Why wasn't I worth it to them?*

As Ashton held her in a fatherly embrace, she felt a comfort that told her Ashton was her father. And he truly thought of her as his daughter. Even if it wasn't by blood.

*****

Morning came, and Ashton sat Valkyrie down to talk to her. "I want you to know," he began hesitantly. "I—well, something happened to you while you were out."

Valkyrie's stomach churned. Somehow she knew what he was going to say. "Did I hurt anybody?" she whispered as she looked down.

Ashton looked surprised. "So you know?" he said.

Valkyrie nodded. *I can't believe I transformed. They're definitely going to kill me now.*

"Ashton," she whispered, "please tell me what happened."

He nodded solemnly, seeming to understand the predicament she was in. "You weren't in the hospital, and no one else knows except me," Ashton started.

Valkyrie sighed with relief. "But what happened? Did I hurt you? And where was I then if not in the hospital?"

Ashton sighed. He was clearly frustrated. He was still having trouble believing what he had really seen. "It's fine, you were in your room. I still haven't had time to clean up the mess. But, Valkyrie, I want you to tell me right now, how is that even possible? Did your family work for Rotto?" Ashton asked. His voice was low and completely serious. It kind of scared her.

His last question shocked her. She wasn't sure if her family worked for the Mislea. Frazil had claimed he was doing something to save them but wouldn't say what. Father and Mother never even spoke of the war. She herself had spoken to Swiftmaw twice now. *But did I betray them? I most certainly never meant to.*

"Valkyrie!" Ashton said, raising his voice. "Answer me! Have you turned us to that devil?"

Valkyrie trembled. She felt the tears rising in her eyes. *No, I can't cry. That never helps—never, ever, ever!*

"I don't know," she whispered. She looked up to see Ashton had his own tears in his eyes. He looked hurt, betrayed, and upset. "I-I would never betray Stexphin Characters. I am a Stexphin. At least I used to be. But I have never done anything to trick or turn anyone in." *At least I'm sure I haven't ever done anything to turn them in. Have I?* Valkyrie tried to think of every conversation she had with Gavin, Courtney, and Diesel. *I don't think I ever mentioned much about Stexphins.*

"I have spoken to Swiftmaw scouts before, a-and I've seen one of the armies, but I never—" Ashton stood and turned his head away.

"Ashton, I—" Valkyrie began, voice breaking.

"Go," Ashton said, pointing a finger to her bedroom door. "Go to your room."

Valkyrie was shocked. *I'm being sent to my room?* She could no longer hold in her tears. It tore a hole in her heart knowing that Ashton didn't trust her anymore. *I was wrong about him thinking of me as his daughter. He sees me as nothing but a traitorous monster.*

Running into her room, she quietly shut the door behind her. She would've run to her bed and cried, only to find the room a mess. The dresser was knocked over along with a few other things, and her blankets were on the floor.

Valkyrie sank to her knees and sobbed. *Is this really who I am now? Am I a pawn of Rotto? Is that what my family was?*

Your family doesn't define who you are, the purple flashed.

She roughly wiped her eyes, and standing, she looked around her wrecked room.

I do not work for Rotto! Ashton may not trust me now, but I have to show him that he can. I wasn't perfect for my family, but I need to prove myself worthy being loved by him. She glanced once more around the room. *It won't do much, but I may as well start with fixing up the mess I made.* Valkyrie began to clean, starting with the bed as she tried to think of ways to earn Ashton's trust back.

She finished picking up the floor. then stared longingly at the fallen dresser. *I'm never going to be able to pick that up.* But she shook her head and went to it. *I can't ask Ashton for help, and I need to prove it to him. I can do it.*

Valkyrie squeezed her fingers beneath the bureau and began trying to lift it. It was definitely heavier than it looked. She was able to raise it high enough to get under it.

Putting her back against the dresser, she tried to stand it up. *The stupid thing won't stay up.* She wanted to scream. Her feet began to slip out from under her, making her boil. All she wanted was to get her dresser back up, but she couldn't! She began to feel weak and helpless, and she thought of how much she needed Ashton's help.

But that also reminded her that the captain probably hated her and would never help her. Tears began to run down her face again as she groaned with the effort. She felt the weight and knew she wasn't going to get the dresser up.

*****

Ashton sat there at the table with his hand over his face. He didn't know what to do. *She says she hasn't turned anyone over. But she's spoken to Swiftmaw and seen armies! How close is she getting to Rotto's side? And who was her family? She can turn into a Griefolowtros. What does that mean? If one of her parents is a Grief, that would mean she was originally raised in Wingspread.*

Ashton remembered the look on her face when he had sent her to her room. The hurt and tears in her eyes broke his heart. He just needed time alone to mull things over. He loved her so much but needed to know the truth.

Ashton lifted his head to hear a crash coming from her room. He sighed and put his head back in his hands. *She's trying to lift up the dresser. But what am I supposed to do if she is part Grief? I can't allow her to go anywhere near Rotto's armies anymore. She can't help both sides.*

God, he prayed, *I thank you for saving her and for giving the Oracle when I asked for help. But I come to you now and ask that you please give me wisdom. I know your Holy Scriptures say to forgive...but I don't know how right now.*

Even as he prayed, his own past came to mind. The painful memories reminded him of the hurt he received from those who never forgave *him*.

Maybe I should try to talk to her again. People can always change. I did after the truth of God was revealed to me.

Ashton had grown up in a rough family. He had many siblings before and after him. He was right in the middle and didn't get as much attention from their teachers as the others, which caused him to wander astray a lot from what he was taught until he began to realize that he didn't want to live this way.

This was before Rotto's time, but Ashton's father was a slave to the Grief, Greenwing. They were taught to do despicable things. Their main job was to hide the Character's dark secrets, whether it was a malfeasance or usually murder.

Ashton was only ten years old when he ran away. It was hard for him to leave his siblings, but his father never really cared for any of them and only paid attention when they failed to do what they were told.

One day, he had stumbled upon some of the deepest dungeons in the fortress where an old Swiftmaw prisoner spoke of a father who loved him more than anything. Ashton was shocked. A father who loved his children? Suddenly, he was desperate for such love.

He had asked the Swiftmaw many questions, and they were all answered. But one he remembered the most was asking how the Swiftmaw was still alive after being there for so many years. He was the only prisoner left.

"It's because of my faith. Acrimony is growing. He needs more souls. He has tried many times to reach me, but he can't take me mentally. He will come one day, and I will be buried physically, but only God owns me spiritually."

And whoever this Acrimony was, he must have taken Bronzepaw because when Ashton returned again, the Swiftmaw was gone.

But he never forgot the man's words. He needed to leave this place full of wickedness and sin. His father didn't care for him, many of his siblings didn't even notice him, but he was close to some of them, especially his youngest brother, Arcturus, but to Ashton, his name was Ace.

He called him that for the mark around his eye. He had known he couldn't just leave his little brother. Ace was only a year old at the time.

The night before Ashton was planning to run away, he had heard his father talking of sending Ace away to a different Grief just as mad as Greenwing.

After that, he knew he had to take his brother with him. Wrapping him in a blanket, they escaped that night. Ashton took weapons and food with him. He didn't have much but would do anything to save his innocent brother.

He carried Ace and the sack on his back for days. He didn't know where he was going but knew he needed to find his brother a home. More than anything, he wanted him to grow up with a happy life, believing in the God who loved them because they were his children.

Ashton lost count of how long he had been traveling. He stopped eating the food just so he could feed his little brother. When they finally came across a small house hidden well in the woods, he was nearly starved to death.

He watched two older Stexphin enter the house, then cautiously took his sleeping brother to the door. He hesitated to knock and ended up leaving him on the step instead. *They will never accept me. I've done too many wicked things. But perhaps they will take on Ace,* were his thoughts as he walked away. All he left Arcturus was the blanket, his own crossbow, and a note.

The note said as much as he could remember:

> Please care for Arcturus (also titled Ace), and bring him up as your own. I would take him myself, but he doesn't deserve someone as wicked as me. He's the youngest from the Lott family; we serve a corrupt Grief named Greenwing. But it's not too late to change his way of living and teach him about the loving God. His family is evil, and he deserves so much more. Please accept

him into your own family, and let him know that
he is very loved.

Ashton could never remember the rest, but he always regretted
the way he had written that card. *I shouldn't have put that he was from
a wicked family.* He had thought the same thing over and over for
years. But he was only ten at the time and didn't really know how
someone might accept a Stexphin from Greenwing.

Ashton shook his head as he remembered that. Fresh tears began
in his eyes. He thought of Caleb and Ace. *Could that have been him?*
But he already knew it was.

He had seen his brother and was very proud at what he had
become. His thoughts turned back to Valkyrie. *I have to talk to her.*

Ashton walked to her bedroom door and took a deep breath.
He opened it slowly. Valkyrie was lying on her bed, back facing him.
The dresser was on the ground with a new crack in it.

He sighed and walked toward the bed. "Valkyrie," he said softly.

She turned and faced him. Her eyes were glossy.

Ashton sat on the bed. He put a hand on her shoulder and said,
"I want to hear your side of the story."

Valkyrie looked a little shocked. But then she relaxed. "I'm not a
traitor," she said. "I've thought about it long and hard, and I'm not."
She paused, then began her story.

This time, she told him everything from the invention to meeting Gavin, and all the way to meeting Courtney and Diesel as well.
She got most of the story out without tears, silently reminding herself, *Crying won't bring them back.*

"Wait." Ashton frowned with confusion. "So you turn into a
Swiftmaw as well?"

"Y-Yes, I thought you knew,"

"No, you weren't a wolf but a Grief."

"I was? No, I only know how to transform into a Swiftmaw. I
mean, Father did say he fused us with Grief as well, except my older
brother. He's only a wolf, not exactly Swiftmaw," Valkyrie replied
thoughtfully.

"So there's more of you," Ashton frowned. "If your brothers are still alive, we need to know. Gifts like this can be dangerous to our side of the wars. We don't know if they would help Rotto."

"I understand," Valkyrie said, looking down to hide her hurt.

"If they're still alive, where do you think they'd be?" Ashton asked.

"I'm not sure. Mother and Father barely told us anything at all. My twin and I only knew stuff from my older brother, Frazil. Mostly, we eavesdropped on private conversations," she admitted.

Ashton nodded. "And how did your brother, Frazil, know this stuff?" he asked.

Valkyrie opened her mouth to speak, but stopped. She wasn't sure at all. "I'm really sorry," she apologized with tears in her eyes.

"It's fine. At least I know now," Ashton said, wrapping an arm over her shoulders and rubbing her arm the same way Dane used to. "No more secrets." He looked at her.

"No more secrets," she agreed, leaning into him.

Ashton bent down and picked up *the Scriptures*. "Have you been reading this?" he asked.

"I tried," she said. "The way it's laid out is all confusing. It's like a series all put together in one book. But I started at the beginning. It was really interesting,"

"Why'd you stop?" he asked curiously, smoothing the ruffled pages.

"It started talking about sacrifices and altars and how to kill certain animals. It got weird and confusing." She looked at him for an answer.

Ashton smiled. "Before you read that section, you should start with the newer testament." He began flipping toward the back.

"But what is it? I'm confused what this book is even about,"

"It talks about our true Father, a heavenly Father who created us to be his children."

Valkyrie frowned with her confusion. "Someone created us? What do you mean *children?*"

Ashton smiled at her. "He's our God, and he loves us more than anything in the world. He knows everything about us, including our thoughts and the number of hairs on our head."

Valkyrie looked at him in bewilderment. "That's impossible. If you knew everything about me, especially my thoughts, you'd hate me."

"And you'd hate me if you knew *my* darkest thoughts," Ashton agreed.

"Then you're crazy to believe in such a thing," Valkyrie stated bluntly. "I could understand a great and powerful God loving you, but me? Ashton, you know who I am. I'm so far from perfect. My own family abandoned me. They only cared for me because I was needed for an experiment. I'm so far from being worth anything." Her voice cracked. "Especially not loved. And you only love me because—" She looked up at the old captain with glossy eyes. "Why do you care about me? Even after learning what I am?"

"Because of this," Ashton said, pointing at the open book in his lap. "I never would have been able to understand how to truly love someone unless I learned what love is. It's not just a feeling you get toward someone."

"Then what is love?" she asked, confused.

"God is love. Without knowing him, we can never truly understand the definition nor the feeling, even the actions made for such a thing."

"Where did you learn this?" Valkyrie asked with a frown.

"Someone told me," Ashton responded quietly. "Then, later, I was guided by friends how to find the answers to my questions through the Scriptures, which was written by the holy men chosen by God."

"Who told you about it, though?" Valkyrie urged on. Surely, whoever shared this with him was crazy.

"No more secrets," Ashton laughed under his breath. "I guess it's my turn to share my story with you."

263

30

CHARACTERS IN THE CAVES

Valkyrie walked to the hospital with a lump in her throat. Ashton had suggested she go talk to Matthias, that he had been worried about her.

Walking through the large doors, she peered around the all too familiar room. It was different from the dirt tunnels but still had an uncomfortable underground look to it.

Looking around, she spotted Alania and silently wondered if she should talk to her as well. Her thoughts drifted to her gray pouch on her waist. Ashton had taken the small daggers.

"Valkyrie," came the doctor's familiar voice. Matthias found her first. She had heard him say her real name before and silently wondered how much Ashton told him.

"Hi, Matthias," she replied, smiling nervously at him.

"I really thought we were going to lose you this time," he said, his own nervous smile appearing. He wasn't mad, she was relieved to notice, but he was concerned and perhaps slightly troubled by her. "I am once again amazed that you made it."

"And it's all thanks to you, Doctor," she said.

"Promise me you'll never come to me again with a life-threatening injury?"

Valkyrie glanced over where she once again recognized the three brothers from her first time there. This time, two of them were being treated; Alania and another nurse were wrapping cuts on the twins arms.

"It's no competition"—she turned back to Matthias—"but I'm pretty sure they've been here more times than me." She jerked her head in the brother's direction.

"*They've* been here their entire lives," Matthias shook his head. "But only once did we almost lose one of them. Not all of them twice."

Valkyrie turned back to the boys, her eyes full of curiosity. What could they possibly be doing to come here so much?

"I have a lot of questions I'd like to ask you," Matthias went on.

Valkyrie shook her head. "I already talked to Ashton," she said. "I'm sorry."

"Well, I'm glad to see you alive and well." The doctor leaned close for only her to hear. "Between you and I, I've never lost a patient before. I was scared you were going to break my lucky streak."

"Gee, thanks." Valkyrie smirked. She liked Matthias. She found it odd he was Ashton's best and apparently only friend. The doctor usually joined them during meals, and sometimes, he brought Alania. *I'm pretty sure they're a thing.*

As Valkyrie left, she looked back at the brothers, but Alania was gone. Her stomach churned in hungry protest for her to find food as she walked back down the dirt tunnels.

It didn't take long to find one of the strange underground caves. Walking in, she stopped and looked around with a satisfied smile. She loved how magical these caverns seemed.

With a special glowing fungi along the walls, ceiling, and floor, it almost seemed to guide Characters throughout the strange herb garden. Ashton had shown her a few months ago how to get food here.

Instantly, Valkyrie went to a strange blue plant covered in yellow stripes. She couldn't remember the name of it, but it's leaves were long and sturdy. If she picked one, it came off easily. Even better, it tasted like wafers.

Walking around the large cavern, her ears pricked up at the sound of other voices. She turned her head to see a small group of older Stexphin Characters. By the sight of their outfits and weapons, she knew they were a traveling group of soldiers.

Ashton had explained to her they didn't come often, but sometimes, soldiers who had grown up inside Smuir would leave but later return again.

Silently, she wondered where they *all* came from.

They must have sensed her staring because they all looked up at her and began talking in hushed tones. She was troubled that her "spectacular" hearing caught every word.

They were talking about her. She turned away and frowned as they soon began talking about Captain Ashton and how gruff and strange he was to have adopted a *stray*.

She shut them out as best as she could, but their laughter rippled through her ears as they began laughing at something the younger one said. Looking back at them, she saw the Character staring at her with an amused smile. She began to feel uncomfortable.

To make things worse, the blond-haired Stexphin left his friends and began walking toward her. *Great.* But, silently, *she* was amused that his uniform looked a little big for him. The boy had long legs and was taller than even she, but his oversized shirt was stuffed inside a belt around his waist.

Maybe they ran out of clothes his size. She inwardly laughed. Another strange thing was that he didn't wield a short sword as the others did. But she noticed sturdy leather straps were around his hands and down his forearm as well as around the outside of his shoes.

"Yur Jay-lae, ain't ya?"

His strong accent was even more surprising. "Yes, sir, I am," she replied.

"I'm Jamin," the Stexphin said, sticking out a hand.

She took it and shook. Despite being the youngest in his group, he had a strong grip. *He has to be around seventeen.*

His blond hair was neatly combed back, sticking out rather bright against his nicely tanned skin. He didn't have Stexphin ears.

266

Even his eyes seemed to pop with a strange green blue look. An indigo-colored scarf was draped around his neck. *Even fashionable. There's no way he's from here. Not with that accent and these looks.*

"Yer Ashe's girl, correct?" he asked.

"Yes, sir. I am," she repeated, beginning to wonder if he had a point coming up and talking to her.

"I've been hear'en sum ru'mers bout ya and zat attack outside the mt'n."

She struggled to understand his accent and gave him an apologetic look.

"My lang-u-age ain't so per'ect. I am still learn'n your strange tun'g on this eye land." Jamin nodded his apologies as he seemed to read her mind.

Island? What does he mean by language?

"What are these rumors you've been hearing?" she encouraged him to continue. She feared they might relate to her being around Swiftmaw and transforming.

"Yur sav'ed a man's life." He smiled, revealing perfect rows of rather sharp teeth.

"Oh." She blinked.

Jamin glanced back at his friends who weren't paying much attention. He put a hand on her shoulder and began to lead her away. She wasn't sure what to do, so she went quietly.

Out of earshot from his group of friends, Jamin faced her again and said quietly, "List'n. I know how to tr'in Stephens like ya."

"I'm sorry?" She looked at him, puzzled.

Jamin looked upset that he couldn't speak clearly. He stretched his mouth then tried again, speaking slowly this time. "I her'd what ya dead to save thee man's life. I was wond'ring if yur wud let me, tr'in y'all."

"Trin? Do you mean train? Like to fight?" Valkyrie was shocked. That wasn't something she really wanted to do.

"My ghoul is tah teach as miny yung Stefers how to defend them-sleeves and others. Rotto es come'en, and he ain't plannen on dress'en up fer a dinnah partee." He waited a moment for Valkyrie to process what he had said.

"But why me?" she finally said after a moment.

"Beh'cuz I her'd what ya dead. Yah did not give up. Zat's the kind-er-of spir't I look fer tah trin." Jamin stumbled over his words, stopping a few times to stretch out his tongue in annoyance.

Valkyrie was quiet. "Can I think about it?" she asked.

"Uv corse. But do'nt keep meh wait'en fer day's on a...on a—" He frowned.

"Response?" she suggested.

*****

Valkyrie later found Ashton had told him what the strange man had said. He was hesitant, telling her how he didn't like the soldier groups that pass through Smuir.

"They think they can just suddenly show up with a ton of strangers. It's terribly risky. And this Jamin fellow, I've met a few times. He's a strange young man."

"That's for sure," Valkyrie agreed.

"Taeson is the name of the one who used to live here beneath Smuir. He's not too bad. He gave the king lots of useful information on what's going on out there." Ashton trailed off for a moment. "The rest in his small group claim to be survivors from Elkhorn. Except that Jamin fellow. He won't say where he's from."

"Is he even a Stexphin?"

Ashton looked down at her. "I don't know. That's what I don't like about him."

"So you won't let me train?"

"No, I want you to train." His reply surprised her. "I won't always be there to protect you, and Jamin's right. Rotto will come someday. But I'm worried about...what if it gets too rough, and you get hurt or even transform?"

Valkyrie was quiet. She hadn't thought of that.

"I'll kill him if he hurts you," Ashton growled under his breath. "Tell him that too."

"So I can do it?" Valkyrie felt a small surge of anxiety. She didn't even know what training would be like.

"For a few weeks, and if it's not too rough, you can continue," Ashton replied. He was quiet for another moment before saying, "When you go back and tell him, try stopping in one of the northern caves. The other day, I saw a group of children around your age."

*****

Ashton had been right. Before she even entered the cave, she could hear the playful shouts of younger Characters.

Suddenly, she felt panicked about the thought of meeting another Stexphin her age. *It'll be just like meeting Gavin. No, this won't be anything like that. We became friends by accident. But I'd so rather be taken back to Runyan's army than do this! Why am I so scared to make friends?*

She hesitantly walked through the entrance. She was surprised by how much more different it was then the other. This cavern was much larger, around the same size as the hospital. Instead of plants growing everywhere, the ground was uneven with a short dark algae growing everywhere.

She stepped onto the growing plant and gasped to find there was a puddle of water beneath the kelp. At the same time, the algae where she had stepped glowed bright colors of pink and yellow.

Valkyrie glanced up at the group of children. They were playing in the center where the ground dipped in more with strange hills surrounding it.

There had to be at least five characters her age. The rest were younger and playing in a separate corner from the older kids.

As the preteens ran around, she watched in wonder as the algae glowed where they stepped as well. Water splashed up beneath their feet as well. They were throwing a ball to each other and shouting with annoyance and glee.

Valkyrie walked along the wall and found a dry spot to sit down. She watched them for a few minutes, trying to understand their game. This was no simple "throw the ball back and forth" like she and Virga used to play.

There appeared to be two teams, and they were trying to get the ball across to their own side. Opposite team members had the right to tackle each other.

A few times, one of them would glance in her direction, but none of them stopped to invite her to play or even ask who she was.

Valkyrie watched as one of the girls, perhaps two years older than herself, ran with the ball. She had to be the oldest and also looked the strongest.

Her light blond hair brushed across her face as she tried to dodge one of the boys. Valkyrie noticed she was also the only one there without Stexphin ears. *Is it possible to be given Bandit ears instead of Stexphin?* she wondered.

She gasped as the girl slipped on the algae, forcing her into the boy who had tried to block her path. They both fell and slid through the kelp, causing a wall of water to grow as well as millions of colors to light up where they slid.

The moment the two of them stopped, the girl was sideways over the younger Character. She gasped and lifted her head. Her blond hair now stuck to her face.

"Deirdre, get off! Get off! Get off!" the boy cried in pain as he began smacking the girl's shoulder. Instantly, she moved, staring with wide eyes as the Character grabbed his shoulder with a pained expression.

"Walker, I'm so sarry!" the girl, who she supposed was named Deirdre, cried in a strong accent. Valkyrie tried not to smile at their reactions.

"Are you all right, Walker?" another boy asked as he pulled his friend up.

Deirdre got up herself, her dress sticking to her soaked body.

Valkyrie studied the boy, Walker. He was tall, about her height, with gray hair that would've looked nice if it wasn't sticking to his forehead. Strangely, a white stripe grew down the center of his strands; his ears were white as well.

The algae below the characters began to dim down from their stillness, but as Walker stumbled forward, it lit up again with bright orange and purple. Valkyrie tilted her head with a curious smile to see Walker had orange eyes as well.

"Deirdre, you've seriously got to calm your punches down," the boy who had helped Walker up said.

"I don't mean tah al'ways hert him," Deirdre insisted, trying to pull her wet dress away from sticking to her stomach. Growing abs showed through the thin fabric. "How about I sit this one out?" she suggested, her eyes falling on Valkyrie.

"I'm done too," Walker grunted painfully.

He's not very tough. But what can I say? We're about on the same level of strength—both sickly skinny. I need a sandwich about as much as he.

As the characters resumed their game, Deirdre came over and sat next to her, still trying to pull her dress away from sticking to her body.

"Hey," she started as she sat down. "I ain't see yer round here much. Y'all new to the moun-teen or sum'thing?"

"Not really," Valkyrie replied. "I just don't get out much."

"Oh. I'm Deirdre, by that way." She crossed her right hand over. and Valkyrie shook it. She was shocked by the girls firm grip. "What's yer name?"

"Oh, just call me Jaylee," she offered with a friendly smile.

"Do you want to play?" Deirdre asked with a wide smile. "It's fun as long as you don't get wet." She jerked a head over at the others. "My team's winning, but we are a player short."

"What about Walker? Isn't his team short one as well now?"

"Nah, Walker will play. I can tok hem into it." Deirdre smirked at the boy who was watching them with accusing eyes near the entrance. "He knows we're talk-en 'bout hem."

Deirdre stood and pulled Valkyrie to her feet. "C'mon. I'll teach ya the ropes an' y'all be hanging by them soon enough. Hey! This gurl's name es Jaylee. Tell her the rules," Deirdre called to the group before turning back to Walker.

Valkyrie caught on to the game quickly. It was the name of everyone else she struggled with. No matter how many times they told her, she couldn't put a face with their title.

That's Hagan Parry... Or maybe he was Cash. No, wait, Cash is his nickname. Or was it that kid? Wait, that's Walker. He has orange eyes. Cash has brown hair...but so does that kid... And that girl. Why am I so bad at this?

Deirdre caught the flying ball easily, sliding through the algae smoothly this time. Without even taking a step, the girl chucked the ball in her direction.

Valkyrie widened her eyes and prepared herself to catch the fast moving ball. She ran, delighted by the colored algae and splashing water beneath her feet.

Then she leaped. Easily curling her fingers around the sphere. Valkyrie mimicked one of Virga's favorite tricks. Well, the stunt had been more of an accident that day.

She turned in the air, catching the eye of Hagan—or Cash—and chucked the ball toward him. Deirdre cheered her as the young Character caught the sphere.

Valkyrie was a little embarrassed that her throws weren't nearly as strong nor as graceful as Deirdre's, but she was grateful she wasn't the only one.

They played for what felt like hours before the group began to break up and head back to their own homes in the underground city.

*****

Valkyrie wasn't sure if she should feel more nervous or excited as she tried to find the training room the next morning.

When she found the room, she was surprised by the strange metal door. *Looks like it's supposed to be some sort of important closest, not a training room.*

She pushed on the unlocked door and entered the room. Instantly, the cold air met her, and she shivered. "It's freezing in here!" she exclaimed to the Character whose back was facing her.

Jamin turned around, nodding in agreement. "Sum buddy did tern zah con-dish-en-er up. Fer'got to tern up zat heat'uh," he explained.

Valkyrie smiled at his pronunciation.

272

"I fig'ured we cud star weather strain'gth trin," Jamin went on.
She took a moment to understand what he said.
"Strength training?" she asked.
He nodded.
Should I be offended?
No, this will be good for you. Purple flashed through her mind.
I hate you, she inwardly mumbled but agreed.

31

A SHADOW INSIDE

Crowley—Year 318

Crowley glowered at the Hollowed Characters before him. They were the most ornery group he'd ever trained.

Really, they were impossible to train. But showing them who was in charge helped the Griefs keep them under better control.

"Hunsaker!" Crowley bellowed. "Get in line!"

He hated new batches.

The Hollowed didn't listen but instead began an argument with another character named Obst. Crowley was losing his patience too quickly today. *If Rotto doesn't learn a better way to control them, I'm going to kill—*

Crowley stumbled backward as Hunsaker shoved Obst into him. He caught his balance, quickly unsheathing his sword.

Obst turned on him, rage in her eyes. "Get out of the way," she growled.

Crowley pointed his tip at her face. "In line. Now. Or this one dies." The Hollowed knew he wasn't kidding. Still, Hunsaker refused to back up, and the others were getting restless from his behavior.

"And why should I listen to you!?" the Character barked. "I don't care if she dies. I don't care if I die. I only care that *you* die, you piece of scum! We're here to take your kind, beat them, and—"

274

Crowley easily sent his short sword through Obst. The character stared at him with wide angry black eyes. Finally, she slumped, and he released his blade, letting her body fall to the ground soundly. He didn't even bother to wipe the black blood from his weapon.

He had learned easily that Hollowed were stubborn. But they thirsted death and blood more than anything. Showing them he wasn't afraid to bring it upon them easily put them in line. Besides, they became dead the moment they turned into Hollowed. He felt no guilt.

Crowley had also come to learn a lot more about the creatures and how they were forced to transform into deceased wolves.

They were much different from Swiftmaw and yet still alike. Instead of the kind brown fur and eyes, Hollowed were an unfriendly dark color with eyes that looked like two endless pits carved in their faces.

The fur around their mouths and front paws were usually stained. Nobody needed to be told what from. But the most wicked things about these creatures were their scars, more like brands, really, covering most of their body. Each Hollowed had their marks in different multiple sections. Some were there from the wounds they received from the camps while others were forced into their skin from the Griefs. They said it was how they kept track of them.

"Hunsaker!" a Hollowed Character snapped. "Fall in line!"

Lookingbill, an unusual Hollowed without many markings.

Crowley studied him. *He's fresh. Usually the fresher, the more deadly they are. But, no, he's not even fully turned. The Griefs underestimated this one. He still has Swiftmaw inside of him to stand up like that.*

Hunsaker turned on Lookingbill with crazed eyes. "I'm going to kill him. I'm *going* to *kill* him!"

"I'll kill *you* if you step anywhere near me," Crowley glowered.

Hunsaker turned on him with such fury. Goosebumps crawled along his skin. He had never met such a crazed Hollowed before.

Hunsaker was also the strongest of the entire group. Crowley had no doubt this Character *could* kill him. But he couldn't show it.

In one swift moment, Hunsaker leaped forward, death in his eyes as he transformed into his even more dangerous form of a demonic wolf. Crowley turned his blade up, ready to pierce the monster.

A loud shriek sounded from above.

Instantly, large talons came down on Hunsaker, inches from Crowley's face. The Hollowed roared and tried to flip over to face his new attacker. But the four-winged raptor dug his razor-sharp talons into the beast's flesh. Then he squeezed before ripping them back out.

Crowley watched the gruesome sight with only half of a brow raised. As soon as Hunsaker stopped moving, the black-colored Mislea flapped all four wings, releasing the beast. He rose five feet before transforming into character.

He fell and landed on both feet beside Crowley. "Keith wants this batch back around for another extent," the young character said calmly.

The Hollowed transformed, but before they could return to their clearing, Crowley called, "Lookingbill."

The Hollowed stopped, his black eyes flashing to white for only a moment before returning.

"He's still—" the Mislea began.

But Crowley interrupted, "Reinke, take him back to the camps."

Reinke transformed into her Character, a wicked smile on her face. Lookingbill transformed as well. "Please, no," he begged, his black eyes once more turning completely white. "Not the camps. They'll—"

Reinke grabbed his arm, and two others joined her in dragging the character back to the Grief camp. He screamed and begged them not to take him the entire way. The rest of the Hollowed left quickly but not before dragging the dead bodies with them.

"You have a good grip around them," the Mislea Character said. The young boy's voice bothered him. Crowley had learned this raptor was from beneath the island, as was Keith.

Keith, another Mislea Raptor, had found Slecherick, Rotto's friend from his original island who had been believed dead. After finding him wrecked in the gulf of Gossamer, Keith had taken care of him until they learned Rotto controlled the Griefolowtros.

Really, Crowley tried to stay out of the confusing muddle of the rare race, but as second in command, he was told everything.

"No, they're impossible," he frowned at this Mislea Character. *Please, kid, grow up and go fix your scarred face.* "They only know I'll kill them or send them back to the Griefs if they don't stay organized."

"You're seen as rather soft compared to how the Griefs treat them," the Mislea Character said. "My name is Shadow, by the way, but only in my Mislea form."

"I don't care. I have to go. Runyan has to know which Hollowed to take off his list." Crowley turned to leave but stopped as his ears turned in the direction of cries. His heart thumped loudly inside his chest. *Blackwing has returned with his army.* He instantly knew.

The Mislea character followed him to watch the Hollowed and Swiftmaw captors return with their fresh hostages from their recent raid in the Meadow of Hidden Rocks.

Three beat-up and gagged Stexphin, all of them over forty, were being dragged through Flamefoot Harborge, the owned bivouac of Griefs.

Crowley slightly glanced over at Shadow, annoyed the teen had followed him. He froze when he recognized the all too familiar mask covering the Mislea's face. He himself had the same coverage every day.

The character watched the Stexphin as one man struggled to break free. The other tried speaking to the unconscious woman. Crowley had learned not to care nor think about it when he saw them suffering. It was almost obvious that Shadow was hiding a million emotions against this activity.

They disappeared through a long tunnel in the cliff barrier. On the other side was April Bend where all the Stexphin were sent.

"Why did you turn against your own kind?" Shadow suddenly asked.

Crowley turned on him angrily. "I didn't!" he snapped. "I only worked for what I deserved."

"What do you deserve?" Shadow risked, looking up at him. He had purple eyes. *Peculiar.*

"I deserve to do what I'm capable of to its full extent."

277

"Which is?" Shadow asked calmly.

Crowley had learned to control his emotions, but he struggled to do so now. He could feel his face heating up at the young boy's questions. *Who does he think he is?*

"Being a leader. Powerful," Crowley stated, as if it were obvious. Shadow didn't answer as another invisible mask covered his face. "What about you?"

Shadow looked scared. "What?"

"What do you hope to achieve under Rotto's command?"

"I wish to be of use," was all the boy said, and Crowley saw the flashes of pain in his eyes.

"You've been hurt?" he guessed.

"I want to be useful."

"You want to belong."

"I don't do well with slaving m—another race."

Crowley was surprised by Shadow's sudden statement.

"I'm only confused how *you* can do such a thing to your own kind."

"I don't believe you. You *do* know how one could do such a thing," Crowley said, finding it almost odd how much he could understand this Character. *We've both been through a lot,* he guessed.

"You don't care," Shadow said carefully.

"Live behind a mask so I can continue to do my work needed for me. I guess I, too, wish to belong and be of use." He looked down at the young Character. "You created a mask for yourself so you won't be hurt again."

"And you for power." Shadow paused before saying, "You're good at this."

"I've been taught by the best." Crowley smiled at the thought of Selah. Instantly, that joy was extinguished. "She taught me how to read eyes," he finished quietly.

"Who?" Shadow urged.

Before Crowley could tell him it didn't matter, a loud screech sounded through the air.

Shadow looked up at impossibly high trees overhead, then turned to leave.

"I enjoyed our chat," Crowley confessed.

"And I. I think we both have something we can learn from each other," Shadow replied with the slightest smile.

"Will you return?" Crowley asked.

"If I am allowed." Then the young Character transformed, spreading his marvelous black wings. The feathers almost seemed to glisten in the light. *He's even more magnificent than Rotto and the Griefs put together*, Crowley silently thought.

"Wait," Crowley stepped toward him. "Earlier, you said your name is Shadow, but only in your Mislea form. If that's true, what's your real name?"

The Mislea cocked a feathered head toward the Stexphin man. "Virga," his voice rumbled deep inside his throat as his eyes flashed a sudden color of brilliant purple.

Shadow beat the air, sending strong currents of wind against the ground like waves. He hovered for a minute before giving one final bash and shooting upward.

*****

It wasn't until weeks later when Crowley was given the chance to speak with Shadow. He hadn't realized how much he missed having someone he could relate with. The young boy reminded him much of Malachi and Selah.

"Captain Crowley," Shadow's voice said from behind him one morning. Turning around, he saw the younger teen looking rather disturbed. Blood covered his hands and the front of his jacket.

"Shadow, what did you do?" Crowley frowned.

"It doesn't matter," the teen said plainly without emotion. He seemed rather older and mature when he acted this way. "I'm here for different matters."

"Not just because you wanted to see me?" Crowley mocked bluntly, anger touching his words. He turned back to the map. Shadow didn't join him.

"No," the boy said from behind. "It's taken me too long to learn not to get close to anyone. Not even for friends."

"What about that Mislea, Keith? Aren't you two friends?"

"It's more of mutual relating."

Crowley turned back to the teen, beginning to feel irritated by his presence. "Why are you here then? *Different matters,* you said?"

"Yes. A question."

"Go on then," he snapped.

"Are you controlled?"

"Excuse me?" Crowley glowered.

"Don't ever forget them. Don't be stuck somewhere you don't belong. It's never too late to—" The boy cut short. Shadow blinked a few times and looked away, frowning as if something had suddenly taken over his train of thought.

Crowley scowled harder. *Why does he look so familiar? I've seen him somewhere before. Not here, though. Somewhere before I came. He's different, though, so I can't put a name on it.*

"Sorry for bothering you," Shadow said as he turned and left. Crowley glared after him.

*****

"Do you know Shadow?" Crowley dared to ask a Grief by the name Runyan one day.

"Who, the Mislea?" Runyan hated him. It was easy to tell. But he didn't care. "Not really. Claims he came from inside the island, just like that other fellow, Keith, who found Slecherick. Why do *you* care?" the Character asked with accusing eyes.

"Wouldn't you like to know?" Crowley scoffed in the man's face. He didn't care that this Grief was taller, stronger, and deadlier than he. He was a prat.

Runyan's face blazed with anger, and he reached out to strike him. Crowley, prepared for having been assaulted by Griefs before, easily ducked. Quickly, he punched the man in the side, making him curl over as he gasped for air.

"If you ever try to place a hand on me again, I'll cut it off," Crowley threatened under his breath.

Runyan struggled to stand straight, his eyes shooting daggers. Before either of them could act again, shouting echoed from above.

Looking up into the trees, Crowley knew it was Rotto's central room above them. The shouts weren't normal but easily defined as war calls.

Runyan made to transform, but the intense pain in his ribs stopped him. Crowley quickly unsheathed his sword, determination setting on his expression as he prepared himself for whatever might dare come down and face him.

A body. No, an older teen jumped from the entrance ramp overhead. Crowley instantly recognized it to be Shadow. In one quick motion, the character was transformed into his Mislea form.

Uncurling his wings, the tips stretched out, catching the air and shooting him upward and forward with such incredible force never seen before. The enormous glistening black feathered wings were beautiful even from a distance.

Two seconds later, a second Mislea emerged from the platform. This one was gray, and Crowley instantly recognized Keith.

A loud enraged shriek came from the Mislea, forcing Crowley to drop his blade and cover his ears. Although his hearing was much more sensitive than the Grief, Runyan also covered his ears, wincing as he did.

Keith was after the fleeing Shadow in seconds, murder clear on his face. In three seconds, the two Mislea were gone, and nothing but the ringing in their ears remained of the two raptors.

"What just happened?" Runyan let out a guttural breath as he slowly dropped his hands.

"Something bad," Crowley stated, picking up his weapon as he retreated to find out what was going on.

32

COMBATIVE FIGHT

Valkyrie—Year 316

Jamin quickly ducked, barely missing a flying plant from his friend, Joaquin. "Jaybird!" the man called. "You're supposed to catch it!"

"Not when yer throw'in a'round like it do not mattar! And I ain't kidden, yer better quit callin' me names or I'm going to go on and tie yer up an' throw yer in a broom closet!"

"I'd like to see you try! We all know I could easily stuff and hang you before you could even lay a hand on *me*," Joaquin scoffed.

Jamin squinted at him with accusing eyes and bent down to retrieve the large round plant, preparing to throw it back. It was soft all around, but the shell was poisonous if ingested. You had to peel it before eating.

Looking up, Jamin saw Captain Ashton, Valkyrie, and Dr. Matthias enter the cavern. Quickly, he dropped the plant and looked away but not before the captain caught his eyes and sent a death look.

His friends noticed. "What'd you do to get on Captain Ashton's bad side?" Joaquin asked, running a hand through his own dark hair and over his ears.

"I ain't sure," Jamin lied.

*****

"Stop it," Valkyrie scolded, elbowing Ashton as she saw him cast Jamin another scowl. "Why do you keep doing that?"

"I'm just warning him," Ashton replied gruffly as they turned out of sight.

"Here," Matthias said, easily changing the subject. "Grab some of those blue spikes."

"These?" Valkyrie asked, bending to retrieve the strange plants sticking from the ground. They were firm and sharp-looking on the end with splashes of blue soaking the outside.

"*Eldorados*," Matthias smiled as he held out the basket for her to drop them in. "They grow quite commonly in the Hidden Rock Valley and are very delicious if you know the correct way to prepare them. Not many people see them as edible, though."

"They're weird," Valkyrie stated, placing the handful of spikes inside the basket.

"I'll come over later and teach you how to help Ashton learn to cook," Matthias promised.

"*I* don't know how to cook with these strange plants, though," Valkyrie responded as she helped Ashton grab a few flowers that tasted like mangoes.

This place is magical, she thought as she plopped a crunchy petal in her mouth.

"It's easy if you know how to compare these plants with original ingredients. They are rather similar in their cooking. You just have to know what to combine for better flavors," Matthias replied. "Besides, someone has to feed Ashton *real* meals after I'm gone."

"Where are you going?" Valkyrie frowned and stood up.

The doctor and Captain cast each other knowing glances. "He's going on a scouting mission by King Demoor. Matthias has to replace Dr. Trinity since—" Ashton trailed off.

"But why don't *you* go?" she asked him.

"This is more of a stealth mission, not a usual trip around the mountain. King Demoor is sending his most skilled scout, Delta, to lead instead of me since I have to stay behind and train more rookies in the caves," Ashton responded as they followed Matthias toward a patch of the glowing algae.

Valkyrie wondered how Ashton felt about the thought of Matthias leaving on a dangerous mission. The two older men were the most unusual of friends.

Ashton had told her how Matthias was the only one willing enough to be his friend when he was younger, that everyone else gave him hate because he used to work for a Grief.

"We grew up together, trained together, and helped each other grow in many ways. It was even Matthias who introduced me to my bride." Ashton always went quiet whenever his wife was mentioned. Valkyrie had seen a picture of her and their daughter in his room before.

Matthias then went on to tell her how scared he was to tell Ashton he didn't want to be a warrior like him but go into doctoring and medicine.

"It took me two weeks of anxious prayers before I finally told him. But he didn't put me down like I had feared. Instead, he supported me more than anyone. And when I learned he was going to be promoted to Captain in the city of Smuir, I went with them and became a doctor the same year."

Matthias had told her quietly that his wife was expecting after the first three years at Smuir; and then she and their daughter both died in an avalanche a year later on their way to Elkhorn to visit family.

Valkyrie wasn't ever sure what to say when they spoke of the captain's loss. She kind of felt like she was the replacement and needed to live up to them.

She still found it odd how the two completely opposite men were still friends after all these years. Matthias had told her they wouldn't even care if it weren't for their strong faith in the Lord. She wasn't sure about that.

At the sound of loud laughter, the three of them looked up to see Jamin and his friends on the other side.

Valkyrie thought back to the last few weeks of training. She was happy by how much healthier she was feeling and looking. Her bones didn't stick out anymore.

"That blond fellow"—Matthias nodded toward him—"there's strange rumors going around about him,"

"Jamin?" Valkyrie asked, silently wondering if Ashton had told him anything about them training.

Ashton grunted carelessly. "He's just part of a traveling group."

"They've been here for a few months now," Matthias said.

"Upon the king's request. They plan on staying around a year, the longest any of them have. But I'm afraid the only good thing about them is the information they've been able to share on the Silent Wars outside," Ashton responded.

Valkyrie frowned at him, and he gave her an apologetic look. *Does he still not like Jamin training me?*

*****

The next morning, Valkyrie entered the training room to find Jamin was there with another Character. *Was I not supposed to come today?* she wondered.

Jamin looked up, and Valkyrie was shocked when the other did as well. It was Deirdre.

"Aye, Jaylee!" Deirdre grinned welcomingly.

Valkyrie returned a confused smile. *What is she doing here?* She glanced at Jamin for answers.

"This is mah yung-er sistar, Deirdre. But I'm gessing y'all met?" Jamin nodded.

Sister? Actually that makes sense.

"Yeah, we all met in the caves about a few weeks ago. She comes on down every so often and plays a good few games with us," Deirdre went on rather quickly. Valkyrie was glad her accent was much easier to understand.

Jamin cleared his throat, and Deirdre lifted her chin with a playful smile and sideways glance at him. "I ask-ed Deirdre to cum to'dah so zah y'all cud prac-tis fight'en physical-ally," Jamin said.

"Oh," Valkyrie squinted at him, "but you've been teaching me for three weeks, and we've fought each other. What do you mean physically?"

Jamin cleared his throat again. "Y'all need tah prac'tice how tah fight wayth more than jus' a way'pon. Yah lern soon e'nuf that out there y'all will be knocken down tah zah ruff er'th."

Valkyrie nodded in acknowledgment. She had been knocked down plenty of times.

"He did not think that yer father wud want *him* knocken yah down." Deirdre gave her a friendly yet mischievous grin.

As Jamin finished explaining to them that he wanted them both to fight past their limits, Valkyrie looked at him with alarm. She hadn't yet been taught how to defend herself without a short blade.

"Yah will ler'n a-long zah way," Jamin assured her.

Valkyrie hoped he was right. She hadn't ever seen Deirdre fight and didn't need to. The muscles along her graceful form were enough to prove the warrior inside.

"Yeah, okay," Deirdre said with an uncomfortable shrug. "But I ain't exactly want'in to punch Jaylee full on in zah face." She glanced from her brother to Valkyrie. "I mean, I could, but I'd feel mighty guilty."

Valkyrie wasn't offended by the remark at all. She felt the same way.

*****

"I want y'all tah close yer eyes, an' think," Jamin said, waiting patiently for the two girls to do so. "Now, think of zah per'son y'all hate most. Then imagine zatswho year fightin' right now."

He waited a moment for them both to think. "Good, Deirdre," he said when he saw his sister's expression close into a scowl. She had her Character. "This cud be sumone who hurt yah or sumbody y'all love. It cud be the Char-ec-tar behind the causes of these kidnap-pen-ens happen'en."

Jaylee's own focus turned into a frown. "Now, fight," he said, and both girls' eyes shot open.

Jamin had started with the two of them standing eight feet apart. Deirdre easily covered that distance to reach her. Reacting without thought, Valkyrie went to the ground, sliding beneath the jumping girl.

Quick to get back on her feet, Valkyrie kicked off as hard as she could with her strong back legs, grabbing Deirdre's middle and sending them both to the ground.

She was trying to remember the moves played out by Gavin and Diesel in the cave when they had fought each other.

But Deirdre didn't hesitate a moment. Once they hit the ground, she jerked both legs between them and kicked Valkyrie in the stomach, off and away from her.

How could I have forgotten that? It's exactly what Diesel did.

Clutching her stomach, Valkyrie stumbled backwards. Tripping over her own feet, she fell.

Suddenly, Deirdre was there, and she easily pinned her to the ground. And for a moment, Valkyrie was reminded of when Virga had pinned her.

Deirdre stopped and looked up at her brother, a frown plastered on her face.

"Remember, yer not attack'en yer friend but yer enemy. Deirdre, who did yah choose as yer great-est foe?" Jamin asked.

"Easy," the girl scowled, getting off Valkyrie. "That stupid Grief, Runyan, who ruined our lives."

Valkyrie gasped. *Runyan?* Her thoughts trailed off to her Swiftmaw friends.

"Jaylee, who did yer have in mind?" Jamin interrupted her thoughts before they went too deep.

"What?"

"Who were ya think'in of as the Char-ac-ter y'all hate most?" Jamin asked.

"I... I thought of a Stexphin named Verrader who betrayed us," she replied hesitantly, not mentioning she had almost chosen her brother who had abandoned and lied to her.

"Is that where yah got yer scar?" Deirdre asked, nodding at the ugly mark on her forearm.

Valkyrie nodded. Usually, she wore Cooper's cloak or long sleeves to cover it, but she had taken the cover off before training.

Jamin nodded and resumed the fight with a wave of his hand. *Wait!* A blow from Deirdre made her head spin.

Jamin watched Valkyrie struggle to get Deirdre off her, but finally, on her third attempt, she moved her head to dodge another blow from the girl.

Deirdre cried out as her fist collided with the cement ground. Jamin smiled as Valkyrie used the distraction to grab her shoulder, pull her down, and knee her in the stomach.

Jamin knew it was a move he had tried explaining to her, but they had never actually tried.

He wasn't worried about his sister. Deirdre knew how to handle pain, more mental than physical, but she had been in fights uglier than this.

He also knew she wasn't going all out. Valkyrie, however, was rather "raw" to this kind of fighting. But he wanted her to get an idea what it looked like and felt like before teaching her techniques.

Jamin turned around at the sound of the door opening. Fear penetrated his heart at the thought of getting caught. *King Demoor will kick me out if he learns I'm teaching teens how to fight. Especially girls.*

But instead of Captain Ashton (as was his greatest fear), three young boys walked in. He almost sighed with relief. He knew and trained these boys. But they weren't supposed to be here.

The boys looked almost as surprised as Jamin who quickly rushed over and shut the door loudly behind them. He didn't need any passersby peeking in at the sound of fighting.

Jamin turned on the boys and scowled at them. Their faces all read guilty. "What do ya think yer do'in here?" he snapped.

The boys all looked down. "Sorry, sir. But, um, you see—" One of them stammered. "We didn't know you'd be here, and we didn't think that you, um, trained other people, and we were kind of hoping to come in and train, uh, practice before our own training later. Sorry."

Jamin glowered. "Yah shud al'ways ask meh before goin' on an' decide-en *lamon safon iao* tr'in room *arc caogham!*" He realized a few words from his original language might have slipped out by the look of confusion on the Stexphins' faces.

Even still, the boys seemed more distracted with the continuing fight. Valkyrie had tried stopping to see what was going on, but Deirdre punched her in the back of the head.

"Ow!" she cried as she spun around and kicked her in the face, easily followed with her own punch.

Jamin looked back at the boys. He had been training them for almost two months now. They always came in the afternoon, and he was disappointed in them coming early. He didn't like them watching the two girls.

Two of the boys were twins and identical with white hair and light blue eyes. The third, and oldest, had dark brown hair with a strange mark on the side of his head.

Their names were Boady, Cale, and Griffen. Jamin found it easier to tell the twins apart because Boady was a little smaller than the others. Cale also had a strange black spot on his left Stexphin ear if looked at carefully.

"Go," Jamin pointed to the wall, "sit ovah there until I'm read-dae tah deal with y'all."

Ignoring the three, he turned back to the fight. It was easy to see Valkyrie was getting tired. Walking toward the wall, he selected two short blades.

"Right!" He called to alert them before throwing the weapons. Deirdre was ready and cartwheeled backward, catching the handle before landing gracefully, poised and facing her opponent.

Valkyrie was alarmed and missed as the weapon clattered to the ground. She hadn't been taught to catch flying weapons yet, and Jamin knew she was much better at throwing them.

He felt a little guilty about this fight. He had known from the start Valkyrie wouldn't win and be embarrassed, but that's what he was aiming for.

His next lesson: humility. *All fighters must have it.* Deirdre needed a bit more of it, but not even he could defeat his talented sister in physical combat.

Glancing once more at the boys, he was upset they had come on this day of all days. Silently, he felt a little bad and wondered if he should end the fight now or at least give Valkyrie an advantage by letting her use throwing knives, in which she was very skilled.

"All right," he said. "I can see y'all gettin' tired, but I want yer to continue. Use that way-pon as a break, instead of hafing to punchin' an' kicken yer way out of this one. Don't go all out becuz I can't afford tah take either of y'all to the hospital. Not anymore." He frowned at the smirking boys.

Jamin was glad the room was soundproof to the outside. Motioning for the girls to continue, he kept an eye on Valkyrie. She was okay with a short sword, but he knew she favored even smaller knives. She could much more easily throw and slice with a dagger than a sword.

He watched intently while Jaylee rolled away from Deirdre's deadly strike then jump up to be ready for her next attack. "Good," he praised her.

"*Loraglo faosiy.*" He frowned at his sister to calm down. "Don't attack yer o-pone-ent first thang. Try to dodge an' duck tah avoid usin' most of yer energy on tha first swing. Let yer attacker wear themselves out."

Both girls settled down and, for a moment, watched each other to see who would make the first strike. Jamin predicted Deirdre would.

Sweat made their skin glisten. Deirdre's usually messy bun wasn't even a bun anymore, and it stuck to her face and neck. Jaylee had wisely worn a tight high ponytail as usual.

Both of the girls wore short-sleeved dresses, but he knew neither of them had the proper fabric. He wondered where he could possibly find such clothing for them.

Deirdre could fight for a long time, but she hadn't worn the correct outfit for today. He was proud Valkyrie had even gone on this far. She was certainly pushing herself.

Deirdre took a sharp breath and raced forward, her sword extended behind her head. She swung the blade around in a swift motion.

Instantly, Jamin realized Valkyrie hadn't seen the attack coming. She wasn't going to move in time. Her shock had slowed her mind, and she hadn't been able to calculate it fast enough that she was being rushed.

His own agile mind sprang into action. Grabbing his sword faster than he thought possible, he threw it to collide with Deirdre's.

Everything was happening so fast, barely even he could keep up to make out the scene. He almost missed seeing Cale jump to his feet.

Deirdre herself realized the last second Valkyrie wasn't moving. But it was too late to stop the deadly swing.

Before the tip of the sharp metal sliced the girl's neck, another sword hit the hilt of her blade, sending a wave of vibrations from her wrists through the rest of her body.

Deirdre fell to the ground, moving her arms up to protect her face from the clattering weapons. A loud scream made her feel disoriented. Had she hit Valkyrie?

No matter what would have happened, Deirdre realized her sword would have killed her. Cale had seen it, too, and had tried to shove Valkyrie out of the way.

The girl now sat up, holding her face with a look of horror. Blood seeped through her fingers. It was Jamin's sword that cut her face.

Instantly, the young man was by her side. Disbelief matched everyone's expressions. Even Cale who still lay on the ground was pale as a ghost.

"I'm cut," Valkyrie's voice quivered as she stared at Jamin with wide horrified eyes.

"Move yer hand. Lemme see," he instructed. "It's not too deep," he tried to assure the group.

"Cale's cut too!" Boady cried, pointing at his brother.

Instantly, Cale sat up. He stared at his left arm in horror where a clean slice went straight across his bicep. His shirt had been cut perfectly along with it and was already soaked in red. Although Deirdre's sword had missed Valkyrie, it had found Cale.

*****

Valkyrie sat still, her eyes wide as she felt Jamin pull the small needle through her upper cheek. *Don't faint. Don't cry. Don't move.*

Jamin had instructed them they couldn't go to the hospital unless absolutely needed. After numbing the cuts, he took the two characters in turn to stitch their wounds.

As he finished, he sat back on his knees and shook his head with a pale expression. "Cap'n Ashton es goin' tah kill meh," he whispered under his breath.

33

FOUL PLAY

The moment Valkyrie walked through the door that night, Ashton instantly grabbed her arm and stared at her face. "What happened?" he asked, frowning.

"Nothing," she said, pulling her arm back and trying to escape.

"This isn't nothing." Ashton scowled deeper, grabbing her chin and turning her to face him as he examined the stitches once more. Valkyrie feared he might recognize the clean slice of a blade.

"It's late, can I please go to bed?" she asked, once more pulling away and quickly edging toward her bedroom door. "Please? I'll tell you in the morning."

"Don't think I'll forget," he replied.

I can give Jamin one more night before Ashton makes him dig his own grave.

*****

The next morning, Valkyrie woke up early to avoid Ashton. *I'll tell him at breakfast,* She decided as she walked into the magical cave full of the underground plants.

Usually, she and Ashton would meet Matthias and Alania here where they'd collect ingredients, then go to the doctor's small kitchen and make breakfast.

Lately, it had only been Valkyrie and the captain. Occasionally, Alania came, but it was easy to tell she didn't feel comfortable doing so without Matthias.

Valkyrie was surprised to find her there that morning. "Good morning." The nurse smiled at her.

"Alania, it's good to see you," Valkyrie said brightly.

"Jaylee, what happened to your face?" Alania frowned.

"Something I'm trying to keep from Ashton," she muttered.

Looking up, she saw Jamin and his group of friends enter. Silently, she wondered when Ashton would arrive. *Maybe I should warn Jamin. It's not a good idea for him and Ashton to be in the same room. No doubt he'd figure out right away what happened.*

Jamin and his friends always hung out in this cave. She had asked about it one day, and he told her it was the only place with enough air fresh to breathe. "*Rarlo aso Famasom. The twires jus ain't doin' it no more.*" She didn't bother asking what he meant.

"Is Ashton coming today?" Alania asked, turning her attention back.

"He should be."

"Do you know if there's been any word on Matthias yet?"

Valkyrie sighed. "If there has, he hasn't said anything."

She was about to ask how Alania was doing in the hospital when someone yelled. They both jumped and turned toward the entrance to see Ashton storming in. *Uh-oh!*

Ashton instantly stared at Jamin's group of friends. She followed his gaze but didn't see him anywhere.

"Where's Jamin?" Ashton roared.

He found out. This is bad!

"What's going on?" Alania asked with a confused frown. Eyeing the stitches on her cheek, she instantly seemed to understand it had something to do with Jamin.

"I hope he got to enjoy his meal because it's the last one he'll ever have," the nurse whispered under her breath as they watched the captain storm toward the group of Characters. "Should I head back to the hospital and prepare?"

Valkyrie thought she barely glimpsed Jamin hiding behind them. *I don't blame him for hiding. Anyone should. But he better get out of here before Ashton—*

She watched as Jamin leaped out from his friends and dashed for the exit like a madman. Ashton was after him in a dead sprint. "No!" Valkyrie shouted. "Ashton, wait!"

She leaped over a large sage growth and rushed for the exit. She was joined by Jamin's group of friends as they ran out.

"What's up with Ashton?"

She recognized Joaquin. "It's a long story," was all she said, glad she could keep up with the group of travelling warriors but sad when Ashton and Jamin disappeared around the corner at the same time.

There was no possible way for Jamin to outrun him anyway, but she was still hoping. A loud cry echoed in the halls. They rounded the corner to see Jamin on his elbows and trying to get up and scramble out of the way before Ashton could attack again.

Already, his nose was bleeding. Ashton had clearly given him quite the knock. "I can't believe you!" The captain began roughly, but before he could finish, Jamin's group of friends were upon him.

Valkyrie stood there, shocked. *What should I do?* She watched as Jamin's friends struggled to tackle Ashton who was stronger than he looked. Soon, he had all of them sprawled out on the ground. As he turned back toward the trembling Jamin, Valkyrie finally spoke up.

"Ashton, *stop!*"

The captain looked at her while Jamin cowered on the ground, covering his face from the blows he was expecting. "That's enough!" she cried. "Why are you attacking him? He saved my life! If it wasn't for him, you'd be visiting my grave right now. You should be thanking him, for goodness sake!"

Ashton scowled at the whimpering Character, then reached out a hand to help him up. Jamin took it and stood. "I-I'm sarry," he stammered fearfully, quickly backing up. "I'll stop if yah want meh too,"

"No!" Valkyrie said at the same time as Ashton.

She and Jamin turned to the captain with surprise.

"She needs it. I've learned I won't always be there. But I don't want her to die because of it!" He stepped closer to the Character and scowled dangerously.

"I ain't mean'en—We didn't—It happen-ed so fast," Jamin tried to explain.

"Let's go get you cleaned up, Jaybird," Joaquin interrupted, pulling him away from Ashton.

Jamin looked at him with fire in his eyes but held back and nodded.

After they left, Ashton shook his head.

"Really?" Valkyrie said to him. "*Really?* You had to *attack* him?"

Ashton turned toward her. He didn't look sorry at all. Without a word, he walked past her but stopped and eyed the stitches on her face once more. Shaking his head again with a sigh, he walked away.

Valkyrie wanted to scream. But she stopped. *I saw that coming. I guess I'm just surprised how fast he was to act about it. I mean, the day Jamin dies, it's going to be done by Ashton.*

*****

"Are you up for a game?" Walker asked, a challenge in his voice when she entered the algae-covered cavern.

"You bet I am!" she smirked, putting on her game face.

"Here!" Walker yelled, chucking the ball at her. "You start!"

Valkyrie caught the ball but hadn't been prepared and stumbled back. Walker's face read triumph all over. *He just wants to show he can beat me. But two can play at this game!*

"All right!" she called, using Virga's usual starting cry. Jumping up, she threw the ball as hard as she could toward the running Walker.

His face filled with panic, but he was quick to put his hands in front of him and catch it. But he himself stumbled and somersaulted backward. He looked dazed for only a second.

Quickly, he jumped up before the others could attack him. Scowling at Valkyrie, she couldn't help but feel a wave of pride wash over her. *He still thinks I'm a weak girl. But I'm more of a Deirdre Junior now.*

296

Walker chucked the ball back to Valkyrie but threw it far to her left so she had to run toward it.

"Hey!" Jolee yelled. "You're on the same side, it's not a competition, Walker!"

Valkyrie leaped and grabbed the ball. But this time, she didn't have the right kind of balance to land, and she fell into the algae, causing a cascade of vivid colors.

Her shoulder plowed harshly into the ground from the rough slide, and pain swelled inside into her old arrow wound. As water splashed around her, the sleeve on her left arm was pushed up to her elbow.

As soon as she stopped, she lay there for a moment and gasped, spitting water from her mouth. Hagan, who she learned was Jolee's brother, was the closest and quickly ran up to her.

"You're worse than the twins!" he exclaimed, grabbing her hand and pulling her up.

Valkyrie wiped the water from her eyes and laughed. She had seen the twins and their brother, Griffen, play before. They had a strange trick where they could boost Boady into the air. From there, he had a much better advantage and made the most scores.

In the last game, Cale broke his arm when they failed to catch him. When one brother was out, none of them played. She was shocked by their determination to continue such dangerous tricks.

"We're trying to perfect it. Someday, we'll be able to do even more!" they had told her.

"Hey, game es a still on!" Deirdre called, clapping her hands together and looking at her with eager eyes.

Valkyrie smiled and chucked the ball in her direction.

"Valkyrie!" someone called.

All the Stexphin turned to see Ashton walking towards them.

"Valkyrie?" Deirdre questioned as she caught the sphere.

Valkyrie's ears went down. She could see the sorrow in the captain's eyes, even from a distance.

The Stexphin passed many nervous whispers as Ashton neared. "It's Captain Ashton!"

"Why would he be here?"

"Are we in trouble?"

"He's one of the king's closest known warriors."

"I heard that anyone who tries to fight him dies before they can even look him in the eye!"

Valkyrie was a little embarrassed. She hadn't realized how great a warrior Ashton was.

"I need you to come with me," the captain said as he neared her. Out of the corner of her eye, she saw a few kids look very surprised.

"Jaylee must be in trouble."

Her sharp ears caught every whispered word. "What's going on?" she asked quietly, seeing the sorrow etched inside his eyes. She almost missed Deirdre telling the others Ashton was her father, but her sensitive ears caught it. "What? She's his daughter?" The other Stexphin stood around, looking shocked.

"I'm sorry, little one," Ashton whispered. "It's Matthias."

Valkyrie felt the color drain from her face, and she feared her legs might suddenly fail her. "W-What about—" But she couldn't think of anything to say.

Ashton could tell she wanted to leave, and he quickly led them out of the cavern, giving the Stexphin teens a small wave of farewell for her.

As soon as they exited, she asked in a tremulous voice, "What happened?"

The captain wouldn't look down at her as they continued to walk through the dark halls. "I just got word the group was attacked, just like ours was. Delta and a few survivors returned. Matthias wasn't among them."

Valkyrie felt lost. She couldn't contemplate what Ashton was saying. Matthias was gone? He wasn't coming back?

"He and a great many others were taken by Ragged Arrows," Ashton let out a shaky breath, and a few tears dropped from his eyes.

*****

Valkyrie woke with a cry. At the same moment, she hit the floor with a painful thump. She groaned and closed her eyes, trying to clear her head from the wretched nightmare.

It's just a dream. Just like all the other nights. It's not real.

She opened her eyes to find herself lying on the floor in her room. Around her was a mess. She stifled a cry and buried her head in her arms.

A knock forced her to wipe her runny nose as she scrambled to the door. She didn't have to ask to know it was Ashton. Unlocking the door, she opened it to see the tired captain standing there.

"I'm sorry," she choked.

"It's all right," Ashton said, hugging her. "I couldn't sleep anyway." He looked down at her and frowned, wiping away a tear. "Why are you crying?"

"Because I'm a monster!" she cried, burying her face into his shirt. Ashton sighed and led her to the almost destroyed bed. Setting her down, he looked her in the eye.

Valkyrie looked away and glanced around the room instead. Ever since the news of Matthias, she found herself waking from horrible nightmares every night. The worst of it was she transformed during these nightmares.

Every morning, her room was almost destroyed, and Ashton would tell her how he could hear her screaming and throwing stuff around. She shuddered thinking of it now.

Ashton was pretty bad off as well with Matthias gone. No one knew what happened to the Stexphin who were taken, but they were as good as dead.

Ashton grabbed her chin and turned her to face him with a soft, "Little one." A fire swelled inside her. "You are not a monster." He gave her a stern look to keep her from arguing.

"Then what am I?" she asked, trying to keep her voice steady.

Ashton was quiet for a moment before saying, "You're my daughter."

Valkyrie shook her head and leaned into him. "What am I supposed to do?" she asked. "When I grow up a-and… I can't live like this forever."

Ashton leaned down and grabbed the fallen binder of *Scriptures* like he had before.

Not that again.

"What do you think you should do?" he asked quietly, seeming to sense her reluctance toward the book he held.

"I mean," she started slowly, "I don't think I'm brave enough to go to Rotto, pretend to be on his side, and find out what happens down there."

Ashton looked at her with surprise. "And no one can expect you to do such a thing!" he exclaimed. "That's too risky,"

Valkyrie sighed. Then what *could* she do?

*****

Jamin scowled and stepped forward, "Nah. Stop, Jaylee," he said as he shoved her back. "What's wrong with ya lately? Yer gett'in weaker and predictable."

He shook his head and put a hand over his face, sighing. Valkyrie got up off the ground and scowled. "It's not like I'm meaning to be such a failure," she snapped.

Jamin looked at her with shock. "Yer also gettin' an attitude." He frowned. What was up with her?

"And you're also getting on my nerves," he heard her whisper under her breath.

Jamin ignored her and crossed to the other side of the room. "Jaylee, go a'head an' choose won or two way-pons of choice." He heard her mutter something as she went to the wall covered with knives and daggers.

She selected two smaller throwing knives while Jamin went ahead and grabbed his sword. Jaylee hated using swords. They're so heavy and long and just get in the way," she had told him once.

"All right," he said. "Be'gin, but do not go on an rush sah much and throw in sum of thee othah drills I have taught yah."

Jamin knew the girl wasn't getting enough sleep if any at all. He always had a few lessons every once in a while with each student to test their anger.

He found today seemed perfect for Jaylee. It wouldn't be long before she bubbled over entirely. He always tested his trainee before teaching them. Only he was surprised at how easily she had gotten frustrated today. Usually, his students were hard to get to.

Jamin ducked and rolled as a dagger just barely skinned the side of his face. *Imma gess'en I've reached her maximum.* He ran at her, lunging with his sword.

She pulled her arm back, preparing to throw her last dagger, but he was fast. In less than a moment, he grabbed at her arm, and she was forced to drop the dagger.

"Tah predictable, Jaylee," he said, letting go and stepping back. "What have I told yah bout—" He began but was stopped.

Jamin wasn't prepared as he saw a blade flash. He fell to the ground as his flesh cut open alongside his face. He didn't have to see it to know it was deep and dangerous.

"Jaylee!" he demanded, grabbing at his bleeding face. *An' Ashton was worried 'bout her? Cud she really be so angry she'd try—*

Jamin's ears sank behind his head, and his eyes went wide. He trembled as he stared face-to-face with a large dark gray Swiftmaw wolf with green flashing eyes.

He tried to think straight but couldn't. This was impossible. As large jaws dove for his head, he regained consciousness. Rolling back, he grabbed his sword. The monster was upon him in an instant, but this time, he was ready.

*****

Valkyrie groaned softly and opened her eyes. She blinked a few times as she slowly sat up.

"Ugh, what happened?" she asked aloud.

Looking around, everything was a blur. But as she looked down, she could just barely see the outline of red blood. Then everything came rushing back to her.

*No! I transformed! But th-that also means—*Valkyrie rubbed her eyes until her vision slowly began crawling back. Looking around the destroyed room, her hands flew to her mouth.

"No!" She trembled. There she saw him, the motionless form of Jamin. "No! *No!*" she cried, desperately stumbling toward him. "No, no, no!" Valkyrie sobbed as she bent over the still form. Jamin was soaked in red as he lay on his side. His sword was a few feet away from him, also covered in blood.

"Jamin?" she whispered. Large claw marks went across the back of his neck and down. "I killed someone. I killed Jamin!" she screamed in horror, covering her face with trembling eyes. *I need to get Ashton. He'll know what to do. H-He can help Jamin. He can save him.*

*****

Ashton was heading for the hospital to visit Alania. She had struggled after hearing the news of Matthias, and he felt it as his job to care for her now.

Walking into the large clean room, it was easy to find the nurse. She was putting a splint on one of the twins. When she saw him, she smiled and released the boys with a warning about playing too rough.

"Captain Ashton," Alania said calmly, her eyes shining. "It's good to see you. I hope you're not here on Jaylee's behalf."

"No, I actually came to see you. I wanted to know how you're faring," Ashton said quietly. He realized he wasn't nearly mentally strong as this woman.

She had to be for such a job.

Alania opened her mouth to speak when someone ran up behind him. "Captain!" the man addressed him quickly.

Ashton turned around. "What is it?" he asked.

"Your daughter, she's looking for you. Screaming and desperate, she is," the messenger said. "I tried to ask what was wrong, but she said she only needed you."

"Where is she?" Ashton frowned.

"Near the surface in the third tunnel," the messenger responded, nodding with urgency as the captain left.

Alania followed him out of the hospital, and it wasn't long before they heard Valkyrie yelling. The moment they entered the hall, Ashton called her name.

"Ashton!" she cried, running up to him and squeezing his waist. She was shaking and blubbering all over.

"Valkyrie!" he snapped. "What is it? What happened?"

"Jamin!" she choked out.

Ashton furrowed his brow. "I'm going to suck the very life out of that Character the minute I—"

Valkyrie interrupted with sobs. "I killed him!" she cried. "I killed him! I killed Jamin!"

Ashton felt his heart skip a beat, and his hands began shaking. Instantly, he knew what she meant.

"Ashton!" Alania gasped. "What is she talking about?"

"Valkyrie, go to your room. Now. Talk to no one," he demanded.

The girl shook all over, her eyes wide with horror.

"You can make it. Now go and don't come out until I come get you. Alania, come with me."

They took off in opposite directions, Alania once again following the captain. He found the door that he knew led into the training room. They went inside, and he quickly shut the door.

Weapons covered in red liquid scattered the room. Marks of blood stained the ground, proving the fight of a man and beast.

Alania reached the form before he even saw it.

"No," Ashton whispered under his breath, quickly approaching Jamin.

"He doesn't have a pulse," Alania said, wiping away the blood that ran down the man's neck. "Captain Ashton. You know what happened." She looked up at him with woeful eyes. "Did your daughter really do this?"

Ashton didn't reply. He closed his eyes. "What do we do with his body?" he asked under his breath.

"Care and give it to the family." Alania looked back down. Her hand hovered over the claw marks on the man.

"He's from a travelling group. I don't think he has family."

"I can't care for him here. We need to get him to the hospital. But, Ashton, I need to know what happened."

Ashton slowly picked up the lifeless form and stood. Jamin's eyes looked like glass. Blood was splattered along the side of his face. He couldn't believe this young soldier was really gone. And he felt it was his fault.

Ashton froze as the door slowly opened, and four youths walked in. The girl froze as the three boys beside her stared, mouths gaping.

He recognized the twins and their older brother instantly. The blond-haired girl, however, he had never seen before.

Boady instantly shut the door at the same time the girl screamed. "What'd yah do tah him?" she cried. "What'd ya do tah my brother?"

Ashton looked down in guilt. He had been wrong. Jamin did have family. "I'm sorry, little one," was all he could say.

The girl bit her hand, and a muffled scream escaped her mouth. The three boys looked sorrowful and scared.

"Deirdre," Griffen whispered, "we should go."

The girl ignored him. Holding her head high, she stared Ashton in the eye, and her tears left. "Did yah kill him?" she demanded. Her body was tense, and he knew she wanted to jump at him with fury.

Ashton shook his head. "No, I didn't."

"Then who did?" she yelled angrily.

"Deirdre," Alania said quietly, coming alongside Ashton. "Don't do this."

"That's my *brother!*" She screamed. "Who *murdered* my brother?"

"Sir," Griffen interrupted nervously. "I don't think he's dead."

"What?" Ashton glowered at him.

He laid Jamin on the ground, and Deirdre was instantly at his side. Fresh tears came back as she saw his injuries.

"How? Tell me!" Ashton snapped, standing over the boy.

"Sorry, sir," he trembled. "But the same thing happened to our father." He glanced back at his brothers. "Everyone thought he was dead. No pulse or breathing, but in the end, he was still alive. But, of course, by then, it was too late, and they couldn't save him," Griffen choked out the words.

"How can I save him?" Alania begged.

"After hearing of ways he could be saved, we began to study botany, starting with the underground plants here in the caves. *Eldorados* have the spike you'll need to bring him back," Boady pitched in hurriedly.

Ashton looked at Alania, and she nodded in determination. "Get him back to the hospital. Griffen go with your brothers and get as many Eldorados as you can. Cale, don't use your arm," she snapped with authority.

Instantly, the group split up.

"Please," Deirdre cried, "you have to save him. He's all I have left. *We're* all that's left."

34

DARTS

With shaking hands, Valkyrie pushed the long needle into her arm. Taking in a sharp breath, she closed her eyes and tried to shut out the pain. She could feel the fluid running through her veins.

Opening her eyes, she turned the gray pouch upside down and dumped the rest of the darts out onto her bed. She was sitting cross-legged over the nicely made covers.

Counting the darts, she realized seven were run dry. Only two were full. *I need to make more. Frazil told me the ingredients, and I wrote them down, but none of them are underground.* She looked up with a pained expression. *I'll have to tell Ashton I need to leave.*

Knocking on the captain's door, Valkyrie tried to plan out what she was going to say.

"Come in," came Ashton's weary voice.

Turning the knob, she pushed the door open and peeked in. Ashton was sitting at his own desk, his head in his arms. Silently, she wondered if he had been sleeping.

Ashton looked up at her, and she loosened to see his bleary eyes. He hadn't been doing well at all for the last week and a half. *He's so stressed. After my accident with Jamin, it's only added to his troubled thoughts. He already lost Matthias.* She closed her eyes sadly. *I'm just making it worse.*

She hadn't seen Jamin nor Deirdre since her last transformation. Ashton told her Jamin's traveling group had finally left, and he had most likely healed of his wounds and gone with them.

Alania refused to say anything until they told her what happened. But Ashton was just as stubborn, leaving them both on knotted ends.

"Ashton," Valkyrie began hesitantly. She walked into the room and shut the door behind her, leaning against it. "I need to ask you— more like tell you something."

Ashton blinked slowly as if he was half asleep. "Yes?"

"I, uh… I need to leave Smuir for a few days." She squirmed and glanced down, waiting for his outburst.

"Why?" he simply asked after a few minutes.

Valkyrie looked up with confusion. He wasn't upset?

Removing the pouch from her waist, she walked toward him and set it on his desk. Slowly, Ashton opened it and took out one of the darts.

"I'm running out," She explained. "I have to make more."

"Do you have to leave?" Ashton asked, looking up at her.

"Yes. I mean—" She held her wrist behind her back and glanced down nervously again. She hated talking to Ashton about her transformations. He was already going through so much. "I stopped taking them for a while, and that's when I started transforming every night until I finally went rogue on Jamin and—" Her voice choked.

Ashton looked back down and dropped the dart back in the pouch. A satisfying *clink* sounded as it hit the others.

"You can go," he said, laying his head back on the desk.

"Wait, really?" she frowned at him.

"Be back in seven days," he instructed. "That way, I can know your still alive."

Valkyrie was quiet. She didn't know what to say. He was really going to let her leave? Just like that?

"Ashton," she whispered.

The captain looked up at her. He looked so much older than he was, as if he was becoming diseased almost.

She bent down and wrapped her arms around his neck and under his arm, resting her head on his shoulder. "I'm sorry."

Ashton didn't sit up, but he grabbed her arms and sighed. "You have nothing to be sorry for. It wasn't your fault they died. I never should have let them leave." He was staring at three frames sitting on his desk.

Valkyrie looked at them as well. One was of him, his wife, and daughter; another of him and Matthias when they were younger; the last a pencil sketch of a baby boy with a strange mark around his right eye.

She knew he kept a picture of her in his jacket pocket at all times.

With one arm, Valkyrie reached for the paper he had been writing on. "What's this?" she asked.

"I have to keep training for my new scouting group. I'm trying to find characters who look for the job and can learn how to handle a blade. My last group was taken, probably killed. If Jamin were still around, I'd ask him to train some warriors for me." Ashton closed his eyes.

When was the last time he had even gotten a good night's rest? "I should go," she whispered, trying to ignore the pang he left in her heart.

"The man told me to let you go," Ashton mumbled, his eyes still closed. She realized he must be asleep. "The old man came and said you'd leave. He said to let you go. That I must stay here. You won't be alone."

*****

Valkyrie walked through the dark tunnels of Smuir in a hurry. *I have a week to find plants I know nothing about. I need help. But Ashton's sick. He won't come. Who could help me? Who would help me?*

No sooner had she thought the words, she saw Walker leaving the entrance of the caves. *It's worth a shot.*

"Walker!" she called, running up to catch him.

"Sup, Jaylee?" he replied, biting into the dark brown plant he held. The inside was orange.

"Are you eating a potato?" she asked, raising her brows and scrunching her nose in disgust.

"A sweet potato," he corrected. "Did you need something? It's late to be wandering the tunnels alone."

"Why are you alone?"

"Fair point," he said, glancing backward.

"Walker, do you know anything about plants? Besides the ones underground?" she asked, beginning to realize how hopeless this was.

"Uh, not really. You need the twins for that. But they're not here. They left with a traveling group a few days ago. I think Jolee knows a fair amount, though," Walker replied, stuffing the last bite of the potato into his mouth.

"Do you know where she is?" Valkyrie asked hopefully.

"Probably in the library like always around this time. Why?" Walker looked at her with accusing eyes. He scanned her cloak and traveling dress. "Are you leaving?"

"Yes, but only for a week. I need to find these certain plants for my, uh, sickness." Valkyrie quickly began walking towards the direction of the library.

"What? But how do you plan to get out of the mountain?" Walker asked, jogging to catch up. He was a little taller than her and had very long legs, making him fast. She knew from playing.

"Deirdre showed me an exit she found once," Valkyrie replied as they entered the library. "Huh. You were right," she whispered when they saw Jolee reading at the table.

It didn't take long to explain her situation with needing to find the plants in less than a week. Jolee knew each name and where to find them in Hickorywood. All except one—*the Althea plant*. It was a strange purple flower, but it's whereabouts were unknown. *Hopefully I'll stumble upon it?*

Soon, Walker and Jolee both followed her to the surface tunnel. There, she led them down a hall full of structures. "It's behind one of these shelves," she explained.

Walker grunted as he pushed one aside. "Not here."

Jolee peeked behind a shelf before moving it. "I think this is it," she said softly. Valkyrie joined her in pushing it aside.

Sure enough, a dark passage was hidden there. Valkyrie turned toward her friends. Stuffing her hands in her dress pocket, she said, "I can't ask you to come along. There's a war going on out there, and last time, we were attacked by Hollowed."

"You don't have to ask us," Walker said. "*I* want to come. I've never left this mountain before or at least not that I can think of. And you need Jolee. She's the only one who knows what these plants are."

Jolee frowned nervously. "I don't think I can go," she apologized. "My mom is really protective. I think she'd die before letting me leave Smuir."

Valkyrie's heart sank. Walker, he couldn't do much. He was fast, but it was Jolee who could help. Plus, it would be fun to have another girl come along.

Jolee walked with them down the passage, once more repeating what she knew about the plants and where she would most likely find them.

Walker had run back to his home, telling her not to leave without him. Valkyrie wished she could be as enthusiastic as he was for this trip. Mostly, she hoped she could find something that could help Ashton.

After walking for a while, Jolee carrying a torch for light, they found the exit. "How are you supposed to reach it?"

"I'm not sure," Valkyrie frowned, staring up at the closed gate overhead. "If we had a ladder or something, we could attach it to those hooks beneath the trapdoor."

"My brother, Hagan, makes a lot of things out of knotted rope. I'm sure he can make a ladder. Here, I'll be back." Jolee handed her the torch and took off running down the dark tunnel.

Valkyrie sighed. She had hoped to be out of the mountain in less than an hour.

Her ears caught the vibrating footsteps of someone tall and fast running toward them. "Walker!" She called to him as he approached. "What'd you grab?"

"A, uh, first aid, food, water bottles, and clothes for myself. I-I don't have a coat," he confessed, pulling his flannel over his arms tighter. "Do you think it'll be cold?"

Valkyrie turned her head in a thoughtful way. "Last time I went out, it was almost winter. I reckon it should be early summer now."

"So warm." Walker licked his lips. "All right. Where's Jolee?"

"She's coming now. I think she brought Hagan as well." Valkyrie looked past him at the sound of more footsteps.

Sure enough, Jolee came into view with her brother close on her heels. He looked as if he had just woken up as he rubbed his face.

Hiding a yawn, he looked up at the trapdoor and the rope ladder in his hands. "Walker, let me climb on your back," he said.

The boy instantly got down on his hands and knees.

Hagan stepped onto his back, waving his arms to keep balance. Standing on his toes, he grabbed the ceiling to steady himself. Reaching up, he tried to touch the door.

"Jolee give me some more rope," he instructed.

His sister pulled the thick cord off her shoulders and handed it to him.

Valkyrie watched with amused eyes as the boys struggled to attach the ladder. After a moment, Hagan had it, and he jumped from Walker's back.

Standing next to him, Valkyrie realized Hagan was half a foot shorter than Walker. He and Jolee both had soft brown hair with large dark eyes. *They could almost be twins.*

Walker, however, stood out with his orange eyes and height.

"Can I come?" Hagan asked as Walker climbed up the ladder.

"Cash!" Jolee snapped at him. "You can't just leave."

"Please, Jaylee? I'm so bored down here. Besides, you could use me. Dr. Trinity used to train me, so if any of you break something, I could be of great help," he begged.

Valkyrie hesitated. "I don't think I could protect all of you guys," she began.

"We're not asking for protection. We're asking you to take us with you," Walker replied, hanging from the ladder. "I mean, it can't be that bad. Besides, I've never seen summer."

"But if something happens to any of you, it'll be on my shoulders," Valkyrie tried to explain.

"Why? We're all about the same level of helplessness." Walker shrugged it off. "But if we all go, we can help each other out. Jaylee, you don't understand because you've been up there before. You've got to let us come."

Valkyrie looked at Jolee who nodded, nervously pulling her arms behind her back. "I think I'll go too," she said reluctantly.

Finally, Valkyrie agreed. They didn't know that she was trained. But the problem was, she only knew how to defend herself, not everyone else.

It took Walker a few moments before he was finally able to push the trapdoor open. He paused before disappearing over the edge.

"What's up there?" Hagan called up as Valkyrie began to hoist herself onto the ladder.

"Uh…a house? I think…maybe. It's really dark. But, hey! Look!" His voice began to fade. "Wow, I'm outside. Look, there's stars."

Valkyrie quickly pulled herself out. Taking in a quick glance, she saw they were in some sort of building. One half of the wall was missing, leading outside.

Walker stood in the dark cobblestone street, staring up at the twinkling sky. His backpack strapped in front of him, he looked like a strange silhouette.

Hagan and Jolee came up next, bringing the torch with them. Shutting the trapdoor, they looked around.

Jolee took a deep breath and smiled, her beautiful eyes twinkling in the dark. "It smells fresh up here!"

"Wait until we get in the woods," Valkyrie encouraged.

The four of them went out and stood in the street with Walker. "Put that light out!" he demanded. The moment the fire was gone, it took a moment for their eyes to adjust to the dark, but looking up, even Valkyrie had to gape in amazement.

"For living out here most of my life," she whispered, "I've never seen this many stars before!"

The dark blue sky was littered with twinkling white diamonds. Not a cloud was in sight, and a half moon reflected the lonely city.

"Where are we?" Jolee asked.

"It's Smuir," Walker smiled. "Before the wars."

"Our home," Hagan whispered.

*****

"Shut up," Tylar laughed, punching his friend in the shoulder.

Jagger responded with his own hit, slamming his fist into Tylar's gut. He grunted and bent over, grabbing his stomach painfully.

"Be quiet," Rhys snapped. "You boys fight like wolves over a dead carcass!" How did he come to be in charge of these three immature preteens?

The group of four wandered through the dark quiet woods. Rhys just wanted to get out. He had barely escaped Elkhorn before he found three boys wandering the woods.

They claimed to be from a group called the Oracle, which had just been attacked. Two of them were only fifteen. Jagger, on the other hand, was seventeen but was still as childish as the rest.

"*Rhys*," Petrichor asked rather loudly, "where are we even going?"

"Keep your trap shut or I'll shut you up myself," he threatened under his breath.

"Why is he so mean?" he heard Tylar whisper under his breath.

Rhys turned on them. "Don't you understand?" he hissed. "Rotto is sending armies out like that!" He snapped his fingers. "I just barely escaped the devil's clutches in Elkhorn, and I don't want to go back. The only reason he releases groups is to feed us to the Hollowed. I plan to make it out of here alive." He closed his eyes and took a deep breath. "Petrichor, I'm trying to find the lost city of Smuir or even the Cliff Shore Peaks. Anywhere but here."

"Elkhorn is that bad?" Jagger asked, discouraged.

Rhys nodded. Horrors of the preyed upon town flashed through his mind. "I just need to get out of these woods."

A sinking feeling began to enter his gut the farther they walked. He looked back at the clueless boys, then forward again. He was beginning to feel anxious.

If I hadn't stopped for them, I would be out by now. But I couldn't leave three boys out here on their own. Besides, they're different.

Tylar was the only and first Stexphin he had ever met to have inklike hair. Even in his form, his fur was jet black.

It was rare enough to be white, but never had there been a black-colored Stexphin. His eyes occasionally flashed a violet color whenever he expressed strong emotion.

Now *Petrichor* was white. Sort of. His hair had a strange light silvery look to it with gray faded lightning streaks going up along his ears. His eyes were a soft gray blue.

Jagger was completely dark brown, a more ordinary color for Stexphin. His eyes were large and dark-colored, and he had a stronger build than the rest of his companions.

His ears, however, didn't stick up straight like all Stexphin. Instead, they laid back as if limp, only slightly rising when the boy was listening with intent focus.

Silently, he preferred Tylar over the others. Although he was just as childish, he had a strange sensation of leadership and authority that most Stexphin his age didn't develop until they were *much* older.

Usually, a Stexphin teen didn't actually start acting capable until they were over the age of twenty-five. He had met quite a few who were incredibly mature for their age, though.

"Ow!" Tylar suddenly snapped, his voice going rough as he glowered at Petrichor. "Why'd you kick me?"

"I didn't kick anybody! It was Ja—"

"Get down!" Rhys cried out as something flashed from the corner of his eye. *They found me!*

A large Halberd flipped through the air, barely missing Jagger's head. The boy cried out and dove to the ground, pulling Tylar with him.

Rhys shoved Petrichor out of the way as another large weapon sailed their direction. *Griefolowtros.* He knew. *Only they use Halberds. We need to get out of here!*

"Go!" He screamed to the boys, pulling Petrichor back to his feet as Jagger and Tylar scrambled to theirs.

In an instant, three of the large lion-faced monsters jumped into the clearing. One of them released a roar that made the very ground vibrate.

Rhys tried to dodge a swiping claw but was struck to the ground. "Run!" he cried as the beast spread it's long wings in a threatening posture.

The Griefolowtros beat its wings and rose into the air, digging it's back talons into the man's legs as he did. Rhys screamed from the pain, trying to reach up and grab at the wound, but he wasn't released.

In one swift moment, the Grief swiped his large wings with enough force to slam him back down into the ground. For a moment, Rhys blacked out as his head slammed into the earth below.

A young scream brought him back.

Forcing his head to turn, he saw Jagger. The boy was thrown to the ground, three large flesh wounds running down and across his face.

This is the end.

As the Grief above him rose in the air again, Rhys barely glimpsed Tylar duck behind a tree. *Where's Petrichor?*.

Right as everything began to fade out, he glimpsed a large black wolf jump into view. It descended upon the blurry form of a white-haired boy.

35

WOUNDED INCOMERS

After arriving at a section of the ruined gate surrounding Smuir, it didn't take Valkyrie and her friends long to find themselves inside Hickorywood Forest.

They decided to find a good place to rest, then start their search for the ingredients in the morning.

Valkyrie was grateful to have friends willing to come out and help her. Even if they were more interested in just getting out, it was still risky for them to join.

Especially if we run into any of Rotto's armies or even if I just see Gavin and anyone else I know, what do I do if that happens?

Jolee yawned behind her, which seemed to send an echo through the young group. *We should stop soon. I just wanted to cover as much ground as possible before tomorrow.*

The trees were scary as they cast dark shadows along the forest floor. Their branches looked like claws, waiting to snatch any of them who risked to go near.

"Jaylee," Hagan addressed her. "Suppose we are attacked…what should we do?"

Valkyrie was quiet for a moment. "Well, I think you start with deciding right now if you would stay behind and help fallen friends or save yourself."

Everyone was quiet as they thought. Jolee answered first. "As terrified as I would be, I think I'd have to stay behind. I couldn't go on if any of you were in trouble."

"Same," Hagan replied, looking at his sister with a troubled expression. "I've worked with the doctors plenty of times before. I'm never allowed to do any real work, but one thing they always said was that I had to have the right mindset. That I had to think of myself last."

They all glanced at Walker. "Being dead honest, I think I'd run and save myself." The boy put up his hands apologetically.

"I believe that," Valkyrie said, a small smile playing at her lips. "Your probably the only one who could run away with enough speed to escape anyway."

"Hey, look at that," Hagan pointed ahead where a tree with a thick trunk had fallen over. Other trees bent awkwardly beneath its massive weight.

"Race you!" Walker called, shoving the boy.

Hagan hadn't been paying attention and instantly hit the ground with a loud thump.

Valkyrie quickly sidestepped him while Jolee broke into a run, never about to let down a challenge. Walker slowed down, glancing back to be sure Hagan was actually okay.

Distracted by the sudden commotion, Valkyrie caught the sound too late. "Jolee!" she cried, looking up at her friend who was faster then she looked.

Jolee's short dress was tangled around her legs and her wild curls in her face, but she began to slow at the sound of Valkyrie's warning call.

But it was too late. Someone came through the woods at a frantic speed. Their paths crossed in less than a second, and Jolee fell to the ground in a rough tumble with the stranger.

Hagan instantly scrambled to his feet, almost tripping himself in his desperation to reach his sister. Walker, who was the closest, only froze for a second before also running to the girl's aid.

Valkyrie was behind Hagan in a moment.

As Jolee let out a sharp cry, Walker dove into the stranger on top of her. They only rolled once before the taller boy had him pinned to the ground by his shoulders.

"Are you all right?" Hagan asked, getting down beside his sister. "Where does it hurt?"

Valkyrie, seeing Jolee had only suffered a rough tumble and wasn't bleeding, quickly went to Walker who still had the stranger pinned down.

She was surprised by Walker's quick reactions to jump in and save Jolee; instead of fleeing like he had said, she was even more shocked to see the stranger was a young boy around their age.

Whimpering and crying, he trembled beneath Walker's grip. Or maybe it was from the pain he was most likely in.

319

The top of his hair was matted down with thick blood. Above the mess, the top half of his left ear was ripped off completely. She gasped at the sight.

"What happened?" Walker stared in horror. He let go of the boy and stood, backing up. He rubbed his hands on his pants. Red streaks stained his shorts.

Valkyrie didn't blame his reaction. She wanted to back up herself and get away from the horrible sight. *I can't even begin to imagine what that feels like.* Her ears sank down at the thought. She reached back to be sure they were still there.

The boy rolled his head side to side, eyes wide in horror as he continued to whimper. His hands shook in front of him, and his legs jolted every other second.

"Hagan!" She turned toward him desperately. "You have to help him!" She knelt beside the sniveling boy. "It's all right, you're going to be okay." *I hope.*

Hagan sat beside her, his own eyes wide in horror. "I-I've never even seen such an injury," he stammered.

"You're the only one who knows enough to help him, though." Valkyrie looked at him fervently.

Hagan nodded firmly. "Walker, throw me your backpack," he said. "We have to stop the bleeding first."

Walker, looking bewildered, began to take off his pack. Before he could toss it to Hagan's outstretched arms, Valkyrie's ears perked up at the sound of crashing.

"Someone else is coming!" she called out. "Walker, behind you!"

The boy turned around to face a man his own height.

Instantly, this Stexphin Character grabbed him by the shoulders and threw him against a tree. Walker tried to kick out at him, his face full of shock.

Valkyrie jumped to her feet, and Walker dropped his backpack as two large hands wrapped around his throat. The boy kicked and squirmed beneath this older man's grasp, grabbing at the arms, holding him against the trunk by his neck.

The man turned his head to stare at Valkyrie. "Stop or I'll kill him!" he barked, his crazed eyes flashing.

She froze, holding up her hands to show she wasn't a threat. *Please don't see my daggers beneath my cloak.* Walker let out a wheezed squeak and stared at her with desperate eyes as he continued to squirm.

"Please," Walker coughed out. "I didn't do anything!"

"Let him go!" Jolee cried, scrambling to her feet. "You're going to kill him!"

The man looked back at the blue-faced Walker, then, seeming to come to his senses, released him. As soon as the boy hit the ground, he rolled on his back, coughing and choking for air. Jolee ran for him, ignoring the risk of passing the madman.

The Character didn't even notice her as he stumbled back. Valkyrie realized he was injured. His leg was swollen and bleeding, yet he didn't even seem to notice.

She glanced back at the white-haired boy where Hagan sat frozen with wide eyes, watching everything play out. *They must have been attacked together,* she realized.

The man saw the boy as well, and his eyes bulged. He looked to Valkyrie with another wave of frenzy as he rushed at her with outstretched hands. *He doesn't realize we're Stexphin. He thinks they're still being attacked.*

The man almost tripped on his bad leg as he tried to take Valkyrie, but she was quick. Sidestepping, she grabbed his right forearm and pulled him down completely.

He crumpled to the earth without even a cry, but his expression was full of pain. In less than a second, Valkyrie had one of her Swiftmaw daggers ripped free and pointed at the man. "Stay down," she demanded.

"Jaylee!" Jolee gasped. "What are you doing?"

"He's not a fighter nor armed. But he is crazy. He doesn't realize we're Stexphin. Hagan, finish helping that boy, then see if you can tend to this man. Hopefully, by then, he'll be in his right mind." Valkyrie looked at the man who stared at the dagger with wide horrified eyes. "I think he hit his head," she remarked when she saw the bruise covering most of his face and growing.

Walker sat against a tree, still trying to breathe normally as Jolee brought her brother his backpack. Hagan began to dig through it, pulling out clothes until he found the first aid.

Valkyrie's ears perked up again. "How many are there?" she exclaimed, moving away from the man who had closed his eyes and calmed down.

"Rhys!" a boy called, coming into the clearing. He stopped where he was, not daring to approach the group. Three deep gashes ran from below his chin, up and across his face. One of his eyes was swollen shut from where one of the scratches had gotten to close.

"This is too much," Hagan stressed as he instructed Jolee to hold the wadded up shirt against the boy's ear. Quickly, he moved to the man who seemed to have gone unconscious on the ground.

"Who are you?" the boy at the trees demanded. He was swaying, and Valkyrie knew he was losing too much blood. He held a Halberd in his hands, which he suddenly dropped.

"We're friends traveling through the woods in search of certain plants. Please, you have to let us help you," she pleaded.

The boy shook his head but cried out in pain, grabbing his bloody face. Staring at his blood-covered hand in horror, he swayed and fell to the ground. "Walker!" Valkyrie called to the boy who was still leaning against the tree. "You have to help me!"

He nodded and stood with a wheezed grunt. Together, the two of them went and grabbed the boy. He was still awake but was too weak to stand.

"One," Valkyrie counted, grabbing the boy's legs while Walker took him under the arms. "Two…three!" They lifted the injured boy without too much strain.

"Jaylee," Hagan's voice trembled, "there's nothing I can do for this man."

After settling the body they were carrying, Valkyrie quickly hurried to his side. "Look," Hagan said, pointing along the man's face. "He has internal bleeding. I can't stop that."

Valkyrie felt as if someone had just squeezed her lungs. *They're looking up to me. I have to stay strong. Focus on the matter at hand.*

"You did the best you can," she said, putting a hand on his shoulder. Her voice quivered, though.

The boy with the three long gashes down his face struggled to roll over and look at the man next to him. "Rhys," he said again.

The man's ear moved, indicating he had heard him.

"They won't...take me," Rhys forced out. "They can't take me back. Don't let them. Where's Tylar?" His body slumped, and his head rolled to its side.

Jolee let out a cry and covered her mouth with her free hand. Tears streamed down her face, and Valkyrie looked away, trying to keep herself under control.

"Did he just die?" Walker asked in horror, stepping away from the body.

The boy on the ground began shaking with sobs, and he tried to cover his face. His cries were soundless, and blood streamed into his open mouth.

"Hagan," Valkyrie choked out, inwardly scolding herself, "you can't help him, but *he* needs care." She nodded toward the boy.

Hagan took in a shaky breath, and she saw his eyes were red. "They always said this was the hardest part of the job," he said quietly as he moved toward the struggling Character.

Hagan went to work, and Valkyrie took over for Jolee. She held the shirt against the white-haired boy's ear. He stared up at her, his beautiful gray blue eyes shining.

Reaching up, he grabbed Valkyrie's arm. "What's happening?" he asked weakly.

She sniffed, squeezing her eyes shut as tears forced themselves out. *I hate this. I can't do it.*

But you have to. A low, radiant, purple glow came from her necklace. She looked down and felt a small confidence surge inside her.

"What's your name?" she asked the boy, her voice evening out. She gently wiped the blood away from his face.

"Petrichor." The boy closed his eyes, letting out a long shaky breath. He opened them again. Suddenly, his face was lit with terror. "W-We were *attacked* by Griefolowtros!"

"Calm down, Petrichor, tell me what happened."

He began crying, and she put a firm hand on his face, turning him to look at her. "I need you to tell me what happened. We need to know what we're dealing with. How many of you are there?"

"Only four," he said, shaking. *We have three.* "My friends and I were escaping another army. That's when Rhys, a man from Elkhorn, found us. B-But then these *Griefs!* They came from nowhere!" He began trembling again.

"How'd you escape?" she asked.

"T-Tylar. H-He betrayed us." Petrichor broke down into more terrified sobs. "I n-never knew!"

*****

Half an hour later, Valkyrie found herself leaning against the fallen tree. Around her were the two injured boys. She learned the other was named Jagger.

She didn't even notice when Walker came and sat next to her. "Doing okay?" he asked.

"I-I just didn't think of all the things we'd be attacked by would be Stexphin." She looked over at him. "Thank you for coming. I couldn't have done this on my own."

Walker let out a small scoff. "We have to be glad Hagan came along. Imagine if he didn't. No, don't actually think about that. That's not a good thought."

They were both quiet for a second before she asked quietly, "Did you do it?"

"Yeah… Hagan helped," Walker said quietly. "It's rough on him. He feels it's his fault."

"There was nothing he could have done," Valkyrie said, looking over where Hagan was lying against the tree. She doubted he was actually asleep.

"What about Jolee? How's she?" Walker asked.

"She's scared. Seeing Rhys die…really affected us all."

She looked back at Hagan. "Thank you for burying him."

"Someone had to." Walker shifted against the back of the tree as if to get more comfortable. After a moment, he said rather loudly, "Is it weird I'm enjoying this?"

Valkyrie turned on him and frowned in confusion. "What?"

"Just, you know, being out here. And I never would have imagined something like what just happened would have ever happen to a kid like me. I mean, I think I like the newness of it all. But I'll be glad to go back home."

Valkyrie inwardly smiled at his words.

"I need to tell you guys something," Hagan's voice made them both turn. She was surprised to see Jolee was awake as well. She was lying next to her brother, eyes open and filled with tears.

"What's up?" Walker asked.

Jolee slowly sat up and moved to sit next to her brother. *Something's bothering them.*

"I, uh, we…we aren't exactly from Smuir," Hagan began slowly. "Our mom took us there after Rotto started sending out armies. Our dad, however, took our older siblings to go fight. We, uh, never heard from them again."

Valkyrie was quiet. Walker looked at them with confusion.

"That's why I was so scared to leave," Jolee trembled. "I was afraid Mom wouldn't be able to handle it if we left."

Valkyrie began to understand. "If you guys want to go back, we can leave in the morning. I can come out another time and find these ingredients." She didn't really agree with that, but her friends needed to come first.

"No, that's not what we're saying," Hagan said, looking up. His large brown eyes reflected the moonlight overhead.

"We think—" Jolee buried her head.

"Oh wow!" Walker said with wide eyes as he exchanged a glance with Hagan. "You think Jagger's your brother?"

They nodded, and Valkyrie gaped. *What?* She stared at the injured sleeping boy. It was hard to notice anything with the wrappings around his face, but now it was mentioned, she saw the similar features between them. She was surprised she had missed it before. He almost looked exactly like Hagan. "How can you be sure?"

"We were too young to remember them, but Mom told us their names," Jolee said, a weak smile on her face. "Our father's name was Zior. Our oldest sister was Tully. Then we had two older brothers,"

"Kedesh and Jagger," Hagan breathed.

Valkyrie exchanged a shocked glance with Walker.

"I think it's a good thing we came," Jolee smiled through tears as she glanced over at Jagger.

"Are you going to tell him?" Walker asked, looking astonished yet excited at the discovery.

"I think he already knows. When I was wrapping his face, he froze up and kept staring at me with wide eyes. I instantly recognized him, and when he asked me my name, he got all sappy about it. Then I heard *his* name, and I just got quiet." Hagan looked down. "I tranquilized him after that."

*****

Valkyrie was surprised how fast she fell asleep after the Parry siblings admitted their relationship to Jagger. When she woke up, the sun was shining in her eyes.

Holding a hand in front of her, she blocked the light and looked around. Hagan and Petrichor were both awake and talking quietly. Jolee was sleeping nearby.

A soft snore in her ear made her jump. She looked at Walker, with wide eyes, who had fallen asleep laying his head on her shoulder. She carelessly pushed him away, causing him to wake up.

"What time is it?" He yawned. "My back is *killing* me."

"Jaylee," Hagan motioned to her. She went and joined them, smiling at Petrichor who only trembled fearfully. "Petrichor knows what we're looking for. The Althea plant."

"Really?" she asked excitedly. "That's awesome, where is it?"

A low moan from Jagger made Petrichor stare at his friend with a heartbroken expression.

Walker stood and looked around. "I'll be back," he said, jogging off. As his shadow crossed over Jagger's face, the boy flinched and ducked his head as if to dodge it.

His eyes opened, and he looked around with his one eye. He frowned and blinked a few times before suddenly sitting up. "Pet, you're alive!"

"Barely," the boy whispered. Then he frowned. "And don't call me Pet. I hate that nickname."

Jagger went quiet as he glanced from Hagan to Jolee. "Do you know who I am?" he asked softly.

"Yes," Hagan nodded. "Our brother. Pet told me how Father dropped you off at the Oracle barricade when you were younger and promised to return once you were older."

"He never did," Jagger said sorrowfully. He looked back at Jolee who now sat up, awake. "How... How are you?" he asked.

Jolee pursed her lips together and looked at him with an expression that read joy and sadness. "Better than you," she said quietly.

Jagger smiled.

"Can I... Can I hug you?"

Jagger didn't answer but crossed the short distance between them and wrapped his arms around her in a brotherly embrace. Jolee cried and squeezed him back.

Hagan watched with tears in his eyes, and Valkyrie nudged him to go join them. "It's your family," she said quietly.

Getting up, Hagan went and joined the hug.

Walker returned and looked at them. "Aw. Did I miss it?"

36

BURNED

Crowley—Year 319

"Lieutenant Fang, I want you to lead the Swiftmaw and those of turning to the opposite side of Canyon Gap until the Stexphin fortress is affirmed. Runyan"—he turned to the glowering Grief—"take your Hollowed and wait below the Fontana Cliffs. If Fang sends you a messenger, then prepare to attack."

"Yes, sir," Lieutenant Fang growled with a wicked smile. Crowley wasn't ever sure what to think about this Character. He had so much control over his mind that he had enough Swiftmaw in him not to go crazy yet too much Hollowed that the two combined created a terrible dark mind.

Runyan stiffened and muttered a "Yes, sir."

Crowley glowered at him.

As the two characters left to go prepare their armies, a Swiftmaw messenger began to approach him. *Finally.*

"Commander Crowley," the man panted as he transformed into his character form.

"Van Dyk. Report." He preferred Swiftmaw so much more. They were tough yet kind and very trustworthy. *It won't be long until even Van Dyk begins turning. He was my favorite messenger,* he thought sullenly.

"Holloway's army is camped in Hickorywood Forest. They wait for word before moving on," Van Dyk said firmly.

"Did that Grief learn anything about Elkhorn?"

"The town is still under siege. Holloway sent a few Hollowed in there against orders. They said the Stexphin are impossible to take because of a burning smog that keeps them entrapped."

Always honest.

"I've heard of rumors of this burning fog," Crowley mused. "Report back to Holloway and tell him to go inside ShadowOak Woods. I've just received word there is a group of survivors from *Elkhorn* hiding out there."

"How'd they escape that haunted village? Thought the place was a topper too tight to pop off with a corkscrew," stated a nearby Character.

Crowley inwardly brewed and motioned Van Dyk to leave. "It is," he stated with annoyance. This red-haired man was a Mislea Raptor named Block. And it suited him well. The Character was a large block. *Always in the way.* "Either I'm given false information or whoever their captor is released them to have them killed or kidnapped. We're not wasting any blood. If it is a trap, Rotto has enough Swiftmaw and Hollowed to spare. The loss won't be that great."

Block laughed. "I like the way you take things in, shake 'em up, and yet keep it in," Crowley scowled at him. "All right, yer makin' a point." The man put his hands in front of him and turned to leave.

Crowley didn't fear the Mislea, especially not Block. He was nothing close to Rotto. Personally, he couldn't even help but notice Rotto had an almost friendly manner about him. Nothing like that redheaded—

Crowley's entire body stiffened, and he stood up straight, staring after the retreating Character. *Was that?* No, he was most certainly seeing something.

He blinked a few times and watched as the Mislea pushed off the balcony built high in the strong trees of Wingspread. The Character disappeared over the edge and, a moment later, appeared as a large raptor. His four wings spread out to its tips, and he shot upward, caving in an arc before disappearing onto another balcony.

Crowley stared after him with fury. He could've sworn he had seen two Stexphin ears, even if it had been for just a moment. That man had short hair that was shaved on his sides, hiding whatever it was on the back of his neck.

It could've been. He closed his eyes, trying to imagine what he had seen. *No. I know what I saw.*

But do you? the all too familiar tone whispered. This voice was always there, bothering him day to night.

"Captain Commander," someone growled behind him.

"Report, Murphy!" Crowley snapped without turning around.

"Fang's army is ready to go."

"And?" This Character always had a catch. He was Swiftmaw but nothing like the ones he had met before. This one was as evil as a Hollowed but smarter than an average Swiftmaw. He was almost as dangerous as Fang.

"And I ask that my Stranglers and I have freedom to scout around the mountain," Murphy growled. Meeting his kind side was rare.

Crowley knew he hated taking orders from a Stexphin just as much as every other Grief and Hollowed. But he had learned not to let them treat him like garbage.

Turning on the young man, he stared at him with hatred. Murphy matched his height but stood even straighter at his reaction.

After ten seconds, Crowley answered in a voice harsher than his expression. "You can't get this permission from Fang?" he snapped angrily.

Murphy slightly flinched, and he let the Character see his victorious smile.

Murphy took a deep breath, hatred spewing from his eyes. "*Fang* is out of his place. You are the Rotto's second commander. *He* is nothing more than a leader of an army. I wish for permission from a higher source."

"You think Fang would decline your request?"

Murphy didn't answer.

"It's the price you fear from him. Yes, I have heard of his so-called lessons. You may have some peace to mind then. You have my permission."

"Would it be too much—" Murphy began, his anger slowly disintegrating.

"Yes, I will tell him myself. I do not fear that mixed monster. Do not think it's because I am Stexphin. Believe me, he has threatened more than just lessons for me. But I know secrets on how to snap him back," Crowley smiled rather devilishly.

Murphy smiled himself, showing he had changed his mind about him. "And what are these secrets?"

Crowley turned away, looking out across the trees. "You have my permission. Return to the army," he ordered harshly.

As soon as Murphy left, he whispered under his breath, "The secret is to have secrets."

No one knew where he had originally come from nor what he knew about the kingdom of Smuir. They didn't know why he was so harsh and demanding nor why he refused to make friends.

Characters had tried before, mostly the Swiftmaw leaders. Some, he could tell, just thought he needed a friend while others hoped to get on his good side so they could protect more Characters from having to go to the camps. But he treated them all the same—harshly with threats.

He wasn't here to make friends. He didn't *need* friends. Besides, no one was even worth it. *Except maybe Shadow if that annoying teen was still around.* The exact same age as Malachi with something unspeakable that reminded him so much of Selah. The boy was special, and yet, Crowley still couldn't place where he had seen him before.

But Shadow was gone. Officially. Keith had returned and reported he had killed the Character. Rotto told him later that the boy had betrayed them. Crowley didn't need proof to know that boy was a threat.

He didn't think his death was too great a loss, at least until that night when he had a nightmare about the Mislea, reminding him where he had seen the Character before.

*****

331

Crowley's eyes shot open. He didn't scream. He didn't gasp to find himself in cold sweat like he usually did.

Without even glancing around his room or checking to see if his short sword was still by his bedside, Crowley jumped from his bed and ran to the wall.

Tracing his fingers alongside the wood, he found what he was looking for. Sticking his index into the crevice, he popped out the large piece of sharp wood easily.

Reaching into the hidden crevice, he felt all the treasures he had forgotten about. He had hidden many things in this open slot when he first came to Wingspread.

As his fingers wrapped around a chain, his heart felt a sudden pang of loneliness. It was the same necklace that held the ring from Malachi's mother that he had given Selah.

Keeping the chain around his finger, he pulled out a piece of parchment. Unfolding the paper, he studied the photo of "The Son of King Declan's Daughter." It was dark, and he could barely see the smudged details, but instantly, he knew it had changed.

Where before the stretches behind the boy looked like shadows, he now realized they were wings. His eyes were pale white, and strange markings were above the boy's head.

No longer did his shirt say the words of the strange school, but now it looked like a snake. *What could it mean? Wait…maybe it's a clue. Like a direction. Riverforge Rampage!*

The more he stared at the drawing, the more he came to realize who all the clues pointed to, also revealing who this boy was before.

At the same moment, he realized there had been a presence in his room since he had woken up. Turning around, he stared at the Character who watched him across the shadowed room. It was the wicked Grief, Runyan.

"What are you doing here?" Crowley asked in a tremulous voice.

"I'm here to kill you, sent by Acrimony himself!" the Grief announced in a strident tone. He held a short Halberd in his left hand.

Crowley couldn't think straight. His dream had cleared his head from the burning fog that had entered his mind the day he arrived. And he knew it would return.

Runyan jumped at him, the roar of a deadly lion escaping his lips as he thrust the Halberd forward. Crowley quickly transformed, easily missing the sharp point.

Leaping forward, he transformed again, this time grabbing Runyan around the neck, then swinging his body around the man so he was put in a headlock. The Grief was forced to fall back, but he was more clever than that.

Runyan transformed, and Crowley's grip was lost. The Griefolowtros instantly turned on him, horrific jaws open and ready to tear him apart.

The Son of King Declan's Daughter

Before he touched him, the Halberd which Runyan had dropped during his transformation was suddenly being forced between them.

The sharp point pierced the lion-headed creature in the neck. At the distraction, Crowley quickly rolled away. He turned to see who had just saved his life. It was Slecherick, a white-feathered Mislea Raptor who had originally been second-in-command.

Runyan transformed back into his character, the halberd in his own hands now. His neck was a mess, but something seemed to be giving the Character the strength to keep going.

His eyes were completely black as he swung his weapon around to hit Slecherick, barely missing Crowley in turn.

Before the weapon passed him, Crowley reached out with his hand, holding the long chain. It hooked on the halberd, stopping it from continuing to end Slecherick's life.

Runyan turned on him with hatred in his eyes.

Crowley grunted as he pulled the chain toward him, trying to force the weapon from the possessed man's hands. But Runyan's strength was outmatched, and he pulled the halberd back, jerking Crowley along with it.

The ring dug into his palm, but he ignored it, refusing to let go. Slecherick leaped forward again. With flailing daggers in his hand, he jumped on the man's back and brought his blades around his front.

Runyan didn't even seem affected by the older man's continuous cutting.

Crowley didn't hesitate. With sweat running down his face, he hooked his ring on the end of the Halberd. The Grief tried to swing the weapon back to begin another slicing attack, but Crowley grunted and pulled on the chain, forcing it to stay down.

Runyan let out a horrifying sound of rage and tried once again to stab him. Crowley fell back, barely ducking.

Slecherick was suddenly thrown off the man's back, and Runyan kicked Crowley in the ribs to keep him down as he swung his weapon around toward the Mislea character.

Crowley screamed like never before as the chain cut through his fingers from the Grief's strong momentum.

Still, he didn't quit. With the two fingers he had left on his right hand, he grabbed the piece of wood popped from the wall and chucked it at Runyan's head as hard as he could.

The sudden movement made him cry out from the pain in his cracked ribs.

The sharp wood missed the Grief's head completely but instead planted itself into the man's hand. With a scream of hatred, Runyan dropped his Halberd and turned on Crowley with such a demonic look he never felt so afraid in his life.

He barely caught Slecherick grabbing the Halberd in a mad scramble. As Runyan began the attempt to transform, Crowley screamed, "Cut his head off!"

Midway in transforming, the axe of the halberd arced around and struck the Griefolowtros' neck. Slecherick took the weapon back from the screaming character and swung it around again. This time, it cut through completely.

Crowley yelped as the lion-faced head landed on his lap. Quickly, he threw it aside, watching it disappear beneath his bed. *I'm never sleeping there again.*

Finally, with the foe dead, Crowley let himself go limp and fell on his back. He took in great breaths of relief as Slecherick dropped the bloodstained weapon noisily.

It was still dark in the room, but looking at Slecherick, Crowley forced himself to sit up. "What?" He panted. "Why did you come?"

The older man, at least over forty, looked at Crowley with a desperate expression full of sorrow and fear.

"I had a dream," he forced out. "You were in it. And I know you saw the same thing."

Crowley was stunned. He had never even spoken to this Mislea before.

"You have the answer we need," Slecherick continued, nodding to the crumpled paper on the ground.

Crowley reached out to grab it, but seeing his bloody right hand, he was reminded of what happened. His shock gave way to the incredible pain he felt. He cried out.

With only his thumb, index finger, and half of his middle, he was disgusted to see what had become of the rest.

Slecherick, seeing the condition he was in, went forward and grabbed the parchment. He collapsed to his knees beside Crowley and held out the drawing for both of them to see.

"It's Shadow," Crowley grunted through pain. "He's the answer. He's the one. The only one who can save us, who has the power to free us from Acrimony."

"But Shadow's dead," Slecherick cried in desperation, dropping his head in agony.

"I"—Crowley took a sharp intake of breath—"I was told he and another were the only two who could stop this darkness. But if Acrimony were to ever reveal himself, this would mean they had been murdered,"

"It's too late then," Slecherick breathed. "Acrimony is here. He's been here all along. Inside of us. Wherever that dream came from, it's cleared us from the smog…but not for long,"

A girl who haunts dreams of the future. Could this be her who sent us the dream? But who is it?

"What is he going to do with us?" Crowley whispered, sounding harsh as he tried to shut out his pain.

"We can't escape this entrapment he's set in our minds. He controls us. And he's going to make us kill ourselves," the man whispered.

Slecherick's words made him uncomfortable but in a way he felt as if he had already known.

Acrimony is so much more than we realized. But I think I knew. All along, I've known it wasn't just a voice in my head. I deserve to die. I've become a monster. I'm no better than a Hollowed.

"So be it. It's too late for me anyway. My life was over the minute I arrived here." He looked up at Slecherick with a masked sorrow. "The devil owns us now."

*****

Knowing they could never escape, the two Characters parted, heavyhearted. Crowley found a Serf willing to care for his wounds and then asked for a place to sleep.

It wasn't until then did he realize who this woman was. She wasn't some ordinary slave but a strong leader inside April Bend and feared by many Characters, including Swiftmaw.

And while knowing who he was, the Stexphin led him to a spare room where he could spend the night. She didn't ask questions, which he was glad for. How would he explain their was a decapitated Griefolowtros in his quarters?

As Crowley lay on the straw mattress, he was tempted to tell this woman everything before the burning fog returned and once again took over his mind.

But would she even believe him? She, no doubt, saw him as the monster who betrayed their kind and killed her children.

Besides, how could he know Acrimony didn't control her as well? No. It was clear this woman owned her mind.

Lifting his head, he glanced painfully at his hand which she held, replacing his missing fingers with fakes.

By morning, I won't be myself and I won't remember any of this even happening. I have to tell her. She may be the only one who is strong enough to help.

"Mrs. *Brooklyn*," he addressed her. "I need to tell you something."

337

37

PORTAL

Valkyrie—Year 316

The next two days, Valkyrie and her group of friends enjoyed each other's company while collecting the wildflowers and unique plants.

The second day, Walker told Jolee that she had a new "Flower Partner."

"Who?" she asked, frowning in confusion.

"It's Pet. He knows more stuff than the entire library of Smuir put together!" Walker smiled.

Petrichor was quiet as he walked beside them. It was also because of this boy that Walker had been able to find a certain weed to give the injured enough strength to travel.

"How do you know so much, Pet?" Hagan asked as they searched a few tree roots sticking from the ground. Petrichor had told them the Cazador Cactus only grew around surfaced tree roots.

"Please, don't call me Pet," the boy said quietly.

"*Petrichor* has an excellent photographic memory. Back at the Oracle barricade, he loved to learn as much as possible and read every book he could get his hands on," Jagger explained.

"And what did *you* do?" Hagan asked.

"I trained with a young man named Jase. He taught me how to fight with a Halberd. It's a Grief weapon, but it's very handy," Jagger said, lifting the short weapon he had stolen from one of the dead Griefolowtros that had attacked them.

"It'll be nice to have another who knows how to fight," Valkyrie smiled at him.

"You fight?" Walker asked, looking at her.

She ducked her head in embarrassment.

"Jagger," Jolee changed the subject, glancing over at her older brother, "will you stay with us?"

He shook his head apologetically. "I'll travel with you until you find everything you're looking for, but I don't want to go to Smuir."

"Where will you go?" Hagan asked.

"I plan to search for our father, Zior. I don't believe he was taken, and I hope to find where he has settled."

"Mom will understand," Jolee said, but the disappointment in her voice was obvious.

"Here!" Walker called, pointing beneath a raised tree root. He dropped to his stomach and tried to peek beneath it. "I felt something. Yup! I found them. Cazador Cactus. Dang, you weren't kidding when you said they were small."

As Jagger helped them extract the short sharp plants, Valkyrie walked over to Petrichor.

"Pet, you said you know where the Althea plant grows. That's all we have left to find now." She smiled at him with gratitude.

He didn't look up at her from where he sat. "I really hate being called Pet," he said quietly. "I'm not someone's animal that they love for what I bring them."

Valkyrie sat down beside him. "I'm sorry. I didn't mean it that way at all. It just kind of rolls off the tongue because Petrichor is such a long name." She paused. "Can I call you Pedro instead?" A teasing smile played at her lips.

"It beats Pet." For once, the boy looked up at her, his own small smile appearing.

"And I'm not just glad you're here because of all the information you've been giving us. I like you for you."

Petrichor looked away again. Another wave of terrified chills raced through him. Valkyrie had spoken to Jagger about this. The boy told her this never happened to him, but something during the Griefolowtros attack seemed to have dug a new fear into his heart.

"I promise, he used to be such a loud, fun boy to be around. It breaks my heart to see him like this. But he's also always been a little closed up. I don't think he'll ever say what's wrong," Jagger had said.

"The Althea plant only grows in Riverforge Rampage," Petrichor said. She looked up to see his chills had left. "I've never been there before, but I know where it is."

"I've heard of that place before," she said, remembering how Ashton had brought it up before their scouting trip was ambushed. *Dr. Trinity was going to take me there.*

"I don't know what this disease is you have," Petrichor began, "but it's got to be dangerous." He looked up at her with his gray blue eyes.

She was discouraged to see the dry clods of blood still sticking to his hair and matting around his ears. His left, the one that had been torn away, was still wrapped tightly.

"Why do you say that?" she asked.

"Because I know botany. Combining all these ingredients, it's a strong concoction I've never heard nor thought of before. What will it do to you anyway?"

"Keep me alive and stable," she said, looking away. Ashton had talked to her about it and said it didn't have to be a lie if they looked at it as a disease that was forced upon her. It made her feel more confident with telling people.

*****

"Here it is," Petrichor said later that day as they arrived at Riverforge Rampage.

After walking most of the day, they had finally arrived at a section of Hickorywood Forest that was also stretched out into the Meadow of Hidden Rock.

Valkyrie gasped, along with a few others at what they saw.

A large trench made entirely out of ragged stone went into the earth for almost twenty feet. The walls became narrower the closer to the bottom.

It was evening, but the setting sun shone perfectly through the rising boulders around the trench. The light almost even seemed to reflect off the stones, shining down into the pit.

At the bottom, shadows and smaller crevices formed the shape of what almost looked like a curved snake.

All around the top outside of the crater was solid stone. Cracks ran throughout it, an unlevel ground. A strange white flower with dark red splotches grew out of these crevices. *Althea.*

"We should camp out here," Jagger said, motioning around the large section of flat rock. "Just stay away from the edge. If anyone falls, I'm not going in after them."

The group went to work, collecting a large amount of the strange flowers. "If we head back tomorrow," Valkyrie smiled, "we'll be a few days early. Smuir wouldn't have even missed us."

"It'll be good for us too," Jolee smiled. "I think Mom will suspect a week-long sleepover."

Thankfully, the nights were warm. None of them had blankets nor pillows, but Walker freely shared extra clothes that weren't stained with blood for pillows. He complained openly the first two nights about having to sleep on the hard ground. But tonight, he didn't.

Valkyrie watched the sky darken overhead, her hands behind her head. Nearby, Petrichor trembled in his sleep, Jagger and Hagan quietly laughed, and Walker snored. Jolee slept soundlessly every night.

I think Virga would be proud to see I have friends, Valkyrie thought, rubbing her necklace with a small smile. Instantly, it was replaced with a frown. *If he hadn't left me, he could've been friends with them as well.*

He never meant for you to be on your own for so long,

Did he mean to leave me? Did he even think of me as he ran into the cottage?

Yes and no. It's the truth that he left you without a second thought. He had other matters on hand.

Valkyrie inwardly scowled at the purple glow. *I don't even know who or what you are. Am I talking to myself or do you live inside my head?*

Neither. But that's not important. You're at Riverforge Rampage. Get up and go along the edge of the trench. If I'm correct, tonight is the night. There are some things you need to know.

What do you mean the *night? Know what?*

When the purple glow inside her mind didn't answer, Valkyrie hesitantly sat up. She glanced around the group to realize Hagan and Jagger had both fallen asleep.

Careful not to wake the others, she scrambled to her feet. Wrapping her cloak over her shoulders, she left her shoes and began to walk across the stone.

As she neared the edge of the trench, she looked down just to notice it was so dark she couldn't even see the bottom. She began to pull her hair back into a ponytail and, squinting, she glanced up at the dark sky. *Where are the stars? And the moon?*

"What are you doing?" a shaky voice asked from behind her. Turning, she saw it was Petrichor. He looked terrified.

"Pedro," she said, his new nickname already sticking. "I'm... just looking. Come on." She motioned for him to join her. He did so hesitantly. Glancing down the pit, he quickly stepped back.

"What are you so afraid of?" Valkyrie asked softly. "You've been acting standoffish since we've arrived,"

"I-It's this place. There's so many stories. Such bad dangerous stories about this trench." He trembled. "It only happens on certain nights, and tonight is that night."

"What are you talking about? What stories?" Valkyrie's heart rate began to speed up.

"No moon. No stars," Petrichor mumbled under his breath as he stared back down into the shaft. "All that's left now is—"

A loud noise that almost sounded like thunder ripped through the air. Valkyrie screamed, and Pedro cried out, covering his ears.

In less than a moment, a strong wind full of dust rose from the trees, causing the large trunks to sway with crackling noises. The whirlwind turned it's direction and began to push against them with immense force.

Valkyrie's cloak was instantly caught in the wind, forcing her to step backward as she covered her face and struggled to keep her balance. Her heel went over the edge of the trench, and she released another scream.

"Pedro!" she cried, trying to reach out as she tripped backwards.

The boy was quick, but not quick enough. He reached out and clutched her hand, but she had already gone over the edge.

She barely glimpsed Jolee sitting up. A bright light flashed below them. "Jaylee!" her friend screamed.

The two Characters fell over the edge and down toward the growing light below. Valkyrie turned her head around to see what it was.

Before she knew it, they hit the bottom. White flashed everywhere. She lost her breath as strong sensations shot through her body. Then everything was silent. And dark.

A small breeze blew across her back, pushing her cloak up her legs. Valkyrie opened her eyes with a gasp.

Quickly, she sat up and looked around. Pedro lay in a heap nearby. *This isn't Riverforge Rampage. Where are we?*

The air here was thick with dusty fog. It was dark, and everything had a strange brown color to it. The ground seemed to stretch out for miles, covered in something *What is this? Am I sitting on rocks?*

Valkyrie picked up the hard shape beside her. She stared at it for a moment, trying to see what it was. "Oh!" she cried, instantly dropping the small animal skull.

She gasped in horror to see what she was sitting on were bones. She didn't recognize the shapes at all. But they appeared to come from an unheard of animal.

"Ew, ew, ew!" Petrichor suddenly cried beside her. Lying on his stomach, his face filled with disgust and horror as he, too, realized it were bones he was lying in.

He scrambled to his knees, trying to push away the bones. But it was useless. "Where are we?" Petrichor looked around.

"I-I have no idea. Where are the others?" she asked, fervently glancing around.

"They're not here," Petrichor said quietly, another wave of chills running throughout his body.

"Hey," Valkyrie said, softly crawling to his side. She placed her own trembling hand on his shoulder as she continued to look around. Silently, she feared whatever monster that had killed these creatures might suddenly come roaring through the fog.

She looked back at Petrichor. "We've gotta stick together if we're going to get out of this mess. I can't do this on my own. There's nothing to be scared about. Well, maybe there is, but that doesn't mean we *have* to fear it."

The boy pulled his knees in and covered his face. Wave after wave of chills coursed through him.

"Pedro, be brave. Like you once were."

Slowly, he stopped shivering. Looking up at her, his blue gray eyes looked different. Although glossed over with tears, a recognizable confidence seemed to be returning.

He's coming back. A small smile tugged at her lips.

But then the confidence disappeared, and his eyes widened. He dropped his hands to the ground and gasped painfully. Staring straight, a thick fog covered his eyes.

"Ped—" she began, but a sharp pain shot through her head. It was so severe she lost her breath and collapsed to her side. She couldn't think straight as a strange thick feeling entered her brain and burned her mind.

You can't escape me, hissed a dark voice. *For you have no protection. Only one is more powerful than me, but you aren't a believer and don't have any spiritual.*

Suddenly, a bright purple light flashed around them. It looked like energy as it surrounded them with exotic sparks. She tried to clear her mind to focus on the sight but couldn't as they lay on their sides, mouths open and shaking severely.

For the briefest moment, the gleam froze. Valkyrie's eyes began to cross, and black spots began to cloud her vision. Before passing out, she saw the purple energy spark forward with extreme force.

She cried out as the purple light blazed through her mind with a painful spike. Slowly, her head cleared, and purple glitter slowly faded to the ground.

*****

"Jaylee. *Jaylee.*"

Petrichor's voice cleared her mind, and she blinked a few times.

Looking up, she met the boy's worried blue gray eyes. "What happened?" she asked, suddenly terrified as she remembered. Quickly sitting up, she glanced around and was disappointed to realize they were still sitting in the foggy meadow full of bones.

"Your necklace." Petrichor pointed at the uneven charm around her neck. "It has a Magia Ore inside. It attacked whatever that *thing* was in her heads."

She was shocked he had said all that without trembling. "But a Magia Ore? I don't understand how it got into my necklace." She glanced around the dark area again. "Do you know where we are?"

"Yes. We're in the Deserted Hinterlands."

"But that's—how did we get here? Riverforge Rampage, is it a portal?" She looked at him fervently.

"Something like that. It's uncontrollable, though, and rarely opens." Petrichor looked around, his brows scrunched together with fear. "We need to leave this graveyard."

"Graveyard?"

"This is where the Colossal Wars ended…and two races went extinct. Until Rotto, that is." Petrichor stood and held out a hand to help her.

She took it and smiled at his firm grip. Getting to her feet, she looked around. "A-And my name isn't actually Jaylee. It's Valkyrie."

"Why did you falsify your identity?" Petrichor asked quietly, almost as if he already understood why.

"I felt the need to." She gazed into his eyes. "And I felt like I needed to tell you." They were both quiet, so she changed the subject. "You don't happen to have a map, do you?"

"No, but I have this." Petrichor pulled out a small compass. It was cracked across the top. "Let's hope it still works. We need to get back to the Meadow of Hidden Rock, which would be"—he turned in a circle before stopping—"northwest. That way."

The two of them walked carefully through the bones, Valkyrie trying not to feel disgusted. Finally, the skeletons ended, and they were walking on solid earth.

She glanced back at the pile, trying to see through the musty air. "Those weren't the bones of Mislea nor wolves. None of them were." She met Petrichor's eyes. "I think much more happened during the Colossal Wars than we know."

Petrichor looked back as well. "I... I noticed too. I've only heard of one such creature with bones like those. Did you notice? They were stronger than steel, and none of them were cracked or broken. Only pulled apart by the joints."

She hadn't noticed.

"Look, what is that?" Valkyrie pointed over at the ruins.

"Fortresses," Petrichor said.

Does he know everything?

"I think... I think we should check it out." He looked back at her. "Reporters and publishers have come here before, searching for more answers on the Colossal Wars, but rumor always said they didn't return. And if they did, they never said what they found and eventually went insane."

Valkyrie looked at him with horror. "Then why should we stay any longer? As much as answers would be—"

"Because of that." Petrichor touched her necklace with his index finger. "Your Magia Ore is protecting us."

As wrong as it felt, Valkyrie nodded firmly, and the two of them walked over to the crumbling stone walls. Soon, they were standing in front of the closest one.

In black spray paint, Valkyrie read aloud, "*The Destroyer owns this land.*"

Petrichor walked away from her and looked at another near wall. From there, he finished reading the message, "*And is coming for the realms.*"

They cast each other uneasy glances. "Who's the Destroyer?" she asked quietly.

"Whatever it was that tried to *own* us," Petrichor trembled.

38

A WAR GRAVEYARD

"Why do you think the portal opened up here?" Valkyrie asked quietly.

"I'm not sure. It always seems to go someplace else for different people," Petrichor said as they stood side by side, staring at the words painted in black across the ruins.

"But there must be a *reason*," Valkyrie replied.

Petrichor looked at her necklace again. "I still can't believe you have a Magia Ore." He slightly smiled. "I've always wished I was gifted." He looked at her curiously.

"I promise I'm not," she said. "I still don't know how this thing got in my necklace." *You still won't talk to me? For once when I actually want to hear your voice.*

Ever since Petrichor had pointed it out, the purple flashes and lecturing instructions seemed to have disappeared altogether. *Was it you? Did you send us here? Why? At least give me some sort of sign!* she inwardly begged.

Purple energy shot from the charm. She stepped back, trying to escape it, but knew she couldn't as it was coming from her.

The purple formed in front of them, then stretched out into a strange faded wall. Petrichor stepped back as well, eyes wide.

They watched as the energy coursed into shapes and forms of characters.

"What is this?" Petrichor asked.

"This is what happened," Valkyrie breathed as the characters began motioning to each other. They ran out of the fortress at the same time a large Mislea Raptor carrying military flails crashed through the stone, destroying half the building.

The Characters ran, but only a few escaped. Transforming, it showed at least eighteen of the creatures fleeing toward Sealgaire Gorge.

"That's—they aren't wolves," Valkyrie gasped.

"But then what are they?" Petrichor frowned. "These *must* be the blue wolves, but they don't look anything like Swiftmaw. Why would they be named wolves?"

Everything began to play out in a rush. The blue "wolves" were chased out, most of them murdered. The Mislea Raptors were deadly and their numbers great.

A small group of blue wolf Characters ran forward. "Aim for the wings!" the one who appeared to be leading called.

Each character in this small band carried large crossbows much larger than an average Stexphin's. Instead of metal pointed arrows, each bow carried large spiked pieces of wood. They almost looked like pitchforks but with additional splinters carved to stick out around it.

This small brave group traversed on while others tried to retreat. Already, bodies lined the ground. Very few were Mislea.

The blue wolves were losing greatly. This small group continued to strike forward. Many of the Mislea fell from the skies from their beautiful aim.

"Rally on me!" their leader called. "There!" He shot the first spike at the quick diving Mislea. Instantly, the rest of the group came and knelt on one knee or stood beside him. They all followed suit, seeming to know which wing they were supposed to shoot at.

Instantly, the Mislea fell, it's wings shredded. The raptor transformed as he hit the ground, but his injuries were even worse in Character form. He screamed, his arms and torso a horrific sight. Valkyrie gasped and quickly looked away.

The scene skipped ahead and showed the strong leader of the fighting band attacking a Mislea Character. He used a long unheard of spiked Pitchfork while the Mislea used a short military flail.

Valkyrie grabbed Petrichor's arm in horror as the spiked ball struck the gallant blue wolf character across the face. He fell to the ground, motionless and torn.

The small group was separated in their own combats, but the fall of their courageous leader couldn't be ignored. Crying out, one of the blue Characters began fighting toward the destroyed fortress.

Going in, he struggled to lift fallen debris. Instantly, another came in. "You can't!" this character cried.

"We have to!" the blue wolf barked. "There's no other way!"

"But if they get their hands on—"

"I won't let them!" snapped the character angrily. Finally, it was revealed what they were searching for as they pulled out a dark gray jagged stone.

"A Magia!" Petrichor gasped.

The blue wolf took the Ore and ran out of the fortress. Turning the two sides and reaching into the center, a strong glow was activated inside.

Instantly, the Mislea saw the glow, and they screeched loudly, all of them running to attack him. But the small group rallied around him and fought off the beasts.

Taking the stone, the energy began coursing throughout the man's body.

What happened next, Valkyrie couldn't understand.

The man's eyes turned white and shone like gems. The energy glowed around him, and he began to be lifted into the air. Valkyrie and Petrichor stumbled back. Although it was only a hologram, it looked frighteningly real.

Slowly, the group of brave fighters began to fall, one by one.

But then a new sound came. A vast pack of small animals smaller than a Stexphin came rushing into the battle, coming up from beneath the ground.

Their faces were small with incredibly long legs and thick straight claws. Their bodies were white with strange black markings.

The creatures began to fight against the Mislea, their razor-sharp claws shredding straight through the Characters' large, rough wings.

The blue wolves released a cheering call. "The Dearbits! They came!"

One of the creatures transformed and walked up to the group, surrounding the rising man with the Ore. But their words remained unheard.

Even with this new creature defending them, the large Mislea kept coming. Finally, the man with the Ore lit up with such a bright light that it covered the entire land.

Then the animation left, and Petrichor and Valkyrie were left standing in the musty deserted war graveyard.

"What happened?" Valkyrie asked breathlessly.

"It was an explosion… That's how the war ended," Petrichor whispered. "They knew they couldn't win."

"But those bones." Valkyrie turned around to look back at the pile.

"That man said those creatures were Dearbit. I never realized they were a part of the Colossal Wars. But their bones are hard as steel. Their flesh was disintegrated. Their skeletons survived."

"Why did the Mislea attack them in the first place?" Valkyrie felt like the hologram hadn't given many answers, only more questions.

"Because of the Magia Ore," Pedro looked at her, his eyes wide with recognition. He seemed to understand everything she didn't. "The Dearbit, not all of them, were destroyed. They most likely came back and took the Ore after the explosion." He began to get excited and spoke quickly. "Then Captain Dana found it! Years ago, in that Dearbit cave! That's how the Gebrochen Sea became impossible to pass. Because after his ship wrecked, they lost the activated stone in the ocean!"

"What are you talking about?" Valkyrie asked desperately.

Before he could continue, the noise of bones falling against each other echoed through the quiet Hinterlands. They both spun, facing the pile. But neither could see anything through the dusty fog.

"We should go," Petrichor whispered in a shaky voice. He gripped her arm, and she felt him trembling as his fear returned. He tried to pull her away, but she stopped him.

"Wait. Look." She pointed toward a form walking toward them. It was a Character, one she couldn't recognize. Their silhouette was almost hidden in the musty air, but she made out two ears sticking from the side of the man's head.

That's not a Stexphin.

The closer he got, she could see he was holding something. In his right hand, a long rod with a strange orange glowing shape at the end. In the other, a bucket. She could hear a liquid sloshing inside.

Another rod stuck from the bucket. But even through the outage, she could see another burning shape. "Go," she said faintly as she recognized what these rods were.

Petrichor didn't need to be told twice, and they both broke into a run. Petrichor was much faster than her, she was surprised to realize, and he easily got ahead. *He's like Virga. Only taller. Maybe faster.*

She was distracted and didn't see the stone. As Petrichor leaped over, she tripped over the small boulder, scraping her palm painfully on the rough ground while trying to catch herself.

Wincing, she quickly turned on her back, staring into the brown darkness. Sure enough, the Character was coming. His brands glowed brightly through the fog.

She scrambled backward, eyes wide in terror.

The man reached her. His face was shadowed, and she couldn't make out any details. But he stopped and stood over her for a second, his eyes glowing with an unseen anger.

He lifted the brand in his hand. The end was shaped like an M and glowed dangerously with hot orange.

Valkyrie cried out in fear, realizing what he was going to do. She couldn't get up. Her legs felt glued to the ground.

Suddenly, Petrichor was there, a long bone in his hand. In one swift swing, he brought it around against the Character's head. The bone didn't snap as the man crumpled to the ground with a pained grunt.

"Go, *go!*" Petrichor screamed in terror, grabbing her arm and pulling her up. "He's still awake! Run!"

The two of them scrambled blindly through the dark. *I can't believe he did that! He's been so scared!*

"There! Hide in there!" Petrichor shouted, pointing to a strangely shaped ruin. They both ran through the arc.

A bright light flashed around them. The strange sensation filled her body again, just like last time the portal had opened.

Then she saw Jolee, standing with her siblings and Walker. They looked at her and Petrichor as the two of them ran toward them, the bright light following them.

Before they even reached the group, the light engulfed all of them, and suddenly, they were falling. Another flash, and the group hit the ground.

Then all went silent. All except the panicked breathing as the youths tried to understand what just happened.

Walker scrambled to his feet. "Where are we?" he asked, nervously wiping the dirt clods from his shirt.

Looking around, Valkyrie didn't recognize any of the dark scenery. Trees surrounded them, but it wasn't Hickorywood Forest. The ground was unleveled with bits of stone.

We're on a mountain. What happened to the Hinterlands?

Getting up, Valkyrie wasn't given the chance to reflect. Her ears shot up, and faint sounds reached her ears. "Get up!" she snapped. "Quick, quick! People are coming!"

They all scrambled to their feet, Hagan grabbing Jolee and pulling her back as they stood in a defensive circle. Valkyrie stepped closer to Petrichor and Jagger.

A thump and a short grunt followed. They all spun around. But Walker was gone.

Hagan wrapped a protective arm around his sister, staring into the trees with wide terrified eyes. Jagger stood in front of Valkyrie, gripping his halberd tightly.

They cast each other confused, terrified glances. Then, looking toward his siblings, he began to step toward them.

Jagger yelped as his feet were suddenly pulled out from beneath him, forcing him to fall roughly onto his back. He tried to sit up and grab whatever it was wrapped around his ankles, but before he could, he was yanked forward.

The rope had come from between Valkyrie's feet, pulling Jagger straight into the front of her legs. She tripped forward, falling over him. Quickly, she scrambled to her feet as Jagger's cry of help faded into the darkness behind her.

"Jagger!" Hagan cried, eyes wide in terror.

She turned to Petrichor who looked like he was seeing ghosts. Jagger's cries for help were getting deeper into the woods. She needed to do something but couldn't leave the others. She looked down at the Halberd Jagger had dropped.

"Jaylee, they're only taking people they can grab," Jolee suddenly said. Instantly, Valkyrie understood what she meant.

Hagan and Jolee were standing too close to each other for a rope or whatever it was to hook itself around their legs. She looked at Petrichor who stood at least four feet away. He seemed to understand too.

Reaching out, he grabbed hold of her wrist while at the same time, Valkyrie saw something shooting out of the trees from behind him. She clutched his wrist in turn as tight as she could.

At the same time, her eyes barely caught the small grappling hook. It wrapped itself around Petrichor's ankle perfectly, and the boy's leg was lifted off the ground.

Digging her heels into the earth, she grabbed him with both hands, refusing to let go, even as he was lifted. Her feet began to slide, and she leaned back, struggling to keep a grip.

She realized she had been holding her breath against the strain as she tried to fight off the strong pull. Trying to gasp for air sounded more like a desperate grunt. Petrichor cried out in pain, and at the same moment, he released her wrist.

She lost her balance and fell forward at the same time. He hit the ground loudly, landing on his stomach, the air knocked out of him.

He was pulled back into the trees, but Valkyrie refused to let go of his hand and was dragged right along with him.

Catching his breath, Petrichor stared at her with wide, terrified eyes. "They've got me!" he cried, scrambling desperately to keep a hold on her arms as they were dragged over rough terrain. "V! They've got my foot! Don't let go, *please*, don't let go of me!"

Valkyrie kept her hold but fought as they were hauled over a broken path.

"Jaylee!" She could hear Jolee's faint cries behind them. *No!* Her hands slipped as they jerked over a tree root. Petrichor was whisked away.

She lay there on her stomach, trying to catch her breath, curling up and grabbing her stomach. *I can't lose them like this. That's it!* Her mind screamed angrily. She bounced up and transformed into Stexphin form. But no matter how hard she tried, she couldn't catch up.

There was only one form in which she knew she could catch them. Without hesitation, she transformed into her Swiftmaw. Now in this form, she pursued after the disappearing Pedro. *I need to save him!*

Catching up, she detected the sliding form. He saw her too. Eyes wide, he began to yell in fear at the sight of a gray Swiftmaw chasing him. *It's so dark he probably thinks I'm Hollowed.* They were nearing the sound of whoever was at the end of the rope.

She realized it was too late. *I should've transformed earlier.* She took a few more great leaps before leisurely slowing down. Petrichor disappeared.

The strange sensation of Sorrowcrest swarmed her head. She stubbornly pushed it away.

Valkyrie waited until the sound of voices had settled down before edging her way closer. Her Swiftmaw paws were large but soundless in the woods. Hiding between a large boulder and tree, she transformed back into her Character, scanning the scene ahead.

It was a small campsite of at least twenty Stexphin Characters. *What are Stexphin doing here? Where is here?* They wore colors of brown and lapis blue. But she didn't recognize the symbol on their chests. It showed a moon with a strange circle around it.

It was getting lighter out as morning neared, and Valkyrie immediately scanned the campsite for her friends. She saw them.

With bags over their heads, they were bound and leaning against each other. No one seemed to be paying them any attention.

Questions filled her mind as she glimpsed around the campsite once more. These Stexphin looked friendly, but why would they kidnap her friends if they were?

A Character with strong build and wearing a long cape exited a canopy. *He must be the leader.*

"Who are they?" snapped the man as he glanced at the three Characters bound together.

"Found them on the Woodsen Outcropping," the nearest Stexphin said. "We don't know where they came from, but they're only children."

"Spies?" the Stexphin asked suspiciously. "Rotto uses them as young as they get."

"Possibly," the scout replied. Another Stexphin carrying a long grappling hook approached them. Valkyrie frowned.

"Easton, sir." The Stexphin carrying the hook approached the other scout.

"Kieran, what is it?" the scout said, whom Valkyrie guessed was Easton.

"We lost the other three," Kieran replied.

"How many of them are there?" the leader asked.

"Six younger teens, Lord Kryspin," Easton responded.

"Then they're definitely not Rotto's. He'll send groups, but not that many of just children." He looked at the bound boys and said. "Take those bags off. They must've escaped Elkhorn. We can't risk taking them in and letting the smog find us." Kryspin glowered.

"Then what do you want us to do to them?" Kieran asked. He looked troubled.

Kryspin was quiet for a second as he thought. "Beat them and send them back Rotto's way. He always enjoys receiving the weak."

39

ONLY THREE LEFT

Valkyrie quaked when she overheard this. *Beat them? Send them back to Rotto? Who is that man and what makes him think to do such a thing?*

"Jaylee," someone hissed in her ear. She jumped and gasped in horror as she spun to see Jolee and Hagan.

"What are you guys doing here?" She had forgotten the two siblings in her desperation to save Petrichor.

"We followed you. It took us forever to catch up, but we just kept going straight. We brought this," Jolee said, lifting Jagger's Halberd. "You left us," she added.

"I didn't mean to. They got Pedro, Walker, and your brother." She nodded back out. They both came up on one of her sides, scanning the campsite.

"What's your plan?" Hagan asked.

*****

Jagger blinked a few times as the bag was ripped off his head. He couldn't see the others but recognized Pet's trembling and Walker's loud groans.

"Who are you?" an icy voice asked. Jagger turned his head away from the glowering Stexphin standing over him. *What happened to Hagan? And the girls?*

"Ow!" he shouted as he was booted in the head, causing him to fall to the ground in a heap. His hands were bound behind his back and legs in front of him, forcing him into an awkward position.

"Tell us who you are," the voice demanded again. *I hate being the oldest. Pick on Walker. He can handle it.*

"Tell me who *you* are," he stated back stubbornly, trying to roll onto his side so he could stare this man down. He wished he had his Halberd.

The man stepped forward, fury on his face. But another Character held out an arm to stop him.

"My name is Kieran. This is Easton." He nodded at the other man. Looking past him, Jagger guessed there were others, but he couldn't see them. "Then there's Jack, Benton, Brooks, and Julien. How old are you?"

Jagger frowned before stubbornly stating, "Seventeen."

"Julien, are you eighteen?"

"Yes," came a boy's response. *Why does our age matter? Unleash me vermin.*

Kieran turned to Easton, "I don't want to touch them. Lord Kryspin gets carried away when he speaks of Rotto. He doesn't actually expect us to give them to that evil character, does he? I don't think we could even do it,"

Easton scoffed. "I could do it. This rotten boy deserves such a fate,"

Jagger felt his throat close up. *Rotto?*

Kieran left, leaving Easton in charge of them. "If you won't tell us who you are, I'll force it out of you," the man growled. He nodded to whoever it was behind them.

Kicking Jagger over so he could see his friends, he cried out, "No!"

The other two characters, Julien and Jack, had seized Petrichor by the arms and shoulders, holding him off the ground. The boy shivered and trembled, squeezing his eyes shut as if trying to block out his fear.

"Let him go! Pet didn't do anything!" Jagger demanded. Walker still sat on his hunches, staring with wide terrified eyes. The boy looked homesick and was quieter than a mute.

Easton nodded to the men who put Petrichor back on the ground but didn't unleash their firm grip. Brooks grasped Jagger and forced him to stand while Benton pulled up Walker.

Easton came up close to his face. "How does it feel to be so helpless?" he asked.

Jagger grimaced at the Stexphin. He wished he could slap the smirk off his stupid face.

"Cut away the binds on their feet," Easton nodded toward their bound ankles. The Characters did as they were told. At last, they could stand straight.

"Oh, what happened to your face?" Easton asked, eyeing the bandages wrapped around Jagger's head. "Looks like you and your Pet got into some trouble."

Jagger's eyes went wide. *Pet!? How dare he mock him like that!* Easton crossed over to Petrichor.

Pet couldn't stand. His legs were shaking too hard, and the guards had to hold him up. Jagger's stomach churned inside as he watched his friend helplessly.

Petrichor didn't look scared but dead. He still hung limply in the guards grasp and just stared down at nothing.

Petrichor! Come on! Get up! Jagger looked drastic. Once his friend would have acted stubborn as well but with a much calmer, kinder affect then he had.

Easton looked Petrichor over, then said, "Quite a strong Stexphin to act so cowardly."

"Don't say that!" Jagger cried. *He's much stronger than you'll ever be!* "Leave him alone! If you're going to torture anyone, torture me!" Easton seemed to be enjoying Jagger's desperation.

He turned on Petrichor and punched him in the stomach. His friend's eyes bulged before closing. He went limp as a sack.

"Stop! Stop! Petrichor! Wake up! Please, wake up!" Jagger yelled. "You're an evil man! You cruel, murderous traitor!" he screamed at Easton.

Easton crossed to him quickly. "Shut up!" he yelled. Nodding to the guards, they dropped him. Jagger grunted as he hit the ground. He looked up right as Easton booted him in the face.

*****

"We need to move now," Valkyrie whispered, desperately to the Parry siblings as Jagger crumpled to the ground.

Easton scoffed and rolled his eyes before turning to leave, instructing the guards to bind them to a tree.

They left the three Stexphin gagged and fastened to a trunk with two keepers to guard them. Walker was quiet the entire time, and she realized it had to be the longest he had ever gone without saying anything.

"I'll go see what I can find out," Hagan said with a quick nod. He embraced Jolee in a hug, whispering in her ear to be safe before sneaking around the outside of the camp, careful to watch for any guards who might be patrolling the perimeter.

"All right, let's go," Valkyrie motioned to Jolee. The two of them snuck through the woods until they found a safe tree.

Following their plan, Jolee boosted her up. As soon as she was settled, she carefully reached down and pulled Jolee up beside her.

Here they separated, each climbing across the branches into other trees, Jolee away from the camp, and Valkyrie toward their friends.

She climbed from one limb to another, astonished how wide these trees were. When she reached the trunk her friends were tied to, she slowly edged down, being mindful to watch where she stepped.

Okay, I can do this. I can do this. She looked below the tree once more. Jagger and Petrichor were out, but Walker was awake and looking paler than the moon. *Now if only there were some way I could signal him.*

He was tied tightly and his mouth was gagged. Valkyrie reached to her side and pulled an Althea flower from her pouch. The flower wasn't too large, and she knew it should land inaudibly.

361

She leaned ahead as much as she dared, then dropped the flower. It fell gradually and quietly before it landed in Walker's lap. He frowned, then his eyes went broad.

He craned his neck upward as much as he could. Valkyrie locked eye contact with him. He looked scared, confused, and happy all at once. One of the guards glanced at Walker who began to move his head around slowly, staring blankly.

Valkyrie quickly ducked behind a branch as the guard looked up, trying to figure out what Walker had been staring at. *Okay, now the critical part.*

She glimpsed back under at the guards. Walker was giving her a fierce scowl. *I know, I know! I'm trying to hurry!* She ducked back behind the branch. *Come on, Jolee.*

Loud sounds began coming from the woods. *Right on time!* With her sharp hearing, she could tell her friend was throwing rocks against the trees and yelling at least half a mile away. *She was right. She was fast.*

Both guards looked up at the noises. "Stay here," one instructed as he left.

Valkyrie reached at her belt and took out a dagger. Walker's eyes went wide as he spotted the blade. He quickly shook his head. *I'm not going to try to give it to you and risk cutting your face to match Jagger's.*

She looked over for a good place to throw it but couldn't get it anywhere with all the branches in the way.

Holding the blade with her teeth, she wrapped her legs around a branch and leaned over, using her legs to keep her grasp.

Hanging upside down, the top of her cloak fell around her face. Taking the blade from her mouth, she threw it the best she could toward the woods. It landed noisily in a brush.

The guard turned toward the noise and frowned. While upside down, Valkyrie spotted Jolee coming back through the trees.

The girl stopped when she saw the guard. He didn't see her as he turned to look back at Walker. Meeting Valkyrie's gaze, she nodded in understanding, then dropped from the tree.

Jolee landed behind the thicket, and the guard frowned as he turned back toward the noise. Finally, he went to go check it out.

Walker watched with wide eyes. His expression turned into horror when they heard a chase begin.

She saw Jagger slowly blink as he came around. It took him only a second to look up and see Valkyrie hanging there. He scowled at her.

"Honestly," Valkyrie said as she dropped from the tree. Walker jumped. "Did you think we'd leave you? And Walker, Jolee's fast. She'll get away." She swiftly began to cut at his bonds with her dagger. The minute they were free, Jagger began to shake Petrichor, trying to wake him up.

"Pet! Come on, Petrichor! You have to wake up!" he urged.

Valkyrie stood there, her face creased with worry. Petrichor looked awful, and his breathing was shaky.

"Jagger, we've got to go," she said.

"He's not waking up!" Fear welled in his voice. "He was hit hard."

"Can you guys carry him?" Valkyrie suggested.

Jagger looked at her frantically, then put his arms beneath Petrichor's. Walker grabbed the boy's legs.

Then they were off on a quick walk, opposite from the direction the guards had gone.

"Hagan's figuring out where we and who these Stexphin are," she whispered hastily. Walker led the way, carrying the boy's legs behind him. "Once Jolee loses those guards, she's going to find Hagan, and they'll meet us about a mile away from here."

"A *mile*?" Walker complained, the first words he had spoken in hours.

"I'll switch out with you once you get tired," she assured him. They had to be quick. It was light out now as the sun rose even higher, and they weren't hidden as well.

But the trail was hard as it began to climb uphill.

After a while, they were forced to stop for a break. Valkyrie panted as she laid Petrichor down with Jagger. The older boy was drained but refused to switch.

"Try to wake him up," Jagger breathed heavily as he sat down.

She shook the boy. "Wake up, Pedro, wake up!"

Suddenly, the boy's eyes flew open, and the minute he saw her, he frowned and kicked her back hard.

She somersaulted, then sat there, stunned. It wasn't that painful, but the momentum from a Stexphin's kick usually made the pain delayed.

She looked at Petrichor who suddenly began trembling and covering his eyes. Jagger's eyes were wide. *He kicked me!*

The sound of yelling brought them back. The Stexphin jumped up, and Jagger grabbed Petrichor. "Pet, come on! We gotta get out of here!"

Petrichor stared at Valkyrie, unblinking. "You—" He gasped, face full of fear. "I thought I saw you. You were...were a monster!" he said.

Valkyrie gasped. *He saw me transform?*

Jagger's own eyes went wide. He stared at Valkyrie, then stepped away from her.

"I don't know what you're talking about!" Valkyrie pleaded. "We need to go! Now! They're coming!" she cried.

"Jaylee!" Jolee and her brother broke into view, both breathing heavily.

"We're in the Fontana Cliffs!" Hagan cried desperately. *I'm never making it home in a week!*

"There's more." The boy stopped and took a gasp for air. They had sprinted the entire distance.

"These Stexphin," Jolee took over for him, even though she was gasping herself. "They live in a fortress called Gloriole, but they came out here as a small group."

Hagan picked up, "They're leaving false trails to keep Rotto away. But it's not only Stexphin!"

"We saw Griefolowtros!" Jolee said, eyes wide. "But they don't work for Rotto! They're against him!" Valkyrie tried to take it all in at once. "Oh! And they're chasing us. We need to go!"

Valkyrie's eyes went wide. "But where *do* we go?" she begged, glancing at Petrichor, hoping he had some answers.

The boy only stared at her with wide, terrified eyes.

I can't believe he saw me transform. Her heart broke in an indescribable way at the exposure of her greatest secret. *But I was desperate! If I hadn't, I never would have—*

"Woah!" Jagger shrieked as a blur leaped upon him. They were here.

Jagger was pinned to the ground by a large Griefolowtros, and Petrichor instantly threw his arms up in surrender.

Hagan lifted the Halberd he had been carrying, but a second Grief, this one a female in Character form, easily knocked it out of his untrained hands.

Jolee was carrying the dagger Valkyrie had thrown, but the girl knew it was hopeless. She dropped the blade and mimicked Petrichor.

Valkyrie, however, wasn't about to surrender. She pulled out her second dagger and threw it at the Griefolowtros who had originally pinned Jagger. The creature had gotten off the boy but stood over him like a guard.

The blade aimed for the lion face, and Valkyrie ran forward as if to follow it in suit.

Something clanked against the metal, throwing her knife off course. Leaping up, she twisted in the air, bringing herself around to grab the Griefolowtros around the neck.

Swinging her body around, she used her momentum to throw the beast off balance and cause him to fall to the ground.

She had never done it before, but it was one of the first moves Jamin had taught her after her combative battle with Deirdre. Now, as she tried it, she realized it was much harder than it had sounded.

Still, she succeeded in throwing the creature off course, and he fell to the ground, instantly transforming into his Character.

He looked panicked by Valkyrie's quick action but didn't hesitate himself to try to kick her away. But she didn't let go and dodged as many strikes as she could.

She stopped short as she felt a point press into her shoulder blade, perfectly resting in her scar from the arrow wound she received on Ashton's last scouting trip.

The feeling sent chills racing along her spine. She released the young Grief who quickly jumped to his feet. *Maybe I should have surrendered like the rest.* She guessed it was too late but held her hands up, closing her eyes and hoping whoever it was over her wouldn't stab her in the back.

The point left, and someone grabbed her shoulder, gently pulling her up. She stood but kept her hands raised. She nervously glanced at the Stexphin Character who held the short sword in his hand.

"We're not here to take you," the boy said.

Hesitantly, she dropped her hands.

"We won't hurt you unless you try to hurt us." He nodded at the bruise she had received on her bicep from a well-aimed kick.

"But you...you just kidnapped us!" Walker stammered, refusing to put his hands down until he knew exactly what it was they wanted.

"Kieran talked to Lord Kryspin." He nodded toward the Stexphin. "Your injuries aren't those of characters escaping Elkhorn. Your victims like the rest of us."

"I hope Easton didn't give you a hard time," Kieran said. "He's a difficult man, but so is Lord Kryspin. But he has offered to let you join our community after learning you weren't from Elkhorn. I believe you aren't. We're well out of Rotto's way and could always use more young men willing to help us. And if not, it's a great start to find a greater group,"

Walker slowly dropped his hands as well. Jagger was standing again, frowning in confusion. "Your community?" he asked. "What is it?"

"May I first apologize for what happened earlier?" the young boy asked.

Oh wait... Is this Julien?

"I did it unwillingly, but my job is to follow orders."

Slowly, the group began to relax. The two Griefs stood back and let Julien and Kieran do the talking. The two of them went on to explain what they were.

Valkyrie walked back to Petrichor who was standing rather distantly from the group. "Hey," she whispered. "I... I don't know if you saw—"

"I don't know what I saw," Petrichor said quietly, staring at her with searching eyes. "I think and hope I was only imagining things. But, V, I've never met someone like you."

"Nor I you."

"This is goodbye, though." He looked back at Jagger. "We're going to stay, and you have to return back to Smuir."

Valkyrie didn't know what to say. They were staying? It made sense and sounded just right for them. "Is there any way we could stay in contact?" she suggested, knowing it was hopeless with the condition Smuir was in.

They both turned at the sound of Jolee crying. The girl covered her mouth and tried to stop her tears. Hagan stood beside Jagger and Julien.

Somehow, Valkyrie instantly understood what was happening.

"Jolee, stay with us," Hagan pleaded. "Don't go back to Smuir."

"No. I could never leave Mom like that," Jolee said, taking in a shaky breath as she wiped her eyes. Valkyrie instantly went to her friend's side and grabbed her arm affectionately. Jolee leaned onto her shoulder and sniffed. "They're both leaving," her voice trembled.

Valkyrie glanced at Walker with worried eyes, half expecting him to stay as well.

"No," Walker shook his head, instantly knowing her look. "I've never been so homesick in my life. This 'trip' has gone way too far past my comfort."

"Jolee," Hagan said gently. "Tell Mom what happened and that I love her. She'll understand."

"I don't mean to cut in," Julien said. "But how do you plan to return to Smuir, the lost city? It's miles away. You'll never make it back alive."

Jagger told them?

"We'll go," the male Grief volunteered. "We can fly that distance faster than a Mislea. We'll stay close to the river so we'll remain unseen."

It was decided. Valkyrie and Jolee would ride together, and Walker would take the other.

The boy was upset to learn he had left his backpack at Riverforge Rampage. But then he sighed and said to just leave it because he never wanted to go back there again.

Valkyrie collected her fallen daggers, returned them to her belt, and turned to the group of Stexphin they were leaving behind. *I can't even begin to comprehend everything that has happened. I have a lot to write down when I get home.*

The thought of recording it all down in her journal once they made it back made her smile.

Petrichor never broke eye contact with her as the Grief rose into the air. She was troubled at the thought to realize they had started this trip with four, risen to six, and were now left with three.

Slowly, the characters below disappeared as they rose past the mountain trees. Valkyrie clasped the feathered mane in front of her. Glancing back to be sure Walker was all right, he looked sick but gave her a weak smile.

Jolee hugged her waist, and Valkyrie heard her whisper. "I can't believe it's only me now. They both left."

"You'll see them again." Valkyrie tried to sound comforting, but not even she was sure if her words were true.

She gazed across the open land of Gossamer with amazement as the wind brushed against them like a friendly kiss.

We'll see each other again.

40

THE ILLICIT GROUP

When Valkyrie returned, Ashton was relieved to see she was all right and had received all the needed ingredients. She told him everything that had happened, and he scowled, saying he would never let her go again.

They both went quiet. Finally, Ashton said, "Thank you. I know this is strange, but thank you for leaving. It's exactly what I needed to come back to my right mind. And now, hearing your stories," he chuckled softly, "makes me feel even better. I'm sorry for not going with you."

"It's all right. I'm just glad to see you as yourself again." She smiled at him.

*****

Valkyrie sat in her room one day, having finally finished her formula. She refilled the darts and placed them in her gray pouch, which was fastened to her belt.

She sighed as she gazed at the last Althea plant on her desk. Her thoughts drifted to Jagger, Hagan, and Petrichor. *I wonder what's going to happen to them. Will I ever see them again?*

At the sound of a knock, she jumped up and ran to her door. "Ashton!" she said happily.

The captain stood there and gave a weak smile.

"Valkyrie," he said sadly. "I-I—" His voice trailed off.

"Ashton, what is it?" Valkyrie asked with a frown.

"I'm leaving tomorrow on a scouting trip issued by the king's adviser," Ashton said quietly.

"But...what if you're attacked again?" she asked fearfully. "W-What will I do without you?"

Ashton sighed and put an affectionate hand on her shoulder. "You will be yourself. Go on in your happy ways, keep your friends, and find people you trust. If anything bad were to *ever* happen to me, you must promise that you wouldn't break down completely. You will remember all the good times we had together. But, most importantly, know that a part of me will always be with you."

"I-I can't promise that. Because it's not going to happen." She glowered at the thought. "I'm coming with you to make sure it doesn't."

"No," Ashton said firmly, "you're not. Not after what happened last time. You have to stay here. It's the only way I can protect you."

"But that promises no protection for yourself!" she yelled.

"Valkyrie, don't raise your voice at me!" the captain ordered. He sighed and quieted. "I said you're staying. So you are. You hear?"

"Yes, sir." She looked down.

"Come here." He pulled her into an embrace and stroked the back of her head. "You need to understand."

"I do. I just don't want to lose anyone else." Her heart ached.

Ashton knelt down on one knee, grabbed the sides of her arms, and looked up into her eyes. "Whatever happens, the Lord is with us. He's with you too. Lean on him, Valkyrie. Trust him."

Her jaw tightened. "I don't think I'm ready for that big of a step," she mumbled.

Ashton stood and rubbed her back. "Please, if anything happens, don't ever quit reading the Holy Scriptures. Only God can help you."

*****

Valkyrie sat on her bed a week later, thinking of Ashton. He said he wasn't sure how long they would be gone, and she was worried about him. All she could think about was when she last hugged him goodbye. An aching feeling seemed to have told her that would be the last time she would see him.

But she had pushed it away and scolded herself. *He's going to be fine! Quit it! You know he's going to be fine!* But she knew he wasn't going to be fine, and Ashton knew it too.

Hesitantly, she stood and opened the top drawer on her dresser. Reaching in, she took out *The Scriptures.* Glancing at Brooklyn's journal, she grabbed that as well.

She had forgotten about reading her Mother's journal.

Setting the binder aside, she realized pages were bookmarked inside *The Scriptures.* Opening the book, she read the highlighted verses aloud.

"The Lord is my strength and my shield; In him my heart trusts, and I am helped; My heart exults, and with my song I give thanks to him." She frowned and flipped to the next highlight.

"Trust in him at all times, oh people; Pour out your heart before him; God is a refuge for us,"

She shook her head. "Maybe for some of you," she muttered.

Valkyrie set the Holy Book aside, grabbing Brooklyn's journal instead. She didn't want to think about Ashton right now, and reading his highlights especially didn't help.

Moving back, she set up her pillow so she could lean against the wall. Pulling her knees in, she flipped through the journal, trying to find where she had left off.

Her eyes caught the word *Jaylee,* and she stopped. She began to read the next few pages and was shocked at what she found.

When Frazil was three years old, he was best friends with a younger girl in Elkhorn Village. Her name was Jaylee. She was deaf and blind.

Nonetheless, Frazil never left her alone. He acted as if he were her guide and led her around everywhere.

Valkyrie let out a heartbroken breath to read the young girl, Jaylee, died unexpectedly by a Jemoran plant.

> Watching Frazil meet his newest younger sister was special in so many sorrowful ways. The moment he saw her, I could practically see that familiar love and protection in his eyes. I told him her name was Valkyrie, but he shook his head, stroked the sleeping baby's cheek, and simply said, "Jaylee." I wasn't sure what to tell him. Although so young, I know he's still trying to understand that Jaylee isn't ever coming back. I'm not sure if he sees that now or if he really believes sweet little Valkyrie is his friend.

The all too familiar hurt for her older brother returned. Valkyrie shut the journal and put it aside, blinking against tears. *I miss you, Frazil.*

*****

The days only passed slower. Valkyrie tried to keep herself busy and went to the caves one day to visit her friends. She was curious to know what happened to Jolee and her mother and how Walker was faring with being home again.

As she neared the cave entrance, an older man spotted her and approached her quickly. "Excuse me, miss?" he asked.

"Yes?" she asked, looking up at him with confusion. *Do I know him? I'm terrible at remembering faces.*

"Are you Captain Ashton's daughter?"

Her heart began racing. "Y-Yes. Did something happen?"

"I'm sorry," the man began steadily, his voice low and gravelly. "The Illicit Group was attacked. Captain Ashton isn't ever returning."

Valkyrie's breath got caught in her throat. Her mind couldn't contemplate what the man meant. She cleared her throat with struggle. "W-What happened?"

"They were attacked brutally," he began.

Valkyrie squeezed her eyes shut and covered her mouth. Tears streamed down her face.

"When I arrived, all that was left of the band was weapons and blood."

*****

Valkyrie lay curled up on her bed, sobbing like she never had before. Whenever she had a hard day, Ashton was always there to comfort her. She had never thought that the one day he wouldn't be was because he actually *wasn't* there. *I've lost everybody! Ashton was all I had left!*

She had truly lost everything. It was so much to bear.

But all she could think of was the promise Ashton had asked of her. *I can't stay brave. I just can't!* Her mind screamed.

The more she thought about what the old scout had said, more rage and sorrow churned inside her.

I could've protected him! Her thoughts screamed at her until she pulled at her ears with the tension. Everything felt so complicated. So wrong.

Before she knew it, she transformed and ripped apart her room. When she finished her tantrum, she transformed back into her Character form and sank to her knees, sobbing.

"What is wrong with me?" she cried. So many thoughts began to turn against her.

If Ashton had just stayed like I told him—Didn't he care what would happen to me? Thoughts of losing her family and friends also began to haunt her, and she choked on sobs.

Looking over, she saw *The Scriptures* lying open on the floor from where they had fallen out of the dresser. Ashton's words echoed in her mind.

She scrambled to her feet and picked up the binder. Anger filled her heart, and she threw the book across the room, screaming, "If God really loves me, why does he keep taking my family away?"

Maybe I'm meant to be a lone ranger, just like Virga always played his entire short life! But it hurts so much!

I don't care what Ashton said. I don't need people. I have to let everyone go so I can never be ripped away from them again. She looked up toward heaven and yelled, "What do you think of that? You can't take them away if they're not there!"

She collapsed to the ground, burying her face in her arms.

It's true. No one loves me, no matter what I've done to make up for my mistakes and to hide the monster inside me. Even Pedro left. I'm truly nothing but a sinful girl who's not worth any sort of love. Why am I even still here? Why can't I just be ripped away as well?

Purple energy flashed through her mind, clearing away all suicidal thoughts.

Are you really a Magia Ore?

The purple light stayed in front of her eyes. *Your brother left me for you.*

He left me! she inwardly rebuked.

No, he died for you. Valkyrie didn't want to believe the voice. *If you can't find the love that never left, at least remember the love that saved you,* the energy begged.

Valkyrie slowly got to her feet. She looked around her destroyed room and walked out the door. Soon, she was curling up on Ashton's sheets. The earthy smell the captain always carried filled her nostrils.

You can't give up, the purple energy whispered. *I'm still here.*

Valkyrie sniffed. "What should I do?" she whispered aloud.

Keep training. Become more skilled than ever before. And when the time comes, go out and find them.

"How will I know when the time is right?"

I'm not going to leave you. Trust me, you'll know. For now, learn how to defend yourself, not only physically. Rotto isn't the only enemy out there.

"What are you saying"

Only God can fully protect your mind. I did my best when you were in the Hinterlands, but you need him.

"God doesn't care about me!" she snapped back.

You're wrong. He's—

Valkyrie didn't want to hear anymore. Ripping off her necklace, she threw it across the room. It clunked against the wall before hitting the floor.

The charm glowed a radiant purple before dimming to darkness in the corner.

"I'll admit you're right about one thing," Valkyrie said aloud, looking at the dark corner. "I can't give up."

EPILOGUE

VITALUS SPIRIS

Year Unknown

It was dark, miles beneath the island of Gossamer. No one knew what was down there. No one except those who sat in the prisons made of titanium surrounded by thick fog.

Here, far beneath the surface, sat many characters of different races. Their prisons were impenetrable and small. They were shaped like domes, almost over each captive.

The walls were full of large oval gaps. But they had learned that what they couldn't see in each gap was felt. Pain.

Besides, it was safer behind these enchanted walls. Because outside, the air was so thick it burned to breathe or even touch. Even if it were possible to escape, the smog would kill them.

Here, Bronzepaw, one of the many prisoners, felt no hunger. The back of his throat burned constantly for a drink. And although he couldn't remember the feeling of ice, he longed for anything cold to slide down his esophagus. Even just a drop of water would beat this hot air.

Bronzepaw sat miserably, leaning back against the titanium. He could hardly remember how he came to be a prisoner of the Destroyer. Sometimes a faint image in the back of his mind would become clear enough for him to see it.

He saw an island, not the one they were trapped beneath, no. This island was a little smaller, and its inhabitants were strong, kind, and loyal. Sometimes he saw familiar faces. But their voices were nothing but a brush of heartache inside his lonesome soul.

Every day felt the same. When he tried to think of yesterday, he couldn't. When he tried to imagine tomorrow, he saw nothing but the smog surrounding his prison.

How long had he been here? Was he to be stuck for all eternity? Not even that would fully process through his mind. He tried to grasp the pain such a thought would bring but couldn't.

Repeatedly, he thought and felt the same things. Each time, they felt more new than the last. Had he felt or thought this way before? He wasn't sure.

Bronzepaw's thoughts restarted with thinking about the faded image once again.

He moaned and tried to lie down on his side, but the motion caused too much pain. It burned his throat even more than his muscles.

Weeping followed the pain. It always did. The sounds came wailing and loud from other prisoners as well. Sometimes he forgot he wasn't the only one.

Over the sounds of sorrow came the scornful voices of hate. Characters screamed above, asking why they were placed in such a hold. What had they done to deserve such misery? Bronzepaw never joined them.

And yet even with the daily gnashing of teeth, something was different today. It took him over an hour until he finally grasped what it was.

Today, he had a name. *Dawn Shadows.* Yes, he could remember that term as well as what came with it. It was the title of the small island he saw every day in the back of his mind. It was a place of refuge.

But how did he remember the Island of Swiftmaw Wolves? What was changing for him to be privileged with such an opportunity to remember the haven of his kind? To see clearly the smiling faces of those he loved?

The voices of those around him began to drown out. Something dark and full of wickedness entered the fog. He shuddered, trying to shut out the voice, a voice so pure with evil it made him wish harder than ever before that he had changed when given the opportunity. Why did he fall away from the God of love?

The truth was so clear now. Why had he followed his flesh and listened to the whispered words of the devil? He had been warned that those who didn't remain faithful would be punished. But he had ignored them.

Everything was coming back. He could remember. He could think with his own words, something he hadn't done in what felt like all his life.

God, please forgive me. I have fallen so deep in my sin.

The voice of evil was gone. The weight on his shoulders felt lifted. But he was still trapped behind the walls created from his sin. It was impossible to break through on his own.

That's when they came. He saw them, through the gaps of his caged prison, creatures of such magnificence that the fog around them was cleared away.

He could hear the cries of hatred trying to fight off these beautiful animals, but they disintegrated instantly. The marvelous creatures ran in on four legs with oval-shaped hooves. They had long slender legs with a deep torso build and were muscular beneath their shining coats.

With long, thick necks and large elongated heads, they had manes and tails that looked as if they were created from soft energy. Each of these creatures were different colors with elemental meanings and a spiritual aura about them.

Bronzepaw struggled to his knees, trying to get a better glimpse at these magnificent creatures of beauty. He watched with bleary eyes as they began to destroy a few prisons that were supposed to be impossible to penetrate.

One of them came to his own prison. Rearing up, muscles rippled as the creature brought down its front hooves. The titanium crumpled to dust.

As the creature approached him, he realized a radiant glow surrounded the beast. It looked like the exact same as the energy from those of Magia Ores.

The graceful animal folded its legs to where it was almost lying down. It began to speak in a strange tongue, a language never heard of before. But Bronzepaw didn't need a translator to know what it was saying.

Trembling, he mounted the gorgeous beast, forcing his aching legs over its strong back.

As soon as the creature stood, it's mane flowed around him in lights. The burning in his throat disappeared, and a strong confidence he never felt before entered his body.

His mind was cleared of the burning smog, and he glanced around with amazement. Suddenly, he knew. He understood.

The mane around him fell away, and the herd of beautiful animals came back together. Only a few others carried prisoners. Many of the cages remained standing.

"Why are you leaving them?" Bronzepaw dared ask. His voice sounded strange, but it felt good to have his larynx stretched.

"Because they choose to stay," a firm, strong voice answered.

A man riding one of the creatures came up beside him. He introduced himself as Lumes. The beast beneath him was whiter than snow and glowed brightly.

The man himself looked gallant, wearing clothes of white. His hair was cut short but had the same soft energy look as the creatures. His eyes were bright and his physique strong.

Suddenly, the herd broke into a gallop, running close together. Bronzepaw clutched the mane in front of him. It felt softer than thread, almost as if it wasn't there.

The beasts were steady, even as they ran at such an incredible speed. Bronzepaw moved smoothly with the rhythm of the creature beneath him.

His eyes went wide as he realized the herd was running straight for the wall of earth.

But they didn't slow down nor speed up. Instead, the light around them coursed through their bodies like energy. Their coats turned into a brown more delicate than the earth before them.

They ran straight through the wall without even the smallest strain.

Bronzepaw was amazed as the herd began to climb upward through the ground, which should have been solid. But they hiked onward as if it were nothing but air.

The smell of earth filled his nostrils, and he smiled widely. Already, he could feel his Swiftmaw instincts returning.

"What will become of them?" an older man's voice suddenly asked.

Bronzepaw turned to see this other prisoner. The older man looked rather rough compared to Lumes. His gray hair grew to his shoulders. Beads were embedded in strands.

He wore a long coat with a tricorn hat. Boots with buckles over the top were strapped to his feet. Two Stexphin ears were almost hidden.

"The Destroyer will fully take them in the final days," answered Lumes, his gallant white creature leading the herd as they climbed upward.

"You mean—" Bronzepaw began.

"Yes," the man replied. "What you experienced wasn't even a small grasp of the true inferno waiting for those who refuse the Lord. You fell away from God and chose to take your own paths. But he never left you. Sometimes we must see both sides to find our way back, *but blessed are those who have not seen and yet have believed.* But do not feel that of guilt. You have repented, and God has forgiven you."

"May I ask, what are you?" the older man said.

"Vitalus Spiris," Lumes nodded to the creatures they were riding. "As you know, God cannot be with sin. His glory would destroy you instantly. We come from our own realm and are connected to the energy of your Ores in which you named Magia. You will see shortly."

"Where are you taking us?" Bronzepaw asked.

The man looked to the Vitalus as they were riding. "After reaching the surface of Gossamer, they will take each of you to a different year. For as I'm sure, you've figured out by now you live in a realm lost in time. That is why certain things exist for only a short while. When it's formal realm sucks it back, it disappears."

Lumes turned to look at him. "Bronzepaw Dawnguard, a Swiftmaw resistance is failing. They need their strong leader returned in order to find the Silverstreak Wolves. Only they can help stop the Griefs of Acrimony.

"And Captain Dana"—he turned to the older man—"your son has fallen away with encouraging war lands. God needs you to plant a seed."

"What do you mean a Swiftmaw resistance?" Bronzepaw interrupted. "What's going on?"

"You know very well of Greenwing but nothing of Rotto, the new captor of your kind. They are losing out there, and the Destroyer collects more every day. You will see soon enough what the Lord has in store for you."

"What of us?" asked a younger man. He, too, was rescued from the prisons along with his mother and brother. Each of them rode their own Vitalus Spiris.

"Your father and sister are gone," Lumes told him. "The Lord says it is time for the blue wolves to be woken up before their prisons of glass break. He will guide you in doing so."

Bronzepaw could feel the vibrations of the Spiris beneath him as it spoke. Its language was beautiful and sturdy, and although he couldn't understand what it was saying, he tried to hear the simple words. *"Kria Si Owa."*

"We are approaching the surface," Lumes translated. "Prepare yourselves."

As the beautiful Vitalus Spiris broke through the earth, Bronzepaw gasped in horror as the truth was revealed to them.

I see now, Lord. I'm here and ready. Send me, he prayed.

ABOUT THE AUTHOR

Tori K. Downs is a young writer who fell in love with the fantasy world through its adventure, creativity, and purpose. Struggling through many trials in her teen years, she decided to cultivate her love of writing and pour her heart into her own world of imagination. She currently resides in Greeley, Colorado, where she enjoys spending her free time reading, writing, and drawing.

In 2019, Tori gave her life to Christ and yearned to make what was originally her stories to escape reality into a series that God could use in other people's lives.

Count it all joy, my brothers, when you meet trials of various kinds, for you know the testing of your faith produces steadfastness. And let steadfastness have its full effect, that you may be perfect and complete, lacking in nothing. (James 1:2–4)

Milton Keynes UK
Ingram Content Group UK Ltd.
UKHW040736090923
428296UK00015B/105